EATER OF SOULS

Other Lord Meren Mysteries by Lynda S. Robinson

EATER OF SOULS

A Lord Meren Mystery

LYNDA S. ROBINSON

WALKER AND COMPANY
NEW YORK

First published in the United States of America in 1997 by
Walker Publishing Company, Inc.

Published simultaneously in Canada by Thomas Allen & Son Canada, Limited,
Markham, Ontario

Library of Congress Cataloging-in-Publication Data
Robinson, Lynda Suzanne.
Eater of souls : a Lord Meren mystery / Lynda S. Robinson.
p.   cm.
ISBN 0-8027-3294-1(hardcover)
1. Egypt—History—Eighteenth dynasty, ca. 1570–1320 B.C.—Fiction.
2. Thebes (Egypt : Extinct city)—Fiction. I. Title
PS3568.O31227E28   1997
813′.54—dc21   96-46828
CIP

Printed in the United States of America
2 4 6 8 10 9 7 5 3 1

TO TAKE A chance on publishing a novel set in ancient Egypt, an editor has to have courage and the ability to withstand criticism from those who dislike subjects that seem too esoteric. Michael Seidman had that courage and took that chance.Then he had the patience to allow me to grow as a writer and the wisdom not to take me seriously when I let my fears overwhelm me. Thank you, Michael. I will always be grateful for your guidance, your experience, and most of all for your willingness to take a chance on ancient Egypt, Lord Meren, and me.

Acknowledgments

I WOULD LIKE to thank Dr. Charles van Siclen for serving as an invaluable resource and Polly Price, my dear friend, for her help in manuscript review. Any errors remaining are mine.

In addition to the research and writing, producing the Lord Meren books involves the hard work of Marlene Tungseth, director of editorial production and design, Krystyna Skalski, art director, and Miranda Ottewell, copy editor. I would also like to express my appreciation to JoAnn Sabatino, Matthew Papa, Liza Miller, and Theresa D'Orsogna, all of whom have played important roles in the Lord Meren series.

So many books are published each year that it takes special enthusiasm and expertise to make any one distinguishable from the crowd. George Gibson, publisher of Walker and Company, has given my books intensive backing that has been crucial to their success. From the beginning his expertise in the publishing business has been invaluable. He also knows and understands writers, their fears and idiosyncrasies, and the toll their own standards can exact from them. His insight and empathy have been a great solace to me.

Finally, I would like to thank my husband, Wess, who is a marvelous first reader and unfailing source of encouragement.

Ammut, the Devouress

S H E   I S   T H E Devouress, Eater of the Dead, Devourer of Souls, creature of the netherworld—crocodile head, lion's foreparts, hippo's hindquarter—she is feared even by the one called Blood Drinker. Ammut the Devouress crouches by the scales while Anubis weighs the heart of the dead one against the Feather of Maat. Toth, Osiris, and the pantheon observe but do not interfere. The scales tilt; the Feather rises. A scream tears itself from the throat of the dead one who stands at the scales. The Devouress salivates, squats on her haunches, and springs. Long, yellow-toothed jaws snap, once at the heart, once at the dead one. Bones crack; flesh is severed; and Ammut the Devouress carries out the punishment dealt to all evil ones—annihilation. The gods turn and face the portal through which the next one will come, the evildoer forgotten. But Ammut lifts her crocodile head and listens to souls in torment in the living world above. Their pain calls to her. Another dead one appears at the portal. Ammut, Eater of Souls, Devourer of Shades, swings her head toward the smell of fresh meat. She is hungry again.

1

Memphis, Year Five of the Reign of the Pharaoh Tutankhamun

SHE COULD SMELL the darkness. Night in the land of the living was a feeble imitation of the obsidian nothingness that possessed her own lair, yet she could smell the darkness. Lifting her hard, jutting snout, she sucked in the textured scents—waters of the Nile, mud and refuse from the docks nearby, the faint smell of dung mixed with fish and smoke from a thousand dying oven fires.

The snout whipped around at the sound of a flute, a shriek of drunken laughter from the beer house. A claw, long, curved, with a honed blade-edge as sharp as a physician's knife, scraped over the cracked mud brick of a wall. It snaked back into the shelter of the alley at the sudden appearance of light. Several of the living approached. Eyes with daggered pupils observed the strangers. Rapid, guttural chattering made her wince. Foreigners—in rank, unclean wool robes smelling of beer and sex. Bearing the torch that had assaulted her eyes, they stumbled past and swerved to disappear down the street

Snorting to rid herself of the stench, she returned her attention to the beer house across the street. One of its wooden shutters was loose and warped, allowing light from within to escape and casting rippled shadows on the packed earth of the road. A larger group burst from the interior, arguing, giggling, swaying to the beat of a sailing song. Men from the docks. Of no interest, no relevance.

She grunted with impatience, something she never experienced below. But the evil one had been in the beer house since dusk. Leaning against the chipped plaster of the wall, she rubbed her haunches against the surface, scraping off more chips of plaster with her rough hide. All grew quiet again, and the light from the beer house began to dim as someone quenched lamps. Far away, in the palace district, a hound howled. At an even greater distance, out in the western desert, land of the dead, hyenas yipped and squealed.

The brittle wooden door of the beer tavern swung open again. She turned a yellow eye and saw, at last, the evil one. He was a small man, as befit his place among the living. A humble farmer with cracked, sunbaked skin, splayed, dirty feet, and three cracked teeth. This was the one who had offended, had transgressed in so callous a manner that she had heard the cry of injustice from below.

She sniffed the air again and caught the scent of a decayed ka, the soul of the evil one. The farmer came toward her. He would use the alley to cross this district of taverns and beer houses on his way to the skiff he'd left at the dock. As he marched unsteadily toward her, she felt the sudden burning rush of power spiced with anticipation. It boiled through her like rolling thunderclouds.

Slinking back into the deepest blackness, she crouched on her hind legs. Heavy, irregular footsteps announced the farmer's approach. And over the sound of his tread she heard that for which she'd been listening all night. The steady, dull *th-thud, th-thud, th-thud*. The voice of the heart. It grew louder and louder, provoking her, taunting her, invading her skull and battering its low vault. Just as the noise threatened to shatter the bones of her head, she sprang out of the blackness and landed behind the farmer.

He turned and tottered, his mouth agape, his eyelids climbing to his brows. He had time for a rattling little screech before she bashed him in the head. The man flew backward and smacked into the hard earth. The moment he lay flat, she lunged, her forearm drawn back, claws spread wide. They cut through the air, impaled flesh, and sliced, severing the farmer's throat. Drawing back, she shook her claw deftly to rid it of blood and stringy tissue while the farmer gurgled and stared up into a long, rigid maw studded with yellow fangs. She listened for that last escaping breath. Once it issued from the body, she stooped over the farmer once more—to do what had been decreed, what she existed to do, what was righteous, what this evil deserved.

KYSEN STRODE OUT of his bedchamber toward the hall of Golden House, the ancestral home of his family in Memphis. Dawn approached, and exhaustion nested in his body like a sated vulture. At the same time he had to endure the pounding mallet of dread that beat in time with his heart. He'd slept only a few hours after last night's conversation with his father. Meren was one of the Eyes and Ears of Pharaoh, confidential inquiry agent to the living god, the pharaoh Tutankhamun, but even one so favored as Meren couldn't investigate the death of a queen without risking his life.

Kysen's thoughts careened to a halt as he imagined the magnitude of the risk to his father. Nearly stumbling into the half-open doors to the hall, he placed his hand on the polished cedar and electrum and entered. The scene of splendor before him never failed to call up memories of his own childhood before Meren had adopted him, memories of bare walls, meager furnishings, poverty of spirit, and the devastation of joy.

Before him slender columns painted in green, blue, and gold rose above his head, while lamplight glinted off furniture trimmed in sheet gold or wrought in darkest ebony. He passed the master's dais, on which stood his father's chair with its elegant ebony legs ending in lion's paws. Each carved paw had claws painted in gold. The solid sides and armrests were fitted with sheet gold engraved with hunting scenes.

The contrast between his memories and the hall faded as he approached his sisters, to be replaced by worry. He had searched for Meren without success earlier this morning. If his father wasn't with Bener and Isis . . . His imagination crowded with thoughts of court intrigue, the enemies Meren had made in protecting and nurturing the boy pharaoh.

Cease. You're weary and not thinking clearly. There's nothing to fear at the moment. He hasn't begun to study the death of Queen Nefertiti.

Raised voices interrupted his worried thoughts. Bener and Isis were arguing as they breakfasted on hot bread, figs, and barley porridge. Holding a rush pen, Bener munched a piece of bread while composing a list of items on a scrap of used papyrus. She glanced up to smile at her brother before responding to Isis.

"You're too young. Barely fourteen."

"I'm not too young. You're just jealous. Lord Reshep is the most pleasing of any at court, and he hasn't even looked at you."

Bener wrote another word in her fine cursive script and contemplated it as she replied calmly. "It would be hard for him to do that, since we've never met."

"I don't care—"

"Have you seen father?" Kysen interrupted before Isis succeeded in provoking her sister.

"Not this morning," Bener said as she added another item to her list. "Did you know that the steward has been obtaining watermelons from a street vendor?"

Kysen, already on his way out of the hall, answered with impatience. "No."

"The kitchen garden produces abundant melons."

"Then I suppose we use more than we grow," Kysen snapped without turning.

Bener's voice rose. "We don't. Damnation, Ky, who has been looking after the accounts while we were in the country?"

"I don't know," he shouted back.

"Find out!"

He didn't answer. If he'd argued with Bener, saying such small matters weren't important, she would have contradicted him and pointed out why watermelons were important. Then she'd have proved her assertion with so well-reasoned a series of statements that he'd feel like a fool for questioning her judgment. Bener had grown into womanhood in the few months they'd been separated, and he'd learned not to challenge her. She'd been right about too many things, even about the culprit in a murder a few weeks ago. He would have to control his temper, or Bener would notice and try to make him tell her what was wrong. She didn't give up once her curiosity was aroused, and he hated lying to her.

Where was Meren? Kysen looked in the master's office, the scribes' rooms, the library, even a few storerooms. All he found were servants, slaves, and old Hapu, the household steward. Finally he realized he was wasting time and climbed an inner stair that rose the height of the house. Coming out on the roof, he left the shelter of an embroidered awning and strode toward the wall, which came up to his waist. He noticed his pace. It had quickened as he searched, and he'd almost run up the stairs.

He made himself slow down. It would do no good to confront his father in this agitated and inflamed state. Meren would observe it, lift one brow in that understated and unmistakably noble and elegant manner of his, and refuse to talk until Kysen had calmed.

He reached the eastern roof wall and forced himself to pause, turn his thoughts elsewhere, so that he could absorb even the smallest sand grain of peace. Looking over the landscape, he beheld a sight that always provoked his awe. Across the dark ribbon of the Nile was baked black land, fertile, life-giving. Beyond that came the east bank villages, and then the red and cream of the desert.

Ra, in his solar boat, approached the horizon of the living world, showering Egypt with his amber-and-gold light. And all around him lay Memphis, greatest of the cities of Egypt, city of Ptah, the creator god in his vast stone-and-gold temple, city of palaces unrivaled even by those of rich and powerful Babylon; Memphis, city of princely mansions and vast foreign trade.

Kysen turned to gaze out beyond the protective walls of Golden House to that other, even greater city, the Memphis of the dead. In the west, up and down the river as far as he could see, stretched tomb after abandoned tomb, deserted mortuary temples, aged and decaying monuments erected by the ancient ones. These had been intended to carry on the mortuary rituals of kings, queens, and nobles whose very names now had vanished from memory. The new cemeteries invaded those of the ancients. Even the uncompleted tombs of great ones like General Horemheb seemed like brash little children clinging to the legs of stronger, wiser old ones.

Kysen watched, holding his breath, as Ra sailed higher. The sun's rays hit the sheer, polished faces of the giants of Memphis—the pyramids. He released his breath, annoyed with himself for feeling so insignificant at the sight. Though distant, the stone triangles loomed, thrusting out of the desert floor. They ascended so high and their bases covered so much ground that even after all the centuries that had passed, nothing had been built to equal them.

His jaw had gone stiff. Kysen had to force himself to stop grinding his teeth. It had been ten years since his father had adopted him at the age of eight, taking him away from the blood father who had beaten him. But he wasn't used to Memphis, White Walls, the royal city, named for the vast protective ramparts of plastered mud brick that protected palace and temple alike. He'd never become accustomed to such grandeur. How could he when he'd been born of a common artisan, a carpenter among the tomb makers in Thebes?

Kysen breathed in the last cool air of morning. Before long, the power of Ra would sear it to the temperature of a furnace. He glanced once more at the pyramids, the walled cities and temples that accompanied them, the first smattering of houses of the living. Then he transferred his gaze to the Golden House compound.

He leaned forward and looked over a white enclosure wall set some distance from the main house. Meren's private garden. He should have guessed. Still as the water of a delta marsh, a tall, lean figure in a pristine kilt and sheer overrobe cinched by a jeweled belt stood beneath a palm.

Placing his cupped hands close to his mouth, Kysen emitted a short, rough panther's cry. Meren turned quickly, looking up at him. Kysen saluted, and Meren nodded, then began to walk slowly to the garden gate. Kysen would await him on the roof, for lately Meren hadn't welcomed anyone into his garden.

As he watched his father's progress across the far-flung grounds, Kysen remembered the first time he'd come here. He'd thought it the most magnificent house ever built, and the largest. And even after having spent years attending court at the various royal palaces of pharaoh, he still felt a jolt of astonishment at its size.

How could Meren have adopted him, made him firstborn son in a house that almost rivaled that of pharaoh? The place was vast, from its columned verandas that surrounded the central house to the five reflection pools, the protective verge of palms, sycamores, and acacias, and the jewellike furnishings. When he'd first set foot inside the high front gate, he had mistaken the private family chapel for the main house.

Small as it was compared to Golden House itself, the chapel was many times the size of the narrow abode in which he'd been raised. To him, Golden House had been a small city complete with granaries, stables, servants' quarters, barracks for charioteers, and a well with winding stone steps leading down to water level. It had taken him years to grow accustomed to his new life, years to forget the beatings, years to believe the love Meren offered so freely.

Now he believed. Now he returned that love, and now he was afraid. Meren had discovered that pharaoh's sister-in-law, the great and powerful Nefertiti, hadn't died of a plague as assumed but had been poi-

soned. The crime had happened years ago—before the heretic king
Akhenaten, Nefertiti's husband, had died—in Akhenaten's new
planned city, Horizon of Aten. But those responsible had survived the
furor of their heretic king's death. One had been killed only a short time
ago, after secretly confessing to Meren that he'd poisoned the queen.

Young as he was, Kysen knew that more people must have been
involved in such a crime. The murderer hadn't been powerful enough
to order the slaying of the Great Royal Wife; whoever had been
responsible for such a decision might still be alive. He and Meren
had been aware of this possibility for weeks. But what alarmed Kysen
was that since learning the evil secret of Nefertiti's death, his father
had grown more and more tense, silent, wary. He'd even stopped
juggling, a pleasure he had to enjoy privately since a great noble
could not be seen tossing brightly colored leather balls like a common entertainer.

Kysen's brow furrowed as he gripped the edge of the wall and heard
the voice of his heart pound in his ears. He'd seen what happened to
those foolish enough to stumble upon hidden wickedness or trade in it.
He squeezed his eyes shut at the vision of a man at the Nile's edge,
stumbling. A long, dark snout shot out of the water, rigid jaws flying
open, snapping as the creature lunged. Long ivory teeth punctured flesh;
that powerful body hurtled backward into the water, dragging the man,
who howled in unremitting pain and terror. Then the victim's cries
changed to short repetitive screams. Even when he was dragged beneath
the waves, he screamed into the blue-black waters.

"Ky?"

He jumped and whirled, breathing hard, ready to fight. His vision
focused on a man bathed in newborn sunlight—the sharp jaw angle, the
smooth obsidian hair, the muscled body wrapped in transparent linen.

"Father," Kysen said, forcing his lips to curve upward.

Meren ignored his smile. "What's wrong?"

"Nothing. I was deep in a memory—that man who was killed by the
crocodile at the country house."

Joining Kysen by the wall, Meren leaned on it and gazed into the
distance. A few moments of silence passed as they watched the pyramids
of the ancient ones burst into white stone flame. Kysen glanced once at
his father, who seemed far more calm than any mortal ought to be given
their predicament.

"You're still worried." Meren spoke with the tranquillity of a sun-bathing lion.

Kysen tried to match his father's composure with a light tone. "Worried? No, not worried." He turned to skewer Meren with a look. "Not worried—terrified."

"I'll be careful."

"The queen's murderer was careful, and he's dead. The Great Royal Wife was powerful, clever, and careful, and she's dead."

Meren shoved himself away from the wall, turned his back, and strolled into the shade of an aged sycamore whose branches arched over the roof. Wind whipped the gossamer robe around his legs and ruffled his hair. He had yet to don a formal wig or the rest of the jewelry befitting one of his rank. Without these it was easier to see the long cords of muscle in neck, shoulders, and arms, kept taut by hours' practice with scimitar and dagger, and yet more hours mastering chariot, bow, and spear. Meren turned back to Kysen, his expression severe.

"The slaying of a queen is a foul sin against the proper order of the world—Maat—the harmony and balance of life as the gods ordained."

"People are killed every day," Kysen snapped.

"Not queens!"

Meren's voice rang out, startling birds into flight from the sycamore. With Kysen giving him a round-eyed look, Meren shut his mouth, thrust his fists behind his back, and went on.

"Forget high principles. I told you, Ky. Whoever ordered the queen killed had to be well placed at court. Someone that powerful probably survived the purge of those who supported the heretic and his attacks on the ancient gods. And he—they—are most likely still at court or close to it."

"But now we have the golden one," Kysen replied. "Tutankhamun, may he have life, health, and prosperity, grows in power daily. Pharaoh is favored by the great gods, beloved of the people. What good will it do to risk your life when Nefertiti has been dead so long?"

Meren strode back to Kysen, halted within an arm's length, and planted his fists on his hips. "You know why I have to find him, this murderer of queens. If he would dare to kill a Great Royal Wife, he would dare an even greater anathema. Such a criminal might dare to kill a pharaoh." Meren inclined his head as he gazed at his son. "You've been training as the Eyes of Pharaoh for a long time. Why are you so worried now? This is what we do—inquire into dangerous secrets, offenses, and transgressions, shield and defend the king."

"Of course I know," Kysen said. He drew nearer to his father, hearing his voice lower and at the same time strengthen in tone. "But something's different. You're different. I see it in your eyes, in the way you take refuge in isolation and the way you stare into nothingness, as if you see something so frightening you can't look away." His voice dropped to a whisper. "I have seen you afraid, afraid for me, for my sisters, for pharaoh. But now you're not frightened *for* someone. You're frightened *of* someone, or something, so frightened that you won't even speak of it, for fear of giving this mysterious terror power. It's as if you're afraid speaking of it will let this evil that tortures you loose to ravage without hindrance and destroy us all."

Kysen kept his gaze fixed on Meren's. As he'd spoken, Meren had drawn over his features a mask of diplomacy, courtliness, and artifice. Kysen had seen him do this when confronted by intrigue among his fellow nobles or when playing a part to draw out victims suspected of anything from stealing royal grain to plotting pharaoh's death, but he'd never been subjected to it himself. That his father would use this mask against him chilled his bones as if they were encased in that frozen whiteness he'd seen on foreign mountains. His hurt and bewilderment must have shown, for Meren turned away, lowered his head for a moment, then faced him, his features released from cold composure.

"I'm sorry. You're not the enemy," Meren said.

Kysen sighed his relief. "Then you'll let this old evil rest."

"No."

"But—"

"Enough!" Meren closed his eyes for a moment, then opened them and went on. "I've had someone search the tax rolls and found Queen Nefertiti's favorite cook. She and her husband have retired to a family farm south of the city. I'm going there to begin our search."

"And what will pharaoh say when you leave court to visit a humble cook?" Kysen said, throwing up his hands.

"I'm going as an ordinary scribe." Meren held up a warning finger. "No objections. You're going to be too busy to fret about me. You're going to prowl among your friends in the dock taverns and beer houses. Find that woman—is her name Ese? Find Ese and ask her about the old days when the heretic ruled. I don't have to tell you what methods to use."

"Ese is mistress of a tavern. What could she know of the wife of a living god?"

It was Meren's turn to sigh, only with an air of tried patience. "You know very well that common villains often are privy to unspeakable evil long before royal ministers. I leave in a few days. And you, my son, will do as I command. You will also abandon these foolish suspicions that I'm hiding something from you."

Pressing his lips together to stop himself from protesting again, Kysen nodded, a slight, grudging gesture.

Meren eyed him suspiciously. "I'm determined on this, Ky."

"Yes, Father."

"And your worries are groundless."

"Of course, Father. If you declare it, it is so."

He bore Meren's inspection with calm, knowing Meren would soon be distracted by the business of the Eyes and Ears of Pharaoh. Then he'd have to take certain measures without his father's approval or advice. It was a thing he'd never done.

Egyptian sons followed the paths of their fathers. They obeyed, or they were disciplined. Kysen knew Meren would expect no less of him. It had taken him years to accept Meren, but once he had, he'd realized that his father was a man of great discernment and authority.

As Meren began to speak of the day's duties, Kysen's thoughts strayed. Unlike his blood father, Meren had never raised his hand against Kysen. Everyone obeyed Meren. It would never occur to his father that they wouldn't. This attitude, Kysen had discovered, was one of the most important sources of a great man's power. Another, even greater source arose from the fact that, if he chose, Meren could decree punishments far worse than any his miserable blood father had produced.

Kysen remembered stealing pomegranates from the kitchen with Bener years ago. Meren had made him copy the unending precepts of the sage Ptahhotep five times. To Kysen it had seemed like five thousand copies. He had suffered sore fingers and excruciating boredom. But never once had Meren struck him. If Meren was in danger, Kysen would protect him at the cost of his own life.

"Are you listening to me, Ky?"

Kysen blinked once. "Of course, Father." He smiled for the first time in two days. "I was remembering how Bener and I used to steal pomegranates."

Meren grinned at him.

"I must confess something," he said. "Sometimes I'd tell the servants to let you steal them without complaining."

"Did you, by the gods? Why?"

Shaking his head, Meren said softly, "Sometimes a child needs the freedom to be just a little wicked."

Perplexed, Kysen studied his father, who looked away toward the reflection pools and gardens in front of Golden House. Then he sucked in his breath. "We are visited."

"By whom?" Meren asked.

Kysen pointed to an ebony-black Nubian wearing a short military kilt and thick gold wrist- and ankle-bands and carrying a spear. It was like watching a colossus walk, for Karoya was a royal guard, member of a select and secretive group. Karoya was one of the few men in the world who answered to no one, not even Meren or the great minister Ay. He was personal bodyguard to the golden Horus, the living god, ruler of the empire, the pharaoh Tutankhamun, aged fourteen years.

2

SOKAR, CHIEF OF watchmen of the city of Memphis, rounded the corner of a street crowded with sailors, foreign merchants, vendors, and donkeys. He took big steps, leading with his ample belly, and changed course for no one. Children playing in the road scattered before his walking stick, which jabbed into the earth with a smack, sending flakes of packed earth into their faces.

One of his underlings hurried before him, shouting to warn of his master's approach. "Way! Make way for the chief of watchmen. Move your carcass, mongrel of the desert."

Each time his stick nearly impaled a passerby, each time his attendant snarled at some unsuspecting citizen, Sokar's shoulders lifted a bit higher and his chest expanded. He wasn't a man of great stature. An onlooker would note that most of Sokar's growth had taken a sideways path. He had a head like a fat mud brick, big, fleshy red lips, and a sparse forehead beneath a wig fatter than his head. His feet, encased in papyrus sandals, hadn't seen a washbasin or cloth in weeks, and he proceeded through the growing street crowds with the gait of a duck that has reached the end of its fattening period.

The belligerent expression on his face was moderated only by those protruding, feminine lips. Sokar was intensely annoyed at having his morning meal interrupted by a report from one of his more excitable watch leaders.

"Goat-witted fool," Sokar had muttered to himself as he stuffed the remains of a slice of date bread in his mouth. "Dragging me out for the murder of some farmer. I'll dock his rations, I will."

Sokar preferred reducing rations to administering beatings as punishment. He kept the confiscated grain and beer for himself. The attendant led him past a house concealed behind high walls and into a street hemmed in on both sides by narrow dwellings and a beer house with cracked and pitted plaster, tightly shut doors, and blank windows.

Upon turning another corner, they left the crowds behind to enter a lane that seemed more tunnel than street, so close were the surrounding structures. Littered with refuse thrown from upper stories and the droppings of geese, ducks, and donkeys, it was almost deserted. The only inhabitant lay across the bottom stair before a front door, his head hanging over a pool of vomit. Sokar followed the watchman into an alley opposite this door and stopped abruptly. Three men from the day watch stood with their backs to a prone figure. One of them held his hand cupped over his nose and mouth. Sokar's walking stick stabbed the ground near this man's bare foot; he jumped and bowed several times to his master.

Wiping a stray crumb from the shelf of his belly, Sokar launched into his habitual bellow. "This had better be worth my time, Min, or I'll have your beer rations for a month!"

"Yes, master. I—we—that is, it—" Min glanced over his shoulder, swallowed, and covered his mouth.

Fat furrows appeared between Sokar's brows. "What woman's weakness is this? Get out of my way."

He shoved the men aside and loomed over the body they'd been shielding from him. He was immediately assaulted by the odor of exposed and decaying raw meat. Sokar covered his nose and mouth while swiping at the hordes of flies buzzing around the body of a man lying on his back. He stepped back, almost stumbling.

The man had obviously been one who labored with his hands, one of moderate height, thinning hair, and skin turned almost black from working in the sun. His nose had been broken and had healed crookedly, but the parallel slashes across his throat were far more conspicuous than this facial flaw. The cuts exposed tendon and flesh and distracted the viewer from the bloody wound above his ear. But what had made Sokar retreat and nearly gag was the hole in the man's chest.

Something heavy and sharp had cleaved flesh and bone in slanting blows deep enough to expose the heart. But the heart wasn't there. In its place, stuck upright into the tangle of vessels, muscle, and chipped bone at the bottom of the cavity, was a feather. Cloud-white, a little more than the length of a man's hand, it seemed to defile the dead man by its very beauty and purity.

A fly launched itself off the exposed meat of the wound and buzzed at Sokar. The chief of watchmen yelped and flailed at it with his walking stick. The fly soared away to perch on the dead man's nose. Sokar straightened from his defensive pose and scowled at the other men.

"Fools!" he barked. "This is a peasant come from his farm to the city on some worthless errand. No doubt he came with fellows and quarreled with them. We do not concern ourselves with the doings of lowlings, however grotesque. Get a shroud—a heavy shroud—and send him to the necropolis. And bother me no more with such insignificances, or I'll set you to guarding dung heaps."

"But, master, the feather," Min wailed.

"An accident." Sokar cast a furtive glance at the body and its obscene decoration. "Some goose or other fowl strayed near the body and left it. You're nearly soiling your kilt over something that has an ordinary explanation. Some quarrel has ended in death and a little magic."

Keeping his gaze averted from the body and making the sign against evil, Sokar shook his walking stick at Min. "No more wild imaginings. If you bother me with something like this again, you'll regret it."

Sokar spun around and tramped out of the alley before anyone else could speak. Once he reached the street, his pace quickened, and he kept looking over his shoulder as if he expected the heartless corpse to get up and chase him. He went so fast that his attendant was forced to trot after him.

Back in the watch compound, Sokar called for beer and more date bread. He scurried into his workroom, shoved apprentices and citizens waiting to see him outside, and collapsed on a cushioned wicker stool. The seat creaked in protest at his weight. He settled into the cushion and wiped sweat from his forehead, nose, and upper lip.

Everyone knew peasants had been ordained to their brutal existence by the gods. The sacred ones had created the orderly society in which Egyptians lived, each man and woman assigned a place with certain work, certain duties. Some, like the dead man, led a rough, contentious life that ended in violence. Who knew why such low ones behaved as they did? No doubt some netherworld demon had caused the quarrel in which the farmer was killed.

Vengeful spirits of dead ones who had been abandoned by their descendants lurked in the darkness. Their kas had been left to starve for lack of offerings, and these miserable spirits often wrought havoc among the living. They incited evil as surely as a pretty woman evoked lust. And Min hadn't the sense to recognize such a common truth and behave accordingly.

Sokar sucked in a deep breath and let it out slowly. Taking a long sip of beer, he picked up a length of papyrus that rested beside him on the floor. He drew a lamp closer, picked up a rush pen, and dipped it in water and black ink from a palette. Now, to continue his reports. Each day he composed one for the mayor, a copy of which would be sent on to the office of Lord Meren, Eyes and Ears of Pharaoh. When one's writings might be inspected by a great one such as Lord Meren, one chose one's subject and phrases most carefully.

Under a column headed "Happenings of the Day" Sokar wrote in cursive script: "One death, a farmer not of the city." No need to disgust a great one with meaningless details. He moved on to list the theft of valuable chisels from a stone worker.

A LITTLE GIRL followed her mother past a fruit stall in a crowded market near the palace district. She yanked on her mother's skirt and pointed up, past the rooftops, at a bird of prey soaring on the invisible winds that swept the sky. Horus, the falcon, "Far-Above One," god of the sky, son of Osiris, protector of pharaoh. This was the sky-falcon, whose eyes are the sun and the moon.

The Horus falcon embodied the majesty and power of Egypt and her king, from its hooked upper bill to the tips of its slate-gray wings. Gray darkened to black as it reached the bird's nape and head, creating a startling contrast with the white of its underside. A curved black slash marked its white cheek.

The bird suddenly dove straight down and vanished near the bank of the Nile, then reappeared, its attack aborted. Banking sharply, it left the market behind to glide easily over the massive ramparts of the royal palace. Uttering an ascending wail, *weechew-weechew, weechew-weechew*, it began a long, graceful descent. The falcon's path took it over colossal pylons, palace lakes and gardens bursting with exotic flowers and incense trees, masses of lofty palms around courtyard after courtyard filled with festival-dressed men and women. At last the bird landed on top of an obelisk carved in pink granite and covered in electrum. Strong wings swept back and forth for balance before folding to the creature's sides.

The sky-falcon tilted its head. The eye of the sun, round and obsidian-black, looked down at a gravel path lined with guards along which two men walked. The taller, darker one followed the other, and they disappeared into the palace. With a rasping *kack-kack-kack*, the Horus falcon sprang aloft, climbing the sky to leave behind the place called Domain of Tutankhamun, Great of Conquests, and the court of the Golden Horus.

AS MEREN STEPPED inside the royal palace he heard the harsh cry of a falcon. If he could have escaped on wings like that bird, he would have. But a summons from pharaoh couldn't be escaped, even if his mood was as foul as a chamber pot. Why had fate thrust upon him this burden of discovering secrets so dangerous that even suspecting them could result in the annihilation of his whole family?

Thus preoccupied, Meren spared no glance at the dozens of guards on alert in the palace corridors and faience-tiled reception rooms through which he walked. Trying to hurry without seeming to do so, Meren reached an antechamber behind the imperial throne room. It was protected by the largest and most formidable of the king's personal body-guards, under the command of Meren's even more formidable escort.

None of the guards took notice of Meren as Karoya came forward and opened the polished cedar door. The antechamber was filled with more of Karoya's men. Each was armed with a scimitar and a dagger thrust into his beaded belt. All wore engraved bronze-covered leather corselets wrapped across their chests.

Meren felt almost naked without his own armor. He was dressed for court, bejeweled and painted, decked in gold, lapis lazuli, turquoise, and malachite. His only weapon was a ceremonial dagger with a hilt of beaded electrum. A brief thought flitted into his heart. If he pursued Nefertiti's killers—there had to be more than one—and made the slightest mistake, it would take an army of royal bodyguards to keep him and the family safe.

He should be making preparations, not wasting time at court. The moment he'd seen Karoya at his house, Meren knew his plans for the morning were ruined. Karoya only appeared when pharaoh sent a personal rather than official message. He had been summoned to a ceremony he'd thought to avoid—the king's reception of the long-awaited Hittite royal emissary. Meren's own web of informers was convinced that the king of the Hittites, Suppiluliumas, had been using rebellious vassals and disgruntled rival claimants to princely thrones to create unrest at the edges of the Egyptian empire.

Several princes loyal to pharaoh had already been attacked and defeated in their city-states in Syria and Palestine. Ordinarily Egypt would have attributed such events to the perennial eddies and currents of warfare that plagued the region. But Suppiluliumas was a conqueror. If he was allowed to continue his depredations unchecked, Egypt might someday find the Hittite armies at her own borders. It had happened once, with the Hyksos. That humiliating conquest had left Egypt with an abiding determination never again to fall victim to an invasion of Asiatics.

Pharaoh must have decided he needed all his foremost servants beside him to present a united phalanx to the Hittite emissary. Thus it was that Meren had donned court garb and come to the palace. Karoya had taken up a stance beside the door that opened into the imperial throne room, a vast, pillared audience hall fabled throughout the world for its magnificence. Nodding to Karoya, Meren waited for the Nubian to open the door, then sighed and walked into a blaze of gold. Blinking in the light of a thousand tapers and alabaster lamps perched on stands, he entered behind and to the right of the throne itself. Karoya went to his place in front of the right-hand support column of the dais.

Pausing, Meren surveyed a sea of the finest starched and pleated linen worn by dozens of courtiers. Ministers, nobles, and government officials rivaled the raiment of the gods in their stone temples with their plaited and smoothed wigs, their heavy earrings, their collars of gold and electrum. None, however, equaled the splendor of pharaoh.

Tutankhamun was seated on an ebony-and-gold throne, and he wore the double crown of Upper and Lower Egypt. Though only fourteen, he carried the heavy gold, lapis lazuli, carnelian, and turquoise of his royal costume as if it were unadorned linen. Meren had to stop himself from smiling. It wasn't long ago that the boy king had complained bitterly of the nuisance of having to wear the tall, heavy crowns, the ceremonial gold beard and cumbersome imperial rings. He'd said it was like wearing the contents of the royal treasury.

A snakelike movement caught Meren's attention. Lying beside the throne and swirling his tail was the king's black leopard—Sa, the guardian. The double crown moved slightly. Meren's gaze flicked upward to meet the solemn regard of pharaoh. Tutankhamun lifted his eyebrows, a signal so fleeting that most wouldn't understand it.

Meren eased his way through the ranks of ministers close to the king and joined the vizier Ay and General Horemheb beside the first step of the covered dais upon which the throne rested. The entire hall gleamed with the jewels of the courtiers, the decorations on the weapons of the guards, the embellishments on the posts and awning over the dais, the throne itself. More royal guards stood in motionless rows against the walls. Behind them rose great painted reliefs showing the king slaughtering his enemies in his golden chariot, the king returning from battle with hundreds of prisoners, the king trampling a Libyan rebel while hacking a Syrian with his war ax.

Tutankhamun complained increasingly that Meren and his other ministers wouldn't let him go into battle and make these brilliantly executed paintings more than examples of royal aspirations. The boy was growing more and more impatient to measure up to the warrior-king images with which he was confronted daily. Soon Tutankhamun would make Meren fulfill his promise to take him on a raid against one of the bandit gangs that plagued the more isolated Egyptian villages.

An abrupt silence fell over the assembly. A hollow pounding echoed through the hall and bounced off the high walls. The overseer of the audience hall paced slowly down the long avenue formed by column after column, each in the form of a bundle of papyrus plants. Meren had to stop his thoughts from wandering back to his own troubles as the overseer stopped some distance from pharaoh.

"Mugallu, prince and emissary of the king of the Hittites prostrates himself and begs to come into the presence of the living Horus: Strong Bull, Arisen in truth, Gold-Horus: Great of strength, Smiter of Asiatics, the King of Upper and Lower Egypt, Nebkheprure Tutankhamun, Son of Ra, Lord of Thebes, beloved of Amun-Ra."

The elderly Ay left Meren's side to stand before the throne. He would speak to the Hittite prince, for pharaoh never deigned to engage in personal speech with mere emissaries, even if they were princes. Trumpets blared, and the towering double doors, each encased in gold, swung open. Mugallu strode quickly into the hall. His clothing gleamed strangely, and Meren swore under his breath. The emissary was wearing Hittite silver.

From head to foot, the man was wearing the white metal that rivaled gold in its beauty, the metal that, unlike gold, pharaoh did not control. It was a reminder of the richness of the Hittite mountain kingdom. A deliberate challenge it was, for much of pharaoh's vast power stemmed from control of Egyptian and Nubian gold. The emissary's kilt was embroidered with roundels in the shape of lions' heads, his cloak with lozenge-shaped plaques in the same design. Even his boots with their curled-up toes reflected silver. Two thick coils of hair on either side of his face hung past his shoulders. The rest of his long, wavy hair was kept back from his face by an engraved silver diadem.

Meren edged nearer the throne and cast a covert glance at pharaoh. The king understood this challenge. Unfortunately, he had allowed it to annoy him. Those large, solemn eyes narrowed. He clenched his scepters, the crook and the flail, until his knuckles turned white. Meren covered his mouth and coughed. Pharaoh's gaze slid to him, then snapped back to the Hittite, who was receiving the formal greeting from Ay.

During this ceremony, Mugallu waited with an uninterested expression on his face. He was a young man, a warrior of the Hittite court and a relative of King Suppiluliumas. Like most Hittites, he was stocky, like a zebra, and bore a pyramid of a nose that jutted out from his face with an aggression that mirrored the character of his people.

Meren remembered Mugallu from other visits; his most common facial expression was a sneer, and unlike pharaoh's subjects or his vassals, he didn't hold Tutankhamun in reverence as a living god. To Mugallu, pharaoh was another prince like himself, and he stood in the way of Hittite ambitions of conquest. Of all the peoples of the world, only a Hittite would dare approach pharaoh so insolently.

Ay was concluding his speech. "The emissary may kiss the foot of the Lord of the Two Lands, the living god, son of Amun, the golden one, the divine Nebkheprure Tutankhamun."

Mugallu swaggered forward, his gaze fixed on the young king rather than on the floor, as that of any mannered ambassador would have been.

He almost bounced up the stairs of the dais, over the inlaid figures of the bound and subjugated enemies of Egypt that decorated the platform. When he reached the king, he dropped quickly to his knees, bent his head over pharaoh's golden sandal, and straightened almost immediately. Backing down the stairs, bowing slightly, he returned to his place. Pharaoh barely nodded, granting permission for the ceremony to proceed, his expression blank.

Mugallu clapped his hands once. A slave hurried forward, bearing an object covered with a cloth. The slave knelt on the floor before pharaoh, proffering the gift with his head bent. Mugallu removed the cloth. A stir moved through the throng of courtiers and ministers that filled the hall. Lying on the cushion was a king's dagger with a gold hilt engraved with roaring lions, bulls, and stags. But it wasn't the gold that provoked awe; it was the blade, made of iron, the metal that could sever bronze. Egyptians called it metal of heaven.

All royal murders and dangers of intrigue fled Meren's thoughts as he gazed at the dagger. He looked at Mugallu, whose expression was mockingly humble as he bowed to pharaoh. Was the Hittite king issuing another challenge? Or did he merely want his rival to fear that he'd discovered the secrets of working the metal in large amounts and could now outfit his entire army? Meren felt General Horemheb move. He followed as the military man joined Ay in staring at the Hittite prince.

"O great king, ruler of Egypt," Mugallu said, his voice echoing in the empty heights of the throne room. "Thus speaks *tabarna* Suppiluliumas, the great king, king of Hatti, son of Tadhaliyas, great king of Hatti, son of Armuwandas, descendant of Hattusilis, king of Kussara."

The emissary lifted his arms. He assumed an aggrieved expression, which sat ill with his pugnacious features, especially the eagle's-beak nose. "Why does the king, my brother, Nebkheprure Tutankhamun, accuse me of destroying his vassals? Are not his friends my friends, and his enemies my enemies? Someone has spoken falsely to the king my brother, for my heart is pure, my deeds clean of evil."

Mugallu lowered his arms and took a step toward Tutankhamun. He smiled at pharaoh as if he were a naughty but amusing puppy. A murmur rose up from the officials behind Ay, but Meren kept his gaze on the king. Tutankhamun's blank expression had vanished. His large dark eyes could look bruised and filled with the grief of the world, but now they ignited with the flames of the lakes of fire in the netherworld. Meren quickly stepped to Ay's side, caught the older man's gaze, and looked up at pharaoh.

"Do something," Meren whispered.

Ay muttered, "You know I can't."

Having failed to gain a response from his royal victim, Mugallu resumed his speech. "Thus says the *tabarna* Suppiluliumas, the great king, king of Hatti. The king, my brother, is young, like a colt among stallions in the treacherous, snow-shrouded mountains. Let not my brother lend his ear to evil-sayers." Mugallu paused to swagger to the front right corner of the dais, near Karoya, where he put his fists on his hips and continued.

"Thus says the king of Hatti. Never do I attack a prince in his city without just cause. In Syria certain carrion-eaters have given refuge to Hittite traitors and refused to send them back to me. I have a right to pursue traitors and those who harbor them. But such small doings need not concern my younger brother. For as men love the sun and a green mountain valley, so I love my brother. Whosoever has mouthed words of evil into thy majesty's ear, let him be cast out of thy presence, forced into the desert to die. Let him be carrion to hyenas—"

There was a sudden movement on the dais. Mugallu stopped in midsentence, his mouth open, as the youth he'd been addressing thrust himself up from the throne. At the same time, a wave of movement traveled over the vast audience hall. Karoya and his royal bodyguards took one step forward and banged their gold-tipped spears on the floor with a crack that made Mugallu jump and stare at those around him. Minister, princes, foreign ambassadors, and nobles dropped to their knees, foreheads touching the floor.

As Meren sank to the ground, he turned his head to the side to glimpse the king. Tutankhamun was breathing hard and glaring at Mugallu. With jerking movements he thrust out the gold-and-lapis flail scepter and pointed at the gaping emissary.

"You dare address my majesty as a master chastises an apprentice?" Although he was only fourteen, pharaoh's voice boomed with the force of royal indignation. "My majesty knows from whence comes the evil and treachery that plague my empire to the north."

Meren held his breath, afraid that the king would reveal exactly how he knew the source of treachery.

"The king of Hatti, my brother, is ill served by so insolent an emissary."

Meren let out his breath.

Tutankhamun lowered his arm. Thick gold bracelets jangled when he jabbed at Mugallu again, putting a gold-sandaled foot forward. "My majesty may be young, but I am the living god, lord of Egypt, son of Amunhotep the Magnificent, descendant of Thutmose the Conqueror. My majesty's ancestors ruled this empire when yours were herding goats in your precious mountains. I will hear no more bleating of colts and carrion.

"Karoya!" pharaoh shouted. "Why is this barbarian, this mannerless foreign pestilence, still on his feet?"

Silence fell. No one moved, except Karoya, who simply lifted his spear. Reversing it, he held it in throwing position over his shoulder and flexed his knee, awaiting the command of the living god. Mugallu's gaze dropped from pharaoh to the Nubian. He didn't move. Then the silence in the hall was ripped by a snarl.

Mugallu's head swiveled in pharaoh's direction, then fixed on a lashing black tail. Cobralike, Sa slowly rose from his place beside the throne. Three stalking paces brought him to pharaoh's side. The restless tail swirled back and forth and snaked around Tutankhamun's legs. The flat black head lowered between lean shoulders, ears pinned back. Sa's wary gaze never left the Hittite.

Another snarl. Without glancing at the predator, Pharaoh lowered his hand to caress the cat's obsidian neck. Sa bared his teeth, but his snarl turned to an irritated rumble at the back of his throat. The Hittite hadn't breathed since that first snarl. When Sa remained at pharaoh's side, the emissary remembered to take in a gulp of air. Meren nearly smiled. He heard a suppressed snigger from the group of ministers behind him.

Mugallu heard it too. His mouth worked, and a flush crept up his neck to stain his cheeks. His jaw muscles contorted with fury, but he darted a glance at Karoya, knelt, slowly, and touched his forehead to the floor.

The silence stretched out, causing even Meren to grow uneasy. Pharaoh was still glaring down at the Hittite. At last he whirled on his heel. Karoya abandoned his battle stance and walked swiftly to meet the king as he descended the throne by the left-hand stair. No one moved while the bodyguard snapped a salute and turned in formation to follow the king. Tutankhamun vanished through the door Meren had used. More guards issued forth to slam the portal closed and plant crossed spears before it.

Meren blinked several times during the royal departure, trying to take in what had happened. Living gods weren't supposed to speak to lowly foreign princes. Living gods preserved an aura of divinity, majesty, calm authority. Even Akhenaten had never broken with this tradition.

"Help me up, boy."

Meren straightened and lent his arm to Ay, whose brittle bones protested at such exertion. Around them the court got to its feet. Mugallu jumped up and rounded on Ay, red-faced, tight-lipped, and furious.

"I am a royal prince, beloved by his majesty and trusted of the great king, Suppiluliumas! Never has the royal message of my king been rejected with such discourtesy. I repeated with all truthfulness the words of my—"

Meren interrupted smoothly. "Highness, are you telling the vizier that your message, which has provoked the wrath of the living god, was the intentional insult of the king of Hatti?"

Mugallu started to reply, then hesitated. His crimson face paled, and he began again. "Never has my master, the great king, offered insult to his brother, the divine Lord of the Two Lands."

"I thought not," Meren said.

Ay sighed and wiggled his fingers at Mugallu in a dismissive ges ture. "Leave now, prince. Before the golden one's wrath renews itself. I would hate to have to send you home in boxes."

"Boxes?"

Meren gave him a gentle smile. "Boxes, probably a dozen or so, highness." He kept smiling until Mugallu was gone. Then he whispered to Ay.

"Pharaoh almost brought us to the verge of war. Was this your idea?"

"Don't be absurd, boy. The Hittite was even more insolent than usual."

"More insolent? What has been going on?"

Ay was prevented from answering. Ministers and nobles crowded around them, asking them what this amazing occurrence meant. Meren answered inquiries with soothing unconcern while his own apprehension remained unabated. Then, abruptly, Karoya appeared at his side. Friends and officials dropped away from Meren. He gave the Nubian an inquiring look. Karoya made no reply. He simply turned and left, expecting Meren to follow. Meren obeyed; for an Egyptian there was no other response imagin- able. When pharaoh commanded, the world bent to his will.

3

FROM THE SHELTER of a persea tree in pharaoh's private garden Meren watched Karoya leave and a pair of royal guards swing shut the carved door in the gate. Surrounded by a high brick wall, the garden was called Delights of Hathor, and it was deserted. As he'd entered, Meren had glimpsed retreating figures as they went through a door concealed behind dense vines. The chief gardener and his assistants, several water carriers, slaves bearing tall fans, women carrying trays—all had been dismissed.

The king would be a while disrobing. The heavy crowns, beard, rings, and jeweled linen overrobe demanded intricate maneuvers to get pharaoh out of them without snagging the royal hair or tangling the beads of a necklace with those sewn on the robe. And each item had to be treated with ceremony by privileged servitors who would be offended if Tutankhamun removed even an earring by himself. This was why the boy often avoided formal robing ceremonies.

Meren wandered over to a stand of sycamores. A delicate pavilion stood in the midst of this small forest, a bright blue, red, and gold jewel amid the dark green foliage. The quarrel with Mugallu would have to be settled. Pharaoh's harsh words could provoke an exchange of insults during which one side or the other would go too far, inciting war before Egypt was ready. Ay was already handling that problem; Meren had his own duties, other tasks, other worries, not the least of which was his own son.

Kysen was daily growing more perceptive. Even a few months ago, Meren could have hidden his anxiety from the boy. Wandering across the garden to a line of imported incense trees, Meren sat on the edge of a clay tub in which a myrrh tree flourished. His wrist itched. He pulled a slender pin from the clasp of a wide gold wristband inscribed with his name and titles, opened the hinged bracelet, and removed it.

He rubbed the white scar on his inner wrist. He could feel the voice of his heart pounding beneath his fingers as he rubbed the skin. Without meaning to, he sank into memories sixteen years old. Then he'd been but eighteen and a prisoner of the heretic pharaoh Akhenaten. The king had suspected him of adhering to the old gods when pharaoh had thrown them all out in favor of his own deity, the sun disk called the Aten. After killing Meren's father for refusing to adopt the new god, Akhenaten had imprisoned the son and tested him. Beatings, starvation, threats, nothing had broken Meren and made him confess to betraying the king's parvenu god.

Meren could still remember the smell of that shadowed cell where they kept him, a smell composed of dirt, sweat, the coppery scent of blood, and the contents of the sandy hole that served as his chamber pot. Meren pounded his fist against the side of the clay tub, willing himself to abandon this senseless reverie. Yet the images flooded through him as relentlessly as the Nile during Inundation. A burly guard kneeling on his arm while others pinned him to the floor. The white heat of a brazier, a glowing brand in the shape of the sun disk with sticklike rays extending from it and ending in stylized hands.

Then the images became feelings—that brief space between the moment when the brand met his flesh and that first searing agony; the pain shooting up his arm, into his heart; his scream; the feeling of distance, of floating away from his body, even as he broke out in icy sweat. Then, at last, the nausea that slammed him back into his body and kept him there to endure the pain.

Cursing aloud, Meren pounded his fist harder against the tub. The memories of pain faded, but not the misery of humiliation. The sun disk scar began to itch again. Meren glanced down at his wrist, smoothed his fingers over the pale circle that formed the sun, rubbed the rays that marked him as a victim of the heretic. Then he replaced the bracelet.

He should never have taken it off, never touched the scar. The burden of the truth about Nefertiti's death had disturbed memories of that terrible time in his life, memories he'd tried to seal in a deep stone chamber within his ka. But he shouldn't lie to himself. It wasn't just the dangerous secret of Nefertiti's death that robbed him of sleep and heart's peace. It was that other, even more momentous death, the one for which he was responsible. How did one justify allowing a living god, a pharaoh, to be killed?

He had suspected that Ay and his allies were going to end Akhenaten's life. Years of attempts to curb the king's excesses had failed, and Ay had no longer been willing to watch Egypt suffer. This Meren had known, and still he'd let Ay send him away to the Libyan border. When he got back, the heretic was dead, supposedly of the same plague that had taken his queen. And now, every time Meren tracked down a criminal, every time he sat in judgment of a thief, revealed the treachery of a courtier or the guilt of a killer, the dishonesty of his position tortured him.

Someday he would go west, to the netherworld and the Hall of Judgment. There the gods would weigh his heart on the divine balance scale against the feather of Maat—truth, rightness, and order. With such sins burdening his ka, his heart would send the weighing pan crashing to the floor. There the Devouress, Eater of Souls, would snatch it up in her crocodile jaws and sink long, jagged teeth into its meat.

The edge of the tub was biting into his legs. Meren winced and got to his feet. If he didn't watch himself, he would succumb to babbling lunacy. No wonder Kysen was suspicious. During the past few weeks these old memories had come back with increasing frequency. It was as if the heretic's vengeful ka had been aroused by the death of one of the queen's murderers. Perhaps Akhenaten was punishing him by forcing him to find and reveal the truth, so that Meren would invite his own death.

He was relieved that this frightening train of thought was quenched when the gate opened and a youth in a simple kilt strode into the garden. He was followed by two slaves bearing ostrich feather fans, another carrying a tray with a wine flagon and goblets, and several guards. His brows drawn together, mouth set in a tight line, he saw Meren and headed for him. The goblets on the tray clattered. The boy stopped, turned, and hissed at the small crowd behind him. The fan bearers backed away. The wine bearer skittered after them. A command like the snap of a whip sent the guards marching out the gate. Karoya appeared bearing the flagon and goblets, shut the gate, and went to the pavilion.

By this time Meren had reached the boy, who turned from glaring at the gate. Meren sank to his knees and bent to the ground. He heard an exasperated sigh.

"Get up, Meren. Making your obeisance to my majesty won't convince me that you're either biddable or humble."

"As thy majesty wishes," Meren said as he rose.

"Things are never as I wish." Tutankhamun stalked past Meren, between dense beds of cornflowers, mandrake, and poppy to a grove of tamarisk trees. In their midst was an arbor covered with ivy. The pharaoh snatched a water bottle hanging from the arbor in a woven net, poured from it into an alabaster cup from a table, and drank. He thrust the bottle at Meren, who poured himself a cup and drank as well. The king downed another cup of water without pause. When he finished, he was breathing fast and glaring at Meren.

"You're not to scold me," Tutankhamun snapped. "I'll get enough from Ay to fill my belly."

"Thy humble cup bearer would not dare—"

"I remembered you doing that very thing not long ago when I visited you at your country house."

It was Meren's turn to frown. "The golden one stole away from his own court, his own vizier and ministers, to sail unescorted to a house where I was trying to conceal the bodies of—"

"Don't!"

Royal irritation vanished, overwhelmed by pain and horror. Tutankhamun's face held the beauty of his mother, the great and powerful Queen Tiye. With it he had inherited her large, dark eyes, heavy-lidded, thick-lashed mirrors of a ka too sensitive for the burdens of a god-king.

Meren waited a moment, giving the boy time to compose himself. "Forgive me, majesty."

"I know it's really Akhenaten's fault," Tutankhamun whispered. "If he hadn't cast out the old gods, beggared their priests and the thousands who depended on them, he wouldn't have provoked such hatred. He must have done horrible things to provoke the desecration of his tomb, the savaging of his body."

He couldn't let the boy dwell on such anathema. "All has been put right, divine one." He drew closer to the king, who gave him a look of desperation.

"They won't let me return to Thebes for the reburial. Ay says I must remain here to draw everyone's attention."

"It's the only way, majesty. You trust Maya. If he can manage the royal treasury, he can arrange for thy majesty's brother and his family to be concealed in the Valley of Kings, where no one will disturb them again."

Tutankhamun sighed again. "Of course."

"And only thy majesty can summon the priests of Amun from Thebes to Memphis."

A grin brightened the king's solemn features. "The high priest was so furious he was shaking when he arrived at court. He wanted to chastise me, and he might have dared if I hadn't told him I needed his advice about the Hittites."

At the mention of the Hittites, the king's smile vanished. "He never kisses my foot!"

"Majesty?"

"Mugallu. He pretends. He kneels and bows over my foot, but he never touches me. I give him an honor I grant to few emissaries, and he never kisses my foot. He didn't this time."

"Ah," Meren said. "And having studied to arouse thy majesty's just wrath, he succeeded. Thus provoking a quarrel between his experienced master and pharaoh, who is not yet fifteen."

Tutankhamun slammed his cup down on the table. "I know, I know." He paced back and forth, then stopped and grinned at Meren. "I shall tell him I'm sorry."

"Majesty?" Meren had never heard a living god even pronounce the word "sorry." He furrowed his brow, trying to imagine such a thing, and failed.

The king laughed. "Don't look so aghast. I'll send word that I regret that his barbaric rudeness provoked me to harshness."

"Ah." Relief smoothed Meren's brow. "I was about to counsel the golden one to refrain from such an unprecedented action."

"But none of this is what I wished to talk about. Come with me to the pavilion."

The king sat on a couch the frame of which had been fashioned as a lion. The gilded wood was surmounted by cushions in the same colors used in the pavilion. Tutankhamun indicated a place on the floor beside the couch, and Karoya put a cushion there for Meren. The guard served plum wine and *shat* cakes seasoned with tigernuts and sweetened with honey and dates.

Pharaoh waited until Meren was in the middle of a sip of wine to speak. "You're avoiding reading the desert patrol reports so that you won't find bandits that need hunting."

Meren paused with wine in his mouth. He glanced up at the king. Deceptively, the boy's cheeks still held the roundness of childhood. His mouth was a replica of the full lips and downward-pointing corners of Queen Tiye's. The richness of eyes and mouth, the oversize, puppylike hands and feet, created an impression of youthful vulnerability. Sometimes Meren forgot that Tutankhamun came from a line of warriors, conquerors, and masters of strategy. He swallowed his wine.

"How did the divine one know?" Meren asked lightly.

"After you promised to take me on a raid to gain battle experience, I bethought myself of how you might wish to delay in hopes I'd forget. Then I sent inquiries to the chief of royal messengers, who confirmed my suspicions. So I dispatched members of my war band to the villages where there has been trouble in the past. Word of any marauding will come directly to me."

Meren slid to his knees and bowed, touching his forehead to the floor. "Thy majesty has surpassed me in wisdom and craft. I await thy discipline, O Horus, Strong-Bull-arisen-in Thebes, Gold Horus, Mighty-in-strength, Majestic-in-appearance, Lord of the Two Lands—"

"Meren, be quiet and sit up."

"Yes, majesty."

"Do you think it easy to balance between childhood and manhood, apprenticeship and kingship? You, Ay, Maya, and General Horemheb must stop protecting me. I can't learn to lead my armies from this pavilion."

"I know, majesty. And thy majesty knows what will happen if he dies on some petty raid, without an heir, without guiding Egypt back from the chaos of thy brother's—of the last few years."

"You will be there to protect me. I will hear no more protests. And I will punish you by making you sponsor Lord Reshep at court. You've met him?"

Sighing at this tedious assignment, Meren nodded. "A few times, golden one. The last time at the feast of welcome Prince Djoser held for him. It is said he seeks a place at court after being raised in the country. And I know he has stirred the women of the court."

"Yes," the king replied. "Unfortunately, he's stirred one of the daughters of Queen Nefertiti's sister. My majesty has no quarrel with Reshep, but he will not court a lady of the royal family. See to it that he meets many eligible women, and obtain an appointment of some kind so that his hours are filled with something besides the sighs of princesses. Later, if your opinion of him is favorable, my majesty will allow him into my presence. This tedious work is your punishment. Next time you won't underestimate me."

Meren thought about the dangers of searching out and attacking desert bandits. "The Generals Nakhtmin and Horemheb and I have spent years training the golden one in the arts of battle, but all the training and precautions we can provide may not be enough, should Set, god of chaos, create disaster."

The king gave him a dark look, and Meren hastened on.

"All will be as thy majesty commands." He inclined his head. "Especially if thy majesty in his graciousness will grant his humble cup bearer leave to make a short journey, no more than two days."

"Why?"

"A matter less important to thy majesty than a beetle beneath the royal sandal. The nurse of my childhood grows aged and weak, and she begs me to visit her before she goes west to join her ancestors."

"My nurse used to tell me stories about Horus the hawk until I fell asleep. Of course, go. But don't forget the raid."

Tutankhamun rose, then stooped and grabbed Meren's arm. Startled, Meren allowed the king to pull him to his feet.

"You look as if a desert fiend just offered you its hand," the king said.

"Thy majesty has honored me with his touch."

Rolling his eyes, Tutankhamun said, "Have you not saved my life more than once? Discovering Prince Tanefer's treachery alone merited reward. But you keep warning me how dangerous my favor can be to the health of a nobleman. Only fear for your safety has prevented me from acknowledging my debt to you."

"Thy majesty is more generous than the bounty of the fields. But if I have to worry about the jealousy of rivals at court, I cannot devote myself to the service of the golden one with complete freedom."

"Very well, then you may go to this aged nurse of yours. But return quickly. I expect to get word of bandit raiders at any moment."

"As thy majesty wishes. I will leave in a few days and return with haste." Meren bowed low and retreated from the royal presence. He was halfway to the gate when a strong young voice called after him.

"And don't forget Lord Reshep!"

NIGHT CAME LATE and hot on the day pharaoh castigated the emissary of the hated Hittites. By moonrise, tidings of the confrontation had flown from the palace district, sailing to other courts with royal and foreign ships, leaping from mouth to mouth around the mansions, houses, and huts of Memphis. Soon princesses and dockworkers, scribes and barbers, were laughing and exulting over the boldness of their young king.

One who had not heard the news was the tavern woman called Anat. She walked through the open south gate of the city, waving to the chatting guards who leaned against the wall. By moon- and starlight, she directed her steps down a path that climbed to the barren higher land at the border between the desert and cultivated fields. As soon as she left the massive ramparts that guarded the capital, her shift was blown against her legs by a strong north breeze. She turned and lifted her face, breathing the water-scented air.

Anat set down the small sack of barley the tavern owner had given her for her night's work. It also contained various items some of the men had given her. She had been busy this night.

Sighing, Anat was about to pick up her sack and trudge the rest of the way to her mother's house. Then the wind picked up. She widened her stance and opened her arms so that she could feel the coolness. The breeze was so strong that it brought relief from the heat still rising from the sun-scorched earth. Without the wind, heat from the ground penetrated her thin papyrus sandals to bake her feet.

Tonight had been a busy night, a good night. With a few more nights like this one, she would have enough goods to quit the tavern and provide a handsome marriage share. There would be enough to attract a man of stature such as a master sculptor, or even a scribe. Then her widowed mother, who was a servant in the household of a village headman, could come to live with Anat and her new husband. Mother was too old to crush grain with a heavy grinding stone.

Bending over her grain sack, Anat opened it and took out a small bundle wrapped in a scrap of old linen. Inside lay trinkets from the men—faience ear studs and a kohl tube of the same dark blue material, a small oval bottle of scented oil for the skin, and a set of copper tweez-ers, hair curler, and a tiny spatula for mixing eye paint.

The scented oil was the most valuable gift, for it was oil of lilies scented with myrrh, cardamom, crocus, and cinnamon. She remembered the one who had given it. A splayfooted, sweaty old priest of Ptah who chafed at the requirement of his profession that when on duty, one practice celibacy.

Anat replaced the bundle inside the grain sack, picked it up, and resumed her walk to the village. It had indeed been a good night, but a hard one. She had entertained three scribes, a coppersmith, a physi-cian's apprentice, a brewer, a goldsmith and an incense roaster, the priest, and two of his fellows who served the goddess Sekhmet. Then there had been a scribe from the mortuary temple of one of the dead pharaohs, with his friend the stonemason. And she couldn't forget that hot-bellied woman who had burst into the tavern looking for her husband.

It had been Anat's ill luck that he'd been the second priest of Sekhmet. The wife, whose arms and legs might have belonged on the body of a quarryman, had chased Anat and the priest out of the upstairs chamber, wielding a stave longer and thicker than a warrior's javelin. Dodging that stave had wearied Anat. She'd left early, much to the annoyance of her next customer, a man of fine clothing but not so fine manners. And the tavern keeper, he'd been furious. Anat didn't care if he was angry. There had been plenty of customers, noble ones and prosperous merchants, to whom he could serve his watered beer.

Her mother's house stood on a patch of level ground at the outskirts of the village. It was a simple, flat-topped rectangle with a small front court. The court was used for everything from grain storage to cooking. The gate in the front wall of the court hung slightly askew. Its latch had fallen off, and Anat hadn't had the time to repair it.

She shoved the door open. The end slat touched the ground and slid along the dusty groove it had worn into the packed earth. Anat sighed and called to her pet cat. He was a foul-tempered menace, but he waited for her on top of the court wall each night. No sleek black body leaped down and came padding toward her. She called again, listening for his irritated yowl.

Then something sailed through the air past her shoulder to land at her feet. Anat bent down to scold the cat, squinting in the light of the full moon. She touched something wet, smelled blood and fur. Gasping, she jumped up and backed away from the lacerated carcass of her pet until she hit the rickety door. The panel rammed into her back with so much force she was propelled forward.

She stumbled and fell to her knees beside the cat's body. As she fell, Anat heard a deep-throated snarl. Terrified, she pushed herself to her feet and whipped around to face her attacker. She still had her grain sack. Grabbing the top in both hands as she spun, Anat drew her arms back, ready to swing the bag in a blow that would stun. Then she saw what was in the courtyard with her.

Anat hesitated, her mouth opening in a wordless scream. There was a blurred movement of razor claws. Anat's mouth worked. She dropped the grain sack, spilling and shattering its contents. She remained on her feet, poised between life and the unknown, staring at the thing that had waited for her. Then she plummeted to her knees again. Her eyes were sightless when the blood-drenched claws descended.

THE CHIEF OF watchmen was ensconced in his cushioned chair, rush pen poised over a sheet of papyrus as he listened to the summaries given by the night's watch leaders. He wiggled his sagging belly until it fit beneath the fragile writing table. His wig was already askew because he'd stuck a stubby finger beneath it to scratch his sweating scalp.

The last of the watch leaders withdrew. The first of the private citizens with complaints entered. A silver-haired old one wearing more wrinkles than a thrice-worn kilt hurried in. To Sokar's annoyance, the old one didn't wait for him to bark questions. He launched into a babbled tale of the death of some woman from one of the outlying villages.

Sokar pounded on the table, producing a loud crack. "Peace, old one!"

The villager started and fell silent to gape at Sokar. Mollified by the old one's fright, Sokar smoothed his sheet of papyrus. Carefully and with time-consuming leisure, he swirled his rush pen in the black inkwell of his scribe's palette. With the pen poised over the sheet, Sokar grunted his satisfaction.

"You may continue, aged one. Begin with who this woman was."

"Anat, master."

"And who is this woman Anat?"

"She—she was employed at the beer tavern called Mansion of Joy. She came home late, in the middle of the night."

The old one stopped when Sokar glared at him and held up a hand.

"Wait." Sokar drew his thick oily brows together and snarled, "Are you speaking of some tavern woman? Some unknown woman who prances about the streets alone at night? Do you know how many petty tavern brawls erupt every night in this city?"

"But she's dead!"

"In her village, you said. It's not the concern of the city watch."

"But there is a feather, and her chest—"

"By the gods!" Sokar leaned toward the old one, and his belly shoved the table as he moved. "Aide!" he bellowed, causing the old one to jump and retreat. Sokar's assistant appeared. The chief of the city watch had turned the color of raw beef. "Throw this fool out, and see that he doesn't return."

The aide grabbed the visitor by the arm and thrust him from the office. Sokar pulled his writing table back. Wiping his face with a scrap of linen he used to clean his pens, he grumbled to himself.

"Bothering a great man like me with such vulture's dung. Must be more than a hundred taverns, countless tavern women, all making trouble, disturbing the order of the city, making me write reports."

Commiserating with himself for his burdens, Sokar picked up a water jar and drank from it in big gulps. Water dribbled down his thick neck. Breathing hard, he set down the jar, wiped his face and neck. A drop spilled on the papyrus.

Sokar carefully blotted the water, took up his pen again, and made an entry in the section for deaths. "A tavern woman, not of the city."

EATER OF SOULS had fed, and now she slept. But the gods had bestowed upon her a link to the favored one, and this connection brought wisps of memory, like tendrils of smoke fed by damp wood.

There is a mother. She is like a newborn bird, ravenous, demanding, never filled. The favored one tries to satisfy the hunger. The hunger doesn't ebb; it grows and grows. The bird clamors for more, cheep, cheep, cheep, cheep, cheep. The noise careens around inside the favored one's head, growing louder, more shrill, more painful. Cheep, cheep, cheep, cheep. Something inside the favored one breaks. He bashes in the mouth that will not close, stopping forever that ravening appetite and those maddening cheeps.

4

KYSEN WAS ON the loggia that sheltered the entry to Golden House, waiting to escort his sisters to the family's private quay. Meren was holding a banquet on his pleasure yacht to become better acquainted with the newcomer, Lord Reshep. In the drive not far away, a groom held the reins of Kysen's restless thoroughbred team, which was harnessed to a chariot decorated with scenes of a desert hunt. In the deep golden light, the acacias and sycamores that surrounded the house cast long shadows on the horses and vehicle. Evening was almost here, and Bener and Isis were late.

He was about to send a servant to fetch them when Reia, one of the company of charioteers that served Meren, hurried around the corner of the house, raced up the stairs, and saluted Kysen.

"Lord, Abu has arrived from Thebes. He wanted to see you at once."

"Yes. I'll come now."

They made their way through the house and across the grounds, cutting through the garden, skirting the pleasure pool with its complement of small boats. Kysen led the way through a door in the long wall that separated the family's quarters from the barracks that housed the charioteers. Unlike the smaller residence in Thebes, Golden House possessed quarters for over thirty charioteers who assisted Meren as the Eyes of Pharaoh. Next to the low barracks that stretched almost the length of the guard wall lay a modest two-story house. This was the home of Abu, Meren's chief aide, who, until Kysen had sent for him, had been overseeing Meren's affairs in Thebes.

A servant was holding the front door open. Kysen hurried inside while Reia dismissed the servant. Abu was waiting in the reception hall in a chair amid piles of leather document cases, several caskets, and a discarded scimitar. He rose when Kysen entered.

"*You* sent for me, lord? I left Iry in charge at Thebes as you instructed."

Nodding, Kysen didn't miss the emphasis. Abu had trained Meren in the arts of a warrior. He'd saved Meren's life in battle, and Meren had saved his. Perhaps no one knew Kysen's father so well, or held close to his heart so many secrets. Few had the rank to give orders to Abu at all, and up to now, when Kysen had occasion to do so, it usually had been on behalf of his father. Kysen glanced over his shoulder at Reia. The charioteer was standing in the middle of the room where he could see anyone who tried to enter from any of the side chambers that opened onto the hall.

Drawing near Abu, Kysen spoke quietly. "Has my father spoken to you of this matter concerning the Great Royal Wife Nefertiti?" He waited impatiently while Abu hesitated. "I can see that he has, so don't bother lying."

"I would never lie to the lord's son."

"You would if my father ordered it. Oh, don't argue. There isn't time." Kysen went on to tell the charioteer what had happened in the past few days. "So I can't convince him to leave this evil undisturbed."

Abu remained impassive. "When he has reached a decision, the lord is as unwavering as the path of Ra in the sky."

"By the blood of Osiris, I think you know more about this than I do." Abu merely gazed at him. "You do! Damnation to you. I suppose it's useless to order you to tell it to me."

"Yes, lord."

"Then you understand even better than I that Lord Meren will be in danger from the moment he makes this journey to see the queen's former cook. And he insists on going alone. Great lords do not travel unaccompanied, especially not the Eyes of Pharaoh."

"There is nothing that can be done to prevent the lord from steering this course," Abu said. His face still held no expression. "The lord will risk his life in this quest, even should the gods try to prevent it."

Kysen studied Abu and at last caught a fleeting look of concern before the charioteer masked it. "You know why I called you here."

"Yes, lord. To protect your father."

"He won't allow me to go with him. He's ordered me to conduct my own inquiries. Among my special acquaintances."

"Then your life is in danger as well."

"Oh, no. You're not dispatching a squad of giant nursemaids after me. They'll send every thief and drunkard scurrying from sight. Just make sure someone follows Lord Meren at all times." Before he could go on, Reia signaled and nodded in the direction of the front entrance.

"Why?" Bener was standing in the doorway in festive garb, her gleaming black wig falling over her shoulders. "Why is it necessary to have Father followed without his knowledge? What is happening?"

Kysen uttered a sound that was half groan and half sigh while Abu and Reia bowed to his sister. "Bener, you shouldn't be in the barracks."

"If Father is in danger, I want to know about it," she replied as she walked into the hall.

Her filmy gown rained pleats down to the floor. The smooth sweeps of kohl that lined her eyes, the glistening green malachite on her lids, the gold, turquoise, and lapis broad collar draped from her shoulders, all combined to make her look older than her sixteen years. Bener wasn't as beautiful as her younger sister. Her almond-shaped eyes tended to bore into people's characters with the precision and facility of a bow drill. Her chin, though small, recalled the strength and outline of a stonemason's mallet, and her nose was endowed with a little of the strong thrust of her father's. Nevertheless, her observant humor attracted the friendship of aged servants and young princely warriors alike. At the moment it was Kysen's regret that Bener also had inherited her father's strong will.

When he didn't answer, Bener walked over to Kysen and folded her arms over her chest. "What's wrong?"

"Nothing, by my ka."

"Oh, of course," Bener said with a guileless smile and wide-open eyes. "Nothing is wrong. Father moves about the house like an abandoned soul in the desert. You alternately glare at him and plead with him for hours. Abu appears mysteriously without Father's knowledge or orders. And my powerful sire, the Eyes of Pharaoh, one of those few in all the world who have the honor to be called Friend of the King, my father has suddenly decided to leave court in the middle of a perilous diplomatic skirmish with the Hittite emissary. In order to visit his old nurse."

"Yes," Kysen snapped. "Now find Isis and go to the chariot. I'll be there in a moment. And stop interfering. These affairs are not in a woman's domain."

He should have expected this of Bener. She had a clever heart and more than a little of Meren's circuitous reasoning power and abiding suspiciousness. Kysen wished she was still distracted by the steward and his excess watermelons.

Bener narrowed her eyes, and he caught a glimpse of shining green-and-black paint that only enhanced the glint she directed at him. "That is what you told me before I discovered who killed Uncle Sennefer."

"Women manage households and bear children," Kysen said. "They do not concern themselves with the tasks of men."

"Kysen, you're a fool. Do you really think that the wives who bear sons to their husbands, the mothers who nurse all male children, be they kings or water carriers, do you think these women have no influence upon the actions of those husbands and sons?"

Having never heard such an argument, Kysen only stared at his sister. She gave a little snort, turned sharply, and left them.

Kysen muttered a curse while glaring at the door through which Bener had vanished. "I must go, Abu. Father will be waiting for us. We must play host to this country lord who seeks a place at court. Lord Meren leaves for the cook's house tomorrow morning. Be careful."

"He won't know he has a second shadow."

Feeling much relieved now that Abu was alerted, Kysen joined Bener in his chariot. He wasn't surprised that Isis was late and would follow separately; she possessed a fragile, slender-necked beauty similar to that of Queen Nefertiti, and the work she did to enhance it consumed many hours. He and Bener arrived at the family's quay as Meren was greeting the first guests.

The pleasure yacht *Joy of the Nile* hadn't the sleek, spare menace of Meren's *Wings of Horus*. She was much wider and longer than that black-and-gold cruiser. *Joy* had a low, curved prow and high stern ending in a carved lotus flower, with a painted gold castle at either end and a long deckhouse set amidship.

The sides of the ship were painted with bands of lotus designs in white and green. But what made the ship burst into reflected flames in the lowering sun were the sheet gold that encrusted the prow and stern and the alternating bands of gilt paint that separated the lotus patterns.

A frieze of Nile-blue faience tiles repeated the lotus design on the deck-house, set off by borders of more gilt paint.

Guests were walking up the gangplank, which was draped with garlands of lotus, poppies, and cornflowers. Meren awaited them at the end of the walk in festival costume. Kysen imagined that moments ago his father's gaunt face had been tainted by a scowl. Unlike many courtiers, Meren preferred a simple kilt and sandals to the complex finery his position required him to wear. Now he stood on the deck of his opulent ship wearing a short kilt covered by a robe rich with thousands of pleats and cinched by a wide belt of gold and red jasper beads. More gold, jasper, and lapis lazuli glittered from his wrists, shoulders, and the band that encircled his heavy wig.

Kysen remembered the first time he'd seen his father in full court dress. He'd fallen to his knees, certain that Meren had turned into a god. The only thing he'd seen as magnificent had been the statue of the god Amun on the feast of Opet. His reverie was cut short by an elbow jabbed into his side.

"I'm not going to stand here all night while you gawk," Bener said. She hopped down from the chariot, straightened her necklace and wig, and glided away.

Hastening after her, Kysen joined Bener and Meren in offering greetings to the guests. This was an ordeal for him; surrounded by so many clean, perfumed, and bedecked people, he felt conspicuous. He was the only one who had grown up with nothing but a loincloth to wear, whose hair hadn't been properly cut until he was eight, whose only bathing facility had been the Nile.

"Cease," Meren whispered to him between arrivals.

"What?"

"Forget what you came from, Ky. It's what you are now that matters."

"The dirt and the beatings are part of what I am."

Meren suddenly changed. One moment he was Kysen's scolding father, the next he changed into a nobleman whose spectacular smile and personal dignity turned the most jaded court lady into an open-mouthed stutterer. Kysen scanned the approaching group and located the person who had provoked this display.

Princess Tio came toward them, her gown swaying in response to her rhythmic, long-legged walk. Going against custom, she wore her hair loose and unencumbered by a wig. She had wrapped strands of tiny electrum beads around lengths of that black river of hair.

Tio was the daughter of one of Akhenaten's Nubian concubines. Unlike pure Egyptian women, who were light-boned and often small, the princess possessed a body taut with long tendons and muscles and a height that enabled her to look down on quite a few men, including Kysen. She had warm brown skin touched with gold, a lithe frame, and eyes so large they nearly distracted attention from lush, protruding lips. Luckily for Tio, she had inherited her mother's features. A girl-child cursed with those of Akhenaten might well have been mistaken for a flabby horse.

Tio accepted Meren's welcome, her gaze passing over Kysen without pause. Kysen took this slight with equanimity. Tio was cup bearer to the Great Royal Wife, Ankhesenamun. The queen's close friend, she took her mistress's part in the ongoing quarrel between the queen and pharaoh. Ankhesenamun disagreed with Tutankhamun's return to orthodoxy. She blamed him for abandoning her heretic father's precepts, and for leaving his isolated new city, Horizon of Aten, for the ancient and fabled capital of Memphis. And now she blamed her husband for the stealthy attack on the tomb and bodies of her father and mother.

However, both Ankhesenamun and Tio blamed Ay, General Horemheb, and Meren as much as the king. Older than her husband by five years, the queen knew the influence wielded by these three men—and she resented Meren's power the most. Kysen wasn't sure why she should save her greatest antipathy for his father, but Tio had been infected with the queen's prejudice. If the princess was attending one of Meren's gatherings, it was a signal of some sort—an opening move in a new game in which Ankhesenamun exercised lethal power.

As Tio moved away from them, Meren whispered to Kysen again. "Be at ease. She's only curious about this new Lord Reshep, who has attracted the interest of one of the royal princesses. No doubt the queen sent her to inspect the man and give a report." A slave brought wine in fluted bronze goblets. Meren picked up two and handed one to Kysen.

"Quickly," he said. "Before anyone else arrives. Tell me why you have sent for my aide without my knowledge."

Kysen hesitated in mid-sip, swallowed hard, and gazed out across the flat rooftops of the city, past the electrum-encrusted temples to the jagged horizon of desert tombs and pyramids.

"It appears I haven't sent for him without your knowledge."

"Don't spar, explain."

Only pharaoh could speak with more quiet mastery. When Meren's voice took on that relentless certainty, no one disobeyed. Kysen had been waiting for this demand, having considered the prospect that keeping a secret from Meren might be impossible.

"You forgot to send for him, so I did. You always leave Abu in charge of the charioteers in Memphis."

He met his father's raking gaze calmly. He'd learned from Meren how to dissemble and had to trust that his lessons had been well learned. Meren held his gaze for what seemed like centuries, then raised his eyes to look toward the quay.

That elusive, charmed smile appeared again even as Meren spoke in a low voice. "I approve."

Kysen let out a breath he hadn't been aware of holding.

"So long as Abu remains in Memphis," Meren continued. "You do understand my meaning."

"Of course, Father."

"I thought you would, my clever young jackal. Now replace that frown with a smile and help me with the greetings. Ah, this superb creature with the fawning retinue must be Lord Reshep."

Toward them came a stately procession. It was headed by a young man of kingly height wearing linen even finer than Meren's. He walked beneath a wig thick with curled and plaited tresses that hung in heavy sections over his back and shoulders. Kysen looked at the man who wore this gleaming black elegance, then exchanged quizzical glances with Meren.

Whispering as he smiled at Reshep, Meren said, "To me he has always resembled a starved frog, but then I don't look at him through a woman's eyes." Meren moved forward to salute his guest and raised his voice. "May Amun provide you with countless blessings, Lord Reshep. Welcome to *Joy of the Nile*."

Kysen was left to battle a threatening smirk. Meren had noted Reshep's elongated arms and legs, his bony knees and elbows. Together with a low forehead, a wide, thin-lipped mouth, and prominent brown eyes, these features would indeed prompt his father's comparison. Kysen found it necessary to force away the image of Reshep squatting on a round lotus leaf floating in a reflection pool. Meren had been conversing steadily with Reshep. He turned and drew Kysen into the group that surrounded the newcomer.

"You weren't at Djoser's banquet, Ky. I met Lord Reshep there. His mother was an intimate of the Great Royal Wife Tiye long ago, before the king was born, may he have life, health, and strength."

Saying nothing, Reshep bowed low. When he straightened, Kysen met a gaze that arced out of Reshep's eyes to pierce through manners and decorum. It sliced past the formal friendliness Kysen offered and stabbed into the depths of his most secret ka. There it carved through and penetrated small but painful weaknesses, pettiness kept hidden from the world, and old grudges. Through this gaze Reshep seemed to expose all the little slights Kysen remembered from being a lowborn among the noble. Then this stranger seemed to delve into his pain—the pain he hoarded like a landowner accumulates rents, the pain he'd come to treat as a familiar and cherished friend.

Heavy black lashes drifted down, then lifted, releasing Kysen and leaving him with an urge to look at himself to see if he was as bare and exposed as he felt. The encounter had happened in the space of a heartbeat. He was disconcerted to find that no one else had noticed it. Kysen had to force himself not to look away from this man, to present the facade of civility and tranquillity Meren had taught him to wear. Reshep spoke at last, although to Kysen the pause in conversation had lasted far too long.

"Lord Kysen, may the favor of the gods be yours." His voice gentle, his smile beneficent, Reshep tilted his head to the side, his eyes lit with amusement he seemed to wish Kysen to share. "Since I arrived in glorious Memphis I have heard much of the clever and brave son of the Eyes of Pharaoh. It is said that none can challenge his bow, and that no young warrior has ever rivaled him in his capacity for tavern beer."

Meren said calmly, "I told you not to race about the city with that herd of ungovernable colts from the king's war band."

"I didn't know I'd earned such renown," Kysen replied. He was conscious of relief and gratitude to Reshep. For what he wasn't certain. Perhaps for having been allowed to keep hidden the humiliating secrets Reshep seemed to have discovered, accepted, and forgiven in their fleeting exchange. Reshep's laughing friends crowded around them, exchanging jests and calling for wine. Kysen's confusion faded as he met old companions.

"So," said a young man in gilded leather sandals, "you didn't know you had a name in the city. I could have told you. Your name is much better than mine. Everyone knows Meren's war training succeeded with you, while they laugh that it failed with me."

Kysen shoved a wine goblet at Prince Djoser. "Not this complaint again."

"No-no-no," Djoser said with a laugh. "Knowing Reshep has made me realize how bowed down with distress I've been. He says many great men—like Amunhotep, son of Hapu, and Imhotep, the powerful sage and magician—haven't been warriors."

Staring at Djoser, Kysen said, "But not long ago you wouldn't listen to Rahotep when he said the same thing."

"That was when I was afraid everyone was laughing at me for puking on the battlefield, and losing governance of my horses, and having to be rescued from my own chariot. Now I realize these are but paltry incidents to a great prince."

Kysen's jaw nearly dropped to the deck. "Is this the man who returned from the expedition to the Syrian vassals all pale and haunted by war demons?" He suddenly glanced from Djoser to Reshep, who had been encircled by a new group of guests. "Djoser, don't set up an altar for someone you've known but a few weeks."

"I worship at the feet of none but pharaoh!" Djoser drew himself up and frowned at Kysen. "I merely choose to become enlightened by good example. Perhaps you're jealous of Reshep already."

"Jealous?" Kysen glanced at Reshep again, noting the elbows and knees, each sharp as the point of an obelisk. "You're fevered."

"And your heart is envious," Djoser said. "Speak to me no more of altars and fevers when I have five more years than you, common-blooded meddler."

Djoser stalked away in his gilded sandals to rejoin his new friend. A woman in front of Reshep moved aside, and Kysen glimpsed him from head to foot, especially foot. Reshep wore gilded leather sandals like Djoser's, but the straps of his were wrapped in sheet gold and encrusted with amethysts. Djoser had encountered someone who shared his taste for splendor.

Kysen had always known Djoser felt unworthy because his mother had been a mere noblewoman who captured the eye of Tutankhamun's father. A scholarly man who longed to be what he was not—a great warrior—Djoser had allowed his failures to slowly curdle his spirit until he threatened to become a snarled ball composed of threads of resentment and bitterness.

Kysen was distracted from contemplating Djoser's unexpected transformation by the deck's movement beneath his feet. The ship swayed, then began to drift. Meren's crew had cast off from the quay. *Joy of the Nile*, a slim reed of illuminated color, glided into the darkening blue of the river. Their guests would watch the fiery pomegranate sun descend into the west, the netherworld, while bathing in the cool north breezes.

Slaves lit torches fitted to the sides of the ship; others lit precious candles and alabaster lamps carved in the fluted form of the lotus. The harpist struck up a feasting tune, accompanied by flutes, double pipes, and lyres. These were joined by drums, tambourines, and the sistrum, a handled, bent metal strip between the ends of which ran wires strung with metal disks. When shaken gently, the sistrum made Kysen's favorite sound, a murmuring chime that soothed his ka.

Meren appeared at his side, his gaze drifting over the milling company. Perfumed and coiffed nobles moved among tables decorated with lotus flowers and burdened with food. The belly-tempting smell of roast fowl revealed the enticement of duck, egret, crane, and prized red-breasted goose. Kysen was about to summon a slave and order a plate prepared for himself and Meren when he heard someone bark his name.

"Kysen, why are you not among that herd of fawning, slack-witted goats surrounding Reshep?"

Meren's arm lashed out and fastened onto that of Prince Rahotep. Hauling the younger man to him, he shot a warning look at his slightly drunk victim, flashed an irritated smile, and hissed at Kysen.

"Keep him at your side. I don't have time to serve as keeper to a man with the tact of a four-year-old child and the temper of a wounded pig."

Slapping Rahotep hard on the shoulders, Kysen grabbed the arm Meren relinquished. "Welcome, my friend. You honor us with your company."

"Huh." Rahotep burped and poured half a goblet of Syrian wine down his throat. "I saw you with that place-seeker. You don't like him any better than I do."

Rahotep scowled at his friend Djoser as he sidled closer to Reshep and fixed his attention on the newcomer's easy conversation. "Only the great god Amun knows why they find the bastard so admirable. He has but one theme to his songs—the perfection and wonder of Lord Reshep."

"Really?"

Kysen followed Rahotep's stare to its object. Djoser was introducing Bener to his idol. Without warning Lord Reshep looked up, over Bener's head, straight into Kysen's eyes. It was but a glance, yet Kysen was left feeling again the force of its perception. It was as if Reshep knew they were talking about him, even what they were saying. Shaken, Kysen felt suddenly angry with himself for reacting with such vulnerability. He dragged his gaze from Reshep. Dislike for the man burst forth, fed by resentment that this stranger could evoke fantasies and baseless fear in him.

"Did you hear what I said?" Rahotep demanded. "Djoser is so besotted he chants Lord Reshep's glorification endlessly to pharaoh, may he have life, health, and strength forever."

Kysen's anger twisted his smile with bitterness. "Father said he looks like a starved frog."

"Ha!" Those nearest them looked their way at Rahotep's loud hoot.

Kysen winced and said through set teeth, "Be quiet."

"Why should I?" Rahotep turned in a circle, glowered at the listeners, and said loudly, "Why should I care what they think? I'm a half-royal, son of Amunhotep the magnificent, a great warrior, clever of heart, unequaled in wisdom." He appeared to remember his manners. Presenting his back to the largest cluster of eavesdroppers, he lowered his voice. "I tell you, Ky, it makes me want to vomit to see a preening grasper turn great lords into vassals and noble ladies into red-faced and hungry tavern women."

"I've never known you to be so hostile to one of so little consequence."

Rahotep banged his goblet down on a servant's tray and wiped his lips with the back of his hand. "That's it!"

"What?"

"That's what makes me hate him. He's of no consequence, and yet he behaves as if he were spawn from the loins of Ra. My father was a pharaoh, even if my mother was a peasant. I deserve the respect due a great one. When we met, the dog gave me the slightest of bows." Rahotep's bushy eyebrows formed one hairy line over his eyes. "He should have kissed the floor before my feet. Perhaps I'll make him do that one day soon."

"Don't," Kysen replied. "My father has been asked by the golden one to become familiar with Lord Reshep. If Meren approves, Reshep may be admitted to court, and into the king's presence."

Rahotep rocked back and forth on his heels. "I care not." He gave Kysen a sideways glance. "I could beat him in a fight, you know. I'm expert with scimitar, sword, and dagger as well as staves, javelins, and throw sticks."

"Yes, Rahotep, I know."

In Rahotep's opinion, no one, perhaps not even pharaoh, could do anything better than he could. It was only his boisterous openness that saved him from being heartily disliked. How could you hate a man whose blatant exaggerations fooled no one but himself? Kysen felt compassion for Rahotep, something he would never have imagined feeling for a prince until recently.

He glanced over at Reshep again. The newcomer was still the center of a chattering group, but as Kysen watched, Reshep lifted a drinking cup of highly polished bronze and seemed to be examining it as if he were thinking of buying it.

"By Ptah's staff," Kysen murmured.

Rahotep tried to see what Kysen was looking at. "What?"

"I think Reshep is looking at himself in that drinking cup." As he spoke, Reshep adjusted a stray lock of plaited hair on his wig.

Rahotep snorted. "Arse."

Kysen didn't answer, taken off guard by a sudden insight. What an addled fool he'd been to assume that Reshep's powerful gaze held perception, acumen, discernment. What he'd seen in those eyes was a ravenous search for his own reflected magnificence. Kysen had mistaken an appetite for adoration for interest and sympathy.

"Are you paying attention?" Rahotep demanded. "Now if Reshep had my visage, I could understand him wanting to admire it."

He listened to more of Rahotep's bragging until a stir and murmur circling through the assembly caused them to search for its cause. Kysen found it first—a young woman who had emerged from the deckhouse. Startling the whole company, his youngest sister appeared suddenly between two posts that held the deckhouse awning. Silence befell one group of revelers after another.

Regal, with the grace of a white lily and the allure of frankincense, Isis calmly accepted the stunned appraisal. For a moment, no one moved. Then Lord Reshep detached himself from the rest, walking with the suppleness of a leopard to bow low before the girl. Kysen heard his sister employ the rough low power of her voice. She used what he thought of as her man-conquering tones.

"Who is this guest?" she asked of no one. "Surely a highborn noble or a prince of royal blood."

Kysen rolled his eyes and gave a snort of disgust. Then he smiled. With smooth yet relentless firmness, Meren stepped between his daughter and Lord Reshep. Although almost imperceptible, the shattering look of fury Meren threw at Isis turned Kysen's smile into a grin.

5

FOR THE VAST numbers of Egyptians who labored in the fields, on the river, and in the workshops of Egypt, when the sun vanished, work stopped and rest began. It was the time when spirits of the dead roamed and underworld fiends ascended to attack the unwary. For Tcha, servant of a tavern owner, night was the time for the most profitable of his activities. He'd never encountered a spirit or a demon, no matter how late into the evening he worked. He wore an Eye of Horus amulet around his neck anyway, to ward off all evil. No sense in tempting such creatures by being foolhardy.

This night, Tcha was abroad not to work but to obtain the proceeds of his labor from his ally. Not wishing to be seen, he walked in the deepest darkness and avoided more illuminated or open areas. He was startled only once, when he suddenly came out of an alley near a private quay and into a glare cast by dozens of torches mounted on a jewellike pleasure ship. Tcha squeaked in alarm, skittered back down the alley, and turned into the nearest road.

Panting, he muttered to himself. "By Ptah's staff, *Joy of the Nile*." He said a quick spell against ill luck. "Amun, Toth, Isis, bring me not to the notice of the servants or charioteers of Lord Meren." Then he fell to rumbling his usual complaints. "Never had no pleasure yacht, never even had a boat. Never had no taste of roast goose nor heron. Never had no slaves to cool me with ostrich feather fans, nor no charioteers to do my bidding . . ."

Tcha indulged further in his litany of hardship, a favorite pastime, as he skulked his way across the city, climbing over walls, creeping through deserted gardens, dodging the few streets where light and drunken laughter announced the presence of a beer tavern or house of entertainment. No one else could have traveled so quickly unobserved, Tcha assured himself.

His secret lay in keeping to the refuse mounds where he could. The city was full of them. Each house had at least one outside its walls. Sets of dwellings of related owners tended to grow into contiguous labyrinths, and these usually had several garbage mounds. In a city as ancient as Memphis, the mounds almost outnumbered the houses. During the worst heat of the day they gave off such a powerful stench that even dogs could be seen avoiding them. Anyone frequenting the refuse mounds this late would do so for unsavory purposes and wasn't going to bother Tcha.

At last he came to the giant mound of trash and filth that loomed behind the house of a great man. This one was astronomer of the god Ptah, custodian of the estates of Ptah in the north, and magnate of the Royal Seal of the Treasury of Pharaoh in Memphis. And one thing Tcha knew about great men, they never visited their refuse mounds. It was an excellent place to conceal the spoils Tcha and his ally, Pawah, collected from their occasional house robberies.

The previous evening Pawah and he had done something brave. They had entered the house of a noble and taken away items of moderate value. At least, that had been the purpose they discussed. Pawah had taken things much more valuable.

"Stupid son of a vulture," Tcha grumbled as he crouched behind a stack of empty oil jars to wait.

Tcha prided himself on never having been caught in a large theft. The city police knew him as a trifling prowler among citizens of limited means and a floor sweeper in the establishment of the fabled and exotic tavern mistress known as Ese. The officials of the city thought Ese a charitable woman for employing Tcha in any capacity. Pawah they considered barely clever enough to follow Tcha's lead. That was Pawah's advantage.

Last night he had shown his true nature. He had crept across the roof, stepping over the servants sleeping in the open air, and slithered downstairs. After pilfering a bronze bowl and a small faience serving plate, he had stolen into the master's bedchamber and filched a pair of gold ear studs. Then he'd sauntered into another chamber, and it had been occupied! By this time, as was his habit, Pawah had worked himself into a state of excitement at the risk he was taking. He had walked into the room, past the sleeping man, and snatched a scarab bracelet that lay on top of a jewel casket.

All the while, Tcha had waited perched on the wall surrounding the house keeping watch for guards, the city patrols, or other dangers. When Pawah hadn't come back quickly, Tcha knew what he was doing. And he'd been helpless. Lying flat on top of the wall beneath the branches of a willow tree, he could only curse Pawah and finger his Eye of Horus amulet while reciting a spell of protection.

The memory of his exposure to danger made Tcha angry all over again. "Wretched bastard, greedy-hearted dolt."

Perhaps it had been Tcha's spell that allowed Pawah to leave the house undetected. The magic hadn't lasted long after they left; somewhere between the noble's house and the refuse mound, they had acquired a follower. He and Pawah had parted, taking different routes home, and the follower had disappeared. Now Tcha felt safe enough to meet his fellow thief.

The house lay on the outskirts of the city west of the temple district. Here the great one had caused part of the city wall to be removed to make room for his villa and hadn't yet bothered to rebuild it. Tcha and his friend were to meet at the refuse mound so that they could divide their loot.

Their arrangement was that Pawah would sit sheltered from the refuse mound by a piece of the wall from the collapsed dwelling. By moonlight Tcha had a clear view of his surroundings, the oil jars being situated on a rise near the protective wall of the astronomer's house. He looked out on a vista of waste that formed scattered smaller hills around the great mound, rather like the sacred cities that once surrounded and served the pyramids.

But the little hills and mounds weren't as deserted as the pyramid cities. Beetles, ants, and spiders clambered in and out of the whole field of refuse, filling the narrow footpaths that wound through the area. Dogs and cats crept up to the freshest spills in search of delicacies. Sometimes they disturbed hawks or vultures perched on a fresh carcass. Then shrieks of fury sailed through the air and caused night terrors among those sleeping in nearby houses.

"Never know if one of them dogs is really an underworld fiend," Tcha mumbled to himself while he scanned the refuse field. "Where is that donkey's arse?"

He rose to see over the wall fragment. No Pawah. A scrutiny of the refuse field revealed a cat fastidiously picking its way through a dump of table scraps, an ant mound the size of a sarcophagus, and the same irregular and noxious landscape as before.

His uneasiness was growing. Had Pawah taken their stores of wealth and run away? Yes! That was why he'd taken those valuables; and he'd left Tcha behind to face any inquiries.

"Hathor's tits!" Tcha scrambled over the oil jars, startling the dining cat into flight.

His legs churning, his heart angry, Tcha darted from one heap to another in case Pawah was squatting behind one of them. When he reached the giant mound, he was breathing hard and gulping in putrid fumes. He crept around the base of the hill of rubbish. On the side away from the house wall, between it and the blank expanse of barren ground that became the western desert, lay their hiding place.

The mound had expanded over the uneven ground formed by more collapsed mud brick. Since before the days of the pyramid builders, people had lived in Memphis. When a house aged beyond repair, its sun-dried mud-brick walls were shoved down and became the new ground. Crumbling mud brick stuck up at odd angles on this side of the refuse mound. Scorpions nested there, and cobras burrowed into the aged earth. Few would risk treading here when they could dump their garbage on the nearer side of the mound.

Tcha had dug a hole beneath a slumping corner formed by the remnants of two old walls. Pawah had lined the hole with pottery shards and placed a wicker lid over it. The lid was weighted with and concealed by dirt. Tcha had made sure that the spot would be left alone by digging an imitation of a cobra's nest into the mud-brick corner.

Tcha cast a quick glance around, then dropped to his knees and scrabbled through the dirt. He found the wicker lid and pulled it off. His hand reached inside and touched rough sacking. He grunted and pulled out one of the packages. Fingers clumsy, sweating with agitation, he unknotted the twine that bound the package. Out spilled the spoils of last night, the bronze bowl and faience plate, and even the gold ear studs and amethyst scarab bracelet.

"By the gods," Tcha murmured. If the valuables were here, then Pawah was here. Somewhere.

Tcha hurriedly replaced the package in the shard-lined hold, put the wicker lid back, and shoved dirt on top. Rubbing his hands on his kilt—it was never clean—he turned in his squatting position to examine the side of the great mound. It rose above him like the soaring ramparts of pharaoh's fortress-palace. Tcha wrinkled his nose; the mountain of filth stank like a row of crocodiles on a mud bank when the sky was hot.

He turned back to the hiding place and heard something that caused his flesh to dimple and turn cold—the eerie call of a jackal. More frightening even than the howl of a hyena, it was the scream of a ka burning in a lake of fire in the netherworld. Tcha took a step backward, then went still with fear as he glimpsed movement behind his hiding place.

His mouth popped open to emit a scream that never cleared his throat. Numerous slender, doglike forms crouched over something. One lifted its head to reveal a long nose and upright, pointed ears, then ducked again. Working together, they dragged their prize away from the corner toward the gap in the city wall, ignoring Tcha. The distant call erupted again. This time one of the creatures lifted its head and howled an answer. Jackals.

Afraid to move, Tcha watched them haul something out into the silver light of the moon. It had to be a carcass; that was the only thing for which a jackal would risk approaching the city. One grabbed something long and thin and pulled. Tcha gave a strangled cry as the dim light revealed the gnawed face of Pawah.

Still tethered by his fear, Tcha tried to swallow with a mouth as dry as a desert quarry. His jaws worked, then fell open when another effort by the jackals pulled his friend's torso into view. Tcha sucked in his breath along with a great draft of foul-smelling air. He gagged, then whirled and fled the refuse field at a stumbling run.

This time he ran hard, his sandals flapping. Not caring if he made noise, Tcha hurtled through the streets, seeking the least shadowed, the broadest, the most direct. He didn't stop until he reached the three-story edifice where he worked. Staggering around to the back, he hoisted himself over the wall and into Mistress Ese's domain. He crept into the servants' block and dropped onto his pallet in one of the storage rooms. Drawing his knees up to his chest, Tcha wrapped his arms around them and rocked back and forth, staring into nothing, and whimpering.

WITH CEREMONIAL GRACIOUSNESS, Meren took his youngest daughter's arm, drew her to his side, and favored Lord Reshep with a smile. His lips curved up, but the smile was fastened onto his face like the gold roundels sewn to pharaoh's robe.

"Lord Reshep, this is the littlest of my children, Isis." Meren felt her stiffen at being named a little child.

Reshep bowed low, and as he rose, he continued to stare at Isis. "I am blessed by the gods to be allowed acquaintance with such a hand-maiden of Hathor, goddess of love and merriment."

"Thank you, Lord Reshep." Isis inclined her head.

When she failed to say anything else, Reshep gave her another compliment. As he listened, Meren tried to understand why he was so furious with Isis. Certainly she had attracted attention before, and the guests had gone back to their eating, music, and conversation quickly after her appearance. But this time Isis was different. She didn't look the same.

Keeping part of his attention on the conversation, Meren pursued this alarming thought. What was different? He studied Isis for a moment before he realized that unlike all the other women, she had worn a simple shift. The dress had narrow shoulder straps and a low, straight neck that cut across her chest at the point where her breasts began. Sewn into the linen were thousands of tiny lapis, turquoise, and gold beads.

The garment was so heavy it clung to her body and moved with even the slightest breath. The current fashion was length upon length of finely pleated and transparent linen beneath which a woman's body was an intriguing blur. Isis revealed nothing except bare, firm arms and a bit of leg, ankle, and her bare feet. And she wore no sandals. Anklets that matched the dress beads drew attention to the muscles in her calves and the perfection of her feet. Meren scowled at one of the anklets as he realized his little daughter knew more than he'd realized about how to entice and intrigue.

He'd sent her and Bener to his sister to learn the management of a large household. Only three months had they passed in the country, yet each had returned more woman than girl in far too many ways. He was losing control of them.

Isis was speaking now that she had extracted a treasure-load of compliments from Reshep. "Are others of your family here?"

"Unfortunately, both my parents have gone west, O matchless one. First my father, then my mother, and I am their only son. Father was a great noble, but retiring. He preferred managing our lands to seeking power and fortune at court. He was a master at producing from the land, of course. And Mother, everyone told me she was even more beautiful than the queen she once served, or even the fabled Nefertiti. She was wise and good and loving, and I miss her." Reshep paused to give Isis an appreciative glance. "Until tonight, I thought her the most beautiful woman in Egypt. Still, I miss her."

"Then we must see that you have so much to do that you have no time to miss her." Isis glanced at her father for the first time since the conversation began, then quickly looked away with a brittle smile at Reshep. "Am I not right, Father?"

"What? Oh, of course. I believe Kysen wished to suggest an outing of some kind, perhaps a hunt. We will send word to you," Meren said.

"You honor me, my lord." Reshep held out his hand, and a fan appeared in it. His slave withdrew again. "I'm certain Kysen will be an excellent companion. Truthfully, I find it difficult to hunt with most men. My skills overmatch most of them."

"Have you killed many wild fowl?" Isis asked.

"I stopped counting, O incomparable lily," Reshep said. "Although I have kept count of the lions, crocodiles, and hippos. I believe I've killed seven lions, thirteen crocodiles, and eight hippos."

Isis gave Reshep a wondering look. "You're skilled indeed."

"At more than the hunt, my—"

"Reshep," Meren said sharply. Lord Reshep's mouth closed as swiftly as a fishnet.

"I see my older daughter about to begin an enactment of the Tale of the Five Temple Traders. Yes, she needs her sister's help. You may go, Isis."

When she was gone, Meren signaled to a slave for wine and led Reshep to the sitting area formed by the awning in front of the deck-house. Woven cushions surrounded two chairs carved of imported cedar of Byblos and inlaid with ivory and ebony designs that formed the hieroglyphs of Meren's name. Meren took one of the chairs, settling into soft cushions, and offered the other to Reshep. His guest folded himself into the seat gracefully.

Dismissing the slave, Meren watched Reshep sip the imported Syrian wine. "My daughter has but fourteen years, Reshep. A marriageable age, I'll allow. But she has yet to gain the wisdom or the maturity I would wish for her."

"I understand, my lord."

"No," Meren said as he leaned back in his chair, lazily stretched his legs, and crossed his ankles. He half closed his eyes and impaled his guest with a stare. "No, I don't think you do. Neither of my daughters has chosen a lover or a husband. Isis is not ready. Of this I am certain. And if she were, I would not wish her to accept someone of whom I know so little."

Reshep lowered his gaze to the pool of dark crimson in his wine goblet. Meren saw his neck and jaw slowly approach the hue of his wine. From what he'd seen of this man, he expected him to take furious offense. Yet the crimson stain ebbed rapidly from his face and neck. Reshep looked up at him, revealing a quiet smile. He spread his arms and tossed his head.

"I should have guessed. Forgive me, Lord Meren. This happens so often that I forget how disconcerting it must be to the fathers."

"What happens so often?"

Reshep turned a little in his chair, rested an elbow on the chair arm, and waved his goblet. "Young women—girls, if you prefer. Becoming instantly taken in love for me." Reshep held up his hand when Meren tried to speak. "I assure you, my lord, I use no spells or amulets. I've no need of them."

"In truth," Meren replied mildly.

"Reshep!" Prince Djoser appeared, breathless and eager. "Come, show my friends how to perform that hunting dance. Lady Isis has requested to see it."

Reshep glanced at Meren, who rose. "A host doesn't prevent his guests from seeking merriment."

When Reshep and Djoser were gone, Meren searched the crowded deck, caught the eye of his son and a charioteer, and resumed his seat. Kysen and Simut approached.

Staring over a table piled with pastries and desert breads, Meren watched Isis drape herself across a couch, arms propped on cushions, one leg bent to display the curve of her hip. "Simut, I was wrong not to assign someone to keep watch over my daughter during this feast."

The charioteer didn't ask to which daughter Meren referred. He spun around and began working his way toward the group of young people watching Reshep lead a men's hunting dance. Kysen let out a short burst of laughter that elicited a scowl from Meren.

"I find your source of amusement unfitting."

With difficulty Kysen mastered his laughter, but couldn't seem to get rid of his smile. "Forgive me, Father. Perhaps we should discuss something else. How did you find this country lord, Reshep?"

"Of little interest," Meren replied. "He's ornamental, pleasant, but he seems to have no other topic of conversation but himself."

"Indeed."

They both turned to find Bener leaning against one of the slender lotus columns that supported the awning. She bore a tray of pastries, which she offered to them before sinking to a cushion beside Meren.

"You agree?" Kysen asked. He looked in Reshep's direction. The dance had finished, and the newcomer had been surrounded by women. Not Isis, however, or Princess Tio, each of whom had their own court of admirers. "Most women seem to find him godlike in his magnificence."

"He wouldn't make a good lover, or a good husband," Bener said with a certainty that caused Meren to sit up straight.

"Why?" he asked.

Bener picked up a fruit pastry and bit into it. "Because he will always be more in love with himself than any woman."

"Rather like Isis," Meren said with a slight smile. "Their kas are much alike."

Kysen shook his head. "I never thought to say this, but Reshep is worse than Isis."

Meren was about to agree, but he happened to glance across the deck and saw Princess Tio walking toward them. Her height and disdainful expression caused everyone in her path to step aside, so that it appeared that she moved through a wave of white linen and jewels.

"Kysen, Bener, go away, quickly."

"What's wrong?" Bener asked.

Kysen stood up and pulled his sister to her feet. "Don't argue. You know that tone."

"Ky," Meren said as his son followed Bener from the sitting area. "Tell the captain to begin the return trip to the quay."

Tio arrived as Kysen left, and Meren rose to bow to her.

"Princess," he said.

She walked past him into the deckhouse. Meren stared after her. She wanted to talk to him alone. He heard trumpets blare a warning, and jackals howled, making his ka writhe. Tio was dangerous. Her mistress, the Great Royal Wife, was dangerous. Cursing silently, Meren followed the princess into the deckhouse.

He stepped inside a miniature reception hall fitted with brightly woven hangings, couches, and piles of cushions. Garlands hung from the ceiling and the furniture, and decorated a table bearing refreshments. Tio stood with her back to him beside an alabaster wine jar half her height that rested in a bronze stand. One hand caressed a rose lotus from a wreath that decorated the neck of the jar. Meren watched her long, dark fingers stroke a pink petal. Her palms were tinted with henna. Her head was turned to the side, revealing a high forehead, the delicate curve of her nose, the lips that, for all their plumpness, contributed to the impression of unyielding remoteness he always gained from Tio.

She was trying to unsettle him by making him wait, by remaining silent and forcing him to speak first. Unfortunately for Tio, he used this maneuver himself when trying to intimidate ministers, evildoers, and his children. He turned away from her and dropped onto a gilded couch. Propped up on one arm, he snatched an electrum bowl filled with dates and popped one in his mouth. He was on his third date when Tio whipped around to face him, her expression still unreadable. At that moment the ship leaned as it turned back toward the west bank of the Nile. Tio stumbled and lost her balance.

Meren lunged off the couch, grabbed her arm, and lifted her. He was grinning. "Have you had too much Syrian wine, O mighty princess?" Tio jerked her arm free.

"You always did have the manners of a furnace tender."

Meren gave her another bow. "And you, Tio, are a lady without equal. O rising star of a fortunate year, with hair like lapis lazuli, with voice finer than gold, thou art more fair than the rose lotus, more delicate than the blue lotus, O mistress of captivation."

"You dung-eating pestilence, I'll hear no more mockery."

Laughing, Meren dropped back onto his couch and picked up the bowl of dates. "What do you want, Tio?"

Tio let her arms fall to her sides. Then she laced her fingers together and resumed her detached expression. "The Mistress of the Two Lands, beloved of the living god, great king's wife, may she live forever, Ankhesenamun, wishes to reward the Friend of the King, Count Meren, for his loyal service to pharaoh. She will take unto her a handmaiden, the daughter of Count Meren, Lady Isis."

"How wondrous," Meren said softly. "I am prostrate with gratitude for this undeserved honor." He thought quickly. The queen hated him for ruining her plan to replace Tutankhamun with a Hittite prince. It had taken her months to convince pharaoh of her contrition, and now that she had gained back some of the king's favor, she made this move.

"Unfortunately my daughter is still quite immature. Her body is that of a woman, but her ka remains childlike. I fear that she would be of little service to the queen."

"That is for the Great Royal Wife to decide," Tio said.

Meren set the bowl of dates aside and poured himself a cup of water. "Her majesty is gracious, but—"

"The queen has already spoken to pharaoh, who has given his assent."

Meren's head shot up. Tio was looking down at him, her eyes glinting like obsidian in sunlight. She smiled at him, and he realized she had glimpsed his dismay. Meren rose from the couch and walked past Tio to a table on the other side of the room. His hand touched the feathers of a small fan lying on the table. He stroked the softness while he searched for some excuse, any excuse that would keep his daughter away from the woman who hated him. What justification was there to refuse such an honor? It was a privilege most men would kill to achieve. What remedy?

Meren continued to stroke the fan as Tio waited and gloated. Finally he turned back to her, his expression rueful.

"Forgive me, princess. I neglected to tell you that Isis will soon marry."

"I have heard nothing of this," Tio replied. "The girl only returned from the country a short time ago, and you haven't asked pharaoh's permission."

"That is because my daughter has several suitors and hasn't decided among them. This won't surprise you after having seen her tonight. You will understand that such a decision takes time."

Tio's remote countenance dropped into place again. "I will inform the Great Royal Wife."

"Thank you," Meren said.

"She may wish to concern herself with any alliance formed by the daughter of such a great noble."

"I wouldn't presume to disturb the Lady of the Two Lands with so unimportant a matter."

Before Tio could respond, there was a call from the deck. Relieved, Meren excused himself and left the deckhouse. Kysen was waiting for him nearby and began walking with him.

"We're about to dock, and we have a late guest."

Meren went to the ship's railing as *Joy of the Nile* gently nudged the quayside. Approaching from an ornate chariot flanked by bearded guards was a man whose garments seemed dipped in silver. Meren and Kysen glanced at each other without speaking. Djoser appeared and leaned over the railing.

"By the gods, Meren, it's that serpent of a Hittite emissary. And he's brought a small army with him."

6

AFTER PHARAOH HAD shamed him in front of the whole court, Meren had not expected Mugallu to remain in Egypt. The Hittite should have stormed home to the mountains of his Anatolian homeland and hissed accusations at his king. What was he doing coming aboard *Joy of the Nile*? As the ship eased through the water to gently nudge the dock, music, clapping, and laughter sent a barrage of sound across the water to greet the foreigner. Only a few guests noticed the Hittite party. Unfortunately, Reshep, Djoser, and the disgruntled Prince Rahotep were among them.

Sighing at the thought of introducing Mugallu to either Djoser or Rahotep, Meren stepped forward as the gangplank was lowered onto the quay. Kysen was behind him, along with Reshep, who seemed unconcerned that it might be presumptuous of a newcomer to insert himself into a welcome party for a Hittite prince.

Flanked by his illustrious escort of high-ranking military men and an assistant minister from Ay's office, Mugallu stepped on board. The rage that had turned his face carnelian in the throne room had ebbed, leaving his heavy features and bird-of-prey nose the hue of mud brick. Meren noticed one of the escort, General Labarnas, who nodded to him and grinned. Meren hated that grin. Hittites were notorious for going into battle grinning just like that, as if they found slashed bellies with entrails spilling out to be the most amusing of sights. The wisest thing to do was to avoid looking at Labarnas at all.

While he and the prince exchanged formal salutations, Meren summoned every skill he'd ever used to survive the crocodile trap that was the Egyptian court. Mugallu wasn't simply an emissary. Judging from his behavior so far, he was a trial, a challenge, a probing stick sent to jab at pharaoh's suspected weaknesses. And worse. Mugallu could be in Memphis to search for an ally, someone willing to betray Egypt, for a price.

At this thought Meren's lips curled in disgust, but he forced them into a smile of tranquil welcome. "Shall we sit and talk, highness? You must be weary after spending all day conferring with the Divine Father Ay."

"Indeed," Mugallu said as he surveyed the men behind Meren. His gaze settled on Reshep, who bore it with an aplomb worthy of pharaoh.

Reshep stepped forward, lifting his hands in greeting as he spoke. "I am Lord Reshep—"

"By the storm god, Meren, do all your nobles dress like women and oil themselves like catamites?" Mugallu asked. He left Reshep standing alone, his mouth hanging open, and walked toward the aft steering castle.

Meren heard a growl and thrust his arm out in time to stop Prince Rahotep from hurling himself on top of the Hittite.

"Get out of my way!" Rahotep snarled. "He insulted us all, not just Reshep."

Shoving his body against the straining prince, Meren hissed, "Cease at once. He wants you to take offense, you fool."

Reshep had recovered from the insult and grabbed one of Prince Rahotep's arms.

"Temper the heat in your belly, my friend. There are other ways to avenge oneself."

"Listen to him," Meren said as Rahotep refused to give up the struggle.

Djoser grabbed Rahotep's other arm while Kysen intervened to try to calm his friend. With Rahotep tethered, Meren left the group and quickly followed Mugallu aft. There, where the ship began to curve up out of the water, lay a gilded pavilion. A curved roof supported by slender columns with lotus capitals provided shelter. Openwork carving formed walls around three sides and showed Hapu, god of the Nile. Mugallu stood beneath the gold-painted roof and contemplated one of the two massive steering oars, now immobile and untended with the ship docked.

"Such a calm river," Mugallu said as Meren joined him in looking across the black water. "The Nile spoils you Egyptians. You're complacent, pampered by its abundance." Mugallu glanced at Meren. "Soft."

Meren leaned against one of the columns and held Mugallu's gaze.

"Walk along the bank, highness, and you'll find that this tranquillity hides danger. One careless move, and you're meat for crocodiles."

"I've spoken to Ay; rather, Ay has tried for hours to placate me," Mugallu said. He resumed his contemplation of the Nile. "Ay is wise and possesses a honeyed tongue, but your child-king ruined all his work by refusing to see me again when Ay asked to be received."

Meren felt his skin prickle, and his hearing seemed to grow more acute. Mugallu's belligerent expression had vanished. His brows arched, and he was trying not to smirk.

"The divine one rarely sees emissaries twice. He consents to allow negotiations, but ordinary business is not for the living god."

The Hittite's smirk contorted. "I'm not ordinary business! By the storm god, I hate coming to this land, with its arrogance, its lazy preoccupation with itself. You"—Mugallu paused to run his gaze over Meren's immaculate figure, the jeweled belt, the transparent linen that revealed long legs—"you . . . nobles. You're pampered, oiled toys of pharaoh, and yet you're stuffed with pride. Every son of a jackal bitch is certain that Egypt is the chosen kingdom of the gods. I know what you call the rest of us. Barbarians, wretched Asiatics."

"And what do you call us?" Meren asked as he studied Mugallu beneath half-closed eyelids.

The Hittite didn't respond. His fingers curled until he'd made fists, and Meren watched him struggle with his temper. Finally the wrath distorting his features dwindled.

"Don't you think King Suppiluliumas knows about your dead heretic king and the misery he caused? Egypt is weak, ridden with old hatreds that have set brother against brother." Mugallu paused. "Cousin against cousin."

Meren stared straight into the Hittite's watchful eyes. "Are you trying to say something about me and my cousin Ebana, highness?"

"You?" Mugallu leaned on the pavilion railing and shook his head. "Why should I say anything about you, the Eyes and Ears of Pharaoh? Even in Hatti we know the power and influence of the King's Friend, Lord Meren. Tell me, do you think, even with all your skill at spying and plotting, that you and General Horemheb and the rest can hold Egypt together long enough for your boy-king to grow up?"

"Do you question the might of Egypt, highness?" Meren asked softly. "I don't think your master is quite ready to challenge a pharaoh at the moment, even a young one."

Standing, Mugallu gave him a smile that recalled the yawn of a sated hippo. The Hittite gazed across the deck and nodded at the crowd surrounding one of the professional singers.

"At home we waste little time singing of the pleasures of life. It makes a warrior soft. Instead, we sing of battle and victory."

"We sing of such things as well," Meren said.

"And we tell tales of great battles."

"Like those of Thutmose the Conqueror, who spread the empire to the verge of the Hittite lands?" Meren was exaggerating, but Mugallu was beginning to irritate him.

The prince didn't answer. Turning his back on the revelers, he took a step closer to Meren and lowered his voice.

"I remember a tale, a favorite of the great king, concerning one of his royal ancestors. This king of the Hittites had an enemy, the prince of a rich and powerful city with a great army. This prince looted and destroyed several Hittite villages and refused to return the people he'd taken from them. Of course, the great king had to retaliate. Do you know what he did first, to weaken the prince?"

"You will tell me, won't you?"

Mugallu threw back his head and laughed so loudly that heads turned toward them.

"Yes, I'll tell you."

Mugallu leaned closer to Meren, who still had his back against a column and couldn't move away. The Hittite was so close Meren could smell the spice bread he'd eaten and the stale wine on his breath.

"To weaken the prince," Mugallu said, "the great king struck not at the enemy himself but at the friend of his heart, his most trusted adviser and confidant."

Meren breathed a comment. "Ah." And he surveyed Mugallu with tranquil composure.

"With his friend dead, the prince was beset with grief, distraught, unable to trust his own decisions without the approval of the beloved friend. He grew weak in battle."

Mugallu stepped back but kept his gaze fixed on Meren. "Naturally the great king defeated the prince, cut his head off, and stuck it on the end of a spear, which he mounted on the royal chariot when he returned home, triumphant."

"A good tale," Meren said in a bored tone.

"I thought you would value it."

Meren lifted himself up and perched on the pavilion railing. "Not one an Egyptian would tell, though."

"Oh?"

"No. You see, highness, Egypt is ruled by a living god, not a mere king. As the son of the great god Amun, pharaoh is wise beyond his years. We who serve him do his bidding. Never has a servant substituted his will for pharaoh's, and the living god relies on the guidance of Amun, king of the gods. So you see, your tale is entertaining, but hardly fitting for Egypt."

The Hittite scowled at Meren. "Perhaps I'll recall another before I return home, but I think this one fits, no matter the divine heritage of King Tutankhamun."

"Would you like more wine, highness?"

Mugallu lifted a hand in protest. "I've had enough, and I'm weary. Don't escort me off the ship, Lord Meren. I've had sufficient ceremony for one day."

"May your sleep be peaceful, highness."

"I always sleep peacefully," Mugallu said as he left. "I only hope I haven't given you black dreams with my tale of the death of the prince's friend."

ON THE SECOND night after the feast on *Joy of the Nile*, Kysen walked down the Street of Foreigners, feeling more at ease in his heart than he had in weeks. Meren had embarked on his journey to find Queen Nefertiti's favorite cook, but Abu was following him. If anyone could protect his father, it was Abu. Still, a dagger of uneasiness pricked at him as he dodged two drunk Cypriot sailors.

After the family had gone home from the feast, Meren had been different. No longer distracted and anxious, his father had been furious. The Eyes of Pharaoh rarely showed anger, not unless by design. Mugallu had said something to Meren in the golden ship's pavilion, something that had so provoked his father's wrath that he'd been unable to conceal it in the seclusion of his home.

Bener had whispered to Kysen about the change in his mood when Meren had spoken sharply to a porter at the front door. Even Isis had noticed Meren's rage, between lyrics of praise for Lord Reshep. True, the reason she'd noticed was that Meren snapped at her to leave off bleating about a lord who thought he was prettier than she was. But she'd noticed.

"Some new intrigue of Mugallu's has irritated him," Kysen muttered to himself. "May the gods curse all Hittites."

He abandoned his musings when he reached the intersection of the Street of Foreigners with the Avenue of the Ibis. He was still near the docks and could hear the calls of water birds and an occasional hippo's roar and feel the moisture of the Nile in the air. But the place he sought was at the edge of the dock district, near the area where Mycenaean Greek traders, ship captains, and sailors lived. If he kept walking and turned down any of the side streets toward the docks, he'd immediately step into a realm few ordinary citizens braved at night.

Everyone called it the Caverns, after the Caverns of Duat in the netherworld. There ferocious god-fiends guarded the afterlife, ready to destroy an unprepared soul. Their names—Breaker of Bones, Eater of Intestines, He-Whose-Two-Eyes-Are-on-Fire—described horrors every Egyptian feared. In the Caverns of Memphis, thieves, receivers of smuggled luxuries, and evildoers from Egypt's far-flung possessions and her own cities lived and pursued strange and distasteful occupations.

As a boy Kysen had been outraged when he discovered the existence of the Caverns. But Meren had shrugged and said that there had always been chaos in the midst of harmony, and that Egypt was fortunate that the god of disorder, Set, ruled over so small a kingdom within the imperial capital. Besides, where else could common men go for entertainment?

Kysen had grown up since asking that question, and now he frequented the Caverns for his own purposes. Nowhere could one hear fresher rumors of corruption, bribery, abuse, and murder. Gossip in the Caverns was more efficient and sometimes more accurate than a royal messenger. Kysen smiled as he approached the tavern and rest house called the Divine Lotus. Its owner, the woman Ese, was the font of all gossip, rumor, and scandal. If she was in a tolerant mood this evening, he might persuade her to make inquiries about the former intimate servants of Nefertiti.

Here in the shadowed world of thieves, dishonest government underlings, whores, and murderers, he went by another name, Nen. Nen was supposed to be the sixth son of the assistant to the steward of a minor noble. As one of eight children, he had little wealth but a taste for luxuries he'd seen at the household where his father worked, no matter how they were obtained. In the Caverns he was known as a clever and easygoing lover of idleness. Everyone knew Nen's time was spent designing clever schemes by which he would profit with as little labor as possible. Outlaws, cheaters, and the corrupt felt at ease with him.

As he set his foot on the step before the threshold of the Divine Lotus, a dirty, sweat-stained body hurtled into him. Kysen fell back against the wall beside the door, the wind knocked out of him. He gulped in air, and with it whiffs of a sickly sweet odor that spoke of months without bathing. Few men smelled like a wet oxhide that had been covered with tallow and baked under a hot sky; the whining shriek that assailed his ears confirmed the figure's identity.

"Tcha, get off me!"

The thief uttered a hyena's yelp, missed his footing on the steps, and fell on his ass in the street. Kysen would have left him there, but Tcha squeezed his eyes shut, covered his head with his arms, and burst out with a spell.

"I am the chosen one, I am the chosen one whose name is unknown! If a creature of the water open his mouth to strike, I speak my name. I speak my name, and the water boils. Evil is destroyed, evil is destroyed!"

"By my ka," Kysen said. "Are you cursing me, you sniveling teller of tales?"

Tcha lifted his head so that two slanted eyes like wet *nabk* berries peered over his arm. "Master! It is you." Tcha untied the knot he'd made of his body and scrambled to his feet. Glancing over his shoulder every few moments, he hurried over to Kysen, bowing and bobbing.

"You've stolen something valuable, haven't you?" Kysen said.

Tcha was Kysen's oldest, and one of his most useful, acquaintances in the Caverns, and the only one who knew who Kysen really was. Almost a year ago he'd fished the thief out of a work gang to which he'd been condemned and arranged for his crimes to be forgiven in exchange for guidance into life here. Now they saw each other infrequently, but Tcha knew that Kysen could find him. He also knew what would happen to him should he reveal what he knew of his benefactor to anyone.

"Tcha never steals, O great master. Everyone thinks I'm a miserable thief, just because I never had no fine house, no fertile fields, no good bread nor beer nor linen robes nor—"

"Tcha, close your mouth."

"Yes, O great master, giver of bounty, gracious of heart, divine of beauty—"

"I said no more!" Kysen again turned to enter the tavern, but Tcha started to follow him, bringing the thief close enough for him to get another noseful of his incomparable odor. "Gods deliver me from your foul smell, Tcha. It's worse than usual." Sniffing, Kysen lifted his brows. "Do I smell honey amidst your other disgusting humors?"

His eyes shifting to the side, Tcha mumbled something inaudible. He edged away from Kysen. As he moved, he clicked, and his movement brought him into the light of a taper in a sconce beside the door.

Kysen descended the steps and planted himself opposite the thief. "What in the name of Amun have you done to yourself?"

Tcha had never been presentable. He was as emaciated as a body fresh from the embalming table, short because of bowed legs, and scarred from beatings that were the rewards of unsuccessful thievery. Although no more than six years older than Kysen, he looked older than Meren. His skin had the cracked, baked appearance of a field at the end of the season of Drought, and three of his upper front teeth were missing. Their absence caused a lisp in his speech. Brittle, dried-reed hair formed greasy plates that issued from the crown of his head and snaked over his ears and forehead and down to the back of his dirty neck.

Indeed, Tcha had always been painful to the eye and to the nose, but he'd never emitted anything resembling a pleasant odor. And he'd never covered himself in more magical amulets than a pharaoh's corpse. Nor had he painted his grimy body with expensive honey. Yet here Tcha stood, his arms, legs, neck, waist, and head encircled with old string, twine, and narrow papyrus rope from which he'd strung countless amulets. And he was evidently reluctant to speak of his strange appearance.

"Tcha, I asked you what you'd done to yourself."

"Precautions, O great master," Tcha muttered. He stuck his arms behind his back as if this action would hide all the amulets.

"Precautions against what?" Kysen asked.

Tcha's eyes darted from shadow to shadow, corner to corner. "Against evil, lord. There be great evil abroad."

"Blessed Toth and Anubis," Kysen said with an increasing grin. "You've thought of a way to protect yourself against the city police. That spell you screeched at me was for use against crocodiles, you know, not men. And if you wear all those amulets while skulking around some artisan's house, you'll clatter like a sistrum."

"The master is wise," Tcha mumbled as he snaked a glance up and down the Street of Foreigners.

"In truth, Tcha, many of those amulets are only for funerary use. Look at this. You have Djed-columns, the girdle amulet, the four sons of Horus, the amulet of the headrest, heart scarabs. Are you planning a journey through the netherworld soon? Don't tell me you plan to rob Osiris and the other gods."

Tcha started, then laughed with a sound like a throw stick scraping polished granite. "Thy jest is most humorous, great master."

"You only need a few amulets to protect yourself from harm," Kysen said as he tried not to smile. He noted that most of the amulets were cheap faience, but a few were of more expensive but damaged stones. He saw a green jasper turtle, a double lion in carnelian, and an amethyst falcon. "I recommend wearing one Eye of Horus, one scarab, and perhaps the ankh, sign of life, so that you will continue in this existence. But why in the name of Amun have you coated yourself with honey?"

"Mistress Ese give it to me. She says that which is sweet to the living is foul to demons."

Shaking his head, Kysen went to the tavern door and opened it. "True, but if you insist on creeping about your business in that condition, you'll end up fodder for crocodiles no matter how many spells you chant. Keep your distance from me, Tcha. The next time I see you, you will have bathed in the Nile. At least five times. With soap paste."

He left Tcha and entered the Divine Lotus, still shaking his head. He forgot the thief with his first glimpse of the tavern interior. He'd heard that Ese had expanded the place and refurbished it. She was known for changing the tavern's appearance so that her patrons were continually surprised and delighted. But this time Ese had surpassed her own reputation for the exotic. She had turned the Divine Lotus into a Mycenaean Greek villa.

Kysen stepped into a megaron, a Greek great hall nearly the size of the one in his own home. The walls shone with brightly painted frescoes of women in Mycenaean dresses with tight bodices that bared the breasts, flounced skirts, and gold rosette earrings. Some of their hair was pulled up and knotted at the crown, while a ribbon bound a long coil of it that hung down the back. Designs of running spirals, zigzags, and stripes bordered the frescoes and the ceiling.

A circular central hearth provided heat, for even in Egypt the nights often brought a chill. Woven cushions and mats were strewn in groups around the hall to form private clusters lit by alabaster lamps. The place was crowded, as usual, but Kysen noticed that tonight most of the customers were foreign, Greeks from Crete and Cyprus, Libyans, several nomads. He saw traders from the great Mycenaean city-states—Argos, Corinth, Pylos, and the city of Mycenae itself. Others he knew to be nobles and merchants from the islands of Rhodes, Melos, and Samos. One group around a lord from Rhodes included captains of ships from Byblos and Tyre, and even a Hittite overland trader.

Those who preferred to conduct their pleasures less visibly sat against the walls or leaned on one of the four tall columns that surrounded the hearth and supported a clerestory that allowed light in during the day and provided an escape for smoke. In corners and places away from the hearth lurked the less grand denizens of the Divine Lotus. The door behind Kysen opened a crack. Tcha slipped inside and scuttled around the perimeter of the hall to join a hive of charlatans, villains, and corrupt minions of corrupt officials. It was as if a ring of corrosion surrounded a central core of bronze ridden with its own, less visible defilement.

Kysen threaded his way through the groups of customers. He paused to acknowledge a greeting from a trader who regularly bribed dock officials to let him ship in unrecorded luxuries that he sold to Egyptian clients. Returning the bow of a dealer in perfumes who had fled Corinth after sleeping with a nobleman's wife, Kysen took a stool beside the hearth and surveyed the megaron.

Strange that the place was so devoid of Egyptians this evening. He saw a few in the rooms beyond, even a particularly bloodthirsty Nubian prince playing a game of senet with one of the tavern women. The prince led royal expeditions deep into the southern wild lands in search of leopards, elephants, and rare spice trees. At least once during a regnal year his expeditions were attacked and robbed by savage tribes who seemed to know their exact route.

Kysen paused in his survey of the patrons. He leaned to one side in order to get a better view of a dark corner of the megaron. There, among the less accomplished villains, sat Prince Rahotep. Wearing a plain kilt and no jewels, he was slumped on a stool against a wall, alone, his hands fastened around a drinking cup big enough for three men. As Kysen watched, the prince hiccuped, bent over his cup, and sucked wine like a cow at a drinking trough. Then he came up for air and cradled the cup against his chest, all the while wearing an expression more suited to an embalming shed than a tavern.

Rahotep had always been given to bouts of sorrowful drinking. Kysen had noted that lately the episodes were growing more frequent. He and most of Rahotep's friends refused to go with the prince on these outings. Inevitably, when he'd had a cup or two of wine, Rahotep would grow quarrelsome. After his fourth or fifth cup, he stopped fighting, stopped talking altogether. He sank into a private world of anguish from which he wouldn't surface for the rest of the night. After hours of black silence, Rahotep vanished. Then in a day or two he'd reappear wearing his old brash manner, oblivious of the irritation of his friends. Kysen turned his back on Rahotep, who was deep in his misery and wouldn't notice him.

A serving boy brought Kysen beer in a double-handled chalice of the hard, eggshell-thin pottery for which the Greeks were famous. Ese had gone to much expense to acquire the finest of such vessels for the use of her guests. Kysen was admiring the tall stem of the chalice that flared out into a graceful bowl when he noticed that the people around him had stopped talking and were staring over his head.

He turned to face a curtain of blue, white, and green flounces. Lifting his gaze, he saw hips bound by a tight skirt. He continued his visual climb and found two small mountains of flesh surrounded by a tight bodice. Above these he encountered a rounded face framed by tight Greek curls of dark brown tinted with red.

Two dark eyes met his. They were eyes that could convey any emotion their owner wished. Most often, in the great hall, they held graciousness combined with a hint of the exotic and promises of the pleasures of Hathor. Kysen had seen them as they truly were—flat, with a serpent's lack of pity, glittering with cold resentment, alight with amusement of a cat playing with a wounded field mouse.

She spoke in a low, rough voice that sent hot spears of reaction through her male guests and caused her tavern women to fall silent. "May Hathor bless you, Nen."

"She has blessed me beyond wishing by your presence, Mistress Ese."

"That Syrian wine you asked for has arrived," she said.

He'd ordered no wine, but Ese had already left, giving him no choice but to follow her. The din of conversation, gaming, and drinking rose around him once more as he stood and went after the woman. Ese walked out of the hall to an inner stairwell. Instead of ascending the stairs, she opened a door and vanished. Kysen hurried after her. As he pulled the door closed, he glimpsed a shadow sailing into the stairwell. By its shape and the odor of honey and decay, he knew it was Tcha.

Shutting the door, Kysen found himself in an open garden court with a central reflection pool. Ese was reclining on a couch beneath an awning at the opposite end of the pool. A Syrian slave waved a white ostrich feather fan over her mistress. When Kysen approached, Ese pointed to a cushion on the ground beside the couch. He lowered himself to it and accepted wine in a vessel of unusual design, a bronze drinking cup shaped like the head of a gazelle. The modeled nose was made to be set in a stand.

"You have become Mycenaean," Kysen said.

"For the moment."

"After this, what will you become?"

Ese lifted her face to the silver moonlight. "Babylonian, perhaps." She glanced down at him. "Perhaps a Hittite."

"Not a wise choice."

"I choose what provokes interest and what tantalizes."

Ese lay unmoving, her stillness the watchful ease of a lioness as she contemplates the hunt. Kysen had yet to become accustomed to the woman's outward calm and inner vigilance.

Kysen stared up at her, trying not to fall victim to perfection of skin, softly curling hair, and an indomitable will. "You'll choose to become a Hittite."

"I will?"

"It is the most daring of choices."

A flash of contempt showed in the woman's eyes. "I'll tell you something. Men are stupid to waste gold on places like my Divine Lotus."

"All of us?"

"Shall we compare? Are women's thoughts dominated by their genitals?"

"We farm and hunt and build great temples," Kysen protested.

Ese gave him an unimpressed glance. "Only after your urges have been assuaged. Without relief, none of you could build a straw hut." She burst out with abrupt violence, "You disgust me."

She wasn't looking at him; she was looking at the past. The violence of her speech had been provoked by whatever invisible scene floated before her eyes.

"I regret that misfortune has been your lot in your dealings with men."

Ese dragged her gaze back to him and nodded, as if he'd confirmed some judgment she had already formed. "I have heard a rumor about you."

"Oh." He was suddenly wary. There shouldn't be any rumors about Nen.

"One of my women said a vegetable seller at the docks told her you chased down a thief who tried to steal her best melon."

"Is that all?"

Leaning over a table set beside her couch, Ese dipped her fingers in an alabaster pot filled with perfumed salve and began rubbing it on her throat. Kysen followed the path of her fingers as they swept down and across a smooth curve. Then he pressed his lips together and jerked his gaze back to his wine. He was angry with himself for falling victim to Ese's manipulations. He knew she never did or said anything out of innocence. He looked up at her again and found her watching him with a faint smile of derision. He felt like a foolish, tumescent boy.

"You may not be as stupid as most," she said. "You're a selfish conniver, a trader in information to the one who can pay the most, yet you prevented an old woman from being robbed of a simple melon. Do you know how much one melon means to such as she?"

Kysen scowled at her. "The wretch pushed the aged one into the dirt. I hate men who use their fists on—"

"Yes?"

"I have more important things to do than prattle about old women. I want you to set your women and your band of—shall we say servants— to making inquiries."

"What kind of inquiries?"

Kysen slowly inspected the garden court for intruders. "Nothing urgent or perilous. I want to find anyone who served her majesty, Queen Nefertiti, the justified, during her last months."

"No."

"No? Why not?"

"I keep away from the affairs of pharaohs, living or dead, and I especially shun prying into the secrets of Great Royal Wives."

"I'm not interested in secrets. I'm interested in hiring servants who know court ways."

"You aren't. You couldn't afford to hire them. What are you really after, Nen?"

Kysen threw up his hands. "There's no hidden purpose this time. I've been paid well for my previous work, and now I've put aside enough to employ a few servants. Think, mistress. If a man intends to rise high enough to attract the notice of great ones, he must learn from others how to conduct himself in a manner pleasing to them."

He bore Ese's scrutiny in silence. Repeating his arguments or decorating them with particulars would increase the woman's disbelief. Setting down his wine, he sighed and shook his head.

"Of course, if you're unable to provide this simple information, I'll get it somewhere else. I only came to you because you're so reliable. And if I must part with a fee, I would rather it go to you."

"I had no idea you cared so much for me."

Kysen grinned at her. "You're a beautiful woman, and you're right. I was more concerned that I remain a valued customer, so that you would look upon me with favor, should I need your assistance in my rise among the great ones."

"Ah, now the plan is revealed. But I think not all of it. You don't actually need the servants of this queen."

"I am counting on the . . . the disgrace under which they fell to make them eager to take any position, even if it wouldn't provide the kind of maintenance usual for a royal servant."

"At last, dear Nen. Something believable comes from your pretty mouth."

Ese put her wine aside and sat up. She stared past him into the moonlit water of the reflection pool. A frog hopped off a lotus leaf into the water with a plop. A faint breeze brought the scent of fresh water and lotus flowers to Kysen, and he inhaled it, cherishing the renewal it brought to his body and ka.

Suddenly his hostess stood and walked past him to the edge of the pool. She turned and came back to him, the softness of her face hardened by calculation. Facing him, she raked him with a glance from hair to sandal.

"Very well. But finding such people will take months, if I can find them at all."

"I don't want to wait."

Ese tapped her forefinger against her chin. "Then I think we will have to go to Othrys."

He hadn't anticipated this. The last man he wanted to bring into this inquiry was Othrys. There was enough danger without involving a man with the scruples of a cobra.

"It seems a trivial matter for Othrys."

Again he was subjected to that ruthless appraisal that made him feel like a sacrificial bull.

"Sweet, conniving Nen," Ese breathed. She touched his cheek with her fingertips. "You're a lovely boy, but even the beauty of the gods won't persuade me to enter into this questionable arrangement without precautions." Her fingers left his skin, but she lowered her voice to a whisper. "If you want me to hunt down the servants of a dead heretic queen, you will accept my conditions. Say yes, exquisite one, or I shall be displeased."

He'd come too far to refuse, and he'd seen the results of Ese's displeasure. "How could I say anything else to you, whose beauty surpasses that of the moon?"

"Someday I'm going to cut out that facile tongue of yours," Ese said. "Come."

"Where are we going?"

"To Othrys."

"There's no need for haste."

"Why the reluctance?" Ese asked. "Do you have something to hide from Othrys?"

"Of course not."

"How fortunate for you," Ese said. She indicated a door in the wall surrounding the garden court.

Struggling to maintain his air of unconcern, Kysen bowed to Ese. Of all the results of this encounter, he'd least expected to be dragged to a meeting with a barbarian who slit throats as skillfully as butchers slaughtered pigs. He could still feel the pirate's cold razor blade cutting into the flesh above the hollow in his throat, feel his own blood trickle down his neck in hot, tingling little rivulets. Even as he withdrew from the memory, a voice from his ka sounded in his head.

You sent Abu to look after Father, and came here alone. A stupid conceit. And it's likely to get you killed.

7

MEREN HAD BEACHED his small sailing boat upriver of the cook's village at dusk. He'd roasted a pigeon he'd shot with his bow and eaten it with the bread and dried figs from home. The journey to the cook's village hadn't taken a full day, but he'd enjoyed the escape from his life of responsibility and ceremony.

At home he dressed in the garb required by his rank. His court robes were elaborate, although made of the finest linen. They confined his movements, often making him feel trapped. The heavy gold and electrum broad collars weighed down his shoulders and chest and reminded him of the invisible burdens he carried. Thick bracelets laden with lapis, malachite, and carnelian added to the feeling that he was carrying a pyramid stone. When he stood in the sun, the metals on his body heated, calling up the old nightmare sensation of Akhenaten's cursed sun disk brand searing his flesh.

Now, as he picked his way down a newly restored canal bank, he reveled in the freedom of a simple kilt, loincloth, and papyrus sandals— and no jewels. Most of his friends thought he was odd. Every Egyptian dreamed of having such wealth and rank. Meren dreamed of a life free of guilt, obligations, and serpentine machinations. And above all else, he longed for a time when he wouldn't fear for his family.

Since Akhenaten had ordered his father killed and his cousin Ebana's wife and son had been murdered, Meren had lived with the certainty that annihilation could strike his loved ones no matter how great his power became. He had only to offend one prince foolish enough to risk the king's fury. So many ways to invite death—a slip of the tongue at court, interfering with some official's scheme of corruption, standing between the priests of Amun and pharaoh once too often. After months spent immersed in a sea of peril, he welcomed being able to walk alone in the approaching darkness.

The charioteer he'd sent to find Nefertiti's favorite cook had given him a description of the old woman's house. It was a little removed from the village, to the south and farther toward the desert than any other. Meren left the fertile fields that took up almost all the land fed by the river's Inundation. He met a few farmers on their way home. They carried digging tools used to repair canals and shore up dikes. Inundation was coming, and Egypt must be ready for it.

A group of men and boys saluted him in the manner of a peasant to a superior, but Meren wasn't alarmed. His skin wasn't as dark as that of a man who worked in the fields. His kilt was clean and his body free of grime. They would mistake him for a scribe.

The land rose as he walked across the higher, less desirable tracts where Inundation didn't always deposit its yearly supply of fertile soil. The solar orb turned carnelian as it vanished behind the distant desert cliffs. It was growing late, and he encountered no more villagers. From a field riddled with cracks caused by relentless Drought season heat, he could see a solitary farmhouse of an old design. The sun was vanishing behind it, taking most of the light.

His foot hit sand. He had reached the desert margin. The cook's house was on a rise that would keep it above water during Inundation. Meren climbed up a few steps, then turned to survey the valley. He skipped quickly over the deserted fields and scoured the tree-lined banks of the Nile. Anyone following him would be forced to keep to the taller vegetation near the water's edge. He didn't think he'd been followed, but if he was wrong, his pursuer was no doubt cursing him for delaying and thus forcing him to remain near the bank in easy reach of crocodiles.

Finally Meren put his back to the river and approached the house. In the fading light he could discern no fire, no lamp. He sensed movement and stopped suddenly, only to see a vulture crouched just beyond the house launch its ungainly body into the air. Meren contemplated the flapping wings. The corners of his mouth descended to form a frown, but he resumed his walk.

He paused again only a few steps from the cook's abode. Like count-less others from the delta to Nubia, this house was a two-story mud-brick building. Half of the upper level overhung the lower, and the overhang was supported by two columns. The walls extended from the house in two low arms to form a yard sealed by a third cross-wall. A wooden half-gate allowed entry to the yard, where Meren could see two domed granaries. Against the left front corner, the owners had built a conical oven with a hole in the top for venting. Exterior stairs went to the living quarters on the second floor; the lower level provided storage and shelter for animals.

Through the high windows dim lamplight was visible, but Meren couldn't see or hear anyone. Geese wandered around the yard and in the ruins of a garden beside the house. More geese snapped at insects there and trod on the dried and half-devoured remains of onions, beans, and yellow peas.

"Kek-kek!"

Meren almost jumped as a goose stuck its head around the gate and fussed at him. It had a white underside, dark plumage on its back, and two black bars on the light wing coverts.

"Cursed fowl," he whispered.

Frightening the bird away with a gentle kick, Meren pulled on the gate. Its hinges needed repair. A quick survey of the yard, stable, and storage area revealed an empty stall for a donkey, a broken granite quern, and fragments of spindle whorls. There was nothing in jars that should have held dried fruit, grain, oil. Other things were missing as well—goats, farming tools, nets and hooks for fishing, sickles, and win-nowing fans.

Leaving the storage area, Meren walked between the two columns and mounted the stairs to the upper floor. The door was ajar. Inside he found a deserted living chamber with mats, worn cushions, and a cold brazier. A few pieces of furniture were scattered around, all of old, inferior wood, probably sycamore. The chamber was dark except for a diffuse glow from a ceramic lamp on the floor near an entryway that probably led to the kitchen. Movement in the shadows caught Meren's eye. He backed up a step, then stopped as he recognized yet another goose. It was perched on a stone quern in the corner, devouring grain.

Meren thought about hailing the cook and her husband, but decided not to. He hadn't expected to find the woman in such a neglected place.

He had assumed that the cook, Hunero, had been given provision from the royal estates when she left, or that she had taken a position with a noble household. Favored royal servants were symbols of rank and prerogative. Hunero should never have lacked for a place. And surely Akhenaten, heretic though he had been, would have provided for his beloved queen's loyal and trusted cook.

Yet this farm had been neglected for a long time. No one had replastered the walls, repaired the gate, or kept adequate provisions. How had its owners survived? Sustenance must have come from elsewhere. He was always suspicious of those who seemed not to toil and yet prospered—if living in this half-ruined old place could be called prospering. What was going on?

Already wary, Meren grew more uneasy as he looked around the living chamber. In a niche built into the wall sat a double statue of the heretic and his queen, Nefertiti. A foolish display, even for a former royal servant. The heretic was anathema. It would only take some officious tax collector or priest's report to invite persecution. Even dead Akhenaten still threatened those he touched, as he had threatened Meren.

He walked over to the niche, which was bathed in the dim lamplight, and stared at it. Seldom since his death had Meren looked upon the visage of Akhenaten. This cheap limestone version had been painted so that the king wore bright trappings. More talented than the sculptor, the artist had painted the eyes so accurately that they held a reflection of the black fire of Akhenaten's gaze. Meren quickly looked away from it to examine Nefertiti's fragile figure. His fascination with the contrast between the two must have been the reason he was caught off guard by the crash behind him.

Whirling around, Meren drew the dagger in his belt and cocked his arm over his shoulder, ready to throw. As he sank into a crouch that would offer a smaller target for an attacker, he spotted a tiny woman in the threshold between the kitchen and the living chamber. She had dropped a bowl of water.

"Thief, thief, thief, thief, thief!" the lady screeched.

Meren winced at the shrill trumpeting sound of her voice. He was sure Egyptian women developed blaring voices that could be heard across a battlefield from keeping order among their children. The shrill voice rose higher; the goose honked and hissed. Meren thrust his dagger into his belt and covered his ears.

"Peace, old woman! Do I look like a thief?"

The woman's mouth snapped shut. Her jaws pressed together and spread out as they do when back teeth have been lost.

"What are you doing here, boy?"

Startled at being addressed in so familiar a manner, Meren blinked, then said, "I'm searching for a woman called Hunero, who was favorite cook to the Great Royal Wife, Nefertiti, the justified, and I seek her husband, Bay, also."

"Hunero is down in the yard milking the donkey, young one." The old woman vanished back into the kitchen without another word. Meren was about to follow when she reappeared, carrying another bowl of water, which she set near the goose.

"There, Beauty. Drink deep, my sweet, my little gosling. She's a little treasure. She's a little daub of honey, she's a—"

"Did you say Hunero was in the yard milking a donkey?"

"A goat, fool. Milk a donkey, what a mad thought."

"Aged one, there is no one in the yard."

"My name is Satet, boy. You should know that if you're a friend of my sister's."

Satet seated herself on a stool and stroked the goose named Beauty with a trembling hand. Meren guessed that she had six or seven decades, a great age seldom achieved by those of humble rank. Like many who attain a revered age, Satet had shrunk as her years increased until she was the size of a twelve-year-old boy.

Unfortunately, her skin hadn't shrunk as her bones did, and now she looked like a hide bag into which had been tossed a collection of children's bones. Her neck was pleated with more wrinkles than a courtier's robe. Wobbly blue veins protruded from her skin like earthworms. Her hair had been shorn in a haphazard manner so that it hung in thin, irregular lengths.

However, her age and frailty didn't concern Meren. He was disturbed by the slight but constant nodding of her head, her strange conversation, and the fact that she had stuck at least a dozen wooden combs in her hair at different angles.

"Satet," Meren said, "where did you say Hunero and Bay have gone?"

"Oh, them? They're not here."

"I know, but where have they gone?"

"They left, all of a sudden, like nomads in a drought. One day Hunero came to me and said they were leaving, going to the city to seek fortune. A lot of folly, that is."

"Did Hunero say which city?"

Satet was stroking Beauty again. The goose shifted her weight from one foot to the other, marching in place as she rubbed her back.

"Aged one, about Hunero."

"Oh, she'll be back soon. She just went to fetch honey from the hives out back."

Suppressing a sigh of exasperation, Meren drew near the seated woman. "Do you live here alone?"

"Of course, young one. Do you see anyone else here? That lazy Bay convinced Hunero they'd be safer in the city, among lots of people."

"Safer, why safer?" Meren squatted so that his head was level with Satet's and caught her gaze. "Please, aged one, tell my why they felt safer in the city."

A voice came at him from behind. "No one knows why they left."

Meren's hand went to his dagger again. Looking over his shoulder he watched a youth come toward him. Unarmed, he carried a sagging basket in both hands, which he set beside Satet.

"I have brought your food and supplies, good grandmother."

Meren's hand dropped from his dagger hilt. This boy was no danger. He bore no weapon except for a small flint knife stuck in the waistband of his kilt. He was tall, but thin as youths are before they attain the musculature of manhood. Satet patted his head and trailed her wrinkled fingers through smooth, soft hair that gleamed as though it had been recently washed.

"Your name?" Meren asked.

"I am Tentamun, master. Bay paid me goods worth many copper *deben* to look after the good grandmother until he came back."

"So you aren't related to Satet. Where did they go, and when?"

"They left, oh, almost a week ago. Five or six days, I think. But Bay refused to say where they were going, and now no one in the village has heard from either Hunero or her husband Bay."

Satet gave Tentamun a playful slap on the arm. "I told you, boy, Hunero is in the yard milking the donkey."

"Yes, revered grandmother," Tentamun replied with patience.

"Did anyone see which way they sailed?" Meren asked.

"No, master, but I happened to be up early the morning they were to leave, and I saw a temple trading ship pass by going south. I haven't seen Hunero or Bay since that vessel sailed by."

"South," Meren repeated.

He pondered his situation. He couldn't chase all the way to Nubia in hopes of finding the city in which his quarry chose to hide. He wasn't going to pry the truth from Satet, if she even knew what the truth was, without a great deal of patience and time. He couldn't stay here. Satet would have to go with him back to Memphis.

"You're certain no one knows where the couple went?" he asked Tentamun.

"Yes, good master. Their leaving has been the talk of the village. Even the headman doesn't know, and we're all worried about Satet." Tentamun swept his arm around in a half circle. "After all, they took almost everything with them, even their cookware. We don't think Hunero and Bay are going to return."

Meren remained silent for a moment, assessing Tentamun's direct look and the way his hands lay comfortably on his thighs as he knelt, resting on the backs of his heels.

"I think you're right. Those two aren't coming back. And I am left with a problem. My master, a great noble, has need of an experienced cook to train several in his household. I was sent to find Hunero. My master detests failure, but perhaps he will forgive me if I bring Satet."

"Oh, but—"

"You can cook, can't you?" he asked the old woman.

"Better than that conceited Hunero," Satet said with a sniff. "I was placed in the household of the high priest of Ptah in Memphis. Hunero says she'll get a place even more grand than that. I told her she's imagining above herself. She thinks she's going to be a royal cook, of all things."

His head was beginning to ache from trying to follow Satet in her voyages through the past and present and back again. Meren spent a while longer satisfying Tentamun that the old one would be safe in his care. Then the youth left, his departure unnoticed by Satet. She was too busy shrieking for her pet cat.

"Treasure, here Treasure, where is mother's little girl?"

Meren covered his ears and glanced around the living chamber. He would sleep on a pile of mats tonight and leave for Memphis with Satet in the morning. He only hoped she would remember him then.

He slept lightly, waking every few hours. Most of the time he woke because Satet was roaming around the house. She napped throughout the day, rather than sleeping through the night. Once he came awake with a jolt to find the old woman's snores from the single bedchamber echoing off the bare plastered walls. Painfully alert, Meren listened to the deep groaning bark that came with each intake of breath. He had a vague memory of something moving beside him.

Looking around, he could see little in the blackness. He assumed Beauty was still nestled in her basket stuffed with linen scraps. The feeling of air disturbed by the movement of a body remained with him. Was it the remnant of a dream, the cat Treasure, or worse, a demon?

"What demon would bother with this neglected and peculiar household?" he mumbled.

Meren rose and went to the door. Pulling it open, he stood searching the yard, the garden, the barren fields. He heard an owl and looked up. A black silhouette crossed the sky, descended, and settled on the gatepost. Meren couldn't make out the flattened face, but he could see the black feather tufts.

Without warning the great bird's head swiveled around, then twisted back in Meren's direction. With a hoot that sounded across the horizon and reverberated from the desert cliffs, the creature sprang into the air. Wings flapping, it climbed the sky, its cries fading before Meren lost sight of it.

He remained at the door to listen for what had startled the owl. In the yard all was stillness. It was so quiet he could hear the north breeze whistle through the vent in the roof. Finally he perceived movement. Treasure, a fat black-and-gray bundle of meanness and gluttony, jumped onto the gatepost and sniffed the spot where the owl had perched. Meren watched the feline stalk along the wall and leap to the ground outside the yard. A black spot, she moved with deliberate care into the fields. Nothing else moved. The cat. He'd sensed the cat leaving the house. After assessing the likelihood that the source of his awakening might be something more sinister, Meren went back to his makeshift bed. Once inside the house, all he could hear were Satet's resounding snores and her intervening snuffles. The cat had startled the owl. He closed his eyes only to open them wide at the eruptions coming from Satet's bedchamber. If it hadn't been the cat that had frightened the owl, it had been those snores.

NOW KYSEN KNEW where Ese had gotten the inspiration for her imitation Greek house. He glanced at the guard on either side of him, then raised his gaze up past the brilliant frescoes to the people on the second floor who leaned over a balustrade and stared down at him silently. His escorts had halted him beside the circular central hearth, and the balustrade went around the entire square walk. Above it rose the clerestory window, now dark and sprinkled with stars. Ese had thrust him into the care of these two spear-carrying want-wits and ordered them to take him to Othrys. That she hadn't come with them said something about the relationship between her and the Greek.

A silver-haired Mycenaean in a long robe appeared and shuffled across the hall. Those in his path gave way. Many of them were accomplished bandits and pirates who stepped aside for no man, so Kysen knew immediately that this Greek was an intimate of Othrys. The farther into the hall the man came, the quieter its occupants became. Silver Hair's steps faltered and ceased as he drew near Kysen. He squinted, then drew a sharp breath and scuttled back the way he'd come.

Conversation failed to resume, and Kysen tried to look unconcerned that everyone seemed to be staring at him. A boom signaled the closing of a door somewhere within the house. It was a deceptive place, appearing to be one moderately large building when it really occupied the entire space of the two adjacent dwellings as well. Why hadn't such a large residence attracted the attention of the mayor and the royal officials concerned with foreigners?

Another boom sounded, closer, and then Silver Hair reappeared, entering from a door painted to look like part of a fresco of leaping dolphins in sea waves. Taking short, careful steps, Silver Hair came to them, made a signal with his hand, and was off again. One of the guards shoved Kysen, and he followed. When they left the hall, Silver Hair picked up the pace and led Kysen through a maze of rooms and corridors.

All at once they came into an antechamber crowded with more guards, then a room filled with shelves bearing clay tablets, papyrus, and flat pieces of stone and shards of pottery. Almost every tablet, papyrus roll, stone, and shard had writing on it—the wedge-shaped script of the Asiatics, the odd scratchlike characters of the Mycenaeans, and copper tablets covered with a script he'd never seen. A good proportion of this varied collection of documents bore signs of violence, either burning, damage from weapons, or both.

The center of the room was clear of shelves and held several low tables. Scribes sat on the floor or on stools surrounded by tablets, shards, and papyrus. Kysen could see only two men without a stylus or rush pen. One was the odorous Tcha. The man in leggings, sandals, and a blue tunic cinched with a gold belt was Othrys.

Silver Hair approached with silent delicacy, hovering behind his master. Othrys paid no attention to his servant or to Kysen. He was a well-built man of middle years, his arms, legs, and chest thick with hillocks of muscle. Puckered scars interfered with the smooth expanse of skin a shade or two lighter than cedar. In spite of the scars, his skin had the tautness of a youth, not a battle-weary barbarian pirate.

Kysen watched Othrys carefully, trying to discern his intentions. He gained nothing from staring at eyes the color of the sky at midday. He wasn't used to sky eyes. They seemed cold and pale compared to the warm shades of brown and black so much more common in Egypt. However, they did go with hair the color of old honey and streaked with gold from the sun. He was still assessing Othrys when Tcha's whine rose above the whispers of the scribes.

"I tell you he's dead! The jackals dragged him away, and I swear upon my own ka, I can't find our—" Tcha glanced at Kysen. "I can't find our belongings."

"By the Earth Mother, he's run off with the spoils," Othrys said.

Tcha had been squatting on the floor, but he had never been able to stay in one place for long. The thief jumped to his feet and darted in one direction, then another as he rattled on. "Not run off, killed. There was a hole hacked in his chest. A hole, I tell you!"

"Who is dead?" Kysen asked. He brushed by Silver Hair and confronted Tcha. "Who is dead?"

Tcha slid a narrow look at Kysen, then at Othrys.

"My cat."

Folding his arms, Kysen said, "You don't have a cat. No cat would keep company with one as filthy and ill mannered as you."

"Be at ease," Othrys said in a light purring tone that encouraged neither ease nor further conversation.

"Most worshiped prince," Silver Hair murmured. "I have brought the one called Nen to you, from Mistress Ese."

The servant retreated. Kysen turned his attention back to his host to find that Othrys had been surveying him calmly, rather like a mongoose contemplating a cobra. Othrys had the most unwavering stare he'd seen, other than pharaoh's. But the golden one's stare was that of a living god contemplating an invisible horizon between mortality and divinity. Othrys's stare was a javelin piercing a man's ka. Kysen always felt that the barbarian's sky-hued gaze masked the fact that he was debating whether he would kill his guest now, or later.

"Thunderbolts and quakes, Nen, be seated while I deal with this fluttered fool."

"It's to be later, then," Kysen said to himself.

"What?"

"Nothing," Kysen replied.

Tcha's relentless movements brought him back to Othrys. "I tell you, great master, there be a fiend abroad in Memphis."

"There are always demons who torment the living," Othrys said.

Flapping his arms in agitation, Tcha burst into a tirade. "He had no heart! And there was a feather. Heart and feather, feather and heart. Do you know what that means, great master?"

Othrys rolled his eyes and shook his head.

"Judgment," Kysen said. He was growing vaguely uneasy, no doubt because Tcha wouldn't keep still and chattered absurdities.

Othrys threw up his hands. "What judgment?"

Tcha licked his lips, but couldn't make his voice work. Kysen answered for him.

"He seems to think the missing heart and the feather—was it a white one? Ah. He seems to think the missing heart and the white feather are signs of a different kind of creature. Which causes me to fear for the health of old Tcha's wits."

"By the Great Earth, cease this cloudy talk. What creature does he fear?"

Kysen met Othrys's impatient gaze with a frown. "What creature? The one who crouches beneath the balance scales of judgment on which souls are weighed against the feather of truth and rightness." Kysen's frown deepened. "She is called many names, but the Book of the Dead calls her Ammut, the Devouress . . . Eater of Souls."

The whispering of the scribes vanished. Even Othrys was silent, while Tcha grabbed a handful of the amulets strung about his body. His lips moved in a silent recitation of a protective spell. Then Othrys managed a question in a faint tone.

"I assume the Devouress eats—"

"The dead found unworthy of the afterlife," Kysen replied. He continued reluctantly. "She eats the living soul, the body, all. One dies again, for all time. One ceases to exist."

"Does one, by the Earth Mother? Eaten alive, so to speak."

Kysen was suddenly angry with himself. What was he doing, taking seriously the ravings of an ignorant teller of tales like Tcha? The man sold the crimes of his friends to the city police. The only reason he was still alive was that he possessed just enough sense not to try his tricks on Othrys.

Smiling, Kysen broke the fearful silence. "Tcha makes sense. Where else would Eater of Souls be drawn than to the Caverns in mighty Memphis, a place stuffed to the ramparts with thieves, ruffians, corruption, and evildoers of every description? So many to devour in such a small space."

"Ha!" Othrys threw back his head and guffawed. The scribes exchanged rueful glances and laughed along with their master.

Tcha stared at them, shaking with indignation so that his amulets clacked.

"I knew it," Othrys crowed. "He tells this tale to conceal his own deeds. Tcha, you killed Pawah, and now you spin this lying yarn to hide behind the Eater of Souls. An original notion, I admit."

All mirth fled Othrys's visage. "But you still owe me my tithe. Pay it, or by the time I'm done with you, you'll welcome the Eater of Souls."

"I spin no yarns!" Tcha squawked. The two guards who had escorted Kysen grabbed the thief by the arms and lifted him off his feet. Tcha's legs whirled in the air. The last that was heard of him was a high whine. "Everyone thinks I'm offal, goat's dung, hippo muck. Everyone despises me. I'm surrounded by malice and disgust!"

Othrys poured wine into a bull's-head rhyton. "Now, that is a man who knows the truth of himself."

Kysen couldn't restrain a grin.

The Greek gave him a tolerant smile. "So, my friend. I didn't frighten you away the last time we saw each other. I've never met a young man who would give himself over in the house of a man who had held a blade to his throat."

"I assumed the blade was your accustomed greeting for those who win games of senet and five *deben* of copper from you."

Othrys handed him the rhyton. It was silver with a gold rim. "You have the facile tongue of a bard, Nen, but your character is shrouded by perpetual mist."

Kysen's heart did a somersault in his chest. He looked over his shoulder at the scribes. They had resumed their work, but Othrys clapped his hands once, and they left.

"I'm what Ese told you I was," Kysen said as he turned back to his host.

Othrys lifted a double-handled drinking cup, drank some wine, and said, "Facile of tongue, dauntless of heart, swift of wit. Being all these things, you should know I would find out who you really were." The cup slammed down on a tray. Wine sprayed out, splattering Othrys's tunic and Kysen's kilt.

"Tell me, Lord Kysen. Why should I not eviscerate you and stuff your body beneath the floor of my bedchamber?"

This was one of those moments for which Father had trained him. Kysen sighed and brushed drops of red wine from his kilt with leisurely strokes. "I suppose because you know that my father would impale you on his spear, taking care not to kill you, then hang you from the prow of *Wings of Horus*. Just above the water, where crocodiles could take turns snapping chunks of flesh from your face and body. At least, that's what he did to the last pirate he caught. Perhaps he would be a bit more angry should you kill me."

"As I said, *my lord*. You're dauntless of heart and swift of wit." Othrys picked up a cloth and wiped wine from his arm.

"Then shall we discuss my need for information, and your need to keep silent about it and me?"

"So long as you understand me," Othrys said. "I reverence not the Eyes and Ears of Pharaoh. See that helmet on the shelf? It is made of the tusks of more than thirty boars. I killed each of them with my sword. Not a spear, a sword."

Kysen inclined his head. "Then I think it is you who are dauntless of heart."

The pirate held Kysen's gaze for a long moment before grunting and bidding his guest state his request. It took little time to make Othrys understand what was needed. The Greek was accustomed to doing such delicate tasks for his customers of the distant cities from Hattusha to the Aegean Sea, the spice lands of Punt, and down into wild Nubia. They arranged to meet again in a few days, by which time Othrys hoped to know something of the fate of Nefertiti's household. Kysen was taking his leave when Othrys put a hand on his arm. Surprised, he withdrew from the grasp.

"I've been thinking about Tcha," Othrys said as he allowed Kysen to escape his hold. "I would forget his ranting if it weren't for the rumors."

"What rumors?"

"Of late the streets have been full of rumors of a demon who strikes at night. Some say it isn't a demon but an animal, a monster. The whole of the Caverns is ripe with talk of evil. I've seen magicians warding off evil from three different houses in two days. And my men are more and more reluctant to venture forth after sunset."

"I suppose Tcha isn't the only one to suddenly begin wearing a multitude of amulets?"

"You're right." Othrys pulled on a leather cord beneath the neck of his tunic. From it was suspended a figurine of the Earth Goddess carved of ivory. "I started wearing this a few days ago, on the night all the animals in my stables and pens tried to escape in fright at the same time. The same night one of my best hunting hounds disappeared."

An inward shiver rippled up Kysen's body, leaving him cold. "Perhaps you should send Tcha to me."

"I will, if I can find him."

"And be careful," Kysen said. "You're in Egypt, where men are judged after death according to their deeds in life. If you die, you may meet the Swallower of the Dead, Eater of Souls."

"I'm swift of foot. She won't catch me."

"Perhaps, but Eater of Souls isn't even a god. Unfortunately the condemned face an abundance of punishments should the Devouress fail. I would hate to think of you being slaughtered with knives, dismembered, and your blood drained away, or cooked like a heron, or burned in a fiery pit."

Othrys's hand closed around the Earth Goddess figurine. Something primitive flashed in his eyes, but he managed a smile. "I bow to your courage, my lord. And your ability to recover from a stumble. The Eyes of Pharaoh has a worthy successor."

Kysen nodded and turned away. "Then I wish you a peaceful and safe evening."

8

OF ALL OF the souls she'd eaten, the father had tasted best. His flesh had been aged in the finest mortal wines. His bones had been brittle; they snapped loudly when she brought her mighty jaws together. She liked crunchy bones. But aside from the pleasure of eating, devouring the father had ended the exquisite torment of the favored one. Devouring the father was one of her most worthy acts.

When the father ended, the condemnation ended, bringing relief to the favored one. No more ceaseless disapproval, no more drunken shouting. The father had been vile carrion fouling the palace of the favored one's soul. Eater of Souls still heard echoes of the bile he spewed at the chosen one of the gods—witless, ugly, clumsy, more lackwitted than a pig, lazy, dirty, womanish, thoughtless, lack-mannered. Every mean little word slurred and carried on a stinking breath.

Eater of Souls growled, clawed the air, and wished she could devour the father again. This time she would do it slowly, so that the creature felt each snap of a bone, endured the agony of her teeth piercing the meat of his stomach, his arms, his chest. Then the favored one's pain would become his pain and bring relief. It was unfortunate that devouring other transgressors against the favored one was but a pale shadow of this first great annihilation.

TENTAMUN WAITED FOR his employer in the shade of a date palm. He had sailed the short distance south to this sprawling estate in order to report Satet's removal to Memphis. This was the kind of event for which he'd been told to be on guard, but his parents had kept him busy repairing the main canal that fed the village fields. Only today had he been able to claim his duty to visit the man everyone else knew only as his patron.

Leaning against the rough trunk, Tentamun gazed up at the leaves of the palm tree, one of many that formed this date field. Foliage shot out of a central point to form graceful, drooping fans. In a few months stalks heavy with dates would appear, ready for picking. Children and trained monkeys would climb high into the air to retrieve the fruit. Great baskets would be filled. Then more laborers would spread the dates out in a carpet to ripen. As fruit of different ages ripened, the field would become a dazzling sheet of color, from darkest brown to bright orange and yellow.

He became uncomfortable with the spikes of the palm trunk digging into his back. The solar orb had reached its pinnacle and was descending toward the netherworld, but the heat that had been building all day remained. He sweated even in the shade. If it weren't for the generosity of his employer, he would have avoided traveling in the last harsh weeks of Drought.

Something moved beyond the mud-and-straw wall that formed a protective barrier around the date field. Through the shadows of the sycamores and acacias that sheltered the estate strode the owner of the dates, the palms, and everything else within sight. As he approached, Tentamun could see his green-and-yellow robe much more easily than he could his features.

Odd that Tentamun couldn't find anyone who knew exactly who his people were. All he'd been able to discover was that the man had an Asiatic father and an Egyptian mother, which accounted for his fluency in Egyptian. Zulaya entered the date field and came toward him, dressed in the manner of his people. His long robe covered him from neck to ankles, hanging in diagonal folds that fit close to his body. The thin, soft wool was patterned in checks, diamonds, and swirls. A headband of the same material kept his long hair pulled back from his face.

In keeping with his foreign ancestry, he wore a beard that he kept clean and arranged in a profusion of tight coils. It concealed his face from nose to chin. The only features exposed were dark rose lips. As Zulaya stalked toward him, Tentamun felt his skin turn cold despite the kiln-heat of the afternoon. It wasn't Zulaya's foreignness that chilled his flesh and robbed his mouth of moisture. But as hard as he pondered, he couldn't identify the exact source of his fear.

Zulaya stepped into the shade of Tentamun's palm. His feet were bare, but his ankles were encased in gold bands. Tentamun considered him aged, for his dark brown hair was streaked with silver. But age had refused to mark Zulaya in other ways. His step was light, his eyes quick and exact. And he bore few lines, although Tentamun guessed that he must have at least four decades.

What was it that made him so uneasy around this man? Could it be the numbers of strange people Zulaya employed? Tentamun had never seen so many come and go from a great man's house. A few were ordinary field laborers or tenant farmers. Others, in spite of their Egyptian dress, seemed rough, some with the manners of bandits, some with scars of old knife and scimitar wounds. Many were foreigners who addressed Zulaya in the language of the Asiatics, or in Babylonian, or other obscure tongues from regions Tentamun had never heard of. Or perhaps Tentamun was uncomfortable because Zulaya seemed to enjoy traveling to foreign places. No good Egyptian liked alien lands. Egypt was a paradise blessed by the gods. Other places were exile.

Tentamun bowed low, but Zulaya had turned to survey the canal that ran past his estate, through the fields close to the river and into the Nile. "Did you know, dear youth, that none of the waters near Byblos or those of the mighty Euphrates rival the dark night blue of the Nile?"

"No, lord." Perhaps he feared Zulaya because he never seemed to approach any goal directly.

Zulaya lifted his arm and pointed across the river, indicating the desert. Swirls of sand formed dunes with knife-edged tops.

"That, Tentamun, is the reason for Egypt's happy nature. A great and terrible barrier against the ambitions and might of quarrelsome Asiatics. They snarl and claw at each other unceasingly, shed blood over scraps of coastline, over rich cities, over mountains covered with cedar. All the while Egypt remains fruitful and at peace behind her rock and sand ramparts. The envy of every monarch, every herder in search of pasture, every barbarian looking for plunder."

Now Zulaya wasn't frightening; he was tiresome. Tentamun waited until his employer transferred his attention from the desert to him. It was the only signal Zulaya would give that he was ready to listen.

"Someone came to visit Satet, my lord. You said you wished to know at once should this happen. He came a few days ago, a scribe in search of servants for his master."

"And did you know this scribe?"

"No, my lord. Now that I think, he never even gave his name."

Zulaya's eyes seemed to catch the sunlight, and he became more attentive. "Tell me everything, from the beginning."

Tentamun complied, but the tale took a long time to repeat, for his master frequently stopped him with questions.

"What do you mean, he took her away?" Zulaya demanded quietly. "Why would he employ that feather-witted old pestilence?"

"He said his master had cooks in need of training in the royal manner."

Zulaya's questions came more quickly now. He had tugged on his headband until the ribbon of cloth came loose. He was threading it between his fingers and pulling it free over and over again.

"Where did he go?"

"I think to Memphis, lord."

"Describe this man again."

"A face all of angles, lord. Black hair cut short."

"His age?"

"Oh, a great age. He could be my father, only he's much less aged than mine. I suppose it's because he's a scribe, but he wasn't weak looking, like those who spend their days inside bent over papyrus."

At this comment, Zulaya drew nearer. His questions became sharp and impatient as he grilled Tentamun on the scribe's appearance. Finally Zulaya once more lifted his gaze from Tentamun to the Nile waters.

"A scribe who doesn't look as if he spends his days bent over papyrus. A man of well-fed appearance. Your description is at odds with itself, dear youth. Was there nothing individual about this man? His speech, perhaps, or the way he walked?"

Tentamun rubbed his brow and thought hard. "No, my lord. He seemed very much like any other man." Then he remembered something. "There was a scar."

"What scar? Where?"

"It was on his inner wrist. I didn't see it clearly. The house was dark except for one lamp, and he wore a leather wristband."

"A scribe who wears a leather wristband," Zulaya said as he rested his bearded chin on a fist and studied the ground.

"The band pulled up on his arm a bit, and I saw part of a white scar. I remember because it was so clearly defined, not like a wound at all, and it seemed to be half of a circle."

His remarks elicited nothing from Zulaya. He turned his back to Tentamun and gazed at the canal, where a group of laborers was dumping loads of earth onto a collapsed section of the bank. As he awaited his employer's next command, Tentamun noticed that Zulaya had questioned him so long that the sun had moved, and he no longer stood in the shade. He stepped sideways, slowly and carefully, so as not to attract attention. He should have known better. Zulaya's fingers intertwined with the green-and-yellow headband, then grasped the ends and yanked the ribbon tight with a snap that made Tentamun jump.

"Some say I'm too suspicious and expect only the worst, but I'm vindicated by your news."

"Yes, my lord."

What could he say? He had no idea who would dare criticize Zulaya. He wasn't only a man of wealth. He was mayor of the town near his estate and friends with the great men of the district, who valued his trading contacts among the Asiatics, the Hittites, the Mycenaeans, and the Babylonians. But there was something ruthless and secretive about Zulaya. It caused Tentamun to doubt that even a great man would dare insult him.

Zulaya turned back to Tentamun, his speech resuming its customary soft tones and embroidered language. "Dear youth, you have done well, and I call upon the gods and my ancestors to look with favor upon you. Ishtar, Marduk, Gula, and Ninurta, the great ones of Ur and Susa and Ugarit."

"My lord is kind," Tentamun said as he fell to his knees and touched his forehead to the earth. He straightened, but kept his head down when he felt Zulaya's hand come to rest on his hair. "My lord?" He hated this. All he could see was dirt and Zulaya's manicured toes. All he could hear was the man's soft voice made harsh by the guttural tones of his accent.

"You don't like coming here, I know. You fear my servants, those with whom I trade, my friends." There was a pause during which Tentamun guessed Zulaya gazed out at the river again. "I will tell you a thing that may help you, dear youth. I have known kings and criminals. I prefer criminals. They cheat, steal, and betray, but at least you don't have to worship them while they do it."

—————

THE EMPTINESS CLAWED at her belly, the gnawing of rats' teeth inside her gut. In the darkness her metal claws scraped the bark of a tree. She rubbed the shining thongs that bound the ax head to its handle and rasped her claws over the engraving on the flat of the blade, but the emptiness remained. The hollow void was growing, spreading, replacing the essence of the Devouress. Others had put it there—the undeserving great one, the pretend god, the foreigner.

Their callousness toward the favored one battered at her belly, causing a crack that spread throughout her gut, spreading slivers of nothingness that grew into holes and then into this horrifying abyss. If she didn't stop them, they would continue to abuse the favored one. Then the emptiness would press outward, through her hide, and envelop her whole. She would cease altogether. She would become emptiness.

There was no moon. The chasm had swallowed it, but she saw with yellow-eyed clarity, inspired by the pain. The task of penetrating the garden had been a simple one. Scale a wall. Kill the sleeping creature who guards the enclosure. Slink into the darkest of shadows. And wait.

A young woman entered the garden. She hummed to herself and stooped to sniff a flower with wrinkled red petals. Eater of Souls wrapped her claws around a knife. This one was of no importance, hardly worth the effort to strike. The Devouress waited until the young woman took the gravel path that would bring her near the tree. Tossing her bushy mane over her shoulder, she raised the knife high and drove it down. When all was over, she lifted the young woman and arranged her on a bench beside the reflection pool. The foreigner would think the girl was pretending sleep to entertain him.

As she pulled a length of transparent linen over the hole in the girl's back, she heard the gate creak. A quiet leap to concealment. A snout raised to sniff the air currents. The scent of a transgressor.

The foreigner crept into the garden and closed the gate slowly, as though trying to keep it from creaking. Eater of Souls lifted her snout, tested the air, caught the stench of a foreign soul. Not appetizing, but begging for judgment. This one had insulted the favored one and caused sorrow. She could hear the favored one's piteous lament—"Life is so terrible. Everyone is so cruel, especially that evil foreigner. I've done nothing wrong. *He* was in the wrong. He should suffer for it."

It was then that the emptiness began. A familiar feeling, the harbinger of misery, of feeling powerless. The descent into gloom was always quick, like falling from a desert cliff and never reaching the ground. But the Devouress knew that the anger would come to save her and the favored one as well. Healing rage was growing in her belly now. It burned the emptiness away, directing the blame to the proper culprit. All she had to do to banish the emptiness and regain her power was destroy the evildoer, the true sinner, the cause of the favored one's pain.

The foreigner reached the girl lying on the bench. He bent over her and touched her shoulder. "My little lotus, have you fallen asl—"

The man sucked in his breath. Eater of Souls was already moving. She lifted her ax high to deliver a stunning blow. But the foreigner wasn't like the others. As he realized the young woman was dead, he backed away from her, and his eyes darted around the garden. He saw her move and jumped out of the path of the reversed ax.

The Devouress hissed, whirled in place, and struck again. The foreigner dodged the second blow but didn't stay for the next. His eyes as large as figs, he uttered a ragged shriek and bolted. She sprang after him, but he reached a door in the garden wall and was out in the street before she could catch up.

Undeterred, she hurtled after him. The pounding of his footsteps kept her on his path through deserted streets, crooked alleys and paths. The foreigner seemed to be running without purpose, blindly, as if propelled by witless fear. So much the better. Eater of Souls sprang up a flight of stairs that led to the roof of a storage building. Once on top, she saw her prey turning down an alley that led to a dead end.

Grunting with satisfaction, she darted across the roof, lunged over the gap between it and the next building, and ran to the wall that intersected another that barricaded the alley. Long, leaping strides took her to the open end of the trap as the foreigner entered it. He ran into the wall that formed the dead end, smacking into mud brick and bouncing off again. He stumbled, shook his head, and took several running steps back the way he'd come.

As he did, Eater of Souls sprang off the roof and into his path. She landed on her feet, her hide rippling. Drawing herself up, she spread her arms wide and showed her claws. She pointed her snout at the foreigner and sucked in his scent through her long, armored nose. Then she drew the ax from between her teeth.

Her prey had staggered backward when she jumped into his path. Now he was staring at her fangs as he tried to back into the darker shadows of the alley. Even in his terror, he sought to escape. The others had never lived so long. It was time for this one to die.

Briefly she wondered what it was like for the transgressor when she snarled, spitting saliva at him, and at the same time sprang at him so quickly he had no time to scream. Eater of Souls smelled a sweet foreign scent mixed with the odor of terror as the reversed blade bashed into the skull of the offender. Raised claws opened. As they brushed together, she heard the hiss of sharp edges sliding against each other.

Then came the first swipe. The impaling. The drag of skin and flesh against incising metal. A dog entered the alley, his nose sweeping back and forth in the air. The animal stopped as she whirled around and raised her claws. Without making a sound, the dog turned and trotted away, tail curled down, head lowered between his shoulders. Eater of Souls let fall the feather of truth and watched it drift down to rest in a bloody valley hacked into flesh.

Eater of Souls took a deep breath and let it out in a long, groaning sigh. Her joints and muscles began to ache, but she welcomed the hurt, the sign of a task completed. Claws stroked the lion's mane. Weariness crept into her bones. And relief. Again the favored one had been avenged, the cause of suffering destroyed. And the emptiness was gone—for now.

ON THIS MOONLESS night, quiet reigned in Lord Meren's household. Meren was in his office, slumped down in a chair, legs stretched out and crossed at the ankles. His chin rested on the broad collar of turquoise, lapis lazuli, and electrum that covered his upper chest, and he was scowling at the tip of a gilded leather sandal. Kysen sat cross-legged on the floor in the midst of a pile of reports from the mayor of Memphis, from agents at the Hittite court and in Babylonia, numerous vassal princes and a wide range of useful acquaintances. Meren felt a tiny muscle in his jaw twitch.

He'd been back two days, and he was still annoyed at the foolishness of his arrival at the house. Satet had refused to come inside through the front door and protested in a loud, annoyingly high voice that had attracted most of the servants, his daughters, and Kysen to the portico. He'd been forced to argue with the old woman in front of everyone.

Luckily, Bener had introduced herself and persuaded Satet to come inside with her to inspect the kitchen.

"Sending Abu after me was deliberate disobedience," Meren said.

Kysen looked up from a city police report and said quickly, "Has Satet remembered anything else about where her sister went?"

"Isn't it enough that she remembered Hunero told her she was going to hide in Memphis?"

"You're angry because you know she's just making things up to impress you."

Pulling himself upright, Meren leaned forward, rested his elbows on his knees, and put his head in his hands. From behind a screen of fingers, he said, "Now she says she's going to look for Hunero herself. I told her no, but—"

"She does seem to get her way regardless of our precautions."

Meren groaned. "I'm still suffering from the spices she used to poison that roast goose." He pounded the arm of his chair. "Damnation of the gods, she's useless. It's going to take weeks for the men I sent to search the towns south of their farm and return."

"I've heard nothing from Esc or Othrys," Kysen said as he tried to stack city police reports into a pile. "Have you read these? Old Sokar must be exhausted. One of these lists of disturbances and crimes took up an entire half page."

Rubbing his forehead, Meren sighed. "I should have known the killer's death would cause the rats to scatter. I should have pursued the cook immediately."

"You can't be sure of the reason they left."

When Meren didn't answer, Kysen tossed a bundle of documents at him. Meren caught them and threw them back at his son's head. Kysen dodged it and grinned.

"What were those words of great prudence you spoke to me not long ago? Ah, yes. You said that I shouldn't vex my heart over things that can't be changed." Kysen waggled his eyebrows. "You said it makes a man intemperate."

Meren sat up straight and pounded the chair arm again. "Am I intemperate? Am I not known for my calm, my lack of ire?"

"Then you're not disturbed by the knowledge that our new friend Lord Reshep is coming to take dinner with us tomorrow for the third time this week?"

Meren shoved himself to his feet so quickly his chair nearly tipped over. He caught it and shoved it out of his way.

"What did you say? No, I heard. I can't endure this much longer. To Reshep, people are but mirrors of his own perfection. I don't understand why Isis encourages him."

"Bener says it's because she's never met anyone more magnificent than herself. She's in awe of him, and entertained by the new experience. I think she likes him because he's so much like her."

"She is not. Isis may be a bit vain, but she has good sense and a kind soul. In some ways she's much more practical than Bener."

Kysen looked doubtful.

"I suppose it's too late to claim the press of royal business," Meren said.

Kysen nodded. "Yes, because I think I hear his self-impressed voice. He must be in the great hall."

"But it's not even morning!"

They both turned to face the door as Abu knocked and opened it. His face expressionless, the charioteer announced that Lord Reshep was in the great hall seeking speech with Meren.

"Tell him I'm sick," Meren said.

"Oh, Father."

Abu didn't leave; he simply fixed his gaze on Meren and waited.

"Father, the king asked you to become acquainted with Reshep."

"I have, and I don't like him. He thinks he's prettier than my daughter. Every time we meet I get the feeling he expects me to fall to my knees and touch my forehead to the floor. Reshep is worse than Prince Rahotep. At least Rahotep's pride and conceit are mere varnish to cover his fears of unworthiness. Reshep really believes in his own perfection, his right to the best place, his unparalleled beauty. He makes me want to vomit."

"This is what you'll tell the golden one?" Kysen asked.

Meren's brows knitted together, and his chin jutted forward. "Yes. That's what I'll tell pharaoh, may he live forever in health and prosperity."

Kysen exchanged glances with Abu, who spoke quietly.

"Lord, are you certain you want to make an enemy of this man?"

"He's of no consequence."

"If the lord will allow me?"

"Speak, Abu. You will anyway."

"The lord would be wise to remember his daughter. Making an enemy of this man might make an enemy of her."

"She'll forget him."

"As the lord's oldest daughter forgot her suitor."

Meren glared at Abu. Tefnut had married the suitor he'd been certain she would scorn and forget.

"Very well, you interfering, presumptuous—"

"Your guest is waiting in the great hall, my lord."

Kysen grinned again, provoking a stream of curses from Meren as he stomped out of the office. With Kysen trailing behind him, Meren walked into the great hall. The chamber was shrouded in shadows that obscured the lotus-flower tops of the columns. Alabaster lamps rested at the four corners of the master's dais, and a servant stirred a breeze with an ostrich feather fan. The breeze caused the lamplight to waver. Shadows danced across the plastered and painted floor of the dais, and over the face of Lord Reshep. Meren strode across the hall and stopped abruptly. His lower jaw came unmoored. Reshep lounged in the gold-and-ebony master's chair, looking as if he were its owner. Meren resisted the urge to haul the intruder out of his chair—a great feat, since Reshep was admiring the hall as if he owned that too. Then Meren saw Isis.

His daughter was perched on a cushion at Reshep's feet, and she was murmuring something in a near-whisper. Meren quietly moved nearer while he signaled Kysen to make no sound. He heard bits of a song, something about love mixed throughout her body. That tune ended, luckily, but then he heard another begin. She was singing that her heart chases his love.

Meren quickened his steps and said loudly, "A late visit, Reshep."

To his consternation, Reshep didn't get up. His wide, thin lips spread out in a smile Meren preferred to call a smirk. As Meren came up the dais steps with Kysen right behind him, Reshep held out his hand. Isis placed a delicate gold wine cup in it.

"I'm so pleased you're still awake, Meren."

He'd been about to tell the young man to get his ass out of the master's chair, but being addressed without his title robbed Meren of speech. He planted himself in front of Reshep and gaped.

Kysen wasn't so aghast. "You forget your manners. Rise and address my father as you should, Reshep."

"I have been doing that," Reshep said with an even wider smile.

Meren watched the corners of his mouth reach the edge of his face. "Why do you smile at me as if you're about to disclose some amazingly pleasurable revelation? Isis, you should be asleep."

"We knew the best time to find you alone would be late at night," Isis said, without concern for Meren's irritation.

Meren looked at his daughter with suspicion. Only yesterday she'd explained how her aunt, Idut, had given her the secret to making a friend, or ensnaring a lover. "Aunt Idut says that a man loves nothing better than talking about himself. He charms himself with such talk the way a snake charms a mouse."

Isis had gone on to say that she'd found that an admirer's attention remained on her much longer if she asked him about his life, his titles, his family. Reshep was the only man who hadn't needed encouragement to propound on such subjects.

Suspicious, Meren asked, "Why would you need to find me alone? And I'm not alone." He exchanged mystified glances with Kysen.

"Kysen doesn't count," Isis replied as she placed her hand on Reshep's arm.

Even at this late hour Reshep was freshly bathed and dressed in a kilt that looked as if it had only been worn for a few moments. Meren felt dirty and disheveled standing in front of him.

"What do you want?" Meren asked without bothering to conceal his impatience.

"I want to give you most fortunate news," Reshep said. His smile spread farther and threatened to climb to his ears. "I have consented to allow Isis to be my wife."

Folding his arms over his chest, Meren buried his fury in humor and laughed lightly. "I think not."

"Naturally it took Isis a while to persuade me, but after she told me of the greatness of your family—what?"

Reshep paled and appeared to sink inward. He looked lost for a moment, disbelieving, then bewildered.

"You refuse me? You refuse me." The young man said it over and over, as if to force himself to believe the impossible.

Meren had controlled his anger at the man who presumed to court his daughter and nearly make her commit herself to a worthless alliance. Now he began to feel sorry for Reshep. The fool genuinely believed he'd been bestowing a great prize upon Isis and her father.

"I could wish you hadn't placed yourself in a situation where I was forced to refuse you before others," Meren said. "But you anger me with your presumption. Few men would try to ally themselves with a Friend of the King upon such short acquaintance. Indeed, I know little of your family, your home, your accomplishments and future plans, but—"

"Father!" Isis jumped to her feet, glaring and breathing hard. Then she burst into imprecations and accusations. "You think I'm still a child. You treat me as if I were younger than Kysen's little boy. You've shamed me beyond bearing!"

Meren turned on her so quickly she started and shut her mouth with a snap. Kysen put a hand on her arm, or she might have backed up. Saying nothing, Meren lifted a brow and directed a soul-freezing look at his youngest daughter. No one moved.

Finally Meren spoke in a quiet, implacable tone. "It grows quite late, daughter. I'm certain Lord Reshep doesn't mean to keep you from your rest. May the goddess for whom you are named give you peaceful sleep."

Kysen took his sister's arm again and pulled her down the dais steps while he muttered, "Come along, before he gets any calmer."

Meren turned back to Reshep in time to catch the young man looking at him. In a brief, almost imperceptible moment, he glimpsed a cauldron of flaming oil. Then it was gone.

"You propose an alliance too soon," Meren said.

Reshep merely looked at him.

"What ails you, man?" He was growing annoyed at the way Reshep kept staring at him in silence, but before he could ask him to leave, Kysen returned.

"Father, we have another visitor."

"Tell him to go away."

Kysen whispered in his ear. "This one you might want to see. It's Tcha, the one I told you about."

"Oh. Reshep, leave my house, and don't return until—"

He heard a great clacking and clattering. It was coming closer. Then the noise was among them, and it smelled. Meren watched what appeared to be a tent of amulets with hair scurry into the hall and propel itself to the foot of the dais.

Everyone backed up as a wave of honeyed putrefaction roiled up at them.

"I sawit! I sawit, I sawit, I sawit! It was huge, and then it vanished. The demon, the creature." Tcha lifted a dirty arm and pointed at Kysen. "You think I'm stupid, you think I lie, but now you'll see. Tcha never gets no praise for his good deeds, never gets enough payment. And now you couldn't give me enough gold to go back there. No, not Tcha!"

Meren, Kysen, and Reshep all stared at the trembling mass of fear that babbled at them. Reshep sniffed, then got up from the master's chair to put it between him and Tcha. Meren found this to be the only value of having his house invaded by the thief.

"Kysen, is this, this . . . Is he saying he's seen a demon? Get him out of here."

Kysen began flapping his hands at Tcha to drive him out of the hall.

"Wait, great lord! I can't go out there. It—she is out there."

"Go away, Tcha," Kysen said. He gave the thief a light shove with the tip of one finger.

"No, wait, wait, wait."

Kysen poked him each time he said "wait."

At last Tcha scrambled out of his reach and exclaimed, "You don't understand. This time Eater of Souls has killed the Hittite emissary!"

9

SOKAR WAS IN an even more foul mood than usual. The idiot Min
had roused him from sleep, and if this was another instance of the
watchman trying to make himself look important by inflating the significance of his discovery, he would miss his rations for two whole months.
Stomach swaying, sandals flapping, the chief of watchmen followed his
underling to an alley near the area inhabited by foreigners.

Rounding a corner, Sokar marched into darkness lit only by Min's
sputtering torch. To his consternation, two men were already there
standing in the shadows near the body. Sokar's face reddened. His
stomach and chest inflated, and he barked, "Here! What are you doing?
Robbing a corpse, no doubt. Min, arrest these two."

As he spoke, the two turned to face Sokar. He could hardly make
out their features or anything else about them until one stepped into the
torchlight. He was big, this one. Sokar was suddenly grateful Min was
with him. Furious that this man had intimidated him, Sokar poked a
finger in his direction.

"You, who are you, and what do you here? There will be no robbery
of corpses or gawking. Another useless one has been killed in the city.
He's probably some country farmer stumbling into a thief, like the others. Min, this foolishness isn't worth my attention. Get rid of the body."

Sokar glared at Min, but then he looked again at the quiet stranger
beside the watchman, caught sight of his scimitar, the horse whip stuck
in a bronze and turquoise-beaded belt. A charioteer!

"Officer," Sokar purred, his stomach deflating. "I didn't know. This is a paltry matter. Please allow me to remove this offal from the street. I beg you, don't let this miserable discovery annoy you." He heard an unknown voice speak quietly.

"What others?"

The question had come from the other man still in the shadows, and it irritated Sokar again.

"Who demands answers of the chief of watchmen? Show yourself."

The stranger stepped into the torchlight. Sokar's eyes caught the glint of a gold broad collar, wide-shouldered height, cloud-fine linen. Curse his ill luck. This was a nobleman. Wrinkling the skin on his forehead, Sokar noted the obsidian black of the man's hair, brows, and lashes. Their darkness made his skin, a tawny brown, seem lighter than it was.

He'd seen this man before. Envied those straight brows and that charioteer's frame. As Sokar struggled with his memory, he noted the man's gleaming eyes, the color fine cedar polished with beeswax. Hollows beneath prominent cheekbones, angular lines to the face, the personal dignity of a pharaoh.

"Lord Meren!" He'd been gawping at the Eyes of Pharaoh like a baffled donkey. He snarled at Min. "On your knees before the great lord and Friend of the King."

Sokar grunted as he struggled to the ground and lowered his forehead. "O great lord, forgive this humble servant. I didn't know it was you in the darkness."

"Tell me, chief of watchmen, do you always make such pronouncements without having seen the victim?"

Speaking to the ground, Sokar launched into denial, only to be silenced when the Friend of the King stalked over to him.

"You said this was another useless one killed in the city." The words were said slowly, pronounced clearly, each like the sting of a scorpion. *"What others?"*

Sokar stopped breathing. He sensed danger, to himself. If there was one thing at which he was accomplished, it was sensing and wriggling out of danger. He shoved himself upright and sat on the backs of his heels. Then he gave Lord Meren a round-eyed yet humble look.

"Others, great lord?" Sokar wiped sweat from his upper lip. "Oh, the others. Foolish country visitors who sailed into the wake of thieves.

I beg my lord not to disturb himself over such unimportant things. My reports—"

"Said nothing of murder, said nothing of more than one, and certainly nothing of several that were alike."

Sokar smiled and bowed even as he shook his head. "Alike, O great one? No, no. Not alike."

Min lifted his head, his mouth open, but Sokar glared at him, and he quickly put his forehead to the ground. Sokar's smile returned as he again faced Lord Meren, but the nobleman wasn't looking at him. He was watching Min with an intense fierceness Sokar had seen in the eyes of a kestrel as it hovered, heading into the wind, looking for prey. Sokar heard the voice of his heart grow louder, so that it seemed to inhabit his ears. His stomach began to burn, and the longer Lord Meren studied Min's prostrate figure, the hotter his belly burned.

Sokar tried to maintain his look of innocence, but Meren wasn't watching him. The great one glanced at his charioteer without saying a word. At that look, the warrior strode over to Sokar, grabbed a pudgy arm, and hauled him to his feet. Sokar was already panting. Now he gasped and quacked.

"Is aught wrong, O great one? What have I done? I am a man of duty. An honest chief. My lord? Ouch! You're hurting my arm, you great elephant! Oh, did I say elephant? Not elephant, you're a great lion. Please, let me go. I must defend myself to the great one."

Sokar kept looking over his shoulder as the charioteer dragged him down the alley. Before he was hauled away, Sokar glimpsed the two men left behind. To his amazement, Lord Meren bent down on one knee in the dirt and spoke to the wretched Min. Min sat up, his gaze fixed on the ground, until the Eyes of Pharaoh said something. Min's head shot up, his mouth rounded in an exclamation. He directed an astonished and amused look at Sokar. Lord Meren said something else, and Min began to grin. In that grin, Sokar glimpsed his own ruin.

DAWN BROUGHT SILVER light pouring into the streets like mist on the Nile. After getting rid of Lord Reshep, Kysen had summoned charioteers to accompany him to the alley Tcha said held the dead man, the Hittite royal emissary. Meren was pacing beside the body while Abu took down notes on this evening's events. Charioteers blocked access to the alley while others questioned the inhabitants of the homes along it.

He didn't want to think about the consequences of Mugallu's death. Better to ask why a prince would be abroad so late in a foreign city, especially the capital of his master's greatest enemy. Better to ask why no one, as far as the charioteers could discover, had heard the attack. Better to ask Tcha why it had been he who had stumbled upon the grisly display.

Tcha squatted in a corner, trying to be inconspicuous. Kysen kept an eye on him while he scoured the alley for any sign or mark left by the killer. It was a passage formed by the back and side walls of five houses. Four of the five had several floors that rose high above Kysen's head like blank-faced cliffs. The fifth, at the intersection of the alley and a street, had only three floors. None of the walls had windows. It would be difficult to hear any noise coming from the alley unless it was a scream.

It was an alley like thousands in Memphis—a narrow walk formed by accident when citizens added onto their houses generation after generation. And like those others that led nowhere, it had been used as a dumping place. Pieces of dried fish, broken pottery, goat dung, shreds of old baskets, littered the ground. Certain ripe piles announced by their scent that this was a favorite place to throw the contents of chamber pots, which sat beneath seats with holes in them. Kysen avoided one such pile, only to be forced to hop over cat dung.

As he landed, he noticed an imprint in earth made moist by the liquid from a chamber pot—a sandal. Trying to breathe through his mouth, Kysen squatted to examine the print. It was a long impression, longer than his own foot, and narrow, like a messenger's ship. And there was something peculiar about it. Kysen studied the foot-shaped imprint for a few moments before he realized he couldn't see the parallel striations of reed or the impressions of palm fiber. This sandal had been made of leather.

Rising, Kysen glanced at Mugallu's body, which was being lifted onto a litter. The man was barefoot. The soles of his feet were caked with filth. He looked at the imprint again. Most ordinary Egyptians couldn't afford leather sandals, and those who could didn't usually wear them in the streets. They or a servant might carry them to a destination before they would be put to use. If they were worn in the streets and one stepped in messes such as the one at Kysen's feet, sandals fell apart. He signaled to Turobay, called Turo, one of the charioteers who was also trained in drawing.

"Make a drawing of this impression." He didn't have to give any other instruction. Turo would copy the imprint using measurements and capturing every detail.

Mugallu's body was carried past, on its way to the house pharaoh had assigned for the prince's use while he was in Memphis. A linen sheet covered the body and concealed the dried cavern of flesh where the Hittite's heart had been. The feather Meren had found sticking out of the wound was hidden in a wicker box sitting beside Abu.

Kysen joined his father as Meren finished his notes and fell silent, staring at the litter and its defiled occupant as it left the alley. Although he appeared as calm as usual, Kysen detected a slight pallor in the delicate, finely lined skin above the eyelids. No one else would have seen it, nor would anyone have understood why Meren had removed a bracelet to rub his inner wrist.

Meren caught him staring, and Kysen looked away, at the place where Mugallu had lain. "He didn't fight much, for a Hittite. The blood is mostly in one area."

"The attacker struck his head first," Meren replied, but he seemed to be thinking of something else. "It was like a battle injury."

Kysen nodded. "You mean the chest wound. Not from a knife or a dagger."

"Hacked, like blows from a war ax, only done after Mugallu had been stunned or knocked senseless."

They fell silent as each recalled the wound and its white ornament, and what had been missing. Was poor Tcha right? Had Eater of Souls come from the netherworld to deliver judgment to the living instead of the dead? Kysen was suddenly glad daylight had come.

"What are we going to do?" he asked. "You say this is only one of several like murders."

"Yes, according to the watchman, Min."

"Remember what Tcha said?"

Meren turned to face him and gripped his shoulder. "I haven't forgotten, but I must go to pharaoh. The divine one must be told of Mugallu's murder. You will have to send someone to the office of the watch to question Sokar, find whatever records he may have kept, find the victims if possible. Use every man, Ky. We have to find this evil one quickly, before the king of the Hittites decides to use this murder as an excuse for war."

"But what if the killer isn't a man?" Kysen whispered.

"Whom can we trust?" Meren countered. "Such evil needs a powerful magician and lector priest. Magicians aren't known for keeping their mouths shut, and the city is already uneasy."

"What about Nebamun?" Kysen asked.

"More physician than magician."

Kysen said, "The chief lector priest at the temple of Ptah is a rattle-mouth."

"I don't trust the ones with great skill, not those in the city. Not even the priests of Anubis." Meren sighed and frowned at the bracelet that covered the scar on his wrist. "No one . . . no one except . . ."

"Who?"

"Ebana."

"Ebana!"

"Shhh!"

Meren grabbed Kysen's arm and pulled him nearer. "He was a lector priest and magician before he was appointed to serve with the high priest of Amun."

"By the soul of Isis, Father. Ebana hates you."

"He's my cousin. He saved my life."

"He has promised to make you pay for the killing of his family, and you had nothing to do with it."

"He thinks I could have stopped Akhenaten from sending those assassins. No, Ky, you don't understand Ebana. He hates me because he hates himself for not being there to protect his wife and son."

"That makes no sense," Kysen snapped. "Please, don't send for him. He'll only try to hurt you in some way."

"He and the other priests of Amun have promised a truce with the king. That extends to Friends of the King."

"And of course, you trust their word." Watching his father closely, he saw Meren's shoulders slump.

"You're right, Ky." Meren gave him a rueful smile. "This is no time to try to deal with Ebana."

"Good. I was beginning to think you'd send for Bentanta too."

"That isn't amusing."

Lady Bentanta was a childhood friend of Meren's, a woman who seemed to be able to create vast discomfort in his father. After seeing her a few weeks ago at his country house, Meren was avoiding her.

"If you've left off baiting me, my son?"

"Yes, Father."

"I'll think of someone to purge this place of evil before I go to the palace. You'll have to attend Mugallu's escort, General Labarnas, and then trace what is known of these other murders."

"And Ky—" Meren was looking at Tcha, who was still crouched in his corner looking dirty and miserable.

"Yes, Father?"

"Go home first and put on your amulets of protection."

THE OVERSEER OF the Audience Hall controlled access to pharaoh. His lineage was said to extend back to the rulers of the delta before the Two Lands became one. Called Userhet, he was of an age to be pharaoh's grandfather, steeped in dignity and knowledge of protocol, and impossible to coerce. He had been at court since the years in which pharaoh's father had earned the name Amunhotep the Magnificent. Thick, furry eyebrows dominated his face in spite of his wedge of a nose. A mane of silver hair was receding toward the crown of his head except at the spot over the middle of his forehead. This pattern made his forehead seem higher than it was.

Userhet wore sandals with specially padded soles so that the hours he spent standing in front of doors that gave access to the king wouldn't ruin his feet. Known for his aversion to children, youths, and young maidens, he had the habit of keeping dried chickpeas in a beaded pouch suspended from his belt. If a noble child became too boisterous, he would pelt the offender with a chickpea. Despite his years, the overseer retained much of his strength. It was put to use occasionally when a rowdy courtier disturbed the serenity of the palace or when Userhet was called upon to eject some unfortunate who incurred pharaoh's wrath. Courtiers and government officials alike feared him.

At the same time, they sought his goodwill, assuming that he could—if he pleased—get them past whatever closed door barred their way and into the sacred presence of the king. Userhet had never denied the truth of this assumption; neither had he affirmed it. He simply let the assumption remain and the rumors of his influence sail around the court.

At the moment the overseer had taken up his position before a door in the massive walls surrounding one of the royal pleasure gardens behind the palace. Outside the walls, courtiers walked up and down paths lined with incense trees, palms, and sycamores. The royal bodyguard lined the entire perimeter of the garden. Userhet leaned on his staff of office and patiently listened to Prince Djoser and Lord Reshep.

Djoser had been born into a family famed for its warrior pharaohs, but having failed as a warrior, he had acquired a desire to insert himself into pharaoh's most intimate circle. Obtaining royal access for Reshep was but his latest step toward his goal of being seen as a man of power. How Reshep would further Djoser's aspirations was a mystery to Userhet. Perhaps the prince expected the man to use his fabled charm on pharaoh for Djoser's benefit.

Userhet was good at listening to noble outrage and entreaty; he could do it for hours. Such endurance wasn't usually necessary, but in Djoser's case, Userhet's stamina was being severely tested. His patience was failing; the prince was making the mistake of whining. Userhet detested whiners.

"Why, why, why?" Djoser moaned. "I was to be allowed into the presence of the divine one at this very hour."

"Thine is the voice of truth, O prince," the overseer said without moving away from the door he blocked.

Lord Reshep sighed. "Tell him who I am."

"I know who you are, Lord Reshep. No one may enter."

Lord Reshep engaged in a staring battle with Userhet. Userhet won when Reshep turned away to whisper something to Djoser. Djoser squinted at the older man.

"Has anyone bribed you to keep me from the king?"

Userhet had been resting most of his weight on his staff; now he drew himself up as straight as this sign of office and turned his back on the two men. Walking to the double doors of the garden wall, he placed his back to the sheet gold covering them and banged the staff three times against the ground.

"All here present harken to the words of The Living Horus: Strong Bull, Arisen in truth; Gold-Horus: Great of strength, Smiter of Asiatics, the King of Upper and Lower Egypt: Nebkheprure Tutankhamun; the

Son of Ra, Tutankhamun, Lord of Thebes, beloved of Amun. It pleases my heart to hold no audiences for the remainder of the morning." User-het pounded the staff again. "Thus saith the living Horus, Nebkheprure Tutankhamun, beloved of Ptah, beloved of Amun, given life forever and ever."

Djoser reddened, and he muttered something.

"Forgive my aged lack of hearing, O mighty prince," said the over-seer. "Did you address me?"

Fists clenched, Djoser walked up to Userhet. "I'll tell you what I said."

Lord Reshep, who had gone pale rather than red, grabbed Djoser's arm and pulled him away. They hovered nearby, brushing against a rare incense tree and causing some of its branches to break. Userhet watched them hiss and whisper to each other while he fingered the chickpeas in the pouch on his belt.

The overseer was debating the consequences of pelting Prince Djoser and Lord Reshep when the stream of promenading courtiers before him on the path began to undulate to the left and right. Someone was coming, someone whose progress made even generals and ministers give way.

Moments later Userhet saw a gleaming black wig surrounding the harsh features of Lord Meren, Eyes and Ears of Pharaoh, Friend of the King. Meren paused to speak to General Nakhtmin, then proceeded on his way. His progress was halted by Djoser. Reshep was nowhere to be seen. Userhet stared straight ahead, but he directed his attention to the two and tried his best to hear what they were saying. Djoser was standing in Meren's way.

"Why have you refused Reshep for your daughter?" Prince Djoser demanded.

For a brief moment Lord Meren's composure slipped, and Userhet witnessed astonished outrage quickly mastered. Meren stared at the prince with indignation of such majesty that had Userhet been its re-cipient, he would have skulked away and hidden for a century. Evidently Djoser lacked Userhet's sensitive qualities, for he repeated his question. By now a few courtiers had paused to listen, and even more were direct-ing their steps in circles that kept them within hearing distance. Meren resolved the confrontation in his characteristic way. He drew close to the prince and began whispering to him. As he spoke, Djoser went pale.

Sweat broke out on his forehead and dribbled into his eye paint. The muscles of his neck writhed as he tried to swallow. Meren drew back, gave the prince a sweet, endearing smile, and continued on his way. Djoser was left standing alone looking sick, staring at Meren's back, his arms limp at his sides.

Lord Meren walked up to Userhet as if nothing had happened. Before he could utter a word, Userhet moved aside, pulled open the door, and bowed.

Meren gave him a look of surprise. "You knew I was coming?"

"No," Userhet replied. "But the divine Horus wishes to have speech with you. Go."

Userhet began pushing the garden door closed, forcing Meren to enter. Giving the door a final, satisfying bang, Userhet turned around and planted his staff in the earth. As he did so, he looked back at Djoser. Sometimes it did courtiers good to be shown how low their rank really was. As for Meren, he would have to rely upon the well-known discretion of the Eyes of Pharaoh.

MEREN STOPPED JUST inside the garden, where royal body-guards examined him as if he were a Libyan assassin. Too many strange things had been happening lately. He was still reeling from Djoser's unconscionable intrusion into his affairs. Now the overseer of the audience hall had taken a serious risk by allowing him in unannounced. Such a breach usually occurred only with pharaoh's permission, which meant something was wrong.

Meren felt as if a swarm of evil curses buzzed around his head. He had risked his life to search for Nefertiti's former cook, only to find himself at the mercy of her demented sister. He'd tried several times to reason with Satet, but the old woman kept sailing back and forth in time and never moored herself to the present for long. For now he'd left her in Bener's charge. Perhaps a few days in a normal household would do the woman's reason some good. He hoped so, for he still couldn't find the cook Hunero, or her husband, and now a new, more present danger threatened.

Who had killed Prince Mugallu? Who was murdering the citizens of Memphis? Evil was abroad in the city. Was it the twisted evil of men, or was it Ammut, risen from the netherworld? If Eater of Souls preyed upon the living, why had she come? Perhaps the gods were displeased with the people of the city, or perhaps some magician of great power had summoned her for purposes of his own.

The horror of Mugallu's death made that of Nefertiti seem placid. He hoped a living mortal was responsible for the killings; the alternative left him helpless unless he could find someone powerful enough to banish Eater of Souls back to the netherworld. And he knew of only one powerful enough to do that—pharaoh. Unfortunately, deep in his ka, he hid the fear that even the power of pharaoh couldn't help his people if the Devouress roamed the earth.

Meren heard someone call his name and looked up to find Rahotep striding down a path toward him. His legs were short in relation to his torso, so he took many more steps than Meren would to cover the same distance. Poor Rahotep had a difficult time looking princely. Without preliminaries, Rahotep launched into an inquiry.

"What are you doing here now? You'll ruin everything."

Immediately suspicious, Meren folded his arms over the transparent linen folds on his chest and said, "What am I going to ruin?"

"Go away," Rahotep said. "Pester the living god with your intrigues and plots later. He's with the Great Royal Wife and doesn't wish to be interrupted."

Knowing Rahotep, Meren grew alarmed. "By the wrath of Set, what have you done? No, not here."

He retreated from the bodyguards to the shelter of a kiosk. Rahotep had no choice but to join him. Feigning unconcern, the prince swaggered to the nearest chair and plopped himself into it. Meren suddenly swooped down at him, planted his hands on the chair arms, and gouged Rahotep with a stare.

"What have you done?" he repeated quietly.

Rahotep tried to retreat through the back of the chair, then covered up his agitation by taking the offensive.

"I've done what you should have. I've begun a reconciliation between pharaoh and the Great Royal Wife."

Meren's brows rammed together. "You? You have served as peacemaker? Her majesty tried to replace pharaoh with a Hittite prince, you fool."

Rahotep shoved Meren and got to his feet.

"Ha! That was a false letter, designed to be discovered and ruin the queen. Her majesty assures me of this." Rahotep glanced over his shoulder at the guards, then whispered, "From her own mouth I heard these truths. She is the daughter of a living god and does not lie."

"She's the daughter of a heretic."

"But a living god nonetheless. And she was wise to consult me. I managed to persuade pharaoh to listen to her explanation of that letter, and now he understands that someone wishes her majesty ill and seeks to divide her from her beloved king."

"Just who is this mysterious enemy of the queen?" Meren asked.

"She hasn't said."

"Not even to her benefactor, the great Prince Rahotep, true of voice?"

"Don't mock me," Rahotep said, his voice rising.

Meren couldn't help a sigh of impatience. "I haven't time for your self-important games. Have you considered that her majesty has always condemned pharaoh for returning to the old gods? Why would she suddenly change and reconcile with the one she condemns for destroying her father's grand vision? Think upon these questions, Rahotep, and while you're doing that, you might want to ask yourself whose name the queen will whisper to pharaoh when he asks her who sent that letter to the king of the Hittites."

Rahotep seemed to have lost the strength to shout. He swallowed, then found a water bottle hanging from one of the kiosk support poles and drank from it. He let water trickle over his face. Wiping his cheeks, he licked his lips and cleared his throat. Whatever he said was spoken so softly that Meren couldn't hear it.

"Speak up, Rahotep. No one can hear."

"I said—that is—well, you know how good I am at charming women."

"No, I don't."

"No? Odd. Everyone else does."

"What are you talking about, Rahotep?"

"I—um—I might have given pharaoh a few hints about how to manage the queen."

Meren lost what was left of his patience. Reshep, Mugallu, Djoser, and now Rahotep. *Gods.*

"Rahotep, you have the wits of a maggot. Get out of my sight."

"I did nothing wrong!"

"Your overweening pride has caused you to take liberties with pharaoh and insert yourself into the intimacies of the divine union upon which the kingdom depends. Leave, Rahotep, before my control gives way and I beat you like a grain tax cheater."

Meren wasted no time making sure Rahotep did as he was told. He stalked down a path that took him into a grove of trees near the great lake at the center of the garden. Once beneath the branches of the grove, he turned and quickly skirted the tree line until he came to the point nearest the lake.

As he caught sight of the water, he realized that the king and queen were sitting in a gilded and painted pleasure boat floating on the water. Their heads were close together, and they were engaged in intimate conversation. Between the lake and Meren stood the Nubian Karoya, his back to the royal couple, a scowl disfiguring his features. Karoya didn't like Ankhesenamun.

The bodyguard saw Meren as soon as he leaned out from behind a tree trunk. The Nubian never smiled, but his scowl did fade until he looked almost pleased. Meren was distracted from this unusual sight by movement in the boat. Ankhesenamun had gotten on her knees beside the king. She took his hand, which elicited a startled look from Tutankhamun. Then she began to lean toward him.

Pharaoh, who was still only a youth despite his air of worldly responsibility, retreated. He bent backward as the queen continued to move toward him until his shoulder pressed against the curved stern of the pleasure boat. Unable to escape, Tutankhamun thrust out a hand to stop the queen. Ankhesenamun caught his wrist, then grabbed the other and pushed herself against the king.

Eyes wide, Tutankhamun turned his head aside. The queen smiled and breathed words into his ear before drawing a wet line on the skin of his neck with her tongue. The king gasped and jumped, which caused Akhesenamun to lose her balance. She landed on her bottom, and her weight rocked the boat. Meren expected her to shriek at the king for causing her to fall; the queen familiar to him had little tolerance for accidents, mistakes, or the uncertainty of youth. But she didn't yell; she laughed, gently, with loving humor.

Evidently his wife's drastic change of nature was too much for pharaoh. He grabbed the oars and rowed the boat to the edge of the lake, talking rapidly the whole time. In moments Tutankhamun had helped his queen out of the boat, summoned Karoya, and had Ankhesenamun escorted out of the garden. Meren faded back into the trees.

Despite his serious nature and maturity, the king would find it difficult to face anyone so soon after that incident. Ankhesenamun always made Tutankhamun feel callow and gawky. On purpose, Meren had always believed. Having to deal with the news of the Hittite emissary's death was going to be hard enough without the king realizing there had been a witness to the way the queen had routed him. Meren waited awhile in the trees and fell to wondering if any man could be responsible for what had been done to Mugallu. After a while, he thrust such naive thoughts out of his heart and walked openly out of the grove and into the king's presence.

10

THE RESIDENCE OF the Hittite emissary boiled with activity, like a disturbed ant mound. Servants stood in corners and argued with each other. Guards marched around the privacy walls and hustled loiterers from the vicinity. Kysen arrived with the watchman Min and a squad of charioteers, to be told by the porter at the door of the death of a female slave and the disappearance of Prince Mugallu.

The chief of the prince's military escort, General Labarnas, wasn't in the house. With his own men behind him, Kysen strode across the kitchen yard to an area beside a storage building. There the general stood over the body of the dead slave, arguing with his men.

The argument stopped abruptly when Kysen appeared. Labarnas, a man with an imposing military reputation and the usual ill-concealed Hittite arrogance, turned on Kysen and shouted.

"What have you done to Prince Mugallu!"

Kysen paused in midstride, then closed the gap between himself and the general before replying smoothly. "I know that his highness is missing, and I have brought news, general."

They didn't know. He and Meren had assumed word from the streets would have reached the Hittites. He'd expected outrage, the usual Hittite accusations and demands, but these men looked like they expected to engage in battle at once. The general and his officers were dressed in bronze armor and boar's-tusk helmets. They bristled with swords, daggers, and spears.

"You Egyptians!" Labarnas snarled. "You beguile with your polished manners and sweet words, lure a warrior into taking his ease, and then, like cowards, strike when a man is most vulnerable. Prince Mugallu is dead, isn't he? Don't bother to spew whatever tale of accident and woe you've created." Behind him, the Hittite officers muttered to each other and gripped their straight swords.

"General, I come with no tale."

Labarnas stalked close to Kysen, causing the charioteers to close ranks. Labarnas ignored them and stuck his face close to Kysen's.

"Very well, son of the Eyes of Pharaoh. Tell me what has happened so that I can return to Hattusha and repeat the lies to my king."

He should never have come without a royal minister and a larger escort. Kysen looked down at Labarnas. Odd how a Hittite could seem as big as a colossus when he was at least three finger-widths less in height. It must be the relentlessly hostile temperament.

Kysen took a moment to marshal his wits. He drew in long breaths and released them without drawing attention to what he was doing. As he breathed, he called up scenes of Meren in the royal throne room sparring with a Babylonian prince, of his father facing down the poisonous old scorpion of a high priest of Amun in his own temple. He wasn't the son of a common artisan; he was the son of the Eyes and Ears of Pharaoh.

When he felt the muscles in his face loosen, the tension fade from behind his eyes, Kysen gave Labarnas a stare he hoped was as regal as his father's. Labarnas had been embellishing on his opinion of Egyptian corruption and treachery, but he sputtered into silence as Kysen refused to respond and assumed an expression of haughty distaste. To Kysen's amusement, Labarnas reddened and spat out an order.

"Speak, Egyptian."

"I have the unhappy responsibility to tell you, general, that Prince Mugallu has been killed."

"I knew it!"

Kysen went on as if the Hittite hadn't spoken. "Apparently he was pursued by some evildoer through the streets, cornered, and attacked."

"Where is the killer?" Labarnas growled.

"We don't know, but the Eyes of Pharaoh seeks the criminal as we speak. No evil deed escapes the inquiry of the Eyes and Ears of the King. The city will be closed off: the docks sealed, the desert routes patrolled. No one can escape."

"Not even me," Labarnas said.

"An unfortunate consequence of my father's vigilance in searching for your prince's murderer, nothing else."

The general pounded the bronze plate strapped to his chest. "I won't be slaughtered like a sacrificial goat."

"Had pharaoh decided to kill you," Kysen said gently, "you'd be dead, and your body cavities filling with desert sand, general. You would not be standing here shrieking insults at me like a hysterical tavern woman."

Labarnas blinked at him, then snorted to cover the grudging respect that came into his eyes.

"General, there is more."

Respect vanished in the face of wary distrust. "What more?"

Feeling like he was trying to converse with a bull whose bowels were blocked, Kysen described where Mugallu had died, the white feather. "He died of . . . of a wound to the chest."

When he finished, every Hittite was still and silent, even the general. Kysen forced himself to wait, to remain undisturbed beneath the hostile stares, to observe with calm the straining of muscles that told of the Hittite desire to attack and kill. Finally Labarnas spoke.

"Demon or man, the prince was slain by Egyptian device. The wrath of the great king of the Hittites will thunder across the sky, shake the foundations of pharaoh's palace, making him cower beneath his throne. It will rend the ears of his subjects and make them fall to their knees to beg for my king's mercy."

"In Egypt we have an ancient teaching that says a wise leader holds his judgment until all is known. If he doesn't, he risks appearing careless, partial—or worse, a fool—if his decision turns out to be wrong."

"We Hittites have our own saying, boy. It is better to strike first than to end up with your head impaled on a spear." Labarnas stepped back and examined Kysen from head to sandal. "This Eater of Souls, this tale of a demon rampant among the living who happened to find my prince instead of another worthless citizen, it's elaborate, full of misdirection. I should have expected a stratagem like this from Egypt. The world knows that behind all this, this magnificence—the gold-covered temples, the perfumed linen, those elegant Egyptian manners—lies a nature full of artifice, craft, and guile."

Kysen inclined his head to Labarnas. "I didn't know Hittites were so prone to compliments."

"You haven't distracted me, Egyptian. You were saying this so-called demon stabbed Prince Mugallu."

"We don't think the weapon was a dagger or sword," Kysen said.

"What, then?"

"Perhaps an ax." Kysen expected Labarnas to erupt into fury. Instead, the Hittite exchanged looks with his officers and gave Kysen a nod of satisfaction.

"Your tale makes more sense now."

"It does?" Kysen said faintly.

"It would take a war ax to subdue even an unarmed Hittite warrior."

What could he say to such reasoning? With so few men in his party, he wasn't foolish enough to describe Mugallu's death in greater detail. He glanced at the body in the linen sheet.

"The evil one killed this slave too? Then the killer was here."

"We found her in the garden," said one of the Hittite officers. "She was stabbed in the back."

"General," Kysen said. "I must see the place in the garden where she was found."

"You should be hunting the killer, not wasting time in gardens."

"I am hunting the killer," Kysen replied. "I won't need long, and I should be gone by the time the prince's body arrives."

"Get on with your hunt, then, Egyptian. I give you two days to bring me the killer. After that, I go back to the great king to tell him what pharaoh has done to his favorite and emissary."

NOT FAR FROM the lake in the royal garden rose an ancient fig tree. It had grown so tall it could be seen over the garden walls. Broad, deeply lobed leaves furnished abundant shade. Meren favored this tree above all others in the royal garden because its thick, rough leaves seemed to block out more heat. His tale of the death of Prince Mugallu had just come to an end. He was kneeling beside the seated king. As Meren fell silent, Tutankhamun jumped to his feet to pace over the woven Syrian mat that had been laid under the tree.

Tutankhamun stared across the hand-watered foreign blooms that formed long red-and-blue borders around the lake. He appeared to be fascinated by the blue sheet of water and the birds that floated on it. A line of green-winged teal paddled toward a lily pad in the water, each uttering that low, continuous quack that seemed to be their fanfare. Several pairs of swans floated in the opposite direction, scattering a flotilla of pintails.

When the king abruptly turned back to Meren, his skin had lost the flush the Great Royal Wife had provoked. Meren had seen that look of bewildered fear when he'd broken the news of the desecration of Akhenaten's tomb, and when Tutankhamun had learned of the treachery of one of his dearest friends. Few others had witnessed the transformation of pharaoh into a frightened youth. He heard the king's ragged whisper.

"No heart? Someone hacked out his heart? When Suppiluliumas hears of this, he'll declare war upon me. I haven't even been on a raid yet! How can I go to war?"

"Be at ease, majesty—"

"Ease? You of all my advisers know what might Suppiluliumas can summon. He conquered the Mitanni Empire, didn't he?"

"I beg thy majesty to listen," Meren said. "Prince Mugallu isn't the only one to have been killed in this same fashion. He's only the latest."

Closing his mouth on a protest, Tutankhamun dropped to the ground beside Meren. "Go on."

"From what I've been able to discover, there have been others, majesty. A farmer visiting from his village, a tavern woman. There may be others. Kysen has gone to the prince's residence to see what happened there and perhaps find out why Mugallu left the house alone at night."

Meren handed the king one of the porous jars sitting in stands by the mat. Tutankhamun accepted it, but the jar hung suspended by the neck in his hand as the king struggled to comprehend the implications of what he'd been told. All at once the youth tipped the jar over his mouth and drank long gulps of cool water. Then he let it splash over his face and neck. Wiping his eyes, he held out the jar for Meren to take.

"In the *Book of the Dead*, the gods protect the justified from the power of the Devouress."

"Yes, majesty."

"How many dead, do you think?"

Meren shook his head. "I know not, divine one. The chief of watchmen of the city is a lazy fool who seems to think a death important only if it involves a great one."

"There can be no harmony and balance in my kingdom if the farmer, the perfume maker, and the fisherman are slain!"

"Thy majesty is wise." Meren held out his hands, palms upward. "I am sure the wife and children of that farmer suffer."

The king's gaze began to shift from Meren to the fig tree, to a dish of bread and dates, back to Meren. "So you think there is one killer and many dead. And the streets boil with rumor that Eater of Souls has been sent from the netherworld to prey upon the living."

"Majesty, it may be that the evil one but hides himself behind the guise of the Devouress."

"And Mugallu?"

"I don't know, divine one. Perhaps he stumbled upon the evildoer." Meren felt a muscle in his jaw twitch. "The other explanation is that he was meant to die all along."

"Why? Who would want to force a war between my majesty and the Hittite king?"

They lapsed into silence, then met each other's gaze.

"Who at court is dissatisfied?" the king asked.

"Perhaps, majesty, we should ask who would gain if pharaoh and the army were drawn out of Egypt to campaign in the north."

"Those who have been forced to give up office and rank," Tut-ankhamun said. "My brother's old ministers, corrupt officials who have lost their positions by my reforms, the priests of Amun, who won't be satisfied until they rule instead of my majesty, any royal prince who thinks he should be pharaoh in my place." The king sighed. "I don't want to go on."

Meren forced himself to continue. "And if I discover that the killings are the work of Eater of Souls . . ."

"Would that mean the gods are angry with me? With Egypt? Have I done something so terrible that they seek to punish my people, and through them, me?"

He heard the strain in the king's voice. "Majesty, you have worked to undo the damage wrought by your royal brother, to restore the old gods, repair their temples, cast out evil and incompetent judges, tax collectors, overseers, and priests. No. If Eater of Souls truly walks the earth, someone worked evil magic to summon her and set her loose among the living."

"Then we must fight the dark magic," Tutankhamun said. "I will gather magician priests from the temples of Ptah, Sekhmet, and Isis."

"Yes, majesty. They must perform divinations in order to discover the true nature of this killer."

Tutankhamun picked up a bread loaf, tore a piece from it, and tossed it to a duck. "If the killer is only a man, he must still be possessed by some evil fiend to have done these things." More ducks came waddling over in search of bread.

"Of course, majesty, but at least it would be an ordinary evil, and not Eater of Souls."

"I suppose that would be a comfort." The king tossed more bread to the ducks.

Meren sighed. "I think an ordinary demon would be much easier to banish than the Devouress."

"Perhaps the magician priests can divine the hiding place of this evil one."

"Thy majesty must not be disappointed if they cannot. If divination produced solutions to such mysteries, my tasks as the Eyes and Ears of Pharaoh would be much easier."

"True, but I will still put the question to the priests."

Meren bowed. There was nothing he could say, for he wasn't certain of the kind of evil with which he was dealing.

The king tossed the last of the bread to the ducks and looked across the garden. "Ah, I thought it wouldn't be long before Ay came to us."

The vizier was walking slowly toward them on a gravel path. Slaves bore a palanquin over him to protect him from the sun's rays.

"I have thy majesty's permission to increase the guards on the city walls and the docks?"

The king stood. "Yes, and double the men on watch. I'll summon the mayor and make certain he understands that the city police are to make themselves vigilant. My majesty will have no more of this laziness and failure to report evil."

Meren rose at the king's signal and bowed.

"And Meren, don't think I'm not aware of your attempts to delay taking me on a raid."

Doing his best to look innocent, Meren said, "Delays, golden one?"

"My majesty will remedy the matter as soon as possible. Neither of us has a choice anymore, do we?"

The king had discerned a consequence of this disaster Meren hadn't considered. He gave pharaoh a reluctant smile.

"I fear thy majesty is correct."

I T   W A S   D U S K . High clouds drifted over Memphis, white, flat-bottomed, their undersides bursting into hues of pink and rose as the solar orb dipped below the horizon. Satet paused in the street beside the stall of a pottery vendor. Shading her eyes, she gazed up at the clouds. She had always nourished her ka on the precious and brief beauty of clouds. This pleasure was even more necessary now that she had to endure Lord Meren's silly questions about Hunero.

Who remembered what daft old Hunero said so long ago? On the farm Satet had more important concerns than the whereabouts of her sister. But now that she was in the city, she might as well find Hunero and go to live with her. It would be better than living at Lord Meren's house. His daughter, Lady Bener, was an exacting mistress of the house. She wouldn't let Satet instruct the cooks unhindered, and the girl insisted on making Satet rest at night when she wasn't sleepy.

Satet trotted down a street, passed through a gate formed by two old stelae, flat, round-topped stones carved with the decrees of viziers who had died before Egypt acquired her empire. It was good that Lady Bener allowed Satet to cook as well as instruct. A few days of the work had ordered her thoughts a bit, and it had occurred to her that the way to find Hunero was to find the best vendors of ingredients her sister loved to include in her cooking. She had been exploring the stalls in different parts of the city, and at last she'd located one whose owner had dealt with Hunero.

The spice dealer had been a close-lipped man with eyes that seldom fastened directly on her own. Satet hadn't liked him, but she understood him. Gain governed his character. If he could enrich himself by opening his mouth, he would, though doing so was contrary to his nature. Satet had simply given him a small faience bowl from the room Lady Bener had assigned to her.

The bargain had produced directions to Hunero's new house in the dock district. In the midst of the houses of ship carpenters and dock officials and buildings used to house offices and storage for temple traders, she found it. Hunero's house was a narrow, two-story building that looked as if the taller buildings on either side were slowly expanding and compressing it.

Satet examined the dwelling from threshold to roof with a disapproving scowl. "Humph. Left the old house for this, did she? That's Hunero. Always seeking to better herself when she's quite well off where she is. And what happens? She ends up with something not half as good as what she had." She marched up the two steps before the door and banged on the dried and peeling wood. "Never satisfied. Never got over being the queen's favorite cook. Always pining."

She got no answer, and all she heard was the buzzing of flies. Dozens of them sailed in and out of the grilled windows high above the door. Satet pounded harder. A woman poked her head out the door of the neighboring house, muttered a curse at Satet, and slammed the portal shut.

"Donkey's consort!" Satet retorted. She began kicking the door and shouting. "Hunero, I know you're in there. Let me in!" Drawing back her foot, Satet gave the door another kick with the full force of her strength.

"Owwwwww!" She grabbed her foot and pressed her free hand against the door.

It gave way, and Satet fell through. She landed on her hands and knees, foot throbbing, in a dark space. What little light the dusk provided showed her a lamp beside the door. Several flies tried to land on her face, and Satet brushed at them absently. With care for her jarred old bones, Satet crawled into a sitting position, lit the lamp, and maneuvered herself to her feet.

Picking up the lamp, she shut the door. "Hunero, I got inside, so there's no use hiding."

Holding the lamp aloft, she directed the light around the room. More tunnel than chamber, it held the furnishings with which Hunero had absconded. On a raised ledge around the room sat beds that could be used at night, reed boxes filled with utensils, tools, and linens. Several low stools had been arranged around a table bearing a senet game box. Two columns supported the roof, and beyond this living chamber lay the kitchen. That's where Hunero would be.

Satet marched into the kitchen, and there, kneeling before the small oven in the back corner, was her sister. "Ha! You thought I'd go away, but I found you. I'll wager you were surprised to hear my voice when you thought I was still in . . ."

Hunero hadn't turned around. She hadn't moved at all. Satet held the lamp out and walked over to the oven. Something was crawling on her sister's back. Flies. The dim yellow light spread over Hunero's back and landed on a blackened spot surrounding a hole in the linen of her shift. More flies darted in and out of the wound, and other insects. The lamp began to shake, distorting the light.

Satet gripped it with both hands and continued to stare at her sister. Hunero had been kneeling before a ledge that formed a work surface in front of the oven. Her face was buried in a thick slab of dough. All Satet could see was the side of her cheek, sunken, dried, discolored with flour. Backing up, Satet continued to stare.

Her thoughts slowed to the speed of the Nile current in a year of drought. Then they grew even more sluggish, like the mud slurry in a desert wadi after a storm. Loud buzzing to her left caused Satet to turn her head. Against the wall, a stairway led up to the second floor from the kitchen. Bay sprawled facedown, as if he'd fallen on his way up. He too bore a hole in his back and dark, clotted stains on the skin surrounding the wound. His body failed to hold her attention for long.

Satet looked back at her sister. "Well, look at this place. Is this the kind of life you prefer to the farm?" She rocked back and forth on her heels while holding the lamp in both hands. "Don't prattle excuses at me, dear sister. And don't expect me to come here to stay with you. I'm taking some things for myself back to Lord Meren's house."

Looking around the kitchen, Satet found a basket with a lid. "No, I'm not going to stay. You may have wanted to seek your fortune in the great city, but I'm the one who's gotten a place with a fine nobleman." Satet cocked her ear in Hunero's direction. "I always said Bay was lazy. Make him wake up and fetch fresh fuel for that oven. I'll come back tomorrow and help you clean this mess. And get rid of these cursed flies!"

Turning her back on Hunero and her brother-in-law, Satet bustled into the living chamber. She filled the basket with two shifts, a pair of hardly used sandals, a faience eye-paint pot, and a wooden comb with long teeth, the top of which had been carved in the shape of a gazelle. After placing the lid on the basket, Satet picked up her lamp and went to the door.

Extinguishing the light, she tossed a comment over her shoulder. "I won't take morning meal with you tomorrow. Lady Bener's cooks will fix me a fine one before I come see you."

Without waiting for a reply, Satet hefted the basket on her hip, stepped outside, and shut the door behind her. Night had come, but darkness wasn't complete, and lamplight glimmered from windows up and down the street. Humming a feast song, she began the walk back to Lord Meren's house.

11

ONCE HE'D LEFT the palace, Meren had gone home, where Abu and Kysen met him. They, along with the watchman Min, spent the remainder of the day and the hours since nightfall assessing what details were known of Mugallu's death and the other killings. Min had brought two white feathers with him. They lay in a bronze tray on top of a chest, their white purity spoiled by stains that had once been red. One was from the body of the farmer, the other from the tavern woman. Min had filched the one on the farmer's body. When he'd heard of the tavern woman, he'd gone to the village and retrieved the second feather.

Meren had decided to call these ugly crimes the heart thefts. It was a term they could use openly without having to name victims or refer to the butchery enacted upon the bodies. If citizens discovered the exact nature of these murders, fear would spark an inferno of violence against anyone perceived as a threat—petty thieves, the addlewitted, the cantankerous, the mean, even some helpless foreign slave.

Reviewing the fool Sokar's notes and reports for the last six months had taken a long time. Abu and Kysen were still working, with Min, who could not read, serving as interpreter of events and decipherer of Sokar's euphemisms. Meren had just finished reading the reports on Mugallu's death and writing his own account. Periodically the silence that prevailed was broken when one of them asked Min a question.

Meren felt groggy from so much writing and sitting. He should have gotten up an hour ago, but Bener had prevented him. She had invaded the office with an entourage of servants bearing food and drink. As she refused to leave until they ate, Meren had realized how limited his choices were. After the meal his daughter sent the servants away—and remained. He'd argued with her previously about how unsuitable it was for her to concern herself with his affairs, but weariness and a respect for Bener's intelligent heart had prevented him from trying to get rid of her tonight. So she stayed, read reports, and eased the burden of the work.

Bener shifted her position on a stool and murmured a question to Min. "What is this note? There is no explanation other than the phrase 'no settlement in the matter of the two hyenas' and a date two months ago."

"Lady, Sokar uses the—the phrase to refer to a house boundary dispute between the temple trader Penne and the overseer of the magazine of Prince Rahotep. They have been arguing about it for many years. Their fathers quarreled over the same boundary, as did their grandfathers. Sokar said their sons will continue the custom because the two families produce nothing but weak-witted laggards who haven't the sense to stop wasting means and time on such a useless quarrel."

"I remember," Meren said. "There has been a case in the vizier's court on the same dispute for generations. By the patience of Amun, I wish the worst troubles I had were like that."

Handing his account of Mugallu's death to Bener, Meren rose, wincing at the stiffness in his knees and ankles. He hadn't been able to go to the royal practice field, or even to drive his chariot in the desert, lately. He began to walk about the room to ease his discomfort. There were similar offices in his mansions in Bubastis and Heliopolis in the delta, at Thebes, and in his country estate near Abydos. Yet he preferred this one.

It was larger than the others, running almost the length of the reception and central halls above which it was built. The walls were plastered, painted pale blue, and decorated with a simple frieze of reed bundles at the top and bottom. The windows set high in the walls bore grilles of gilded wood. The six slender columns set in two rows had been carved in the shape of tall green lotus plants, the petals of which spread out at the top, as if reaching for the sun. The stems of the flowers had been painted with alternating bands of gold and blue at the base and just beneath the petals. As had been intended, the decoration of the room imitated a reflection pool dotted with lotus plants and surrounded by the sun-drenched blue of the sky.

Only in the last few years had he been able to enjoy his Memphis office this way. He and his wife had shared too many private moments here. After she died, he hadn't been able to remain in this chamber for long, because Sit-Hathor had filled it with gifts to him. Leaving the master's dais, Meren went to a long cabinet set against the wall. There rested the last of Sit-Hathor's gifts, an alabaster lamp carved in the shape of a chalice cup sitting on an open, rectangular base.

When not in use, the lamp appeared a simple object of the valuable, cream-colored stone. When lit, a scene appeared as if by magic, illuminated by the gold flicker of the oil and floating wick. A close-fitting alabaster lining had been affixed within the chalice bowl. It was on the outer surface of the lining that the scene had been painted. Meren studied the glowing chalice, upon which he could see an image of himself and Sit-Hathor. He was sitting in his ebony chair with the legs carved to imitate a leopard's and claws fashioned of ivory. Sit-Hathor stood before him, smiling and offering him a lotus flower. This pose had been a private joke, for Sit-Hathor had been a woman more likely to pelt his face with the blossom than offer it meekly.

It was growing late. The office was illuminated by a dozen alabaster lamps, but reading in such light wearied the eyes. The strain worked against alertness, and everyone had to be alert with an unknown killer abroad in Memphis. Meren turned to face the room. His fingers traced the fluted shape of the chalice lamp as he began.

"The hour grows late. We should review and then take our rest. Kysen, you said Prince Mugallu's killer also dispatched a slave and the sentry posted at the garden."

"Aye, Father. I surveyed the places where the bodies lay, but the Hittites had swarmed all over. If the criminal or creature left any signs, they're gone. But the guard and the slave were killed with a simple knife in the back."

"So this evil one reserves the ax and the—whatever made those rows of slices on the throat and face—for special victims."

Abu looked up at him, startled. Kysen nodded without surprise while Min gripped an amulet of protection he wore as a necklace. Meren glanced at his daughter, but Bener didn't seem disturbed. She was rolling up a papyrus and inserting it in a leather document case.

Without looking up, she said, "If they were killed by the same evil one, man or demon."

Everyone looked at her. She rolled her eyes and gave an impatient sigh.

"Which is the greater amazement? That I had the wits to consider the possibility, or that I had the temerity to say it?"

"Neither, daughter," said Meren.

He frowned at her, which failed to evoke anything but a little smile. Thrusting his hands behind his back, Meren abandoned his position beside the lamp and walked a circuit that took him down the rows of columns and back.

"Pharaoh has alerted the royal bodyguard, the infantry companies stationed in the area, the naval patrols, the city police, the desert patrols. But no one knows what to look for, or whom."

"General Labarnas tried to send a messenger after I left," Kysen said. "The men I set to watch the house stopped him and sent him back. His message wasn't written, so we don't know what Labarnas wants to say to the king of the Hittites."

On the return leg of his circuit of the office, Meren gave a bitter laugh. "No words of praise, I'll wager." He stopped between the first pair of columns, unclasped his hands, and began toying with the thick hinged bracelet that covered the Aten scar on his wrist. "Very well, let us review what we've learned."

"We know of at least three heart thefts," Kysen said. "There was the farmer ten days ago, the one Sokar listed as the death of a farmer, 'not of the city,' with no other description." He said this last with contempt. "Then there was the—what was she, Min?"

"A tavern woman, lord."

"Yes, Anat, the tavern woman in that western village."

"And her cat," Bener said.

"And the cat," Kysen replied. "And Tcha's friend Pawah, but we only have Tcha to tell us what he saw. His veracity isn't the stuff of which great men write advice for their sons." Kysen glanced at Meren. "Has he been with you?"

"No. I thought he went with you," Meren said. They stared at each other.

Abu spoke up. "I last saw him in the alley where we found Prince Mugallu."

No one said anything for a while. Then Meren turned to Abu. "Send someone to look for him when we're finished."

"I have to go to Ese's," Kysen said. "I'll look for him there. Most likely he has burrowed under a rubbish heap somewhere to hide from danger, and from us."

Bener shut the lid on the document case she'd been using. "If you find him, don't let him in this house. The servants had to burn incense for hours to get rid of the stench." Setting the case aside, she said, "Three heart thefts? But what of those two entries in Sokar's reports of several weeks ago?"

"We don't know that those were heart thefts," Kysen said. "Min wasn't present when they were discovered."

"But Sokar described them as he did the others. He wrote 'a death' and 'not of the city,' or 'a wretched slave.' I've looked at most of his reports, and he seldom becomes so sparing of words or so vague unless there's something he wants to avoid."

When Kysen's brow furrowed, and he began to rock back and forth on his heels, Meren knew it was time to interrupt.

"It may be nothing, but I want to be sure. Min will ask the watchmen involved about these early entries."

Min answered hastily as Bener opened her lips. "Yes, lord."

Before either of his children could pursue their disagreement, Meren continued. "Returning to what we know of these killings. All began with a disabling blow, followed by a slice to the throat by some weapon, or claws." He set his back against a column, folded his arms, and stared at the floor while he thought for a moment. "The cuts are too clean."

"What do you mean?" Kysen asked.

Meren looked up at him. "You've seen the gashes left by a lion's claws, or a leopard's. The edges aren't nearly as clean. Mugallu's throat looked like someone had sliced it with a freshly sharpened butcher's knife."

"Perhaps the evil one has some strange weapon," Kysen replied. "A knife with several blades."

Bener walked over to Meren and spoke quietly. "The claws of Eater of Souls, are they not as sharp as the gods demand? If the Devouress eats the body of the dead, heart and bones and tendons, her claws would have to be sharper and harder than any metal."

Again no one spoke. Min clutched his amulet. Kysen and Abu exchanged uneasy looks while Meren stared at Bener.

"By the gods, daughter. The image you devise makes my bones cold."

Eyes large with surprise, Bener said, "All I do is think of the sensible consequences of what I know to be true."

"But your imagination," Meren replied. "Your heart is clever, but it's also filled with colorful vision." He was surprised when Bener's eyes began to glisten with unshed tears.

"Thank you, Father." Bener cleared her throat. "What other things do we know?"

Knowing Bener would be furious with herself if she succumbed to tears, Meren walked over to Kysen, listing items as he went. "All the killings are done at night. All the dead are humble except for Mugallu. None except the Hittite's slave and sentry were linked to any of the others."

"And all the killings except that of the tavern woman have taken place in the dock district, which the people call the Caverns, and the foreign enclaves nearby," Kysen added. "But the woman worked in the area, and lived in the village. I suppose the demon—or the man—found her in the Caverns and followed her home."

"And if the killer is mortal, we should consider that the evil one may live near or frequent these places," Meren said.

Abu came over and handed Kysen a flat sheet of papyrus. Kysen took it and glanced at it. "Yes. I found a single leather sandal imprint. There were others similar to this one at the prince's house, but none was an exact duplicate."

"And the Hittites had tramped all over the areas where the bodies were found," Abu said.

Bener came over to the group. "I've been thinking."

All three of them turned to look at her, but she failed to notice.

"Do demons wear leather sandals?" she asked. "Would Eater of Souls wear them?"

"I've never seen the Devouress drawn wearing sandals or any footwear in any of the sacred books," Kysen said.

Abu said, "Nor I."

Another uneasy silence fell. A loud crack made Bener jump and the men touch the daggers in their belts. They relaxed when Min knelt and picked up his stone amulet from the floor. His face turning the color of red jasper, he muttered an apology.

Meren fought back irritation at his own lack of composure. "This is a senseless point. Demons do not wear clothing, and anyway, the sandal print is unlikely to be that of the evildoer." He stalked away from the group, stopped at a column, and whirled around to face them. His body felt as tightly drawn as a hunting bow.

"If Eater of Souls prowls among us . . . that would be a matter for pharaoh. The golden one is the intermediary between his people and the gods. He causes the earth to continue in its endless cycles of birth, death, and rebirth, Harvest, Inundation, Drought, and Harvest again. Only pharaoh has the power to intercede with the gods. He will ask Osiris, ruler of the netherworld, to summon Eater of Souls back to the land of the dead. My hope is that the Devouress rumors are false. After all, only the hearts of the dead are missing, and I don't think Eater of Souls would refrain from devouring her entire . . . meal."

Meren didn't like feeling powerless. He went on, for images of what a devouring must look like threatened to enter his heart. "We will proceed as if the evil one is mortal until we know differently."

"And take magical precautions," Kysen said.

"We'll protect ourselves," Meren said. "Now, what kinds of men use axes?"

"Soldiers," Bener said.

Kysen gave her an irritated look. "Almost all men know how to use an ax."

"Priests?" Bener retorted.

"Those who perform sacrifices, Mistress Know-All. And any priest who is also a noble."

Bener held her forefinger up in front of Kysen's face and said, "If you would allow your heart time to consider, you'd realize that carpenters, butchers, and cooks use hand axes constantly and thus possess skill with them."

Brother and sister took up stances facing each other. Their gazes met and held.

"I do not allow my heart to consider things that are plain to all but you," Kysen said.

Bener gave a little snort of contempt. "Plain? What is plain is that you don't like the notion because you didn't produce it, and I did."

"You would have us question every joiner, carpenter, shipwright, and wood gatherer in the city," Kysen said as he moved closer to his sister so that they were almost nose to nose. "Who would like such a notion?"

"You deliberately misunderstand my words."

"Enough!" Meren snapped. "We grow too weary. We'll begin again in the morning. Abu, take Min to the barracks and give him a bed." When the two were gone, Meren turned a scowl on his son and daughter. "I'll thank you both to remember your rank and dignity before others. I cannot understand how you could quarrel like a couple of baboons in the presence of my aide and a watchman. Kysen, you have yet to make that visit of which you spoke, and Bener, you have a great household to manage. Go away."

Bener whispered an apology before hurrying out of the room. Kysen left without a word, revealing by his expression that he knew better than to make excuses. When he was alone, Meren went back to his chair and slouched into it. His mood, already dim, had been soured by his children's petty bickering in the face of butchery and danger.

Now he couldn't go to bed. He would only lie awake while his irritation festered. Slumping down in his chair until his head rested on the back, Meren glanced to his side and saw a sheet of papyrus laid out on the small table next to him. Flat, polished stones held the curled sheet open. It was a description of Mugallu's body. His gaze picked up the words "white feather," and he immediately wondered what kind of feathers had been used, and why.

Then he realized where Bener had gotten her reasoning ability. A habit learned from her father, perhaps inherited along with her clever heart? He'd never given a thought to this—that his daughters claimed from him virtues and faults his father had passed down to him. And his mother. Without knowing it, he'd assumed and wished them to be images of Sit-Hathor. But there had been times when he'd noticed one or the other of his daughters give him a brief, sharp look. He'd never bothered to interpret that look, yet it had remained in his memory.

He'd observed the look from his oldest, Tefnut, who lived far away and would soon give birth to her first child. Closing his eyes, Meren summoned a memory. Tefnut herding her younger sisters into the central hall to greet the guests attending one of his feasts. She had spent hours drilling Bener and Isis in manners. All of them had behaved well, and

Tefnut had gathered the girls at the proper time and taken them out of the hall to bed. When she came back she had given him that look, but she'd never said anything.

That look. Meren opened his eyes. Expectation, that's what it had been. Expectation, excitement, unspoken pride at a task accomplished. And eagerness. A shy eagerness, hunger. For praise. For an acknowledgment from him. A tiny sign that he had noticed, that she was worthy of his attention.

"Meren, son of Amosis," he whispered. "You have the perception of a block of limestone. Callous bastard."

Bener had given him that look tonight, and again he had ignored it, as he would the glance of a slave or the panting of his favorite hunting dog. Ashamed, Meren set aside these thoughts with a vow to correct himself. But now sleep would escape him completely. Standing, he removed the stone weights and picked up the description of Mugallu's death. Reading it wouldn't invite sleep. He would think about the white feathers.

He set the sheet aside and went to a chest the size of a sarcophagus that had been set beside the master's dais. Sit-Hathor and he had collected old writings, copies of texts passed down for centuries. Sometimes he had a use for them. There was one old document, a record composed by the chief royal fowler of the pharaoh Senusret I, who ruled more than six hundred years before Meren had been born.

The house had grown quiet. All the servants had gone to bed, except those few on night duty such as the porter. One of the lamps sputtered and went out, but Meren paid no attention. Lifting the lid on the chest, he pulled out a case of documents. He read the label inscribed in black ink, put it back, and picked up another case.

"I'm sure it's in this chest," he muttered. Searching through the other cases, he came upon one resting beneath several others. "I knew it."

Meren pulled the container out of the chest and carried it to his chair. He sat, opened the case, and began removing the valuable papyri one by one. "Birds, birds, birds. It is an entire book."

When he was halfway through the documents, his hand wrapped around a thick bundle. He set the case aside, removed the twine binding the roll of nested sheets, and unwound them. As he read, a gust of wind whistled through the window grilles. It sent the lamplight into a silent dance. Meren listened to the flutelike whistling and glanced at the cavorting shadows. Then his gaze fell back to the papyrus, and he began to read again.

WHEN KYSEN ENTERED Ese's tavern, he wasn't alone. Narrowing his eyes against the thick fog of perfume, beer fumes, smoke from cooking fires, and the press of bodies, he looked over his shoulder at Abu.

"Cursed nursemaid," he muttered.

Abu, who had left behind the whip and scimitar that identified him as a charioteer, met his gaze without mercy. "The lord's orders. He said if you objected I was to tell you this is what you deserve for sending me to sniff at his heels like a hound on the scent of an escaped slave."

"It was for his own protection."

There was no reply from Abu, whose expression told Kysen he'd just proved his father's point.

"Oh, never mind."

Kysen shouldered his way through a crowd that had gathered to watch a team of naked Greek acrobats. One girl, her dark hair streaming down her back in tight curls, did back flips around the central hearth. Another bounced across the floor and leaped onto the shoulders of a young man. Kysen was working his way toward the stairs behind which lay the door to Ese's garden court when a young woman in sparkling eye paint and a beaded girdle darted out of the crowd and grabbed his arm.

"There you are!" she exclaimed in a trumpeting voice. "You've kept me waiting, and I've lost two customers because of it. And you've brought a friend. I hope you also brought gold, because you're going to need it."

Kysen gaped at her, his eyes wide and his lips slightly parted. The young woman shook his arm.

"Come along, both of you."

Without waiting for his consent, the girl hauled him upstairs. Abu trailed them, and Kysen tossed him a look that disclaimed any acquaintance with her. The second floor consisted of suites of rooms bordering the square landing that overlooked the hall. His escort passed a series of closed doors, hauling him behind her. Kysen heard noises behind several of them, noises of which he could easily imagine the origin.

The girl stopped, knocked on one of the doors, and pushed it open.

Silently she pushed Kysen inside an empty room and shut him in before
Abu could follow. As he stumbled into the room, he heard her confront
Abu.

"Stay here, mountain of muscle."

Then Kysen heard a squawk and a thud. The door opened to reveal
his imperious escort sitting on the floor spewing epithets at Abu. The
charioteer stepped inside, slammed the door on the girl, and gave Kysen
an inquiring glance.

"I think Ese will be along soon," Kysen said.

"We wait a few moments," Abu replied as he searched the room.
"Then we leave." He walked into the chamber beyond the first room and
returned. "Another door leading to a back stair. We will not remain in
this box trap for long."

"Why have you brought a stranger?"

It was Ese. She stood in the short passage between the two rooms.
Her skin appeared gilded and shone in the lamplight. Kysen tried not
to stare, but even at court he'd never seen a woman whose body had
been rubbed with scented oil into which gold dust had been strewn. Ese
had abandoned her Greek garb for the transparent mist of Egyptian linen
so fine it must have come from royal workshops.

Kysen forced himself to display only the slightest of reactions,
bowed in homage to the woman, and said, "Ese, this is a friend, Abu."

"He isn't my friend. Tell him to get out."

She hadn't stopped staring at the charioteer since she'd appeared.
Abu returned her stare and remained where he was. Kysen cleared his
throat to draw their attention.

"He won't leave, Ese, and I can't make him."

Ese gave him a smile that hinted at anticipation. "I can."

Abu remained silent and oblivious to the threat. Kysen shook his
head.

"Please don't do that. Abu looks upon me as a—a son, and I trust
him with my life."

"This does not interest me," Ese said.

"But I think you're interested in my assurance that, should you
summon your men, this room would soon hold many corpses you would
have to explain to the city police."

Ese adjusted a fold of misty linen that draped across her arm. "Very
well. At least he's not a hippo's ass of a nobleman. What do you want?"

"I've come about the list," Kysen said.

Ese turned away. "It's too soon. Come back in a few weeks."

Sighing, Kysen watched her go, then gestured to Abu. The charioteer walked swiftly to the chamber into which Ese had vanished. Kysen heard a scuffle, a shriek, and a door slam. It wasn't long before Ese swept back into the room, her body quivering, her sweet face disfigured by resentment and rage. She didn't stop when she got inside the room; she reached Kysen, lunged, and struck him across the face. Unprepared, Kysen took the full force of the blow. Abu, who had followed Ese, grabbed her and tossed her to the floor. Ese landed on her side. Instead of screaming, as Kysen had expected, she slipped her hand inside the ties of her robe and withdrew a knife. Kysen tried to warn her.

"Don't draw a weapon!"

Abu was already moving. He ran two steps, then struck with his foot, kicking her hand. Ese cried out as the knife flew across the room to bounce off a wall. While Ese clutched her injured hand, Abu pounced on her. She was wearing several necklaces, and he snagged them and pulled them tight at the back of her neck.

Dragging Ese to her feet, Abu shoved her over to Kysen, pushed her to her knees, and held her while she sputtered and tried to breathe. Her fingers worked between her neck and the jewelry in an attempt to relieve the pressure. Abu simply pulled up on the necklace chains. When her face had turned the color of a ripe melon, Kysen nodded to Abu. Without warning, the charioteer released his grip.

Ese dropped to the floor on her hands and knees. Swaying unsteadily, she gulped in air, coughed, and made gurgling noises. Kysen retrieved the room's single chair and sat down in front of Ese. The red in her face had faded to pink when she jerked herself upright, yanked at her gown to untangle it from her legs, all the while spitting curses at Kysen.

"Please, Ese, you will make me turn as red as you did if you keep up this deluge of soldiers' profanity."

"Get out!" Ese winced and coughed at the strain on her bruised throat. She went on in a lower tone but with just as much virulence. "No man rules here, and no man treats Ese like a common slave. I'll see your gut split and your entrails curled about your neck while you still live. I'll have my men cut the skin from your living body. I'll cut out your eyes and—"

"Woman," Abu said quietly. "Disavow your threats, or I'm going to kill you at once."

Both Kysen and Ese lifted their gazes. Abu was standing behind the tavern owner. He had drawn his dagger, a double-edged blade of bronze. Kysen had seen him slit the throat of a Libyan tribesman in less time than it took to blink. But what alarmed him was that Abu had that peculiar air of his, the one that meant he'd made a decision from which there would be no appeal, not even from Kysen.

Drawing in a quick breath, Kysen spoke softly, never looking away from Abu. "Ese, don't move."

Something in his voice must have communicated the gravity of her situation, for Ese swallowed hard. "Make him stop."

"I can't," Kysen said. "If you don't swear by Amun not to harm me, he's going to kill you. Right now. And there's nothing I can do to stop him."

"Her oath is worthless," Abu said as he turned the dagger so that the flat of the blade was parallel with the floor.

"Not to me," Kysen said. "She didn't understand, Abu. And she didn't mean anything she said."

Abu lifted his gaze from Ese for the first time and shook his head. "You're wrong. This woman has done all the things she threatened to do to you. To men. This I have seen for myself."

"They deserved it!" Some of Ese's hostility had returned, but she darted a look at Abu and softened her tone. "You know they deserved it, after what they did to me, and to my friend, and to my sister."

"Your sister?" Kysen asked.

"She's dead."

It was a blunt answer, and Kysen could see Ese would rather face Abu's dagger than give him more details.

"I'm sorry your sister has gone west. I have three sisters, and if someone killed one of them, I would act as you have."

Ese studied him in silence. Then she sank back on her heels. "I don't believe you, at least not entirely, but I'm willing to admit I lost my temper. It's these murders, and the talk of demons. I can taste the fear in the air." She rubbed her throat. "I've lost dozens of customers. They're too afraid to walk the streets at night."

"Murders? Word has spread quickly."

"What do you expect in Memphis?" Ese lifted her hands, palms up, her voice harsh from maltreatment. "I give my oath by the king of the gods, Amun. I didn't mean those threats. I was on edge and worried. That's why I lost control."

Kysen nodded. "Abu?"

The charioteer scowled at Ese, but sheathed his dagger and stepped back. Kysen released a sigh.

"By the staff of Ptah," Ese snapped, her anger threatening to erupt again even as she voiced her curiosity. "You were more worried than I."

Kysen stood and helped the woman to her feet. Then he guided her to the chair. Rubbing her throat, she sat down with a groan. Her hands began tugging at the folds and pleats of her gown.

Studying her red flesh, Kysen asked, "Are you well?"

"Don't insult me with your concern." Her voice broke, but she cleared her throat. "You're like too many other men—pretty but with a ka more suited to a crocodile."

He protested, but Ese's indifference showed in the way she stared at the opposite wall and rubbed her neck without responding.

"Oh, very well," Kysen said. "I can see you treasure your ill opinion too much to accept any amendment to it."

Ese turned to smile slyly at him and incline her head in assent. "You wanted to know about the list you gave me. I really have little to say at the moment. There were sixteen names, and I haven't received word on most of them. It was quickest to find out about the dead ones."

"What dead ones?"

Ese was removing her necklaces now, with grimaces and sharp little intakes of breath. "The queen had many, many attendants. So far, one of the three personal maids is dead, as is one of the five dressers. One of the privy door openers and a sandal bearer, these two have gone west as well."

Kysen asked, "How did they die?"

Dropping the necklaces in her lap, Ese began to massage her neck. "Let me think, let me think. The privy door opener was filling a water jar at the river and a crocodile got him. All too common a fate, I'm afraid."

"What of the dresser?"

"She died of old age."

"And the personal maid?"

Ese wrinkled her brow while her fingers intertwined with a beaded necklace. "Oh, yes. An ailment of the gut. A pity. She wasn't that old. I think she had twenty years. And the sandal bearer was even younger, but he died of a putrid scorpion sting."

"There was no hint of any of these deaths being more than accidents or illness or old age?"

"No. The only remarkable thing about them was that they all happened within a few weeks of their mistress's death."

"All within a few weeks."

"It will take more time to find out about the rest," Ese said. "But I can't until I'm paid."

Abu spoke up. "Don't worry, woman. You'll get your wages upon the morrow."

"Don't talk to me of wages as if I were a stone breaker, you son of a—"

"Please, Ese," Kysen said as he stepped between the two. "I've already saved your life once tonight."

Ese rose and sent a flaming look at him. "Just don't send him with my fee. And don't bring him with you ever again."

"I won't send him with the fee, but I don't think I can prevent him from coming with me."

Coming close, Ese lowered her voice so that only Kysen could hear. "I accept mishandling from no one. Do you understand? How do you think I survive among men like Othrys?" Her voice gained in force from the rage she held in check. "By being even more vicious than they are. Ask anyone on the docks or in the streets who they would rather face. They'll all choose anyone but me."

"I believe you," Kysen said. "But you can't—"

He stopped; Ese had already turned her back and vanished into the second room. He heard a door slam. He was thinking about Ese when Abu interrupted.

"The hour is late, lord. We should go home."

"Do you fear encountering Eater of Souls?"

Abu opened the door to the landing and stood to one side so that Kysen could pass. "The hour is late."

"Very well," Kysen said. "But even with Ese after us, it's bound to be safer in here than in the streets with a demon."

12

ONCE KYSEN LEFT Ese's tavern, Abu insisted upon going ahead of him.

Knowing it was useless to protest, Kysen said, "Go, then. Perhaps you have a good idea. This way I can watch your back."

Abu hesitated, to Kysen's amusement, but evidently could think of no objection. They set out, and Kysen kept a set distance from Abu until they entered an older section inhabited by Syrian traders. Here the streets deteriorated into mere tracks made treacherous with dried-up gullies from previous high floods and troughs dug by those in need of mud for bricks and too lazy to go to the river.

This was the portion of the trip Kysen disliked, for the tracks reversed on themselves, then suddenly twisted at a right angle, then reversed again, causing him to confuse his location. He could navigate well during the day, but night seemed to increase distance and stretch time as though he had been cast into a dreamworld. And the night was black, the color of the netherworld, and of death.

Kysen hopped across a gully and tried to remind himself that black was also the color of the fertile soil, life of Egypt, that gave to her the name Black Land. A name so old it was lost beyond the time before the delta and Upper Egypt became one kingdom. But not older than the gods, or their servant, Eater of Souls. Kysen darted glances into doorways, over awnings, down alleys, and up stairways to roofs.

"Take heart," he muttered to himself. "You might only meet one of the others, like Blood Drinker, who comes from the slaughterhouse, or Backward-facing One, who comes from the abyss."

Abu took another track, one in which they nearly had to turn sideways to make progress. Feeling penned, Kysen closed the gap between them and hurried after the charioteer as the older man veered suddenly at an angle between an old drying rack and the half-demolished garden wall of a deserted house. Kysen plunged down the new track, but as he passed by the wall, stepping over chunks of mud brick, he stopped. Then he quietly moved away from the wall, putting his back to the side of a house. His hand slipped to his side, and he drew his dagger.

Trying not to make a sound, he hardly breathed in his effort to see. Something was wrong. He scoured the area, noting the high, blank walls that crowded in on him. He couldn't see the moon, but his eyes had become accustomed to the dark. It was possible to distinguish shapes.

Whatever had caught his attention was in the old garden. The west wind had calmed, but he could still perceive the movement of the date palms within. He forced himself to remain as still as any of the dead shrubs and flowers behind the crumbling wall. Surely if someone were stalking him, Kysen would hear him step on dried leaves. Then he heard a footfall on loose dirt. Whirling aside, Kysen ducked and pointed his dagger.

"Lord, it is I."

"Quiet, Abu."

Abu melded himself to the wall beside Kysen. Pointing to the garden, Kysen lapsed into his watchful state again. Abu's sudden appearance had startled him and caused his heart to gallop. He drew in a deep breath, then let it out quickly and sniffed; motioning to Abu, he dropped to a crouch and stole to the garden wall. Abu slithered toward Kysen; they were separated from each other by a gap in the wall.

Kysen picked up a clod of mud and tossed it over the wall, where it landed at the base of a palm tree. Immediately dried leaves crackled, bushes quivered. A disembodied howl sounded behind him. Then a black silhouette eclipsed the stars above Kysen's head. Kysen launched himself into the air, hurled his body into the gap, and grabbed. His hand closed on something pliant, moist, greasy. A hyena's shriek issued from the thing, but Kysen yanked hard, and it hurtled over the gap to land between Kysen and Abu.

Releasing his grip, Kysen peered down. "If you want to track someone, you shouldn't go around smelling like rotting hippo meat, Tcha."

The thief scrambled around in the dirt, whimpering. "Never had no fine house with baths and slaves to pour water over me. Never had no house at all. Just a hut, a miserable hut. Sometimes a corner in a yard, or a place in the street."

As the whining continued, Abu kicked the huddled mound of grease, string, and amulets. Tcha fell silent.

"Where have you been, and why are you following us, you addled dung beetle?" Kysen asked.

"Been with the great master. He sent me. Wants to see you at once."

"Now?"

"He says it must be now. Already it may be too late, he says. Oh, what a day of misery and woe. Poor Tcha, poor wretched Tcha. No guards for him. No protection, only orders and threats, orders and threats."

"Here's another," Abu growled. "If you don't stop whining, I'll cut out your tongue."

Wiping the hand that had grabbed the thief, Kysen said, "I'm not going anywhere with you, Tcha. You're coming with me to answer some questions about your friend Pawah."

There was no answer at first. Tcha worked his way to an upright position, which put his eyes level with Kysen's chest. The thief took a couple of wary steps away from Abu. Fishing among his amulet draperies, he took one of the talismans in both hands. He held it close to his body while he turned in a circle and muttered incomprehensible phrases. Kysen sighed and was about to interrupt, but Tcha broke off his incantation.

"Othrys says if you don't come, he will take wagers that neither you nor Eyes of Pharaoh will live to see Inundation."

With deliberate slowness, Kysen swung toward Tcha and spoke quietly. "If you're lying, I'll give you to Abu."

The thief shook his head violently, but it seemed Othrys was the greater peril, for he began to trot down the path. He beckoned to Kysen.

"Come, lord. We must go to the pyramid city."

"At night?"

"At night." Tcha whimpered and danced from one foot to the other. "No one cares if a demon eats Tcha's heart. No one cares if Tcha is eaten. Go to the pyramid city, Othrys says. Go to the pyramid city. In the dark, in the *dark*."

Abu joined Kysen. "Don't go, lord. You can't trust that bag of grease and misery."

"I have to," Kysen said as he watched Tcha scuttle away. "You heard what Othrys said. Father's life may be in danger."

"Yours as well."

"I'm not fearful for myself." Kysen set off after Tcha.

Abu kept pace at his side and glanced at Kysen. "That is what worries me. A little fear would benefit you, lord, by making you more cautious. Then perhaps I'd get a little rest."

KYSEN PULLED A fold of his headcloth over his nose and mouth and turned east, away from the malicious desert wind. In the darkness, hot gales soared in from the west, hurling their vast stores of sand. Millions of tiny spikes scored his legs, and he closed his eyes as the storm whirled around his body. He could feel dust cake his skin and embed itself in the linen of his kilt.

With surprising suddenness, the wind ebbed, the incessant wailing faded, and Kysen was able to stand erect. Walking between Kysen and the thief was Abu. They climbed another rise. At the top, Kysen called a halt and approached Tcha. The thief seemed unconcerned about the necropolis police. Either he was practiced at avoiding them or they had been bribed by someone else, probably Othrys.

"I don't like strolling through the city of the dead at night, Tcha." Kysen swept an arm around, indicating the endless conglomeration of burials that stretched far to the north and south.

"We're almost there, lord."

Kysen planted his fists on his hips and stared into the night. Now he could distinguish the outline of the step pyramid. Six rectangles with sloping sides rose high above, each successive stage smaller than the previous one. The burial place of King Zoser was at least twelve times the height of any of pharaoh's palaces. With a buttressed and recessed facade, a vast enclosure wall surrounded the tomb and its complex of buildings.

Meren had taken Kysen into the place when he was a boy. Within the enclosure wall lay another, smaller pyramid and replicas of palace ceremonial buildings the king would have used in life, such as those for his thirty-year jubilee. There were also storage buildings to house the king's possessions and food and drink to provide sustenance and comfort to pharaoh's spirit. But the most valuable of these lay with the king beneath the massive house of eternity—pristine in its coat of polished limestone—in a vast complex of galleries and chambers.

Kysen had explored some of the storage buildings. One great magazine had been filled with the remains of grain sacks looted long ago. Others were shells filled with rubble. He remembered the reedlike columns; they had been carved from the surface of the stone walls so that they were still engaged to them. Meren had told him that the whole complex had been built to imitate an ancient royal palace, but in stone, the building material of eternity, not brick, the ephemeral substance used by the living. Kysen hadn't asked his father if he thought the king and his treasures still lay beneath the mountain of stone.

Zoser must have been a mighty god-king to have ordered the construction of so vast a house of eternity. The step pyramid even dwarfed the straight-sided pyramid of a later king sitting beside it. Yet it lay deserted now, its storehouses empty, its endowments turned to other uses by succeeding kings. No great staff of mortuary priests and attendants performed the offering rituals for this once mighty ruler. Kysen assumed the royal spirit had to rely on the magical sustenance of food, drink, and provisions carved and painted on the walls of his tomb.

"Lord," Abu said. "We should go."

They followed Tcha down the slope. Farther to the south and also near the pyramid of Teti to the east lay the new cemeteries. All around them rose countless chapels, some still with their stone facades, others stripped down to their brick cores, and still others that appeared little more than mounds of dried mud. The city of the dead had been here as long as Memphis, its origins stretching so far back in time that no one knew its true age. It was said that the first king of Egypt had founded the city. How many dynasties had succeeded him?

Tcha scrambled over and around a group of aged and crumbling tombs. These clustered in rows, rectangular with sloped sides, plain but once filled with riches. Many still sealed within their underground shafts the princes, ministers, and their wives and families who once served the god-kings. These old ones lived so long ago that no one remembered their names.

A blur of movement raced across Kysen's path. He and Abu both crouched and drew daggers. A black silhouette leaped on an overturned statue and hissed at them. They waited, not daring to move. A black cat. Was it someone's prowling pet, or a disguised spirit of the netherworld? The cat hissed again and fled.

Kysen let out a long breath while Abu growled his irritation. They kept their weapons unsheathed. Tcha appeared around the corner of a tomb.

"Come, lord. We're almost there."

"We'd better be," Kysen replied. "And I'm not staying long."

He climbed over a pile of rocks left from long-dead robbers' invasion of a tomb and followed the thief. Tcha scurried across one of the few clear areas between the nobles' tombs and the bastion wall of the step pyramid. As they walked, Kysen could discern the top of the steep-sided pyramid to the south. In daylight, if he stood on some vantage point, he would be able to see farther, to distant pyramids up- and downriver, even to the greatest of them all on a plateau guarded by the sphinx of Khafre.

Abu stumbled, and Kysen turned to see the charioteer pick up something. He went closer and barely made out the remains of a boning rod, one of a pair of wooden pegs tied with string. Masons used them to make blocks of stone perfectly smooth by resting the pegs on the stone, stretching the string tight, and chiseling away any imperfections. It had probably been here for centuries.

Abu tossed the peg at Tcha's head as it appeared out of the ground several paces away. "This way, lord."

Kysen walked over to the thief and looked down the slanting ramp upon which Tcha stood. The walkway pierced the ground between piles of rubble that looked recent, and then plunged beneath the ground to disappear into complete blackness.

"I'm not going in there," Kysen said.

Tcha knelt and fumbled with something on the ground. "I have a lamp—" Tcha stopped when Abu suddenly loomed over him. "O great master," he added with a gape at the charioteer.

Abu snarled at him. "The lord will not go down into a hole to be trapped and slaughtered. Where is Othrys, you sniveling little carp?"

"I am here."

All three of them whipped around as vague light appeared at the bottom of the shaft. A man came up the ramp holding a torch, and, looking like the men in old wall paintings of Greek bull leapers, Othrys followed him. The Greek wore a cloak of some dark Asiatic design over a plain kilt. The torchlight revealed the pirate's sky-colored eyes and honey-and-sunlight hair. The man at the barbarian's side was also dressed simply. He was a stranger.

"Come along," Othrys said without any greeting or ceremony. "There isn't much time."

Kysen stayed where he was and pointed at the torch bearer. "Who is he?"

"My scribe. Come now, I haven't much time."

"This scribe wasn't with you the last time we met," Kysen said. He signaled to Abu.

The charioteer stalked down the ramp to glare at the stranger. The scribe was slight, his bones small, but strong in the way that the acrobats at Ese's tavern had been. Long, wind-tossed hair fell to his shoulders. He shoved a brown length of it back from his face and met Abu's challenging glare with a spark of humor in his eyes. Kysen immediately became intrigued. He'd never seen anyone react to Abu the way this man had. He'd seen men regard the warrior with fear or admiration, and some great ones, usually those of royal blood, ignored Abu. Never had anyone looked at Abu with indulgence, as if he were a boy of four playing a game of war.

Even more curious—the stranger only observed Abu for a moment before swinging around to Kysen. The torch in his left hand dipped and highlighted his face. Kysen found himself subjected to a scrutiny so intense it was as if he were a minute piece of lapis lazuli being examined by a royal jeweler. He could even imagine this man's heart assessing the most strategic point at which to break the stone, or himself.

Intensity, brooding severity, and menace soared at him from the torch bearer. The impact was as startling as it was unexpected. This man was no ordinary scribe; his features and manner were too refined. He had a sculpted nose, fine brows, and a mouth curved like the open bud of a lotus. Yet he wore a plain kilt, no jewels, no sandals.

"Leave off," Othrys said. "By the Earth Goddess, neither of you is going to ravish the other's soul while I wait like a slave."

"Then who is he?" Kysen demanded.

A voice like the trill of a dove, a strummed harp, the cool north wind, answered before Othrys could. "I am Naram-Sin."

Kysen frowned, took a step closer, and examined the stranger carefully. "You're Babylonian."

All he got was a slow, almost wicked smile, but he hardly noticed because his memory was coming alive. And something was bothering him. Several years ago, when he was still being tutored, Father had given him copies of ancient texts, part of an old family collection passed down for generations. The papyrus had turned yellow and brown, fragile. His task had been to reproduce it.

"Naram-Sin," Kysen said. "I know that name."

The torch bearer raised an eyebrow but said nothing.

The papyrus had been a translation of a record from the ancient times of a kingdom called Akkad in the region near Babylon in the land of the Tigris and Euphrates rivers. It told of a mighty king who had conquered so many lands and cities that Kysen couldn't remember all of them. He'd conquered cities in the land of Sumer and spread his domain as far as the Great Sea and to the mountains of the land of the Hittites. He made great Elam a vassal state. He even fought with Egypt. But his downfall was the sack of Nippur, the great city of the god Enlil on the Euphrates.

Naram-Sin, drunk with his own glory, had performed vile acts of desecration and defiled the sanctuary of Enlil. In revenge, Enlil had called down upon Naram-Sin and his capital, Agade, barbaric hordes from the mountains, ruthless and utterly destructive. When the invaders were finished, Enlil and other gods of the two rivers laid a curse upon the city—that it remain forever desolate and uninhabited. Now nothing remained of it but an eroding mountain of mud brick and broken pottery.

"Naram-Sin," Kysen repeated. "You have an ancient and famous name. I might even say it's notorious."

The torch bearer's smile hardly faltered as he turned to lead the way down the ramp. "I could say the same of yours, son of the Falcon."

Kysen exchanged looks with Abu. Falcon was the nickname Maya, the royal treasurer, had given Meren when they were youths. Only Meren's closest friends used it.

"I am continually astonished at Othrys's intimate knowledge, and how high it extends," Kysen murmured to the charioteer.

Abu grunted. "I like it not, nor do I like the Babylonian. He reminds me of the mandrake plant, lush, perhaps pleasing to the senses, but full of death."

"You're overwrought, Abu."

"He smiled at me."

"A great transgression, I know, but you must endure it."

"I'll bury my fist in that delicate little nose," Abu grumbled under his breath as they followed their hosts down the ramp. He scowled at Naram-Sin's back. "A foreigner's nose, that is. No strength to it."

They descended west toward the step pyramid at a steep angle beneath the ground. One of Othrys's bodyguards waited at the point where the shaft widened. Several lamps had been set in wall sconces of archaic design, and beyond the opening in the walls, the shaft continued, no longer sinking but maintaining a level grade. Kysen glanced down the shaft, then looked again.

Beyond the opening the shaft became a finished corridor. Someone had smoothed the stone walls, ceiling, and floor and covered them with fine, hard plaster. An outline draftsman had begun his work. A grid of faint red lines marked out the proportions of a register, and within the grid had been drawn the beginnings of a scene. He could see the figure of a man holding a cup to his lips, seated before a table laden with food. The scene was unfinished and hadn't been painted. Perhaps the man featured in the scene had changed his mind about it, or he may have died and been hastily buried before this portion of his eternal house had been completed.

"Planning a bit of tomb robbery?" Kysen asked as he rounded on Othrys.

Othrys barely glanced at the corridor. "Don't pretend to be a fool. This shaft is almost as old as the one it intercepts. Your own people did whatever looting has been done long ago."

Abruptly, before Kysen could reply, Othrys took his arm and thrust his own out to forestall Abu. Pulling Kysen away from the others, he stopped beside the unfinished drawing. For the first time Kysen realized that there was something different about the pirate. Lines had appeared on his face that hadn't been there before. One ran across his forehead parallel to his hairline, and a spray of fine lines issued from the corners of his eyes. But what alarmed Kysen more was that Othrys had lost his air of cheerful deadliness.

"By the curse of Tantalus, what pit of vipers have you cast me into?"

"Why are you so disturbed?"

Othrys clamped a hand around Kysen's neck, yanked him close, and hissed into his ear. "Because I sent three searchers to begin your inquiries. Only one returned, and he didn't live long after he reached me. These are *my* men, not simple servants. Do you know what it takes to destroy even one of them?"

The men who served Othrys ranked among the most skilled and deadly. He'd seen even a Hittite avoid a confrontation with them.

Shoving Othrys away, Kysen fought his own increasing dread. "One man dead and two vanished. Where did you send them?"

"It doesn't matter," Othrys said. "But I remembered what you said about the woman Satet and her sister the favored cook, so I sent another man to the village to speak with the youth Tentamun." Othrys leaned against the outline of the tomb owner and stared past Kysen's shoulder with such intensity that his eyes narrowed to slits. "Both have disappeared. Those I sent after them haven't even found bodies. And the village is full of dolts with the wits of sheep. No one even saw Tentamun and my man leave the place."

"They can't have vanished without any sign."

The pirate hardly glanced at him. "You're not that innocent. Of course they could." Othrys beckoned to Naram-Sin, who joined them as if it was his right. "Tell my friend about the man who returned to us last night."

Naram-Sin seemed not to have caught Othrys's dread. He put his back against the grid wall and crossed his legs at the ankles. Folding his arms, he cocked his head to the side and began as if he were a bard telling a tale at a feast.

"He crawled to the back gate, where the porter called for help. Guards dragged him inside, but left him in the kitchen yard because of his state."

"What do you mean?" Kysen asked.

"He was bleeding from all his body openings, and even from small cuts that should have healed. There was a torrent of blood."

His voice faint, Kysen stared at Naram-Sin. "So he died soon after he reached you."

"Yes." Naram-Sin's lazy smile provoked suspicion that he enjoyed Kysen's uneasiness.

Kysen refused to respond to that smile and barked one word. "Plague?"

"Oh, no," came the purring response. Naram-Sin tossed his head to make a shining lock of hair fall away from his face. "No, he had fits and blood in his piss. No, this wasn't a plague. It was poisoning."

"I find your manner of drawing out your tale unamusing, Naram-Sin. Get on with it."

The Babylonian glanced at Othrys and chuckled. "You were right, my friend. He is more noble than peasant. He has barely outgrown the sidelock of youth, yet he treats me like some common musician who plays a tune too slowly."

Othrys scowled at the scribe. "This isn't the time, Naram-Sin. Play your games later."

"Very well." Naram-Sin stretched his arms and yawned before resuming. "The man complained of burning in the mouth. He vomited along with his other miseries. All together these are signs of poisoning by the fruit of the castor oil plant."

Kysen began dusting off his arms and legs while he considered the meaning of this new murder. "How do you know this? Are you a physician?"

Again he was subjected to that hot-oil smile that made him want to backhand the scribe.

"No, not a physician. An old woman whom I knew from infancy taught me about medicine and plants and their uses."

"Fruit of the castor oil plant is used for pains of the head and illness of the belly," Kysen said. Bener had given one of the slaves some for an ache in the head not long ago.

"And it eases afflictions of the skin," Naram-Sin said with a look of patient endurance. "But six fruits ground up and mixed in food that has already been cooked, such as a stew or soup, will bring on illness within hours." The scribe shoved himself away from the wall and turned to examine the drawings. "I would say that our man ate the poison no more than a day or two ago."

"I will find out who has done this to my men," Othrys said.

"I have no doubt," Kysen replied, "nor would I wish to be present when you find the evil one, but heed me, Othrys, I also must know who does not wish inquiries made about the people we discussed."

To Kysen's annoyance, Othrys didn't seem to be listening. He was engaged in some wordless communion with Naram-Sin, to which the Babylonian replied with a slight shake of his head. The pirate's gravity increased, and he faced Kysen.

"Leave this matter. You don't understand it, and the ones behind it are beyond your power."

"My father won't abandon his search," Kysen said, "and no one is beyond his power."

Naram-Sin wasn't smiling anymore. "If you refuse, you endanger yourselves and us as well."

"Why do you think I must pursue this?" Kysen snapped at Othrys. "Is this the same pirate who showed me his boar's-tooth helmet and boasted of slaughtering thirty beasts with naught but a sword?"

Othrys's eyes became slits the color of faded cornflowers. "Have a care for your irreverence, my lord."

He turned his back on Kysen and walked down the plastered corridor. Pausing where the light failed, he lowered his head and remained still for some moments. Then his head came up, and he turned on his heel. Stalking back to Kysen, he spoke once more in a strong whisper.

"You must heed me well, for I fear you will be allowed but one chance to grasp the danger that approaches." Othrys pressed his lips together as if he wasn't certain he could find the words he needed. "There are certain ones among us—not many—who are without sorrow of heart. I have shared bread with men so vile that they would couple with a fiend if the result was to their gain. Among these are a very few who move among the shadows of the world, who love the crooked trail, the hidden path that conceals their direction. Such ones feed themselves by spreading corruption and evil wherever they go, contaminating whatever they touch. A man like this nourishes himself on the power that secret corruption gives. He thrives by sullying the pure, corrupting the innocent, destroying the strong."

Othrys's voice grew quieter as his description continued. "A man like this increases his power by using others while he remains undetected. He sits in darkness growing strong on sin, flourishing on the strength of those he destroys. The more puissant his victim, the more power he steals for himself and the greater his pleasure in victory." The pirate's words were almost inaudible now.

"And if you intend to do battle with one such as this, I can promise you that the Nile will flow with fear. You will find that your heart's friends plot your destruction, and your name will be cursed by those who once praised it. The taste of life will turn to bitter vetch, my young friend, and not even the Earth Mother will come to the aid of the Eyes of Pharaoh and his son."

Kysen felt the skin over his skull stretch tighter than a hogging truss. The pirate's words gave him a glimpse of a life spent wading in eddies of horror, of swimming against a current of putrid evil. How was he going to make his father understand such danger? He shook his head and caught Naram-Sin looking at him. There was that expression of wicked amusement again, but this time it was tempered with pity. Kysen felt his cheeks grow hot and clamped down on his unruly emotions.

"Othrys, how do you know that one of these monsters is concerned?"

"Such a devastation of my men is beyond the power of most of my—rivals. And it happened so quickly and in such a skilled manner that I knew immediately that there could be only a few who might be responsible."

"Among your acquaintances, perhaps." Kysen brushed grit and dust from the folds of his kilt. Removing his headcloth, he folded it so that the inner side faced out, drew his dagger, and wiped the blade on the cloth. As he drew the edge along the cloth, the fibers split. "However, it is clear that you've never lived at court. There such men are as numerous as flies on a slaughtered oryx."

The blade sliced another path through the cloth. Then Kysen tossed it in the air. Catching the weapon by the hilt, he slipped it into his belt.

"You're a fool," Othrys said.

Naram-Sin's soft laughter echoed down off the plaster and stone. "But a brave fool."

"The names of the criminals, Othrys. I'm not going to waste more time listening to menacing tales."

The pirate suddenly dropped his air of apprehension to smile nastily at Kysen. "By the blessed gods, you need subduing. I almost wish I could be there to see it. Follow me."

Othrys walked into the darkness once again. Kysen went after him, stopping before all light faded. He waited, growing more irritated as the moments passed. Then a hand shot out and pulled him into blackness.

"Curse it, Othrys, you're not performing a festival play. Give me the names and be done with it."

"Keep your voice down, boy." The words came out of the obsidian void, sharp, like cobra's fangs.

Kysen held his tongue, and Othrys continued in a whisper. "If you reveal that it was I who gave you these names—"

"I already know what you're capable of."

"Then remember it."

Kysen felt Othrys's breath near his ear.

"Three names. These are the ones with the mighty grasp, the will, and the appetite. There is one called Dilalu. If you wish to acquire large numbers of weapons, he can find them. Dilalu is never in one place for more than a few months—in Alalakh, Ugarit, Kadesh, and of course, in Memphis. I think he played a part in the Hittite destruction of the Mitanni, but of course, I can't be sure. And he's in Memphis at the moment."

"Who else?" Kysen asked.

"An Egyptian called Yamen, an officer and scribe in the Re division."

"An officer?" Kysen asked. "What kind of officer?"

Othrys chuckled. "The kind that serves generals and sometimes is sent to foreign lands as an envoy, which gives him opportunities to meet generous people who seem to give him many gifts. Many, many gifts. And these gifts Yamen generously bestows upon his numerous friends, some of whom I would not trust should my other choice be your demon Eater of Souls."

"I've met worse."

"I won't try to convince you," the pirate said. "You'll believe me soon."

"And the last?"

"The last is Zulaya, a Babylonian who lives in Egypt and trades in horses, wool, copper, spices, many things. But what he is known for among my people is his unrivaled supply of the secret doings of princes, chiefs, and kings."

"If these men are so evil—"

"These men," Othrys snapped. "They have a few similarities. Their influence is felt in many lands. Each has secret friends among the great ones of Egypt. And most important, their enemies have a habit of ending up in evil plight. The high numbers of deaths among their rivals keeps most from interfering in their affairs."

"But it's strange that I haven't heard of them."

"Gods! You will be my undoing. I have almost decided to abandon you to the malice of this evil power."

Othrys stomped out of the darkness, leaving Kysen to follow. He joined the pirate, who was listening to Naram-Sin softly mention the late hour.

"A pity," Naram-Sin said as Kysen appeared. "But then, Egyptians always think they're somehow invincible simply because they're Egyptian."

Kysen ignored the Babylonian. "Othrys, I'll tell my father what you've said. But I have to warn you. Don't expect this talk of a master of evil to deter him. If he had to, Meren would hunt this criminal down into the caverns of the netherworld."

"Would he?" Naram-Sin asked with a smirk.

"Do you know Maat?" Kysen countered.

The Babylonian shook his head.

"Maat is the divine order of existence, which was brought into being upon the creation. Maat governs the seasons, the stars, the relationship between mortals and the gods, and above all, rightness and justice. Pharaoh rules through the authority of the goddess Maat."

Kysen tossed his headcloth at Naram-Sin's feet and surveyed the two foreigners. "This is what you don't understand. Egypt is governed by Maat. Pharaoh guards against lawlessness and chaos. He preserves the divine order, and Eyes of Pharaoh exist to aid pharaoh. Evil is chaos, and chaos is evil, which threatens Egypt's destruction. And Egypt, her pharaoh, her peaceful seasons and endless stars, these are the substance of my father's ka. If he must, he will bring the stars down to the earth and the earth to the sky to preserve Maat."

Turning to go, Kysen lightened his tone. "In any case, both your shadow criminal and this murderer who steals hearts must be stopped. Eyes of Pharaoh has decreed it, and what he ordains always comes about, I promise you. Have a safe journey home, Othrys. And may the protection of Amun be with you."

13

A GREAT SHIP was moored at the temple quay, its dark hull hardly visible above the night-black waters of the Nile. So long and wide that it dwarfed even the largest of pharaoh's warships, it had no deckhouse. Unlike other ships, its prow didn't curve up. Instead it looked cut off, and thick lines could be seen running from it to the quay.

This was the royal barge *Tutankhamun Is Divine*. An overseer of the treasury had brought it to port just before nightfall. The arrival of *Tutankhamun Is Divine* had been a marvel. On the last leg of the voyage from the southern quarries at Aswan, it had appeared over the horizon like some vast floating plain. Long before it docked, rhythmic chants and the drumming of oars from thirty towing boats signaled its advance. The sun boat of Ra had set fire to the pink granite of two needlelike obelisks resting side by side on the barge.

These elegant, tapering monoliths were meant to stand before the pylons of the temple of Ptah. Their pyrimidion tops would be covered with sheet gold to reflect the sun's rays. As he had promised, pharaoh was restoring the temples of the old gods, replenishing their looted coffers, in reparation for the destruction wrought by his heretic brother.

No guards patrolled *Tutankhamun Is Divine* or her cargo. There was no fear that thieves could shift stones weighing as much as several pyramid blocks and measuring four times the height of the tallest house. The hot western wind whistled through the streets of Memphis and burst into the open at the quay to hurl sand across the water. Smaller boats bobbed and dipped. The royal barge remained almost immobile.

One of the towing boats bumped against another. At the muffled smack of wood against wood, a long mud-green snout rose behind the first obelisk. Eater of Souls peered out at the quay.

Bronze claws scraped pink stone while protruding eyes studied the docks, the other boats, the storage buildings, and deserted streets. She had been slithering along in the shadows, on her way to yet another execution, when that large overseer of the city watch had appeared. Marching toward her with that officious, waddling gait, the creature had actually barked at the two men preceding him. Mortals didn't bark at Eater of Souls; usually they screamed, if they got the chance.

Intrigued by the overseer's officious manner and flabby bulk, she had wondered what it would feel like to sink her ax into that thick chest. While she speculated, she had waited almost too late before she faded into the black shelter next to a staircase running up the side of a house. The creature waddled nearer, moved past her, then stumbled. Catching its balance, the mortal turned, slowly, as if afraid to look. Eater of Souls gripped her ax. Her claws scraped against each other. The creature gasped, its eyes bulging, and whimpered like a sick piglet. Before she had even decided to attack, the overseer whirled around, leaped into a sprint, his flesh jiggling, and vanished down the street.

Eater of Souls chased after the mortals but lost them near the docks. When a drunken gaggle of priests staggered across the quay, she plunged aboard the royal barge to avoid them. Too many encounters would keep her from the most important task she'd performed so far on behalf of the favored one.

Her mane brushed a wooden beam as she lifted her snout. The west wind escalated. Howling out of the land of the dead, it screamed with the voices of countless dead and damned souls. Eater of Souls could hear their fury. These she had not devoured; deprived of tombs or ancestors to feed their spirits, they wandered the desert without the sustenance, condemned to eternal starvation.

Eater of Souls lifted herself onto the obelisk. She crouched on her haunches and tasted the wind with her snout. The stench of the living was gone. Leaping across beams and then to the quay, she slithered back into the street shadows.

Time to find the evil one. This transgressor caused terrible hurt to the favored one by its very existence. This one sinned in a thousand ways. First, there was the sin of beauty; the outward visage flaunted its perfection before the favored one. Second came a rank so high that it brought unequaled magnificence and wealth and made the favored one seem a beggar. These transgressions paled beside the third—for the evil one possessed power, godlike authority, a majesty of ka that taunted the favored one into black misery.

All admired the evil one. The fiend walked a golden path surrounded by precious jewels, countless slaves, servants, admirers. Where the fiend went, awe, praise, and fascination followed. The creature existed in a silvery mist of splendor and eminence that was slowly poisoning the Favorite.

Eater of Souls paused in her journey into the city as the pain of the favored one reached her. She backed against a wall, scraping hide and fur. From her fanged jaws issued a rhythmic grunting that ended in a hollow moan. The emptiness and desolation enveloped her, deeper than the abyss of the netherworld, more horrible than Eater of Souls herself.

Then she snuffled into silence, listening to the west wind howl. A message from the pantheon soared on the scouring blast, entered her nostrils, and curled its way to her heart. Now, at last, she understood the great quest that had drawn her to the land of the living. Above all, she must destroy the one who was a lethal Nile cataract, a granite barrier concealed in churning, frothy white water that reflected the brilliance of the sun. Because it captured the rewards, glory, and worship that belonged to the favored one, this creature was the most dangerous. Every moment it existed, the fiend ripped from the favored one's ka the treasure to which only the Chosen was entitled. Each robbery, each stolen bit of praise, pierced the Favorite like a javelin, and the emptiness swelled.

Terror lurked in this emptiness. Terror and perpetual agony. She had to destroy the cause of this desolation before it obliterated the favored one. As the desolation churned like a sea storm in her gut, Eater of Souls pointed her snout to the stars, howled, and bounded down the deserted street toward the place of the transgressor.

MEREN STILL COULDN'T sleep. He dropped a pile of reports beside his chair, rose, and went to the table bearing Sit-Hathor's alabaster lamp. Beside it lay the tray holding the two feathers and the text about birds. The feathers were quite ordinary looking, neither longer than one-third the length from his fingertip to his elbow. To him they looked like those of a goose or swan.

He unfurled the bird papyrus. It was a long text with painted illustrations, their colors still bright. Although the papyrus had darkened, it was still strong. It had been written by a royal scribe, who stated that he was setting down the words of the overseer of pharaoh's bird keepers, Snefru, twelfth day of Inundation, Year One of Seqenenre Tao. Seqenenre Tao had ruled over two hundred years ago. He must have liked fowling.

"Now," he said to himself, "which birds have white feathers? Owls, but the white ones aren't long enough. Not ostrich feathers, although if this murderer truly does weigh the heart against the feather of truth . . . hmm, the feather of truth."

Meren set the bird papyrus down and placed polished stone weights on it to keep his place. He hurried to another of the great chests in which the documents and texts were kept. This one was set apart from the others and made of precious ebony inlaid with ivory. Scenes on its sides depicted the ruler of the netherworld, Osiris, and his companions, Anubis, Toth, and Horus, son of Osiris, and his wife Isis. Stopping beside the chest in which sacred writings were stored, Meren whispered a prayer of praise as he pulled out a thick roll. Opening the *Book of the Dead,* he began to skim the chapters of spells.

He skipped over the hymns to Osiris and Ra, the chapters devoted to restoring the dead, not letting one's soul be taken from him, the ones that opened the tomb and allowed the dead man to go out into the living world. More hymns, a spell for being changed into a falcon of gold.

"Here it is."

Meren held the papyrus closer to a lamp mounted on a column. This was a new copy of the *Book of the Dead,* and the papyrus from which it had been made was thin, yet strong, and of so fine a quality that his father had refused to let Meren touch it until he had completed his education as a scribe. The scene of the Hall of Judgment stood out in brilliant colors—red for men's skin, yellow for women, pure white clothing. Registers of sacred black hieroglyphs bordered a painting of a balance scale. Anubis knelt under one arm of the scale. In one pan lay the heart of the dead person. In the other, the Feather of Truth, its shape resembling that of an ostrich feather.

"But the killer hasn't used ostrich feathers." He started to roll up the papyrus, but his hands went still when he saw the beast crouching behind Toth, the recorder of verdicts in the Hall of Judgment. "Ammut, the Devouress."

A fantastic monster was Eater of Souls. She was composed of the three most deadly animals—the crocodile, in whose jaws so many Egyptians perished; the lion, whose claws ripped flesh as if it was melon pulp; the hippopotamus, giant terror of the waters, who could crush a victim flatter than a papyrus sheet with one stomp. This demon lurked by the balance scales, ready to devour all who were not judged true of voice.

Closing his eyes, Meren imagined Eater of Souls. Wet yellow teeth, stinking breath. He knew the pain of a lion's strike and still remembered the lacerations across his ribs. Faint, ragged white lines in his skin reminded him of the agony he felt when those claws ripped through his flesh. As they cut, his skin and muscle tugged. Then they were dragged along with the claw as it moved, making him feel as if he were being peeled.

The papyrus snapped closed. Meren blinked and looked down to find that he'd been rolling up the book while deep in the memory of the lion attack. He replaced the book and went back to the bird text. While he read, he muttered to himself.

"The evil one has no ostrich feathers. Too poor to get them, or too clever of heart to reveal that he has such a luxury? White-feathered birds, white feathers. Heron, egret." He'd seen egrets following a farmer's plow and eating insects turned out of the soil by the blade.

He moved a weight stone and revealed a drawing of the sacred ibis, beloved of Toth. The bird had a pure white body, black neck, bill, legs, and wing tips. Black and white; good and evil.

"An appropriate choice," Meren said.

There were more white birds. The spoonbill, which was used as a decoy in fowling, and the Egyptian vulture. This was a disgusting bird with a bare-skinned head and hooked bill. It lurked in rubbish piles and fed on the excrement dumped there.

Meren let the papyrus roll closed. This was a useless study. Egypt teemed with birds, especially when foreign places of the north turned cold. They flew to the land of the Nile seeking refuge, and anyone could collect feathers, anyone who could hunt or who could purchase a freshly killed fowl in a market.

Feathers were used to adorn dresses and to make fans, as stuffing for cushions to cover chairs and stools, as pallets and mattresses for beds. Birds of all kinds were kept in walled yards, pens, and cages, fattened, and then slaughtered. Birds inhabited the desert, the Nile, the swamps and marshes. The royal menagerie was full of birds, as were those of many nobles. All over the kingdom they were collected and sacrificed as offerings to the gods. Unfortunately, white-feathered birds were almost as numerous as flies.

"I'm becalmed, adrift without oarsmen or helmsman," Meren whispered to himself. He would ask Bener which of his own fowlers might be able to discern more about the feathers.

Pinching the bridge of his nose, Meren listened to the wind. The severe blasts had died down for the moment. He rolled his shoulders. They ached, and he was weary of trying to make sense of crimes that appeared to have been done for no reason. Never had he been faced with evil devoid of purpose. Evil born of chaos lodged within a mortal—such a man was surely demented.

What kind of man chopped out the hearts of strangers? For the victims hadn't been of the same family, village, or city. And there couldn't be more than one criminal at work. That several could be responsible for such horror was surely unlikely. Apart from Mugallu, none of the dead ones had mortal enemies. According to what his charioteers and the watchman Min had been able to learn, each had been unremarkable, passing through life without either creating great disturbances or performing great accomplishments. These people weren't worth killing, so why do it?

Nothing he knew seemed to give a sign of who or what Eater of Souls was. Perhaps this was one of those instances where ordinary investigation wouldn't suffice. He always tried to use orderly reasoning in his inquiries, but if he was dealing with the anger of the gods, would orderly reasoning be of use?

He felt the rise of irritation. Confusion always sparked a fire in his chest and made him want to drive his fist through one of the mud-brick walls of his office. He had to get out of the house. On a table beside his chair lay his scribe's palette, a stack of blank papyri, and a box no one but he ever touched. It was of stained cedar and decorated with his name in gilded hieroglyphs. Snatching it up along with a lamp, Meren strode out of the room, downstairs, and out of the house.

The grounds were quiet except for an occasional whinny from the stables, lowing from the cattle pens, and the rustle of palm and sycamore leaves in the wind. The breeze whipped his long, transparent robe around his legs. He'd taken off his wig and much of the heavy jewelry with which his body servant, Zar, had burdened him that morning, but Zar had replaced them after Meren had bathed this evening. He'd been too preoccupied with the heart thefts to notice. When he had, he'd removed some.

His wig was somewhere in his office along with at least two electrum-and-amethyst armbands and three rings. He'd kept only his seal ring. He strode down a path lined with small pomegranate trees, a recent addition ordered by Isis and Bener, both of whom intended to learn the mysteries of making wine flavored with the fruit. Meren suspected they were interested only because they were learning from his childhood playmate, Lady Bentanta. His daughters liked Bentanta. They hinted that she would make an excellent wife. They didn't know Bentanta like he did.

Meren reached his private garden, where he dismissed the porter whose task it was to patrol this area of the estate. He didn't want the man walking in on him when he opened the gilded cedar box. Once inside the refuge, he placed the lamp and the box on a table beneath a wooden awning supported by four painted poles beside the largest reflection pool. Glancing around, he saw no one.

The garden was his attempt to capture the beauty and teeming life of the Nile and bring closure to his life. This way he could renew himself, drawing strength from pleasure in the water, the animals and plants. The moon sprayed silver light across the water. Undulating dark shapes were barely discernible in the depths, but he caught a glimpse of a talapia, a fish that hatched its eggs in its mouth, a symbol of rebirth.

A heron with a smooth, ornamental crest behind its head goggled at him from the water, then stalked away on its measuring-rod legs. Several Egyptian geese paddled by. The trees and pools in his garden, along with the reeds and lotus plants, were the haunt of pintails, rock pigeons, doves, and pied kingfishers.

Satisfied that he was alone, Meren lifted the hinged lid of the box. Within lay another hinged lid that swung open to reveal four paneled compartments. Each contained an orb that gave off a golden luster in the lamplight. Meren took three of them, two in one hand, one in the other. He tossed the single orb in the air and caught it, then repeated the action, establishing a steady cadence. Quickly he threw the second and third into the air so that they spun above his head.

Then, his juggling rhythm established, he walked slowly down the paved path that bordered the reflection pool. He moved toward the shorter end nearest the gate in the wall. The orbs made a satisfying pat as they hit his hands briefly before he tossed them again. *Pat pat pat, pat pat pat.*

A breeze arose suddenly, making the limbs of the sycamores and acacias scrape against each other, thousands of leaves breathing hissing murmurs. Swaying flowers and shrubs accompanied them with the whisper of their leaves and petals. Seeking to empty his heart of agitation, Meren continued to juggle while listening to the refrain.

At his feet dead grass blades and leaves danced as he reached the corner of the pool. Then he hesitated, juggling in place while he frowned. Catching the balls as they fell, he held them and listened. Beneath the gentle creaking of limbs and the mesmerizing strain of leaf and petal he had heard something else. Something faint, but as discordant as a snapped harp string. It hadn't been a bird. Holding still, Meren concentrated, keeping his breathing shallow to eliminate any distracting sound.

Still nothing. He turned, looking around the garden at the secluded arbors, the tree-shrouded pavilion, the small orchard filled with more pomegranate as well as persea and *nabk*-berry trees. He searched arbors heavy with grapevines, stands of palms, and smaller pools with their lotus and papyrus thickets, ducks, egrets, and geese.

"You fool," he whispered aloud. "You're imagining demons and spirits where there are only fish and birds."

He turned and flung the first golden ball in the air. Without warning the wind surged, sending a furious blast across the garden. With it soared the biting desert grit. The west wind howled through the desert escarpments, soared through steep valleys created by the stylized mountain ranges that were the pyramids and cemeteries of Memphis. And under the howl came a noise like an animal's grunt. Meren heard it, caught the orbs again, and turned to the west.

Had he heard the rasp of metal, or was it simply branches scraping together? The air smelled of water, dust, and some animal odor. Perhaps it was wet duck or decaying water plants. The garden was alive with movement, but the west wind subsided. Trees and reeds settled down. After a few moments, Meren decided the only thing he'd heard was the wind and resumed his walking and ball tossing.

After one circuit of the reflection pool, the wind picked up again, but not enough to stop him from juggling. He had to pursue this interest in secret, for great nobles did not perform feats of entertainment like commoners. Meren wasn't certain what pharaoh would think if he learned that his Eyes and Ears tossed brightly colored balls like the troupe in the royal palace.

And Zar disapproved. He acquired a look like a bilious toad and said things like, "Great lords do not toss balls like naked children" and "One so noble of lineage cannot sustain his dignity while chasing after toys as the baboon chases cats." Zar had served royalty and understood the importance of decorum, splendor, and reserve in supporting a great one's power.

But Meren needed this pastime. It forced him to concentrate on balance and rhythm while it relieved his heart of burdens, fears, and confusion, if only for a brief time. So he juggled when he was alone.

Unfortunately, this time he couldn't distract his heart from the deaths, the missing hearts, the feathers. If he tried, he ended up trying to make sense of old Satet's demented opinions about where her sister could be. Every time he pressed the old woman for answers, she gave answers that were increasingly absurd. He dared not press her too hard for fear of permanently confusing her wits.

He'd been forced to take the men assigned to searching Memphis for her sister and divert them to the hunt for Eater of Souls. Unsnarling the tangle of Nefertiti's death was going to take a long time. Every day that passed in which he sent out requests for information, asked friends about old memories, and culled old records of the household of the Great Royal Wife increased the chance that the wrong person would discover that Meren was interested in a queen long dead.

"Cease!" Meren hissed to himself. "You're to think of balance and speed, not killings."

He turned a corner of the pool and started down the long side of the rectangle. Moving slowly, he approached the next corner. There an artificial papyrus marsh had been constructed on a base of Nile mud. Rising to double Meren's height, the thicket of triangular reeds with their frothy, tufted crowns bowed and bobbed in an isolated gust of wind. Meren reached out to catch a ball that had been blown slightly off its course and tossed it up just in time to catch the one that followed.

As he neared the papyrus marsh, his foot came down on something soft, wet, and cold. He cried out, withdrew his foot, and staggered sideways. The golden orbs bounced in all directions. He heard a plop as he regained his footing and watched one of the balls sink into the water. As the wind ceased, a giant toad croaked at him. It scrambled to the edge of the pool and jumped in.

"Cursed water monster." Meren rubbed his ankle. His foot was wet from the toad, so he went to the pool and dipped his foot in the water.

As he bent his knee, the papyrus reeds stirred, producing a rattlelike sound. There was no breeze! Meren pulled his foot out of the water and reached for his dagger, but he was too late. Several dark figures erupted from the marsh and rounded the corner of the pool. As Meren drew his weapon, a fist hit his arm. He dropped the dagger, but three swords jabbed him.

Expecting to feel metal pierce his flesh, Meren froze. When the sword points remained embedded in his robe, he pulled himself up, dropped his arms to his sides, and turned to face a man who stepped closer.

He looked like a mastaba, one of the short, wide tombs of ancient nobles that resembled benches. His eyes bore an expression that said he understood his own importance in the world, and that it was greater than that of anyone he'd met so far. Bronze armor was wrapped around his torso. It covered his lower legs and encrusted his helmet, but his body seemed hard enough that the metal protection might prove unnecessary.

"General Labarnas," Meren said. "I wouldn't have expected you to be so foolish as to attack one of pharaoh's servants in the middle of his city."

The Hittite threw back his head and laughed once. Then his smile vanished. "Perhaps, Egyptian, I've come to avenge Prince Mugallu, whom you slaughtered like one of your sacred bulls."

"Have you ever heard of the Eyes and Ears of Pharaoh attacking anyone like a hyena after a carcass?"

Labarnas was only a silhouette of lighter darkness in the night. Meren watched him twitch his head to the side as an eagle does when scouting for prey. He heard him slide his sword into its sheath.

"I didn't come out in the evil breath of this desert wind to listen to the poison and lies of an arrogant Egyptian prince."

"I cannot understand why you're here at all," Meren said. "My son told you we were doing everything we could to find the one who killed Prince Mugallu."

Labarnas darted toward Meren, shoving aside one of his men. "My father died at the hands of an Egyptian dog at Kadesh."

"Neither he nor any Hittite should have been in Kadesh," Meren said. "Kadesh belongs to pharaoh."

"Miserable perfumed catamite!"

Meren smiled his indifference and touched one of the Hittite sword blades. "Enough of this useless and petty debate. What do you want?"

Labarnas said something in his own language to one of Meren's guards. The man dashed behind the papyrus thicket and returned with a basket large enough to hold half a bull's carcass. He set it down near the general and removed the lid. Labarnas swept his arm toward the container.

"O perfected prince, true of voice, beautiful of aspect, great Eyes of Pharaoh, get into the basket."

It took Meren a moment to understand, as no one had ever dared to insult him in this manner.

"Are you possessed by a mad spirit?" he asked.

"I'm leaving this cursed city, Egyptian, and you're my letter of safe passage. My men and the rest of the delegation are waiting for us, and once I have you back at the royal visitors' house, pharaoh will have no choice but to allow me to leave."

"How do you know he won't hurl a dozen companies of infantry at you?"

Labarnas planted his fists on his belt. "Why is it that you Egyptians think all Hittites are dense of wit? The great king, Suppiluliumas, knows the secrets of his brother. Not that pharaoh's affection for you is a secret."

"Perhaps," Meren said lightly. "But I know the living god far better than your king, and I can promise you that trying to compel him to do anything, much less to bend to your will, is a mistake. One does not order a god-king. Not unless one is prepared to suffer—possibly I should say—divinely."

"I weary of talk. Egypt has lost the will and the fire needed for conquest, wasted it on dalliance, perfume, and jewels. Get in the basket, curse you, before I order you bound and silenced."

"I suppose you've killed all the men on guard," Meren said as if carrying on a pleasant conversation with a banquet guest.

"Not all of them. Some will live."

At last Meren allowed himself to look away from Labarnas to the walls surrounding the garden. "By the great Amun, general, you're right."

Fire rained down on the group by the pool. Meren remained still while flame-tipped arrows stabbed into the ground in a circle around them. The soldiers holding Meren at sword point stepped back, then stopped, fearing to move. Their blades dipped toward the ground as they searched the top of the wall.

Labarnas whirled around to stare as well. Standing on top of the wall, shoulder to shoulder, bows drawn and spears held ready to throw, Meren's charioteers waited quietly. The gate creaked, and the old porter shuffled into view, bowed to Meren, and gave the Hittites a contemptuous scowl before he hobbled back the way he'd come.

In a blur of movement, Labarnas was suddenly at Meren's side. Grabbing his arm, the general pointed his blade at Meren's heart.

"Tell your charioteers to go away, Egyptian."

Meren refrained from showing his irritation and spoke more calmly than he felt. "Please don't move again, general."

"Ha!"

"Do you see that young man holding the bow trimmed with sheet gold? Not a plain warrior's weapon, is it? His name is Reia. He's a lieutenant of chariots. How many prizes for accuracy have you won, Reia?"

Reia responded without shifting his stance. "In year four I won three, lord. This year I have won two, so far."

"Hollow boasting," Labarnas growled. "I've won dozens."

Shaking his head, Meren replied softly. "Here in Egypt, there are only three."

The Hittite's eyes slid sideways to examine Meren's expression. Meren lifted an eyebrow.

"I've seen Reia hit a crow sitting on the nose of the sphinx, from a moving chariot."

Breathing hard, Labarnas tightened his grip on Meren's arm. "Pray to the gods, then, Eyes of Pharaoh, for we both die."

"Why?" Meren asked quickly.

The general's face was lit by burning arrow shafts. He looked like a desert nomad suddenly faced with the task of sailing across the Great Sea.

"I swear by the wrath of your storm god," Meren said wearily, "all I want you to do is go back to the visitors' palace and let me find Prince Mugallu's killer."

Labarnas tightened his grip on Meren's arm. "I know what I'd do if someone took me prisoner in my own house."

"True, but as you Hittites never weary of repeating, we Egyptians are more courtier than warrior."

"You're lying," Labarnas said with a glance up at Reia.

Meren laughed softly. "So, you have learned from your sojourn into the Black Land." His mouth drew down at the corners. "As foolish as it may seem, you're going to have to trust me. If I had killed your prince, would I have sent my own son into the midst of your warriors to tell you Prince Mugallu was dead?"

Shifting his weight from one foot to the other, Labarnas was silent for a moment. At last he grunted, lowered his sword, and released Meren's arm. His men sheathed their own weapons. Meren inclined his head to the general, then nodded to Reia. There was a loud smack as spears were turned point up and their hafts rammed into the top of the wall. Bowstrings were allowed to loosen as bows were lowered so that nocked arrows pointed at the ground.

"Reia will escort you home," Meren said.

Labarnas glared at him. "Will I reach it alive?"

"Of course. Do you think I want pharaoh to blame me for the death of a great Hittite general? The Son of the Sun would send me to explain to your king, and that I wouldn't like to do."

"I'm going," Labarnas said. "But if you have no good explanation by a week's end, I'm leaving if I have to fight pharaoh's infantry, chariotry, and archers all at once. Then you'll find yourself explaining my death to the great king while he sits on Egypt's throne."

Meren turned away from Labarnas. "Oh, go away, general. I'm trying to catch a killer who feasts on hearts, and I have no patience with your threats."

Labarnas growled something in his own language, but didn't object when he and the other Hittites were ushered away. Meren refused to allow Reia to surround him with guards. Reia protested, but finally left to escort Labarnas when Meren remained adamant. Finally Meren was left alone in the garden again. The flaming arrows had been removed. The lamp he'd brought was burning low, and Meren had subsided wearily into a chair beneath the awning by the reflection pool.

He had propped his elbows on his knees and lowered his head to his hands and was grumbling to himself. "Wretched Hittite vandals, invading a man's private garden. My heart will never regain enough peace to make sense of either the heart thefts or the queen's . . ."

Meren had been staring through his fingers at the mat that covered the earth beneath the awning. Now there was a small foot encased in a blue sandal on the mat. Meren didn't even move.

"I suppose the noise woke you," he said.

"Aye, Father," said Bener. "A Hittite invasion does disturb one's dreams."

Placing a tray on the table beside him, Bener yawned and ran her fingers through her long hair. "That was a good lie, that story about Reia hitting a crow."

"He almost hit it."

"True. Are you ever going to rest?"

Meren straightened, then slumped and stretched his legs. "Can't."

"What queens?"

"What?" Meren echoed, abruptly alert.

"Just now, you were complaining about not being able to make sense of the queens."

"Who can make sense of the Great Royal Wife or the lesser ones?"

Bener fixed her great dark eyes on him without saying a word.

"Tell me," Meren said. "Can you?"

"If you refuse to confide in me, I can't be prepared for murderous invasions of the house, Father. What if they had gotten hold of Remi or Isis? And where is Kysen?"

"Visiting Ese's tavern."

"I've heard of her."

Meren sat up. "How have you heard of this woman?"

"I don't spend my whole day in the house directing servants. I have friends whose fathers and brothers and cousins seem to feel a great need to frequent the place, although why carousing with strange women holds more attraction than giving amusement to a lady is a puzzlement to me. Why is it so, Father?"

He hadn't been so bereft of thought since—he'd never been so bereft of thought. His heart wouldn't produce words. Meren stared at his skeptical, sensible daughter, stunned at the way her heart pursued matters to their reasonable end.

"Never mind," Bener went on. "You look weary, and it's going to take you some time to think of a good excuse for that one." She yawned again and said, "I'd better tell you now. Isis is planning to take herself and her possessions to Prince Djoser's house, where Reshep is staying."

A demon was pounding a mallet against his skull. Meren groaned and pressed his fingertips to his temples. A woman married a man by bringing her possessions to his house. Girls seldom did this without elaborate arrangements between the two sets of parents, negotiation of a marriage contract, feasting and celebration. But some were fearless, or foolish, or—as in the case of Isis—both.

Bener dropped to a stool and picked up a cup of wine from the tray she'd brought. "I think it was his idea. I bribed Isis's hairdresser to tell me anything serious. She says Isis thinks you'll have to agree to give her a marriage portion and contract if she goes to his house."

"Isis should know what I'll do to Reshep. There isn't going to be any contract or portion. He'll be fortunate to escape with his—"

Nodding, Bener said, "That's why I'm sure this is Reshep's interpretation. He has dazzled her heart, or she wouldn't have misjudged you."

"When pharaoh asked me to inquire about him, I sent men to Reshep's country estate. They should return soon, and I'll know more about this presumptuous suitor. Meanwhile, Isis is going to visit Tefnut, escorted by a squadron of charioteers, half a dozen foot soldiers, and my old nurse."

"What are you going to do to Lord Reshep?"

"I would like to feed him to this killer who haunts the city, but I can't be sure the evil one would do the work." Meren rubbed his chin. "I suppose pharaoh would be annoyed if I pulled his spine out through his throat. I shall have to ponder the matter."

"Then I'm going to sleep late tomorrow and avoid the furor when you confront Isis. But before I go, shall I tell you what I've been thinking?"

This was one of those times. Meren felt her apprehension as she regarded him with that look of expectation. He nodded gravely so that she wouldn't suspect him of indulging her.

At Meren's nod, Bener took a sip of wine. "You still don't know why these killings have been done. But obviously they've been done by someone who can prowl the city at night. This person is someone who can go to the foreign quarters and the docks without being conspicuous, or word would have reached you."

"You're correct so far," Meren said.

"The evil one always kills in concealed places, at night, taking the victims by surprise."

"So this criminal is good at stalking," Meren said, following Bener's reasoning. "He's a hunter. Like pharaoh's huntsmen and fowlers, like fishermen. But not like unguent makers, scribes of the treasury, slaves."

Bener peered at him over her wine cup. "Noblemen hunt. They have time to do it."

"I know, but anyone can use the night to do evil."

"Therefore, there's no mark or sign connected with the killer," Bener concluded.

They shared a comfortable silence. Meren reflected upon how easily he explored possibilities of great evil with this amazing daughter.

Bener finished her wine and set her cup on the tray. Turning to him, she furrowed her brow. "We don't know enough, do we, Father?"

"No, my dear, we don't. Not yet." Something Bener had said bothered him, but he wasn't sure what. He felt faintly uneasy that he might have missed something, but Bener slipped her hand into his.

"Are we safe?" she asked. "General Labarnas was able to steal into the house."

"I sent most of the charioteers with him. He's not coming back. He's a Hittite general, Bener. This killer isn't. Of that I'm certain. And the evil one prowls another part of the city."

"Reia's going to increase the night guards?"

"Of course, when he returns."

"Then I can sleep. Will you?"

"Not at once. The voice of my heart is still loud."

Bener picked up another wine cup and handed it to him. "I put one of Aunt Idut's sleep remedies in this. It's too mild to rob you of consciousness, but it soothes frenzied thoughts."

When Bener had gone, Meren set his wine cup aside. He detested potions. The trouble was that his sister Idut had taught his daughters the wisdom of herbs and medicines passed down by the women in the family for generations. Both were developing great skill, but Bener had taken to practicing on the household, especially him. She grew quite excited talking about herb harvesting and drying. Tinctures, infusions, and decoctions fascinated her. He was afraid she was more interested in them than in the young men who tried to attract her attention by driving their chariots back and forth in front of the house.

However, she was right about sleep. He needed it, and he wasn't going to get it if he allowed his heart's thoughts to wander from worry to worry. Having sent everyone to bed, and with Reia away escorting the Hittites, he might be able to seek the peace he usually found in his garden.

Meren retrieved his juggling balls. The one ruined by the water he tossed in one hand. Each time it hit his palm, it made a splat instead of a pat. Shaking his head, Meren began walking toward a grove of sycamores. He could hear the toad he'd nearly squashed serenading the reflection pool with hollow, watery croaks. An owl soared into the garden, landed on a sycamore branch, and whirred an accompaniment. Leaving behind the smell of water and reeds, he came to the pavilion where a couch was always ready for his use.

Meren sank down on the linen-covered mattress. Sighing, he removed his jewels. Nearly being eviscerated by a Hittite had exhausted him. Zar would be annoyed that he hadn't come in for bathing, but his eyelids felt as heavy as altar stones. He didn't even bother to pull down the reed shades to keep out the west wind. He lay down and realized he had picked up the wet juggling ball again. He dropped it and his dagger beside the couch and closed his eyes.

Soon he was drifting in a world of peaceful darkness and enveloped in night sounds that always brought tranquillity. Breathing deeply, he tried to inhale the sounds of the owl and the toad, the lapping of water against the sides of the pool, the rising wind that caused tree limbs to undulate and their leaves to shiver.

But underneath this euphony he heard something else. It was another toad, one encouraged to join its fellow by the absence of people. Meren turned on his side to face away from the pavilion steps and the pool, his thoughts growing fuzzy. One toad was soothing, a group could wake an embalmed one. When he was settled and drifting in his tranquil world of sound, he nearly fell asleep. He could feel his busy thoughts fade, his cares sail away on clouds of familiar, comforting sounds. He was drifting in a mist of peace, like the ba bird, the form of one's ka that had a bird body but a human head. But something was wrong. One of the toads seemed to have hopped onto the top rail of the balustrade and was blaring its call into Meren's face.

Without opening his eyes, he frowned. Odd conduct for a toad, and this one's croak wasn't soothing. It sounded like a grunt.

A wave of comprehension rushed over Meren so that he was wrenched into vigilance. The speed of the change brought pain, which in turn jolted him into battle wariness. He tried not to alter his breathing, even when the breeze brought an incomprehensible scent, a mixture of decaying hide, sweat, half-dried blood, and . . . something else. Something sweet that when mixed with the other smells made him want to vomit. Lying still yet tensed to repel an attack, Meren tried to make sense of the sweetness. Not decaying reeds, not rotting animal flesh, not even rotting human flesh. No, something that had once been pleasant, like perfume.

Balanos oil, that was it. Balanos oil and myrrh? Decaying hide, blood—and perfume oil? His stomach twisted even as Meren heard that grunt again. This time it didn't stop. It repeated itself, growing faster and louder until it was one long, groaning roar. When the sound moved, Meren opened his eyes and rolled across the bed at the same time.

He hit the pavilion floor as something leaped at him and landed on the couch. All he saw was a crouched, deformed shape and a fanged maw. He kept his gaze on the thing above him and grabbed for his dagger. The shape rose from a squatting position as Meren's hand hit the wet leather ball.

His ears filled with the creature's bawling roar when it sprang at him. He caught a glimpse of an ax and curved, razorlike claws. Meren hurled himself into another roll. The ax missed his head and bit into the floorboards. He tumbled over the floor and hit the balustrade. The thing followed, reaching him as he jumped to his feet.

His back to a support post, Meren straightened in time to dodge a slash from those claws. He turned his head to get a look at his attacker's other arm, only to spring backward to avoid another cutting swipe. His foot caught on the pavilion steps. He flew over the stairs to land on his back. His head hit a buried rock.

Meren cried out, but forced his eyes open. He shouldn't have, for the face of a crocodile filled his vision. The reversed end of the ax hurtled at him at the same time that bronze claws clamped onto his arm and began to incise his flesh.

14

EATER OF SOULS hesitated, confused by the rapid movements of her quarry. This one was harder to kill than the others. First the foreigners had intruded, forcing her to wait until they were gone. Then the wait had brought back the pleasures of the Hall of Judgment. There the unjust quivered before her, and she found that anticipating the satisfaction of appetite rivaled the pleasure itself. This creature was the font of the favored one's pain. Killing it would bring more pleasure, more relief from the emptiness, than any of the others.

She should have resisted the urge to savor the moment before the kill. She'd tasted it too long, and the evil one had awakened. The mortal hadn't been asleep at all. It was clever, and it moved with scorpion speed. Scorpions could be caught, though.

Eater of Souls launched herself after it as the mortal fell out of the pavilion. She raised the reversed ax over her flat, mud-green head as she clamped an arm. As had happened countless times, her victim was caught between pain and horror at the sight of the Devouress, frightened into stillness. In that motionless instant, she tasted the grandeur, the beauty and power, embodied in this transgressor. Destroy this mortal, and all that it had gathered to itself would flow to the favored one.

Eater of Souls felt a demon howl build in her gut. It rumbled up her throat as she brought the ax down—on bare earth. The evil one had twisted like a crocodile suffocating its prey, wrenching from her grasp. Eater of Souls lashed out with blood-painted claws and missed yet again. She bellowed her fury at being robbed of the kill.

The blow had to be delivered, or the evil one would get to its feet. The bronze ax head soared back and up, high over her mane, as she uttered the bellow that always turned her victims' legs to marsh mud. At the same time, a terrible noise assaulted her. High, piercing, like the shriek of a thousand burning cats, the sound stabbed into her head.

Eater of Souls spun around on a grunt and drew her head down between her shoulders. There, near the reflection pool, stood the daughter who had brought wine. The girl's mouth formed a black cave of noise. The screams rose several notes and drove hot spikes of agony behind her eyes. Eater of Souls tried to ignore the pain. She turned back to her victim, but the evil one had vanished.

No, there it was, at the pavilion. And it had a dagger. Eater of Souls cringed under a renewed barrage of shrieks and snarled at the daughter as the girl threw a volley of rocks. At the same time, Eater of Souls heard men shouting.

More mortals approached. The Devouress launched herself at the evil one, claws spread, ax blade biting the air. At the last moment, as the victim braced for her attack, she swerved and hurtled past it into the grove of trees. Leaving the mortals stunned, the Devouress clawed her way up a tree and leaped over the garden wall. On the other side she darted quickly into the shadows and pounded through the streets, rage building with each stride.

The evil one had escaped; no one escaped Eater of Souls. She had failed the favored one. Now the emptiness would be renewed, increased by humiliation and time. Pausing, the Devouress lifted her snout and waved it through the air. She caught the scent of the transgressor, still fresh. She could smell its fear, but mixed with it was rage and a hint of cold reason.

Eater of Souls did not inspire anger; inspiring anger meant that the angry one felt equal. None equaled the Devouress. For this reason as much as for the favored one, she would hunt down this quarry and destroy it. And she must do it quickly, before word spread among the living that an evil one had survived Eater of Souls.

HE WAS DESPERATE to protect Bener. Meren raced after the creature that had attacked him in darkness, not thinking of the folly of pursuing it into the black shadows of the trees. Streams of sweat emptied into his eyes, blurring his sight and stinging his eyes. He dashed an arm across his face as he nearly ran into a palm. What stopped him was a rock.

It soared past his head and smacked into the palm tree. He whirled around, shouting. "Bener, get back!"

Of course, she didn't listen. While shouts of charioteers filled the garden, she charged through the trees and landed beside him, with a fistful of stones, ready to hurl another. Meren hardly glanced at her. His lungs worked; his body tensed in readiness while his heart emptied of all but the need to protect Bener and to hunt down and kill the creature. He searched the grove, strained to hear the slightest grunt or scrape of metal claws. Above them, the limbs of an acacia rasped and squeaked. Bener started, and her movement caused Meren to grab her arm and begin backing out of the grove.

They hadn't gone far before they were surrounded by charioteers. He gave them a brief description of what had happened and sent them after the intruder. He wanted to go with them, but he was afraid to leave Bener. She wasn't crying or frantic, but her body trembled, and she had a dazed look. His men left, but dozens of servants crowded around them.

He gave answers and reassurances he didn't feel, but the chatter and the demands rose anew, fed by darkness and fear. The voices grew louder and louder until he could hear nothing else. Something stung his forearm. He glanced down to see four red slices in his flesh. He turned his arm over and found another, deeper cut. Five, five cuts. He tried to concentrate on them, on Bener, but the wails and entreaties of the servants resounded inside his head, battered his skull.

"Be silent!"

His roar cut through the din and shut even the most importunate of mouths. "Everyone out. Not you, Bener." When they were alone, he asked, "Are you hurt?"

"No, Father."

She said nothing more, and he knew better than to press her. Leading her to the reflection pool, he knelt and stuck his arm in the water.

She sat beside him. "Was that . . . ? Who was—what . . . ?" Bener caught her lower lip between her teeth.

"That, my dear, foolish daughter, was Eater of Souls."

"It was the Devouress."

"It was what people are calling Eater of Souls."

Meren scooped water into his hand and allowed it to trickle over the cuts on his arm.

"A demon," Bener repeated in a harsh voice. Her fists were clenched, and they pressed into her stomach.

"Perhaps." Meren looked up to find her staring at him. "Perhaps it was a demon."

"What else could it be?"

"I don't know."

"How could you not know?" Bener's voice rose and carried over the water. "It attacked you! I saw the—the head, the long snout. Even in the dark I saw the claws. I thought I was going to perish of terror."

Meren rounded on her. "But you didn't. You threw rocks."

"It was going to kill you!"

"Next time run for help," he snapped.

Half closing her eyes, Bener said carefully, "If I'd run for help, you might have been killed." She glanced at the cuts on his arm.

"I'd rather risk death than see you in danger."

"But, Father, I feel the same way."

Startled, Meren was about to retort when Bener's courageous air vanished and she burst into tears. She threw herself into his arms. He held her tightly, having learned in the raising of three daughters that this wasn't the time to attempt comfort by spouting reason and wisdom. Then, as suddenly as the tears appeared, they ebbed. Bener lifted her head to glower at him.

"I saved your life."

"You're a brave young woman," he replied. He was too exhausted to quarrel, his ka filled with trepidation and disquiet.

Bener gave him a suspicious look, but he only smiled at her. "Your maid will be waiting for you. Go to your chamber and try to sleep. The hunt for this creature may take the rest of the night."

"Can you hunt a demon?"

"I don't know."

"But you don't think it was Eater of Souls, or you wouldn't have sent men after it."

"Bener, I tell you I don't know!" Even to him his voice sounded rough, like split wood. He stood with her. "Forgive me. I'm weary."

"Aren't you frightened of the—the—"

"Go to bed, daughter. We'll talk upon the morrow."

He watched her leave and wished suddenly that the gods hadn't given her so much cleverness and bravery. The garden gate shut. He had a little time now, with no one to see. Dropping to his knees, he sank back on his heels. He cupped his hands, dipped them into the water, and splashed his face. Then he stuck his injured arm into the water again. The coolness eased the sting of the cuts. But it didn't stop the trembling. He made a fist and stared at the liquid blackness.

Someone had lit the lamps that rested in tall stands around the pool. He could see his fist, a distorted stump beneath the surface. Cursing, he swept his arm up and sent a spray of water into his face. The shock against his skin didn't help.

When the thing had attacked and he saw it for the first time, the sight had caused a brief moment of terror so extreme that he'd felt a jagged bolt of pain reverberate through his body, and he'd torn his attention from the terror and pain just as he did in battle. But now he was paying the price. Every muscle, from the top of his head to the soles of his feet, ached. The bones in his arms and legs had become hot, formless sand. The voice of his heart pounded in his ears.

Changing his position, he drew his knees to his chest, rested his arms on them, and lowered his head. "What was it? A good question. What was it? Unfortunately, I don't know."

The attack had happened too quickly. He'd been startled, and there had been no time to think, no opportunity to get a good look at the— thing. All he remembered were flashes in which a yellow eye, a long, fanged snout, or slashing claws dominated. A half-hysterical chuckle erupted from his chest. The mighty warrior, Eyes and Ears of Pharaoh, had been struck helpless, blind, and deaf at last.

Hearing his own laughter, he clamped down on it. Allowing it free rein would invite a loss of control he couldn't afford. He must harness himself before Kysen or the searchers returned. Lifting his head, he bent his neck back and exposed his face to the breeze.

Face what's really bothering you. Face it now, before the fear grows.

His dread arose from a suspicion that Eater of Souls had been sent by the gods to avenge the murder of a man who had been a living god—Akhenaten. For years he'd lived with the knowledge that Akhenaten had been murdered. Over a decade had passed, but he still suffered from the burden of the sin. He had allowed Ay to send him away, knowing that when he returned, pharaoh would be dead. No word had been said to lead him to believe that this was so, but words hadn't been necessary.

And in all the years since then, he'd tried to justify his sin by helping to restore divine order to Egypt. The work of undoing Akhenaten's ravages had been difficult. It would take many more years. Yet still he felt the weight of sin within his ka. And now Eater of Souls had come.

He'd refused to believe it. He knew men's hearts. The heart of a man was capable of conceiving a plan in which killings were disguised as judgments from the gods. He had trusted in this possibility. All the while, hovering like a vulture, suspicion waited. Suspicion that nothing could assuage the wrath of the gods at the murder of one who had been born of a god and a queen.

He had always expected retribution. He had feared that, in the Hall of Judgment, his heart would crash to the ground when weighed on the scales against the feather of truth. Had the gods judged him already for his role in a pharaoh's death?

Eater of Souls had come to destroy him. His only hope lay in the failure of the demon. But surely an instrument of the gods wouldn't fail to destroy its quarry. Did this failure signal that the creature wasn't of the netherworld? Or was Eater of Souls playing with him?

He should examine what he knew instead of indulging in fearful speculation. What did he know? The creature had extraordinary strength. He was no longer certain that he'd fallen from the pavilion during the attack. Perhaps it had picked him up and thrown him. He hadn't been able to escape it, for Eater of Souls had the speed of *Wings of Horus* and more skill than the most skilled of warriors. That ax, it had nearly crushed his skull.

But he had touched Eater of Souls. He'd smelled it, heard it. He had touched skin, the skin of a living man—or woman. He'd smelled mortal flesh and perfume oil amid other, stranger smells. And those howls and grunts. Those could have come from a real throat. But he'd also seen a yellow eye, a golden-brown mane. And he'd felt his flesh being slashed by knifelike claws.

Its size. It had been big. Taller than he was. Meren remembered having to look up at it, but then, he'd been on the ground most of the time. Still, the creature hadn't been so large that it couldn't have been a tall man, or a very tall woman. But it had moved so quickly, and with such strength . . .

He started when the garden gate opened. Kysen shut the door with deliberation and came to stand beside him. They both contemplated the reflection pool. There was a plop in the water that made Meren jump again. As the toad began to croak, Kysen turned to him.

"It seems we both have much to report."

Meren smiled ruefully. "It is as the old writings say. I will show you the land in calamity. Great ones are overthrown. The land is destroyed and the river of Egypt flows not."

"Surely it's not so evil."

"That depends, Ky, upon whether the gods have lost patience with us or not."

A FOREIGNER ENTERING the city of Memphis on this morning would ask if this was indeed the fabled capital of the Egyptian empire. Streets normally teeming with pedestrians and herds of donkeys, goats, and sheep bore only light traffic. Vendors at the city markets who usually argued with customers at the top of their voices used subdued tones. Most of the citizens had vanished, leaving behind deserted houses, half-empty temples and palaces.

A curious visitor who searched for them would find that the crowds had left the noisy domain of the living for that shadow city of Memphis, the vast stone city of the dead. Here, on the desert borders, balancing between the world of mortals and gods, people had clambered over crumbling mortuary chapels and scrambled between statues of dead kings and queens to reach the step pyramid.

Thousands stood shoulder to shoulder, bent back their necks, and shielded their eyes against the morning sun to catch a glimpse of the unparalleled sight. At the top of the pyramid, Nebkheprure Tutankhamun, the living Horus, son of Amun, Egypt's intermediary between men and the gods, was performing sacred rites of magic to banish evil from the city and protect his people. Pharaoh had already summoned the high priests of several gods whose magic and power were fabled—Isis, Selkhet, Ptah, Toth, and Amun, the king of the gods. Even now priests performed rites of banishing in the dark shrines of the city's temples.

The royal bodyguard lined the edge of the summit of the step pyramid, their spear tips gleaming in the sun. Within this protective wall stood the king, his most trusted courtiers and relatives, the high priests, and Meren. He hadn't wanted to come. His men were still searching the city for Eater of Souls. He should be doing the same, but pharaoh had insisted he be present, saying that after the attack Meren needed magical protection.

So here he was, standing in the middle of a square ring of royal guards. Inside this formation whirled dozens of priestesses. They danced and plied sistrums and ivory clappers. The noise and stamping of the dance drove off evil spirits, but it also made Meren's head ache. He watched the women move in a line, stamping to the beat of drums, their robes heavy with beads that clattered, their arms raised high as they directed the cacophony up and across the necropolis to the city.

These weren't ordinary priestesses and singers of the temple. Each was a noblewoman or princess and the divine adoratrice of a temple. And one of them was Ankhesenamun, the Great Royal Wife. It was she who led the dancers, assuring the attention of the gods by her presence. At her side danced Princess Tio. Meren was certain neither would have participated in any ceremony that might benefit him, had they a choice. Ankhesenamun whirled past him. Each time she came near, he glimpsed the loathing in her slanting, date-shaped eyes.

She was the kind of woman who could enter a room and turn a man's mouth into a desert, but she was also the kind of woman who hated learning new things. What she knew already, she considered as sacred as the hieroglyphs on the walls of a temple. And she didn't change, no matter what new knowledge was presented to her. It was this aspect of her nature that worried Meren.

Ankhesenamun might be courting her royal spouse in search of reconciliation, but she hadn't changed her nature. She passed by him again, and he lifted a brow. She stumbled a bit, glared, and moved her lips in a wordless curse. Even the curse of Eater of Souls brought some blessings. Meren had to look away quickly, or he would have committed a terrible breach of etiquette and smirked at the Great Royal Wife.

A few yards away, Tutankhamun stood surrounded by high priests. He was clad in white linen, the color of ritual purity and sanctity. He wore a gold-and-silver headcloth, necklaces, bracelets, belt, and uraeus diadem, all of gold. The flesh of a god was gold, the color of imperishable eternity and the sun. The bones of the gods were silver, the color of the moon. Moving slowly under the weight of his magnificent raiment, pharaoh recited incantations before a statuette of Eater of Souls.

Meren eyed the figure, trying once again to envision what had attacked him two nights ago. He still couldn't say what it was. When pharaoh had been told of the incident, he'd demanded an answer. Was it demon or man? And Meren hadn't been able to give him a reply.

The frantic search had expanded in a circle with the house at its center. It had led to the discovery of several wandering dogs and a nobleman's son who had passed out in the street from drink, but nothing else. Pharaoh had summoned priests who deluged Meren with questions and offered learned opinions.

That's when the worst of the trouble began. The high priest of Amun, Parenefer, had arrived from Thebes. Still feeding himself on hatred born of Akhenaten's persecution, Parenefer seemed much too pleased to be able to claim that Eater of Souls came to avenge the wrongs done to the old gods. The high priest of Isis, a cheerful young man who had recently taken his father's place in the office, had disagreed.

"If Eater of Souls could be brought because of those wrongs, she would have appeared many years ago. My divinations proclaim this evil originates within the living. An evildoer seeks to hide beneath the guise of a demon."

"No, no-no-no-no!" The high priest of Selkhet—a fierce and temperamental goddess—was excitable. "Possession, that's what it is. An evil spirit has possessed someone and causes the sick one to do these things without knowing it. I have consulted the sacred writings as well as divinations and oracles."

Meren had listened to all of them. That was the trouble. The priests couldn't agree. Without their guidance, he was left to struggle alone. And still he wasn't certain whether the thing that had attacked him had been someone in a disguise or a demon.

Would a demon have been frightened away by Bener's screams? The high priests and their most learned magician-priests differed in their opinions on this matter as well. When he'd touched the creature, Meren had felt hide as well as flesh. The flesh told him that he faced a man, possessed or not. But the hide, rough yet pliable—had it been the skin of a demon?

His heart was full of conflict. And contending with Isis hadn't helped. Yesterday he'd stopped her from leaving to take up residence with Lord Reshep, who was still a guest at Prince Djoser's villa near the palace. He didn't even want to remember the quarrel that had ensued. Isis had accused him of caring only for his own interests. She'd said he thought her negligible of wit. He'd protested that he thought her quite clever but young and foolish.

This remark had not endeared him to his youngest daughter. At the moment she was shut in her bedchamber and refused to speak to him. Not that he wanted to engage in another such conversation. Still, he loved Isis too much to allow her to win this argument. The men he'd sent to investigate Reshep should return any moment. After he heard their reports he would brave Isis's wrath. But how could he make her understand that the thought of her ruining her life was more frightful to him than facing Eater of Souls?

Prince Djoser prevented him from finding an answer to this question. Not that he really had an answer. Djoser left the group surrounding the king and paced slowly toward Meren. He held in his hands an incense burner, a long bronze rod shaped like an arm and hand. The hand held a bowl into which burning incense had been placed. The prince reached him and swept the incense around Meren's body while he chanted prayers.

Djoser was acting in his capacity as a priest of Isis, a role he played much better than that of warrior. He could perform the rituals and remember the protocol of the dozens of ceremonies, and he knew the mysteries of the House of Life in the temple. But Meren knew Djoser still secretly longed for the renown of a warrior. Perhaps his unhappiness with his nature caused Djoser to seek out posturing and flamboyant knaves like Reshep.

He hadn't realized he was staring at the prince. When his attention returned to the present, Meren found Djoser glaring at him. Caught off guard, he felt a jolt of surprise, for he could almost feel the heat of Djoser's rage. Was the fool still angry with him about Reshep?

Djoser recovered himself and shoved the incense burner in front of him. Meren nearly choked on the sweet smoke. His eyes stung, and he blinked as he caught another whiff of the scent used to attract the attention of the gods. Its recipe was engraved on the walls of temples to preserve the knowledge. Meren had read the hieroglyphs once and had been surprised to find it called for juniper berries, sweet flag, cassia, and cinnamon as well as precious frankincense and myrrh.

He drew breath again as Djoser finished, but this time the sweet scent reminded him of Eater of Souls. It was the myrrh. Those who used it sometimes kept the smell about them for hours. If it was in unguent, it would last until the wearer bathed. Surreptitiously Meren wiped away the tears the smoke had caused, even as he wondered whether a demon would smell of old incense. No, this he doubted.

A priest standing beside him turned and handed Meren a set of golden cords. Meren took them in both hands. It was time for his part in the ritual. With Djoser leading the way, he approached pharaoh and the effigy of Ammut, the Devouress. Kneeling, he held out the cords. Pharaoh took one and tied several knots in it while the high priest of Amun recited spells. This was the ritual for binding Eater of Souls. The knots provided a barrier across which the demon could not pass.

As the dancers kept up their protective din, pharaoh tied the knotted cord around Eater of Souls. He then placed the figure inside a tall chest made to resemble one of the towers of a desert fortress. The priest of Isis came forward bearing a heavy rope. He and Parenefer tied the rope around the closed door of the chest, then held the two ends together while pharaoh applied a clay seal. Next, to the accompaniment of chanted spells, Tutankhamun pressed the bezel of the royal seal ring into the damp clay.

Thus the demon was imprisoned, its might sealed away and kept impotent by the most powerful force in Egypt, the living god. The dancing, chanting, and clapping rose as pharaoh lifted his arms. Meren blinked when Tutankhamun shouted a command with such force that it was heard even above the drums. All noise ceased at once.

Meren, who was still kneeling, glanced down to find he was still holding a golden cord. Why had they given him two cords if pharaoh needed only one? The dancers stood in their ring around the king. The priests, the courtiers, awaited pharaoh's signal for the party to leave the summit of the pyramid. Tutankhamun ignored Parenefer's whispered hints.

Turning his back on the sealed chest and the old priest, pharaoh signaled that Meren should stand. Meren glanced at Djoser, who shook his head to indicate ignorance. Meren had no choice but to stand before the king holding a useless length of gold cord while everyone stared at him. Then pharaoh came close, took the cord, and began knotting it while he chanted the protective spells. There was a stir among the dancers. Meren glanced at them to find that the queen had stepped forward as if to object. She was restrained by Princess Tio.

"Keep him from harm who is bound by my protection," the king chanted. "I beseech the god my father, I beseech Isis, Osiris, Toth, and the golden ones. Keep this Lord Meren from harm. I set my protection about him. The power of my majesty shall keep you safe from any action, any interference, any harm."

Meren had no choice but to allow pharaoh to slip the cord around his waist and tie it. Bener had insisted upon calling a priest to ward him with protective spells, but he'd never suspected that the king would provide one of his own. Tutankhamun finished tying the last knot and stepped back.

"There," he said under his breath. "Let Eater of Souls contend with the power of the son of the great god."

"Majesty, I—"

Tutankhamun almost smiled, but he appeared to remember his god-like dignity before others.

"Is the great Eyes of Pharaoh speechless? Then I am recompensed for having to learn so many endless spells, chants, and prayers for this ceremony."

Meren felt his features settle into a courtly mask. "Does thy majesty know what he has done? He has made me at least a dozen more enemies at court than I had before."

"Better a few more enemies than a hole in your chest where your heart should be."

With this pharaoh turned and signaled the end of the ceremony. Meren was left to follow. The significant result of pharaoh's actions didn't occur to him until the royal party had descended the step pyramid and returned in procession to the palace. Ankhesenamun and her retinue continued on to her own palace. The queen hadn't liked the king giving his magical protection to Meren, but now he understood what he'd seen in her eyes. Not just enmity, not simple hatred, but jealousy.

Meren hadn't considered this possibility before, and he didn't like it. But he had too much to deal with. He wanted to leave. The search for Eater of Souls continued; Kysen was at the house, supervising and overseeing the continuing searches of the docks, the foreign quarters, and the district around Meren's house.

Back at the palace Meren found himself obliged to attend a royal consultation. With pharaoh presiding, Ay, several other ministers, and the priests were discussing Eater of Souls yet again. Meren's attention strayed. He tried to think about the attack in a different way—who hated him enough to try to kill him?

Well, that list was as lengthy as the carvings on a temple wall. Just recently he'd managed to offend the Great Royal Wife, Princess Tio, Prince Rahotep, Djoser, Lord Reshep, poor Mugallu, and General Labarnas. Those were the ones he could remember. Only the gods knew who else had reason to hate him. His duties made certain that he caused inconvenience, even harm, to many of whom he wasn't even aware. Stifling a groan, Meren turned his attention to the men around him and found the priests still quarreling.

His patience was disappearing quickly, and the longer the high priests argued about the significance of the killings and why the demon had appeared, the more restless he became. Old Parenefer, frail and brittle like an insect, clutched his staff of office and spoke above the competing voices.

"The reason we can find no purpose to these deaths is that they are divine judgments of the gods, who have read the hearts of those who have been killed and found them evil. Because of Egypt's suffering under the heresy of the old pharaoh, the gods have lost patience and have sent the Devouress to carry out punishment." Parenefer swiveled around to stare at Meren. "Eater of Souls has been sent to rid Egypt of corruption."

"Then she should have begun with you," Meren said lightly.

He shouldn't have spoken, but he was sick of listening to Parenefer whine about how much he and the righteous had suffered because of Akhenaten. Over Parenefer's head he caught the king looking at him. Tutankhamun's eyes crinkled at the outside corners, and Meren thought he glimpsed a fleeting curve of his lips. He was going to hear his own counsel of diplomacy tossed back at him the next time he was alone with the boy.

The high priest of Isis, whose family was far older and more noble than Parenefer's, rolled his eyes and let out a sharp sigh. "We don't even know if this really is the Devouress. It could be someone who hides behind the guise of a demon to fool us. There was a case in the Hare nome of a farmer who moved the boundary stones of eight different fields and blamed it on the angry spirit of a dead woman."

Several ministers nodded, and discussion erupted again. Prince

Rahotep joined Meren, nudged him with an elbow, and growled at him.

"So, you're an evildoer already condemned by the gods. My commiserations."

"You're not amusing, Rahotep."

"If you'd have sent for me the night before last, I could have had my infantry hunt down this bastard killer, and we wouldn't be here listening to that old vulture Parenefer."

"I forgot," Meren said.

Rahotep folded his arms over his chest. "You didn't forget. It's like you to think you can combat even a fiend from the underworld by yourself, just you and your fabled charioteers. The Eyes and Ears of Pharaoh, whose name is known throughout the empire, whose spies and informants are innumerable and as hidden as the secret names of the gods."

"You're still angry at me. I told you the truth about meddling between pharaoh and his queen."

"I'm not angry," Rahotep said. "You were wrong, if you can imagine it. The golden one was most gracious in his thanks for my advice. Oh, and I hear your Isis is to marry that strutting ostrich Reshep."

Meren stared at the prince. "Don't be absurd."

"Then it's not true?"

"Of course not."

"Did he hear about Eater of Souls coming for you and withdraw from the arrangement?"

Meren turned on Rahotep and spoke under his breath. "Curse your smug face, Rahotep. This attempt at humor has the subtlety of a hippo attack and the refinement of hyena dung. If you continue to wrap your barbed tongue around my daughter's name, I'll tie your ankles with your tongue and pitch you into the nearest dung heap."

He hadn't been as quiet as he thought. The silence in the audience chamber caused both of them to stop glaring at each other and turn to find themselves the center of attention. Rahotep cleared his throat and marched over to the group of ministers near Ay. Meren found that he didn't care whether Rahotep was embarrassed before pharaoh, councillors, and great priests. He stalked around old Parenefer and knelt before the king.

"Golden one, I beg leave to return home to oversee the hunt for this creature. We must find it, or him, before it strikes again."

"Come," the king said.

Meren rose and mounted the dais upon which sat the king's golden chair. He knelt beside Tutankhamun.

"If by chance this killer isn't a demon, but one possessed, or a man of devious heart who marauds in disguise, then—"

"We're looking for the disguise, majesty. We—" He stopped because the king suddenly leaned closer and began to whisper.

"Meren, why would this—this thing come for you?"

Avoiding Tutankhamun's eyes, Meren shook his head. "I know not, majesty."

"Have you—that is . . . Is there any reason—"

"Like any man, I have sins for which I must answer, golden one."

"Great sins?"

Meren raised his eyes to the king's dark gaze. He wanted to say no, but he couldn't. Which was the greater sin—allowing a heretic to cause great suffering, or failing to save a heretic from the consequences of his own heresy? This was the dilemma that haunted his ka. This sin would blacken his heart forever. So he found himself speechless before pharaoh. To Meren's consternation, his silence caused the king to nod as if in understanding.

Then Tutankhamun smiled. "Do you know why I have such affection for you?"

"No, majesty."

"Because of all the great men, warriors, and princes about me, only you find it impossible to lie to me. Oh, I know you deceive me about things you consider for my own good. But if I ask you for the truth about yourself, you always give it."

"Majesty, you don't know what—"

"What you've had to do to survive?" Tutankhamun asked with bitter humor. "I am the son of a pharaoh, the brother of two pharaohs, ruler of an empire. I know, Meren. It's bred into my flesh."

"Thy majesty is as wise as the Nile is long."

"Go, Meren. You've spent too much time in Parenefer's company, and you're beginning to sound like him."

15

IN THE PAST few days Tentamun had come to wish he had never undertaken employment with Zulaya. Indeed, he had begged the gods to deliver him from this man, but his entreaties had brought no rescue. When the stranger had come to his village asking questions about Satet, Hunero, and Bay, he had led the man to Zulaya. Now Tentamun was Zulaya's guest, a guest without the freedom to leave.

He wasn't imprisoned or maltreated. Zulaya's steward had given him a chamber in a small, white-plastered house that lay opposite the main residence. They fed him and even provided clothing. But someone was always around. If he left the house and walked toward the gates, a servant or a guard always appeared and watched him. Tentamun had never been brave enough to continue on to the gate and past the sentries that stood there day and night.

He'd been here four days. Or had it been five now? In all that time he hadn't seen the stranger again. The first night he'd awakened to muffled screams. They'd been distant, as if coming from underground, but the screams had grown faint, then inaudible. Tentamun hadn't been able to sleep again until dawn. Now he waited in a richly decorated antechamber for an interview with Zulaya, and he was afraid of what would happen to him once he entered his master's presence.

The first time he'd seen Zulaya had been over a year ago. A fine pleasure yacht had docked near the village, and the cook from the kitchen boat that served it had come seeking fresh fruit and meat. Tentamun was drawn to the ship, which was painted a deep lotus-leaf green. It had a white deckhouse with a painted gold frieze around it. The people on board wore filmy, cloudlike clothes and jewels that glittered more than sunlight on water. He had never seen the like.

For hours Tentamun watched the ship, a craft built only for leisure, and the richly dressed occupants who seemed to have nothing to do but sit beneath multicolored awnings and sip cool drinks while slaves fanned them. Then he looked down at his own loincloth with its patched tears and soiled spots that no scrubbing could remove.

That day he had promised himself that someday he would own such a ship. It would be just like this one, a shining green leaf forever floating in the gentle current. And he would rest on a gilded couch, his body cool from the breeze of a dozen fans, his eyes closed against the glare of the sun, with no work to do and only orders to give that work should be done. No more trudging behind an ox pulling a plow. No more threshing grain beneath the withering white eye of the sun.

As he dreamed of a life of riches and laziness, Zulaya had appeared, crossing the plank to shore like a god stepping out of the sun boat of Ra. He'd been dressed in a foreign robe tied at the shoulder and secured by a golden lion pin. Tentamun remembered the robe's color, a deep, dark red like the finest jasper. But what he remembered most vividly were Zulaya's hands. Clean, long fingers without the disfigurement of large knuckles, they had been free of calluses and scars. Unlike Tentamun's, the nails were unbroken and free of soil.

Zulaya said he'd noticed Tentamun's interest. He offered employment. Tentamun didn't hesitate. Because he had wanted a boat of lotus-leaf green and clean hands without blemishes.

Nebra came in through the tall double doors of Zulaya's apartments and beckoned. Tentamun disliked Nebra, although he'd never spoken to the man. He disliked Nebra because he moved like a cobra and had eyes like the false glass ones used by artisans for statues and death masks. Nebra seemed to have no position about the household or tasks to perform. He appeared suddenly and stayed for many days, during which his only occupation seemed to be secret conferences with Zulaya. Then he vanished again.

Nebra had an Egyptian name, but his skin was a shade lighter than most men's, and his hair had an auburn tint. It was a natural color, similar to that hairdressers achieved with henna. But what was most disturbing about Nebra was his youth; he was only a few years older than Tentamun.

In spite of his age, however, his appearance always caused a stir in Zulaya's household. Servants grew jittery and dropped things. Guards found patrols in the fields and desert suddenly rewarding. Slaves sent to wait upon Nebra went unwillingly and returned with great speed. And yet Nebra was quiet, undemanding, courteous.

As he passed Nebra in the doorway, Tentamun glanced quickly at him. It was obvious that Tentamun hardly existed in whatever landscape those glasslike eyes surveyed. Tentamun shivered, for he suddenly realized that Nebra reminded him of a shabti, a statuette provided in a tomb so that it would perform any labor demanded of the deceased by the gods. With his vivid coloring and almost total lack of facial expression, Nebra could be a magically animated statuette. When he was still, Nebra gave the impression that he was waiting and would wait for eternity to perform some mysterious and frightening task for his master.

Tentamun had hoped that Nebra would leave once he'd admitted him, but he guided him into a room of high columns and bright airiness. Leaving Tentamun, Nebra crossed the chamber to the long, low window that formed a kind of balcony running most of the length of the room's west wall. Zulaya was there, a hand resting on a low balustrade as he gazed out at the Nile. Nebra whispered to him, then retreated to lean against a column on the balcony. Zulaya beckoned without looking at Tentamun.

"Come."

Tentamun went cold, but forced his legs to take him to his master. Zulaya still didn't look his way. The balcony overlooked the lapis lazuli band of the Nile, and Zulaya seemed fascinated by the activity on the bank. There a freighter had docked. Hundreds of pottery jars had been stacked on the ship's deck in an orderly mountain. Sailors perched on the slope of the mountain, on the deck, and ashore in a line, swinging the vessels to each other in a chain of motion.

Farther along the bank where the ground was level, workmen scooped up rich, dark mud and slapped it into wooden brick molds. Line after line of drying bricks marched up the slopes of dry ground. Beyond the brick molds, gangs of laborers shored up canal banks and dikes, for Inundation would soon turn the Nile into an inland sea.

Zulaya suddenly leaned out and pointed across the river, beyond the west bank, at a trading caravan. Dark-robed, herding a long line of donkeys bearing panniers, the group trudged away from the Nile on its way to one of the desert oases. Two of their company struggled with several bulky parcels wrapped in tattered sailcloth. Finally the last bundle was strapped into a pannier and the donkey persuaded to join the line plodding out to the sand.

"There," Zulaya said with quiet satisfaction. "A scene of peace and beauty. I never fail to gain pleasure from watching the life of the Nile." He cocked his head to the side and smiled at Tentamun. "And of course, it pleases me that we're rid of that annoying spy you brought me."

"Rid of him, master?"

Zulaya wasn't paying much attention. His gaze had returned to the caravan. "Yes. The desert will swallow what we no longer have use for. It was fortunate one of my parties was about to set out."

A lump formed in Tentamun's throat as he darted a look at the last donkey plodding along, its tail flicking back and forth, the panniers on its back bobbing gently as it walked. Was Zulaya referring to the cargo loaded on that donkey? Tentamun couldn't make himself ask. He might get an answer he didn't want.

Zulaya closed his eyes, took a deep breath, and let it out slowly. "When my affairs become too pressing or I find myself growing annoyed or weary, I come here. Gazing upon the Nile is like a small rebirth." Zulaya glanced down at Tentamun, his smile fading only slightly. "And now that I've renewed myself, we will talk. We've never done that, have we?"

"No, master."

"Come, then. You may sit on that stool. Don't concern yourself with Nebra. He too enjoys the scene from my window, and he's most interested in what you have to say."

"But I know nothing more than what I've told you, master."

"Oh, I'm not talking about that spy you brought. He was persuaded to confess the nature of his interest in your village. Forget him."

Tentamun lowered himself to the stool, glad that he wouldn't have to keep his knees from folding but more alarmed than ever. A master did not allow an underling to sit in his presence, especially not on a stool. Zulaya sat in a chair fitted with cushions of the softest leather and placed his feet on a padded rest. His robe, long, loose, and decorated with borders of electrum roundels in the shape of rampant bulls, settled around his legs. The material made a hushed, rustling sound that increased Tentamun's tension.

"Now, my dear youth, are you quite comfortable?"

"Yes, master." He was going to die, and Zulaya was playing with him for amusement. What master asked after the comfort of a hired man?

Zulaya picked up a faience cup from a tray beside his chair. "You may have water, but no beer. I want your heart alert."

Tentamun's palms were damp as he took the cup and sipped. All his thoughts seemed to falter, then stop, although Zulaya remained gracious and seemed unconcerned.

"Are you hungry?"

Tentamun wished the man would simply kill him. "No, master."

"Good."

Zulaya arranged the folds of his robe, then rested his hands on the arms of his chair. His fingers spread over the gleaming cedar. Each of them was encircled with a ring. The rings all consisted of a tinted red-gold hoop threaded through an engraved bezel of lapis lazuli, malachite, or amethyst. Tentamun watched the splayed fingers slowly curl around the chair arm, then open, then close again. When the movement ceased and the hands went limp, Tentamun lifted his gaze.

His master leaned forward and spoke in a confiding tone. "Now, dear youth, we will begin again. I want you to search your heart. Think carefully, with precision and clarity, back to that day when the scribe came seeking the former royal cook. I am going to listen to your tale again and again. And you, my dear youth, are going to repeat all you know until you can describe this unknown scribe in a much more accurate manner than you have previously."

"But I have described him, master."

"Not well," Zulaya said, his smile recalling delightful childhood games. "I want you to do it well, in the manner of harpists who compose songs and epics of the gods."

"But—"

"And if you find yourself unable to comply, I'm sure Nebra will be happy to help you find the words that will give me a most vivid image of this mysterious scribe."

As Tentamun rubbed his damp palms on his thighs, he glanced over his shoulder in the direction of Zulaya's gaze. He met the colored-glass stare of Nebra, who gave him a smile that was the mirror of Zulaya's.

"I find that Nebra's presence somehow inspires people to great descriptive feats," Zulaya said while Tentamun remained trapped in that lifeless stare. "I'm sure he will do the same for you, dear youth."

SOKAR PACED AROUND his office. His was an irregular route because of the chests and wicker boxes strewn across the floor. A plague of charioteers had descended upon him after he'd fallen into disfavor with the Eyes of Pharaoh. They'd taken every note and document from the last six months and left without telling him his fate.

He was so disturbed that he'd been imagining monsters in the dark. Of course, he'd been drinking to assuage his sorrow at being so unjustly treated. That was why the shadows had jumped at him in ghastly forms. That was why.

But his men had seen the monster too. They said it was the demon that was preying in the city. Should he tell anyone? No. They would think he was telling a tale to get himself noticed after incurring the wrath of Lord Meren.

"Min is to blame for this. Oh, misfortune and ruin. I'm undone, and all because of a few lowborns."

Sokar wiped sweat from his upper lip and dried his hands on his kilt. He tried sitting on his stool, but that only brought him a better view of the wreckage of his office. He got up and hurried to a table where his aide had left food for him, including a fresh date cake. Breaking the loaf in half, Sokar took a bite and lapsed into the thoughtless haze that often accompanied his eating. More comfortable, he wandered back to his stool and sat down again. He shouldn't become so upset over a scare in the night.

He was almost through with the cake when he glimpsed a small pile of ostraca, the pottery shards and flakes of limestone upon which notes were often taken. On top of the pile lay a large shard from a water jar. It was covered with notes, notes he'd forgotten. The remains of the cake dropped from his fingers. He licked crumbs from his lips. Wiping his mouth with the back of his hand, Sokar maneuvered himself to his feet and picked up the shard.

"The two old dead ones from the house."

He had refused to go when one of his men reported these deaths. He'd had enough to do without dragging himself across the city to look at corpses of two old fools who'd gotten themselves killed, probably by a thief. What if this incident was like those others! Sokar scanned the notes. No, the old ones had been stabbed. Sokar sighed and tossed the shard back on the pile.

"Amun be praised. I'm safe. Or am I?"

He thought hard. Had he remembered to include this case in his report? Yes, yes, he had, and he'd even inquired if the couple had family in the city. They didn't, so he'd ordered them given burials in the cemetery reserved for the poor. Certainly they wouldn't get embalmed. There would be no elaborate rituals performed by funerary priests, but that was the fate of the poor and the unknown. It wasn't his fault. Nobody could say it was his fault.

Sokar's body slumped as he sighed again and went to his food table. He reached for a water bottle. Downing most of its contents, he picked up the remaining half of the date cake, a jar of beer, several spice buns, and some figs. Piling these on a tray, he added fish cakes, a honey loaf, and a melon. He picked up the tray and went back to his stool, where he placed it on the table next to him and began eating.

He'd been so worried after having offended Lord Meren that he hadn't eaten very much. But time had passed, and no demand that he be replaced had come. Either Lord Meren had forgotten him, or the Eyes of Pharaoh had decided that Sokar's offense wasn't so very great.

"After all," he said to himself with his mouth full of fish cake, "who were they but common laborers? And a cursed barbarian Hittite."

He would go about his business, perform his duties as usual. He couldn't be blamed for anything. Sokar gulped down some beer and yelled for his aide.

"Get in here and clean up. How can I work in this refuse heap?"

KYSEN STRODE OUT of the house with Bener and Isis close behind him. On the loggia Abu waited with a chariot and a squad of men.

Bener spoke before he could. "You found Father. Where is he?"

"The lord is in his sailing boat, lady."

Isis let out a sigh, and Bener turned to Kysen with a smile of relief. "I told you he wasn't in danger. He's weary of being surrounded by guards. You know how he craves solitude."

"On the river?" Kysen asked. His father had eluded the men guarding him not long after the banishing ceremony performed by pharaoh.

"He could have told us what he intended instead of vanishing in the middle of the city," Isis said. Her eyebrows climbed her forehead as they did when she was vexed. "Father never thinks of us, only of himself."

Her siblings turned on her.

"If I were you, Mistress Run-away," Bener said, "I wouldn't accuse others of faults that weigh down my own heart. Especially not Father."

Kysen made a rude noise. "You know her. She thinks if she sulks and berates Father with cruel remarks he'll relent. I am amazed at her ability to ignore a lifetime's experience to the contrary."

"Go quickly," Bener replied with a glare at her sister. "I can send someone to you if there's news of the demon hunt."

Kysen jumped into the waiting chariot along with Abu. They drove to the canal nearest the house, where a boat carried them to the river. It was late in the day, only a couple of hours before dark. Fishing boats, pleasure craft, and freighters alike swarmed in the waters, and Kysen was forced to wait impatiently while the sailors of his own craft wove through the traffic upstream. Finally they sailed far enough from the docks to leave the crowds behind.

The waters were rising with the approaching flood, making the Nile wider. On this blue pool a craft about the size of a fishing boat floated toward him, its sail furled. In it sat Meren, his hand on a steering oar. Kysen's boat surged forward with the breeze and cut across the river to meet Meren's craft in midstream. Meren guided his boat alongside the larger one, and Kysen joined him. Before anyone else could get in, Meren shoved the two vessels apart with his oar. Abu gripped the mast and stared after them, then settled down to follow at a distance.

Kysen sat facing his father, who resumed his placid, zigzag course downstream. Meren began as if Kysen had been in the boat all along.

"We haven't found Tcha again, have we?"

"No. He isn't at Ese's, and she has searched for him too."

"He might have seen something, perhaps even Eater of Souls. If he's still alive, he might be able to tell us where to find her."

"I should have kept hold of him when I met Othrys, but he disappeared while I was dealing with him and his supposed scribe. I think Tcha would have told us if he knew where the creature dwells, though, in order to protect himself."

"Perhaps." Meren turned the boat toward the east bank.

Kysen could no longer contain his impatience. "You should not have gone out alone. The demon could have attacked, and you would have had no aid."

"Look around, Ky. How could anyone approach without me seeing them?"

Kysen glanced over the flat expanse of the river. Several skiffs hugged the steep banks, but here there were no great papyrus swamps or thickets of reeds as there were farther north.

"That dead farmer," Meren said. "Min said that the only remarkable thing that happened to him was nearly getting run down by a chariot. That was why he was drinking at the tavern, to recover from the fright."

"I knew it!" Kysen exclaimed. "You've discovered something. I told Bener and Isis you wouldn't have vanished if you hadn't learned something important."

He waited, but Meren avoided his gaze and turned the boat toward the west bank. "The tavern woman entertained many customers the night she was killed. We're tracing them through the tavern keeper, but some he knew only by the goods they used to pay him." A distant look appeared on Meren's face. "The tavern keeper said Anat left before her work was done. He was furious, because her next customer was a man of good appearance who could have paid well. But when Anat refused him, he left much offended."

"And Tcha's partner in thievery had just tried to rob a nobleman's house," Kysen added.

"I need to question Tcha. I want to know which nobleman he and his partner visited that night."

Kysen stared at his father, who was calmly surveying the course downriver. "You've discovered something."

"I don't know," Meren said. "There seems to be nothing that would relate the dead ones, and yet . . . I keep thinking about them—a careless farmer, a negligent tavern woman who leaves her work early, a thief who dies after committing a robbery. And then there's Mugallu, who was killed after nearly provoking pharaoh into a war."

"And you," Kysen said quietly.

"And me." Meren shifted his weight and pulled the steering oar toward him. "Eater of Souls attacked me, but why?"

"Because you are searching for her."

"Would a demon care?"

"If you interfered in her work, yes."

Furrows appeared between Meren's brows. "You find nothing remarkable about this group?"

"Father, their hearts were stolen."

"Then perhaps I'm wrong," Meren said to himself.

Kysen would have pursued this discussion, but he felt the boat suddenly change direction to veer away from the riverbank. Meren nodded toward a spot where the bank sloped gradually and water lapped at the soil. The waters churned. The black mud suddenly rose up and grew jaws and teeth. Spine-backed crocodiles snapped at something beneath the water. One rolled over and over between the writhing bodies of its fellows. Kysen knew what that twisting wallow meant. Lacking the ability to tear with its jaws, the crocodile used this method to rend its victim's flesh into manageable chunks.

"About these three men of whom your pirate is so afraid," Meren said.

Kysen dragged his gaze from the crocodiles. If Meren wasn't worried, the victim must have been an animal.

"Dilalu the weapons merchant, Zulaya the Babylonian, and the Egyptian officer called Yamen." There hadn't yet been time to deal with the knowledge Othrys had given him.

"Yes," Meren said. "Dilalu and Yamen are in Memphis, but Zulaya is not. I have heard of Yamen, but not the other two. But none of these men had positions at court during Akhenaten's reign. One of them may know something about Nefertiti's death, but his role must have been indirect. Once Eater of Souls has been caught, or ceases to prey among the living, we will discuss methods by which we will explore the activities of these three."

"None of them is important," Kysen said. "Not to me. What is important is keeping you safe. Will you come home now?"

"Am I not sailing back to the city?"

"Don't pretend surprise, Father. And I'm not going to be distracted. You've had the look of a man who has seen the lakes of fire in the netherworld ever since Eater of Souls attacked you. You're not a coward, but I saw your face when Parenefer accused you of sin that provoked an attack by Eater of Souls. What is wrong?"

Meren shoved the steering oar against the current, and the boat turned slowly. Kysen waited, knowing he dared press no harder for an answer. There were some secrets Meren told no one. Some he guarded with his very life. Abu's boat was drawing nearer, and as it approached, Kysen gave up hope of a response.

"What has changed in Memphis that would draw the attention of the gods and Eater of Souls?" Meren asked in a harsh whisper.

"Nothing has changed."

Meren leaned forward to hiss at Kysen. "Something has changed, my son. Search your heart, your intelligent heart. What has changed is this—you and I seek the murderer of a queen."

"I don't understand."

Meren leaned back and worked the oar. "Nor do I. But I do understand that the queen's death was part of an intricate game of power, a game that isn't over. Someone is still playing, Ky, and I can't tell which action is a move in that game and which is not."

"Then what are we going to do?"

"At the moment," Meren said as he guided the boat toward Abu, "we're going to try to stay alive."

Kysen grinned. "I always try."

"An admirable goal," Meren said with a slight smile. His gaze drifted ahead to a trading vessel loaded with ivory tusks, ebony logs, and cages of birds with iridescent blue and orange feathers.

Kysen noted that look of vague reverie. "You're still troubled, and not about the nature of the demon's victims."

"I'm sure I've missed something, but I've gone over everything—the white feathers, that sandal print, the places where the murders were done. No sign or object leads to any particular person. Assuming that Eater of Souls is a person, that is."

Kysen rubbed his chin. "I think you're angry with yourself, Father."

"And I think you're impudent," Meren said mildly.

"You're angry because you didn't defeat Eater of Souls when you fought; you weren't even able to see her clearly."

Meren pounded on the steering oar. "Can you see across the garden by the light of a few distant torches?"

"No."

"I'll tell you what I saw," Meren snapped. "I saw a leathery snout filled with jagged teeth, a lion's mane, and those evil bronze claws." He glanced at the cuts on his arm before going on. "I saw a yellow eye with a slit of a pupil. That's what I saw. Otherwise, all I saw was a cursed ax blade so honed and polished it gleamed in what little light there was. You've been in battle, Ky. You know the things you remember. I can remember those teeth, those lifeless animal eyes, and those bladelike claws as if they were before me at this—"

Meren's hand went still on the oar. Kysen almost spoke, but instinct warned him not to interfere with whatever thought had stopped his father in midsentence. He watched a lock of Meren's hair stray over his forehead. Zar would be offended that his master had yet again removed his finery while out of the house. Meren continued to stare blankly past Kysen's left shoulder.

"Father?"

"Mmm."

"You have remembered something?"

"What?"

"You've remembered something."

"I—I'm not certain."

"Tell me, and I might be able to help."

Meren didn't answer at first, then he shook his head. "I must consider well before I speak. It's too dangerous."

"I consort with thieves, a murderous Greek pirate, and Ese. What more danger could I face?"

Meren's gaze focused on him at last, and Kysen saw a flicker of pain quickly disguised. "Oh, much more, Ky. Much, much more."

16

HIS ABSENCE HAD caused the evening meal to be late. Distracted by his discovery on the boat with Kysen, Meren had eaten without paying much attention to his food until he realized Bener had been putting more helpings of lotus roots, roast crane, and *shat* cakes before him. Now, although it was late, he still felt overstuffed. Bener said it was his fault for failing to eat enough to keep his belly from shriveling. He didn't argue because he was still chasing an idea, following it as one tracks an antelope down a crooked desert path between steep-sided cliffs, carefully and with the wariness of a lion.

Finally Bener had ordered him out of the hall so that the servants could clean. He was instructed to go with Kysen to the roof, where the night breeze would be the strongest. After surveying the darkened city, they had perched on the wall top that formed a balustrade around the roof. Meren took a goblet of wine from Kysen, but he was distracted from his deliberations only when he heard music. Looking across the roof, he saw three musicians seated on a mat. One played the double pipes, another a harp, and the third a flute that produced deep, mellow tones.

"Bener thinks you have forgotten how to be at ease," Kysen said.

Meren glanced at the musicians again. "Bener is perceptive, but I haven't the time to correct my bad habits at the moment. Ky, we've been looking for Eater of Souls in the wrong places."

"But she attacked most of her victims in the foreign district and near the docks."

"All of the dead ones inconvenienced people."

Kysen frowned at this sudden change of subject. "I thought we were discussing where to find the demon."

"We are." Meren set his goblet aside. "The farmer nearly caused a chariot to crash. The tavern woman deserted a customer. Tcha's partner robbed someone."

"I see."

"Ky, Eater of Souls, if she is a living person, has to be noble."

"A noblewoman."

Meren shook his head. "You still don't follow my path. The tavern woman's customer, the chariot driver, the one who was robbed, I think they are the same man."

"A man who disguises himself and kills because he is inconvenienced?" Kysen asked with a stare.

"You sound doubtful."

"Father, you've plucked this notion from your imagination more than from knowledge." Kysen sighed when Meren folded his arms over his chest and said nothing. "What signs are there that Eater of Souls is a nobleman?"

"I told you."

"You told me things you've surmised."

"There's also the ax."

"An ax can be borne by any man, or woman."

"This wasn't an ax used by a carpenter or chariot maker," Meren replied. "Those axes are plain, and you've seen the ones used by wood-choppers. Their handles are long, and many have semicircular blades. This was a battle-ax, Ky."

"Which any common soldier possesses."

"Not this one." Meren stood and leaned against the roof wall. "I should have noticed before, but I've been paying attention to the more frightening features of Eater of Souls—the claws, the crocodile's head and jaws, the feather placed where the heart should be. What I saw was a battle-ax, but not one used by an ordinary soldier. It was like those given to great warriors by generals and kings."

Kysen said nothing for a moment, then whispered, "By the gods. Are you certain?"

"It had an elongated blade, like the ones we use in battle," Meren said. "But I think there's engraving on the flat of the blade, and the handle has sets of parallel groves inset with gold. The wood isn't ash or sycamore. I think it must be stained cedar or dark brown ebony. The leather thongs that bind the blade and support the handle are gilded with red gold. When I stopped concentrating on Eater of Souls and began to search for other memories that were as clear but not so frightening, I finally recalled the ax."

"By the gods," Kysen repeated softly. He turned to meet his father's eyes. "Who have you inconvenienced of late?"

"Should you not ask whom I haven't inconvenienced?"

"This isn't a time for jests."

"Bener says I need merriment and leisure." Meren held up his hand. "Very well, don't frown like a priest-instructor faced with a dozen inattentive pupils. The list of those I've annoyed is long, even if I include only recent weeks. There's the Great Royal Wife."

"Father, please be serious."

"And Princess Tio."

"Hmm."

"You don't appreciate my humor, Ky. I also annoyed Mugallu, but he's dead. Then there's Djoser, who's mad because I won't support Lord Reshep, and there's Reshep himself. Of course, I could include others at court and General Labarnas."

"Not a Hittite."

"Of course not," Meren said. "And I've managed to make Rahotep furious."

"I saw him at Ese's. He was in one of his drinking miseries."

"These black moods of his are growing more foul. I shall have to do something about him if he doesn't cure himself."

"Who else have you inconvenienced, Father?"

Meren smiled. "Apparently one of the three men so feared by Othrys."

"May Amun protect us."

"Yes, and that list contains only those I've annoyed recently and directly. A great man offends many, even if he tries not to, Ky."

They lapsed into silence as each contemplated the possibilities.

Meren rubbed his chin, feeling the rough stubble of a day's growth of beard. "Who have Mugallu and I both offended?"

They stared at each other, scowling, but a sudden din of female chatter caused them to break off. Bener marched up the interior stairway to the roof, turned, and snapped at her younger sister.

"I told you to instruct Mutemwia to watch her."

Isis stalked up the stairs, her perfectly arranged robes askew from the climb. "I don't have to do your bidding. You're only my sister."

"I'm mistress of the house," Bener said as she marched over to Meren. "And unless you're going to do all the work that entails, then that means I can give you orders. Now look what's happened, and it's all your fault."

"I'm not the one who lost her. You're the mistress of the house, so it's your fault."

"What's wrong?" Meren asked.

The girls turned to him and spoke at the same time.

"She lost Satet."

Meren shoved away from the wall. "What are you talking about?"

"I told Isis to tell Mutemwia to watch Satet so that she didn't leave the house and wander the city again, but she didn't do it."

Isis pinched a pleat in her robe and jerked it into shape. "I'm not a slave to be commanded by *her*."

"Luckily," Bener said with a scowl at her sister, "I noticed Satet was gone and told Abu. He followed her and just returned."

Meren headed for the stairs. "Ky, stay here with the girls." His son caught up with him halfway down the stairs.

"Bener and Isis have a houseful of servants and guards to protect them. You're the one who is apt to go about without protection."

"I'm not wasting time arguing," Meren said. They reached the bottom of the stairway, where Abu waited for them.

"She has gone to a house near the dock market, lord."

"Excellent," Meren replied. "We'll go there now."

"Wait, lord. You must have an escort."

"He's right, Father."

Meren threw up his hands. "I don't want to frighten the old woman. You may bring one man. And be quick. I'm leaving the moment my chariot is ready. I don't want her to run off elsewhere before we get there."

He was pleased with Abu's speed. By the time he stepped into his chariot, his aide had returned with Reia. Abu drove Meren while Reia accompanied Kysen. The trip to the dock market neighborhood was slowed by darkness, and in the market itself Meren called a halt.

"It isn't far, lord," said Abu.

Meren glanced around the open space bordered by houses, work-shops, and storage buildings. Those few still up at this hour weren't likely to be drawn to an empty market.

"I don't want the aged one to be frightened away by the noise of our approach," Meren said. "Reia will remain here with the chariots."

Soon he was standing in front of a meager house squeezed between two larger ones. The street was empty and silent. Meren held up a hand to prevent Abu from opening the door. Kysen began to ask him a question, but Meren silenced him with a gesture. Perhaps he was imagining that the quiet of this street was different from that of the others nearby or the market.

There seemed to be a void of sound surrounding this house, an absence of the noises that should have hung in the distance. Here it was as if the night had swallowed sound as it engulfed light. No dogs barked, no babies cried. Even the wind seemed afraid to blow, and Meren could hardly hear his own breathing. He glanced around, noting the deserted rooftops, the doorsteps without cats. This street was near the rough dock taverns. No doubt its inhabitants stayed inside with their doors barred at night.

He turned to Kysen and Abu. "Ky, you and Abu stay here. I don't want to alarm Satet and whoever she's visiting."

"Lord, I don't think there's anyone else in the house," Abu said. "It's too quiet."

"They may be in the rear."

"At least allow me to come with you," Kysen said.

"No. This is probably where her sister is staying, and we must go carefully so that we don't frighten off this cursed royal cook."

"I should at least go to the roof," Kysen said.

"Very well."

Meren pushed open the door to reveal a darkened front chamber. Beyond he could see a dim yellow glow. Nodding to Kysen, he slipped inside and shut the door. As he walked toward the light, a goose honked, causing him to start. Then he heard Satet.

"Be quiet, Beauty. I'll be finished soon. I must fold this sheet, or it won't fit in the basket. Look, I found my cosmetics box. I knew Hunero took it with her when she left."

Meren stepped into a kitchen lit by a single lamp. To his left lay a staircase that led to the second floor; to his right, an oven sat against the far wall beneath a ventilation hole in the roof. Jars of fruit, oil, and beer sat on shelves, while baskets lined the walls. Before one of them, near the oven, knelt Satet. She placed a folded linen sheet in a basket and looked up at him.

"You! Go away. I can't instruct your cooks anymore. I have this house now, and I'll be busy selling bread in the market."

"Where is your sister?"

"I don't know. She's terribly lazy. She might be asleep." Satet turned to Beauty, who was pecking at bread crumbs scattered by the oven. "What do you think, Beauty? Tell him what an indolent Hunero is. Was my sister not asleep when we first found her?"

Meren walked over to the stairs that led to the second story and glanced into darkness. He looked over his shoulder at Satet.

"You should have told me you found your sister."

As he spoke, Satet picked up a small cosmetics box, placed it on top of the sheet in the basket, and straightened. She glanced his way and gasped. Her mouth formed a cavern, while her eyes widened to the size of ripe olives. Meren looked at her expression and at the same moment felt a presence behind him. He whirled and dropped to a crouch. Something buzzed by his head, and he heard a snarl.

Meren threw himself backward. A giant shadow chased him, and he caught a glimpse of blank yellow eyes. With the speed of a leopard, claws lashed at him. It was all he could do to scramble out of reach before the ax came at his head again. There was no time to draw his dagger, no time to do anything but dodge, veer, and duck to avoid being slashed or hacked. He jumped aside as the creature sprang at him. Satet whimpered and fell to the floor senseless. Beauty squawked when Meren stepped on her foot, then flapped her wings and hissed.

Eater of Souls swung the ax, but with both hands Meren grabbed the arm that bore the weapon. To his horror, his strength was as a child's against the creature. The arm jerked free. The ax flew up. A clawed hand grabbed his neck, and he felt the blades cut into his flesh. It was then that he remembered his voice.

He shouted an alarm, twisted in that animal grip, and kicked. Eater of Souls roared, but struck again with the ax as Meren tried to pull free. Meren saw the blow coming, stopped struggling, and lunged down, pulling Eater of Souls with him. They hit the floor as he heard the front door crash open. Something hissed by his ear. Meren grabbed blindly and found Beauty. Snagging the goose by her neck, he threw her at Eater of Souls. Beauty landed on the creature's chest, wings flapping, neck stretched. She hissed once, then struck, lunging past the gaping jaws.

Meren heard a scream as he rolled away and jumped to his feet. The ax dropped as Eater of Souls drew both arms up for protection against the pummeling beak. At that moment Kysen raced down the stairs, his dagger drawn. Abu was in the doorway with his own weapon. Both drew back their arms, but Meren cried out.

"No!"

Eater of Souls thrust the goose away, grabbed the ax, and scrambled to a crouch. Grunting, her breath coming in loud rasps, she prepared to throw the weapon.

"Reshep, don't!"

The ax paused high in the air. The crocodile head tilted to the side. Then a high voice with the texture of sand issued from beneath the snout.

"Ammut, the Devouress, Eater of Souls, comes to destroy transgressors. I am sent by the gods to protect the favored one."

The voice sent waves of cold crashing through Meren's body. It wasn't Reshep's. This voice slithered through muddy, sluggish water. It basked motionless in the boiling heat of the sun for hours, then slid beneath the water close to the shore and lunged at unsuspecting and thirsty gazelles. And yet there was an undertone of grit, a rumbling purr that belonged in the deserts and savanna where it stalked prey through the tall grass.

Meren exchanged glances with Kysen and Abu. Neither had moved once they heard that voice. Kysen lifted his brows in a question. Meren shook his head.

"Reshep, I know it's you under that mask. Stop now."

"The gods have sent Eater of Souls."

"Reshep?" Kysen gaped at Eater of Souls. "Are you certain? Reshep has such a vain, lazy heart."

Abu shifted his weight, his arm still cocked to throw his dagger. "He's possessed."

Eater of Souls paid Abu no heed. The dead yellow eyes seemed to stare at Kysen, but then the snout turned and pointed toward Meren. In the shadowed light he could see that the preserved crocodile's head fit over Reshep's. The lower jaw came down to conceal half the man's face, while the lion's mane attached to it covered his neck and shoulders. A hippo hide emerged from the lion's mane in front and back and was attached to Reshep's kilt by leather thongs.

Reshep raised his arm to point at Meren. His hand was covered by a thick leather gauntlet. Finger stalls of polished bronze ended in curved, clawlike razors. One of them pointed at Meren.

"Evil one, source of pain and emptiness. Usurper of glory, worship, and power. You steal what is rightfully the favored one's, and you must be devoured."

The ax lifted, but Meren spoke quickly. "The favored one is Reshep?"

The ax paused.

"All who cause pain to Reshep must be devoured?" Meren asked softly.

Kysen's voice rose. "Father—"

"Be quiet!" Meren whispered sharply.

"The gods are merciless to those who deserve annihilation," Eater of Souls replied. The ax arm lowered. "The father of the chosen one, he caused much pain. His mouth poured forth scorn and reproach, endlessly, destroying the praises of the mother. There was great relief when the father was devoured."

"And the mother?"

"She praised the favored one, but only when he became a mirror by which her own perfections could be reflected. And she was a bottomless well, always needing, always empty, never content. She drained the Favorite of glory and perfection to feed herself."

"The gods decreed that she be devoured," Meren said.

There was no answer.

"And the farmer, he nearly caused your—Reshep's chariot to overturn."

Eater of Souls uttered a rumbling purr of assent. "The cursed simpleton stepped into the street without looking."

"The tavern woman?"

Eater of Souls raised the ax once more. "Judgment must be carried out."

"What about the Hittite?" Meren said loudly.

The Devouress hesitated, then raised her snout as if to test the scent of Abu and Kysen. Turning back to Meren, she lowered her weapon and rested the handle in both hands.

"The foreigner insulted the favored one. As you insult him by your existence."

When a crocodile is hungry, it lurks just beneath the surface of water near the bank, still, with soulless patience. When some small or weak creature ventures into the open to drink, it lunges out of the water and closes its jaws around a leg or neck. In a heartbeat the creature is dragged underwater, to be crushed and drowned under the weight of that slithering body. There is no sign of the attack, no warning snarl or growl. There was no warning when Eater of Souls lunged at Meren and swung the ax.

Meren threw himself aside, tripping over Satet's prone body. He felt the ax slash the air beside his ear as he tumbled to the floor. Landing on his side, he rolled even as Eater of Souls turned and swung the ax up. At that moment Meren heard a thud. Eater of Souls paused in swinging the ax overhead, two daggers protruding from his chest. Meren jumped up as the demon stumbled and fell. Kysen ran to his side while Abu approached the Devouress.

"He still lives, lord."

Meren and Kysen knelt beside the crocodile head, gripped the snout, and lifted it. Reshep's burning eyes appeared. Meren shoved the mask aside and turned back to Reshep, who was staring at Kysen. Then his gaze fastened on Meren. Sudden recognition flared. Meren heard a low, watery growl. Kysen and Abu shouted. Bronze claws struck, slashing at Meren, but Kysen rammed the battle-ax against Reshep's forearm. Reshep howled as Abu shoved one of the daggers deeper into his chest.

Shaken, Meren rose and stood looking at the body of the man, the crocodile's head, the mane and hide. Abu recited a banishing spell. Meren's lips moved silently as well. Kysen muttered an appeal to Amun for protection, then turned his attention to Satet, who was rousing from her faint. Beauty immediately flapped her wings at him and clacked her beak. Swearing, Abu grabbed the bird by the neck and thrust it into a large cage that sat beside the stairs.

While Kysen helped the old woman to a stool, Meren found a water bottle. He handed Satet a cup and poured her a drink.

"Reshep," Kysen said over Satet's head. "It was Reshep all this time. And he wanted to marry Isis, by the gods. What kind of unspeakable evil lodged in his heart that he could—"

Kysen's half-moon eyes narrowed as he and Meren stared at each other.

"He was possessed," Abu said. "Did you hear that voice? It was the voice of a fiend." He pulled his dagger from Reshep's body and began cleaning it on the hippo hide.

No one spoke. Satet began rocking back and forth while she hugged herself. Kysen stared at Reshep's body with a speculative look.

"A strange possession," Meren murmured.

Kysen turned to him. "What do you mean?"

Meren set the water jar aside, rose, and went to stand over the dead man. "I have been pondering something for a long time. Have you ever heard of one possessed by a demon or evil spirit only by night?"

Kysen shook his head.

"Or a demon who took the part of protector of a man?"

"Then why, lord?"

"I don't know," Meren said. He studied Reshep's unmoving features, now as immobile as those of his crocodile mask. "Perhaps I'm wrong, but I cannot understand why the great gods of Egypt would concern themselves with a petty noble and send the great Ammut, the Devouress and Eater of Souls, to protect him. Perhaps some other fiend made him sick so that Reshep imagined that he was this favored one simply because that is what he wished to believe. From what we've learned about him, his mother certainly told him that often enough."

"Then all this death, all this terror, was about Reshep and the things he wanted," Kysen said.

"I think his heart was crazed, possessed of some evil fiend," Meren said, "but not by Eater of Souls, and I'm almost certain not at the behest of Osiris, Amun, and Ra. The only chosen one of the gods in Egypt is pharaoh, may he have life, health, and prosperity."

"Reshep," Kysen said, shaking his head. "How did you know he was Eater of Souls?"

"Remember what I asked you? Whom had Mugallu and I both offended? I thought of several, but of those, I believed only Reshep truly had the kind of heart that would think small offenses deserving of death."

Meren was looking at Satet. The old woman was still rocking herself.

"Aged one?" Meren asked. She didn't reply.

He tried again. "Satet."

No answer.

"Ky, we should take Satet home. Abu, remain here, and I'll send Reia to you."

"Here, lord? What if our spells haven't banished the demon?" Abu was eyeing the crocodile head and making a sign against evil.

"Post yourself before the front door, and I'll send priests along with Reia," Meren said. He, too, wouldn't want to stay here alone with Reshep, or Eater of Souls.

As they helped Satet out of the house, Kysen paused. Meren heard a sharp intake of breath as his son turned to him, his face barely visible in the dark.

"What do you suppose he did with the hearts?"

Meren had been asking himself the same thing, and the more he asked, the more he wished he hadn't thought of the answer. "What does Eater of Souls do with the hearts of those condemned by the gods?"

He knew Kysen had understood him when his son pressed his lips together and swallowed. Silently they walked away from the house.

17

SHORTLY BEFORE DAWN Kysen strode down the corridor of the women's quarters and stuck his head in Bener's chamber. Bener was pacing but stopped when he appeared.

"You're back. Why were you so long?"

"Where is Isis? I expected to find her waiting with you."

"She went to bed hours ago. What happened? Didn't you find Satet?"

Kysen muttered under his breath and plunged down the hall. Bener caught up with him as he reached Isis's door and started pounding on it.

"Isis! Isis, you worthless piece of offal, I'm coming in!"

"What's wrong?" Bener demanded. "Where's Father?"

"He's gone to the palace." Kysen shoved the door open and darted into the chamber with Bener close behind.

Isis slept as perfectly as she dressed. Lying on her back, her head-rest supporting her head, she rested with a single sheet draped over her body. Her arms lay beneath the linen. Kysen reached out, grabbed a handful of artfully arranged hair, and yanked. Isis howled and shot out of her nest, spitting and clawing. Undaunted, Kysen pulled his sister off the bed and sent her spinning across the room. She bounced against a chest and knocked over a cosmetics table as she landed. Kohl tubes, tweezers, unguent pots, ivory combs, and several mirrors flew in different directions. A blue-and-yellow-striped cosmetics bottle shaped like a fish shattered at Kysen's feet.

Unhurt, Isis launched herself from the floor, snatching a pot as she went. She hurled it at him, screeching invectives. Kysen ducked and heard the pot hit a wall. Bener dodged flying shards. Several maids appeared in the doorway, but they vanished upon seeing Kysen. Isis bent to pick up a jar, but Kysen kicked it out of range and grabbed a handful of hair at the back of her head. He stuck his face close to hers and shouted over her shrieks.

"You spoiled, selfish spawn of a dung pit, you nearly got father killed!"

Bener thrust herself between them. "Stop this!"

She pulled on Isis's hair and Kysen's fist. Isis was screaming, jumping, and trying to kick Kysen. Rather than have Bener take blows meant for him, Kysen released his hold. Isis backed up, sputtering and breathing hard, but her curses didn't stop until Bener rounded on her.

"You shut your lips or I'll beat you myself."

Isis's mouth snapped closed. She smoothed her hair back from her face while glowering at her brother. Kysen was wishing he'd thought to bring his chariot whip.

Bener faced him. "What has happened?"

"We found Satet, and Father went into the house alone to fetch her. But Eater of Souls was waiting."

Neither of his sisters said anything. Eyes widening, Isis made a little sound that might have been a gasp.

Bener asked quickly, "Was Father hurt?"

"It was mere chance that the old woman warned him," Kysen said, his gaze fixed on Isis with ka-shriveling contempt. "But it couldn't have been chance that Eater of Souls knew where to find us. Isis has been seeing Reshep secretly, and I'll bet my finest thoroughbred it was their plan to use Satet to lure Father there."

"It was not!" Isis shouted.

Kysen stared at her. Bener stared at her.

"It wasn't," Isis said again, less loudly. When neither sibling replied, she burst out again. "How was I to know the demon would be there? Reshep said he wanted to talk to Father, to convince him that our marriage would be a great alliance. We knew Father would never agree to see Reshep again. He's so stubborn. But I knew that Father was interested in the old woman, and that if she vanished, he would chase after her. It's not my fault an evil demon followed him too. Is Reshep safe?"

Kysen shoved Bener out of the way and stuck his face close to Isis's. "You stupid she-goat, Reshep was Eater of Souls. If we hadn't killed him, he would have murdered Father."

He watched color ebb from his sister's face. Her great dark eyes stood out against the pale flesh. Her mouth half open, Isis shook her head.

"He's been killing anyone who got in his way, anyone who caused him the slightest annoyance." Kysen straightened and folded his arms over his chest, still burning Isis's flesh with his stare. "He knew he was the favorite of the gods. He'd convinced himself of it. And because he believed it, he knew that the gods would send help to ease his way in the world. That help was Eater of Souls."

"You're crazed," Isis whispered.

"You think I'd make up such a tale?" Kysen gave a snort of disgust. "Why would you find it difficult to believe that Reshep thought himself chosen by the gods when you believe the same thing about yourself?"

"Oh, Isis," Bener said with a look of disbelief.

Her sister's disapproval seemed to affect Isis as Kysen's had not. She winced, and silent tears began to trickle down her cheeks.

"I only wanted to—"

"Have your own wish!" Kysen bellowed. "Without thinking of anyone else." He poked Isis with a finger as he spoke. "And you almost got Father killed. Had he not been quick, had Abu and I not been there, Reshep would have bashed in his skull, slashed his throat, and carved out his heart!"

Isis gave a shriek and buried her head in her hands. Bener rolled her eyes and shook her head. Kysen watched Isis for a moment, then turned and marched out of the room. Bener came with him, and together they went out of the house to the kitchen building. He found a bottle of wine in a pantry room, and Bener brought cups and a loaf of bread. They took their food to the family garden. Sitting under an old acacia tree, they each downed a cup of wine before they spoke.

"All she had to do was see that the old woman got out of the house at a time when Reshep was waiting to follow," Kysen said.

"Does Father suspect?" Bener asked.

"You should have seen him," Kysen said. "We were looking at Reshep in his strange costume. He wore a preserved crocodile's head, you know. And Father suddenly said Isis's name in a voice so faint I barely heard it."

Kysen shook his head slowly. "The first thing he thought of was how Reshep had been in this house, on his ship, near you and Isis, and then he realized . . ." He took a long drink of wine. "He actually shuddered. He closed his eyes so I wouldn't see his pain, but he shuddered."

"She didn't know, Ky. She would never hurt Father on purpose."

"No," Kysen said. "And do you know why? Because to do something to someone deliberately, you have to be thinking of them. Isis seldom thinks of anyone but herself."

"You're angry. In a few days, when you're calmer, you'll see a different picture."

"Why can't she be sensible, like you?"

Bener sighed and poured herself more wine. "You and Father are always complaining about me, too. You're not satisfied with either of us."

"You have a good ka, Bener. Isis has an evil one."

"Not evil, just one in need of strong guidance. But I think this disaster will force her to see something in her mirror besides her pretty face."

"Her sight had better improve quickly, because Father will speak to her when he returns, and if she shrieks and whines and lashes at him with her tongue, I'm going to drop her down the kitchen well and seal it with a granite slab."

Bener rose and offered a hand to help Kysen rise. "Your heart isn't thinking clearly, my dear brother. If you want Isis to suffer, you should take away all her cosmetics, her mirrors, her perfume of Mendes and oil of lilies, and her jewels and robes."

"You are a clever one," Kysen said as he got up.

Bener punched him lightly on the shoulder. "I'll pretend to console her in my chamber if you'll seize her treasures."

A nasty grin grew on Kysen's face.

"Father will only confine her to her chamber. True repentance is attained through sacrifice."

"Then we're but helping Isis to sail on the route to divine order and rightness as a servant of Maat," Bener said with great solemnity.

Kysen patted his sister's arm. "True, and to help her keep on a righteous course, I'll give all her trinkets to the women at Ese's tavern."

MEREN WALKED IN a circuit around Reshep's body as he composed his report to pharaoh aloud. One of the younger charioteers sat on the floor with a sheet of papyrus stretched over his crossed legs and wrote down his words. Other men swarmed through the house, inspecting everything from the flour bins to the cheap senet game in the bedchamber.

As Meren spoke, he tried to ignore the way his chest ached with the dull, insistent pain with which he'd become too familiar. His youngest daughter had betrayed him. She hadn't known how dangerous her betrayal was, but she hadn't given much thought to anyone but herself.

He had stopped talking, and his men were looking at him. He resumed, pushing all thoughts of Isis out of his heart. Satet had been taken home where Nebamun the physician could care for her, and there was no sign of her sister Hunero or the husband. The house had been cleaned recently, probably by Satet on one of her secret excursions. Meren was furious with himself for not keeping a closer watch on her.

His negligence was a sign of how much confusion Eater of Souls had caused. Had he not been submerged in guilt over why Eater of Souls had attacked him, he would have pursued his inquiries with Satet more quickly. He would have to remember not to allow his personal sentiments to interfere with his duty to pharaoh and Maat.

"Thus ends the matter of the one called Eater—"

"Egyptian! Egyptian, who are you to send for me as if I was a miserable vassal?"

Labarnas roared into the kitchen with Abu, Reia, and several charioteers right behind him. The Hittite saw Meren first and headed for him, only to be halted by Reshep's body blocking his path. Labarnas was in mid-roar, and his voice cracked. He stepped back and bumped into Abu, but didn't seem to notice. Muttering something in his own language, he made a magical sign before scowling at Meren.

"Why have you dragged me to this place?"

"You said you wanted the one responsible for your prince's death." Meren nodded at Reshep. "This is the one."

Labarnas looked down at the body, the crocodile mask. He walked around to the head, kicked the hippo hide that covered Reshep's thigh, and grunted.

"I've seen this one."

"On my ship, when Prince Mugallu visited," Meren said as he walked over to join Labarnas. "Mugallu insulted him, and this man avenged himself."

"Is this how you Egyptians settle a quarrel?" Labarnas planted his fists on his hips. His voice was as loud as a rock slide. "Hittite warriors with differences face each other and fight under the open sky of the storm god. Prince Mugallu was struck down by cowardice. I will tell my king, the Sun, how you allowed his intimate friend to be slaughtered like an ox."

"Reshep killed many, for far less than the insults Prince Mugallu gave him."

"After your pharaoh insulted the prince deliberately!"

Meren sighed, walked over to a chair that had been brought for his use, and sat down. "Labarnas, do you know how irritating you are?"

"Irritating? I'll irritate you, you perfumed, soft-skinned lotus sniffer."

Meren held up a hand. It was a gesture he used to command silence among his charioteers, and he'd employed it without thinking. Labarnas stopped his tirade, then looked annoyed at himself for doing so.

"Allow me to finish before you lose your temper. You irritate me, Hittite, because you make accusations without knowing what has occurred. You take offense against pharaoh and all Egyptians as though your only purpose in coming to Egypt was to provoke a war. And you accuse me of negligence regarding Prince Mugallu and imply that there's some plot against your king."

"Everyone knows that you Egyptians are born to deceit. You construct plots as easily as you construct great temples and palaces of gold and lapis lazuli."

Meren leaned back in his chair and smiled. "Exactly."

"Don't smirk at me, you cursed Egyptian." Labarnas frowned. "What do you mean, exactly?"

"Engage in a bit of reasoning, general. If I'm so versed in deceit and trickery, could I not have found a way to murder Prince Mugallu without placing myself or any Egyptian under suspicion?"

"No doubt you tried and failed."

Rising, Meren shook his head and walked over to Labarnas. He swept his arm in the direction of Reshep's body.

"The diplomacy of death, my dear general, requires subtlety, a delicacy of construction, and above all, simplicity of design." Meren lowered his voice and said softly, "You can be assured that if I had wanted to kill Prince Mugallu, he, you, and your whole party would have been allowed to leave Egypt first. Then, once you were past the great border fortresses, well into the barren lands between them and the nearest city to the north, you would vanish. Quickly, in silence, as though a desert storm had swept you away into the vast emptiness of the frontier and buried you beneath a mountain of sand."

Holding Labarnas's gaze with his eyes, Meren paused with a slight smile. "Oh, I would search for you, send word to your king, invite him to send Hittite troops to search. All in vain. Until one day, on an expedition deep into the Sinai, your troops would find the remains of a battle, and nothing but ashes from flaming arrows, and bones dressed in Hittite armor."

No one moved. Sounds of the house search reached them, but no others. Finally Labarnas gave a sharp bark of laughter.

"Did I not say pharaoh's people worshiped the god of deceit? You've just proved me right, Egyptian."

"Then you understand that these murders were the work of this one man. Remember the thief, the tavern woman, and the farmer."

Labarnas bent and touched the crocodile mask on the snout, then rose and eyed Meren. "When I tell the great king, I'll still blame pharaoh for not providing safe lodging for the emissary."

"Of course."

"I want to leave at once."

"I will beg pharaoh, may he have life, health, and prosperity, for permission."

"Hmmmph. For an Egyptian, you're almost tolerable. I would have killed you, had I been successful in escaping with you that night."

"I know," Meren said.

"But now," Labarnas said as he turned to leave, "I think I would have paid dearly for it."

"May Amun protect you on your journey."

"And may the storm god bless your fate, Egyptian. The next time we meet won't be in some gold-encrusted audience chamber but on a battlefield."

"You sound certain."

"I am, Egyptian. I am."

The moment Labarnas was gone, Meren turned to Abu. "Still no sign of the cook and her husband?"

"No, lord. We found the man who rented this house to them. He's a priest of Ptah, holder of the office of keeper of the cattle of Ptah, which means he knows little except that he assigned the managing of the property to one of his servants. The actual owner lives in another town."

"Find the real owner, Abu."

"It will take time, lord."

"Find him, and find out how the cook came to rent this place from him. Curse Reshep a thousand times. Seeing him has addled Satet's wits so that I fear she'll never regain them."

"Lord, she had little left in any case."

"She could make sense on occasion, if she really desired it." Meren glanced around the kitchen. "Someone has cleaned this house recently."

"Satet, lord."

"Perhaps. But the couple's possession's are still here. They should be here."

"Aye, lord."

Meren watched Reia free Beauty from her cage and toss scraps of bread to her. "Abu, it would be well to discover if there is or was any connection between Reshep and the cook or her husband. There probably isn't, but thoroughness is a virtue."

"Yes, lord, but it's almost dawn."

Meren glanced up at the diffuse light coming through windows. Abu was reminding him that his duty demanded that he report the discovery of Eater of Souls to pharaoh.

"What am I to say to the living god, Abu? That Reshep killed people who interfered with his desires? That anyone who irritated him got his heart cut out? What monstrous fiend infested his ka?"

"He was possessed by a demon, lord."

"And by the ghost of a mother who raised Reshep to believe in his own perfection and a father who drank and failed to attend to his son's raising."

The light coming through the windows grew brighter. "I must go to pharaoh with my report."

Officially, Meren's task was to guard against anything that might threaten pharaoh or Maat in Egypt. He, and others like him, used their unique blend of clandestine knowledge gathering and overt intimidation against the myriad threats to the divine order. Yet Tutankhamun seemed most enthralled with the more mundane aspects of Meren's duties.

Bound by rigid royal tradition and duty, he fed his desire for freedom and release from unending ceremony by listening to tales of the struggles and extraordinary behavior Meren encountered. This, as well as Tutankhamun's personal trust, was why Meren was one of the few in all the world who could ask for admittance to the presence of the living god at any time.

Such a privilege meant nothing if he couldn't find the king. Finding a living god wasn't usually a problem, since he was bound by dusty, creaking tradition that worked against deviations from the set royal schedule adhered to by noble servitors, ministers, and everyone else around him. Wherever he went, Tutankhamun moved in a cumbersome swarm of people—bodyguards, high-ranking priests, royal servants, courtiers, family, government ministers, and a host of slaves. But Tutankhamun had developed the ability to elude this suffocating hindrance.

Sometimes he simply rose before anyone else and left the palace with his bodyguards. Sometimes he ended an audience and vanished before his courtiers could come after him. At other times he waited until the middle of the night and stole out of the palace with only Karoya for protection.

Thus, when Meren went to the palace, he sought the king in the royal chapel, not knowing for certain if he would find the living god in his appointed duties or off on some unexpected excursion with the court in a frenzy of alarm. Luckily, he arrived just as Tutankhamun emerged from the dark inner chamber that held the altar and the sacred shrine in which the image of the king of the gods, Amun, was kept. Only the king and priests of the highest rank were allowed in this chapel.

Tutankhamun walked into the light of dozens of alabaster lamps. Heavy doors covered with sheet gold swung shut behind him with a boom. Linen-clad backs bowed low, Meren's among them. Pharaoh hurried down a corridor formed by slender wooden columns painted to resemble tall papyrus plants, but stopped and turned back to stand before Meren.

"Eyes of Pharaoh," the king said.

Thus addressed, Meren straightened. He didn't expect what he saw.

Tutankhamun's skin had been painted in gold with magical signs of warding, protective symbols, an idea that probably had come from the magician priests. He held a golden net such as would be used to catch harmful spirits in a magical ceremony.

The king came nearer. "You have news."

"Of a privy nature, O golden one."

Tutankhamun turned around and addressed his waiting councillors. "My majesty will confer with the Eyes and Ears of Pharaoh."

He waved a hand in dismissal, which caused a murmur of surprise. The dozens of people surrounding the king began to move all at once, except for the Overseer of the Audience Hall and one of the chief judges of the kingdom. The judge whispered to the overseer, who approached the king.

"Great king, thy majesty is to preside in a hall of judgment at this very hour."

"The judges and the complainants will wait, overseer."

Soon Meren was in the uncomfortable position of having to sit in a small pleasure boat while the king rowed on one of the vast palace pleasure lakes.

"This is the answer?" the king asked as he pulled his oars out of the water. "A mad, petty noble who imagined himself greater than he was? It wasn't Eater of Souls?"

"Reshep was possessed, golden one, but I don't think Eater of Souls was in him. I can't believe Eater of Souls would serve such as he."

Tutankhamun looked thoughtful. "True. If Eater of Souls were to come among the living, he'd serve me."

"Thy majesty speaks with the wisdom of his father Amun."

"My majesty will order his name erased wherever it's found. Get rid of him, Meren, and I'll put it about that an outlaw was caught masquerading as Eater of Souls in order to rob the citizens of Memphis."

Meren bowed, and they fell into an uneasy silence. Such was the fate of evil ones. Their names were erased from documents, monuments, family tombs. Their bodies were cast into the desert to become the fodder of hyenas and jackals. Denied their eternal house and the repository of the soul, these spirits were left to the terrible judgments of the gods. When their names were erased from the land of the living, their final avenue to existence vanished, and their souls perished.

Tutankhamun was staring at the reflection of a lone cloud in the water. "I'm glad you refused to admit him to my presence. Do you think he would have taken offense at me?"

Meren went cold as he realized the king's meaning. Reshep had envied Meren's power; how much more hatred would he have had for a living god.

"Never mind," Tutankhamun said. "I can see it in your face. A danger escaped. Which reminds me. My scouts have returned and reported vicious bandit raids on villages just north of the great pyramids. Libyan tribes, they say. Testing my strength, trying to encroach upon my kingdom when they think I'm too young to defend myself. My majesty will not tolerate such transgression."

"General Nakhtmin will send troops at once, divine one."

"Oh no," Tutankhamun said. He shipped his oars, stuck his hand in the water, and doused Meren with a spray of water. "Your promise, Eyes of Pharaoh. I'm to go on the first suitable raid. This is the first suitable raid, and you're taking me, as you promised."

Meren regarded the king solemnly, then sighed and leaned against the side of the boat. He touched his fingers to his brow and allowed his head to droop.

"It's of no use," the king said.

"Majesty?"

Tutankhamun shoved an oar into Meren's arms and laughed when his courtier nearly lost his balance. "Admit it. You were thinking of pleading weariness."

"Thy majesty thinks I would deceive him?"

"If it suited you, yes. Fortunately, you've done yourself the ill favor of teaching me most of your tricks and wiles." The king thrust the second oar at Meren. "Resign yourself, my lord. We're going on a raid. As soon as my scouts can find the bandit camp—and you're not leaving the city until that happens."

"Thy majesty's will is accomplished," Meren said with a scowl.

"This time it is."

Meren shoved the oars in the water. "I should not have given the divine one my promise."

"No, you shouldn't have, but it's too late. Now row my majesty back to the water steps, Meren. I must sit in judgment before Ay hears of my absence and comes looking for me."

Meren guided the boat to the great stone staircase that descended into the water at one end of the lake, and they climbed ashore. Meren

watched pharaoh disappear into the palace and stared across the ornamental gardens, annoyed that he'd lost the battle of delay so soon. He
should have anticipated that Tutankhamun would maneuver around him
and been ready with a creative excuse for further postponement of the
king's battle initiation.

"Ah, well. What cannot be changed must be endured."

He returned home to an unusually quiet house. For hours he'd been
avoiding any thought about Isis and her role in last night's near-disaster.
She needed curbing, and he was going to have to do it. Which made him
even more angry and hurt than he already was. She was forcing him to
be unpleasant, and he hated being that way to his children.

But he couldn't deal with her now. He needed time to think about
what was best. Relieved that he'd thought of a reprieve, Meren went to
the hall where Bener had ordered food and beer set out. Kysen was
waiting for him, his hands restlessly twisting a papyrus roll. He greeted
Meren as his father sat down and picked up a water jar.

"All went well with the Hittite?"

"As well as any matter can go with a Hittite." Meren poured water
into a large cup and drank all of it.

Kysen's fingers closed over the papyrus. "And pharaoh?"

Meren furrowed his brow.

"Father, there's news about the cook."

"Good. What is it?"

Kysen looked over his shoulder, and Abu appeared, leading the
chief of watchmen, Sokar. When Meren saw him, he almost groaned.
Sokar approached and threw himself at Meren's feet.

"O mighty Eyes of Pharaoh, have pity on this poor miserable servant.
I am beset with countless duties. I have no relief, too few men, a vast
city to patrol. How was I to know?"

Raising his eyes to the ceiling, Meren snapped, "Be silent. Kysen,
what is he doing here?"

Kysen put the papyrus roll into his hands, one of the daily lists of
incidents compiled by Sokar. An item near the bottom of the sheet had
been underlined in fresh red ink. It read, "Stabbings, a man and a
woman. Not of the city."

"By the gods!" Meren felt blood rush to his head. He jumped to his
feet, sending his chair scooting backward as he glared at the blubbering
chief watchman.

"They were not of the city, my lord! Newcomers, who didn't even own the house, poor, and of no importance."

"Sokar, you are a lackwitted donkey." Meren clenched his fists in an effort to keep from striking the man.

"He says he knows who owns the house," Kysen said.

Meren shoved Sokar with his foot and bellowed, "Who!"

"A man of Arthribis in the delta, called Nefersekheru."

"Go on, Sokar," Kysen said. "Tell it all."

Sokar tried to worm his body between the tiles that decorated the dais stairs.

"Out with it, you fool, before I pull your tongue out and make you eat it," Meren said.

"Nefersekheru only holds the lease on the house," Sokar said. "He holds it for another, who also is not of the city."

Meren paced away from Sokar and returned to plant his feet wide apart, his hands on his hips. Sokar whimpered and kissed the floor before Meren's sandal.

"Listen to me," Meren shouted. "If you speak those words 'not of the city' another time, I will banish you to the turquoise mines. Now tell me who owns that house where Hunero and her husband Bay were killed."

"Naram-Sin! His name is Naram-Sin, O great one. Oh, misery and woe, I am doomed. Naught but horror befalls those who cause difficulty for the Greek pirate."

"Silence!" Meren bellowed.

He ignored Sokar's blubbering. Rubbing his chin, he fell to pacing while Abu dragged Sokar out of the hall. With the chief of watchmen gone, a peaceful silence reigned. Kysen dropped wearily to the floor beside Meren's chair, grabbed a small bread loaf, and began tearing pieces from it. Meren paused beside his chair to fix his gaze on a glazed floor tile. It bore an alternating pattern of papyrus stalks and lotus buds.

Finally he spoke. "Ky, we've stumbled into a swamp inhabited by all sorts of poisonous creatures. Everything is murky, like marsh water. The truth is trapped below the surface, weighed down by mud, tangled in roots, and screened by reeds. If we reach for it, we could thrust our hands into the mouth of the crocodile."

Kysen tore off another piece of bread and studied his father. "I know, and that's why I don't understand why you suddenly look as if you're anticipating the feast of Hathor."

"Who killed the cook and old Bay?" Meren glanced down at his son. "Was it someone in the pay of the pirate? Was it Naram-Sin? Or was it Eater of Souls?"

"They were stabbed."

"So was that woman who was waiting in the garden for Mugallu."

"By the wrath of Set, Father."

Meren smiled. "Yes. Each time we approach near the matter of Nefertiti's death, something happens to distract us. Is Naram-Sin a distraction, or have we reached past the screen that conceals the hunter from the quarry at last?"

"You're intrigued. Father, you were right in the first place. Whoever killed the queen is more dangerous than any bandit or Hittite. This is not the time to be amused."

"Easy, Ky. Don't adopt my habit of becoming too grave. After facing Eater of Souls, I realized I'm much too serious, and such gravity gives no advantage. And you're right. I am beginning to appreciate our unknown enemy. He must have a complex nature and a ka of infinite sagacity to have remained hidden for so long and to have designed such a complicated method by which to direct his plots."

"Then you don't think we're near the truth yet?"

"I don't know."

Meren sat down again and poured wine for Kysen and himself. Handing his son a goblet, he lifted his own.

"I don't know the truth. At least not all of it. But I do know that I'm going to find the one at the center of this intrigue, and when I do, I think it will be someone who possesses within his ka more of the true nature of Eater of Souls than Reshep ever did."

"And yet you relish searching for this new demon," Kysen said.

Raising his goblet higher in a salute, Meren grinned. "I appreciate the complexity, the serpentine design, the intelligent heart. We've alarmed someone, Ky. I was beginning to think the murderer dead or out of Egypt. But he's here. And he's fighting us. We've disturbed the scorpion's nest, and he's about to strike. Soon there will be no more dueling with shadows. And that above all else pleases me. I prefer to face my real enemy, not lowly and servile pawns."

"Well, it's too late to do as I wanted and let the matter drop."

Meren laughed and picked up a bowl of dates. "If we do that, we'll get ourselves killed all the more quickly."

"Is this your new attitude, go into danger cheerfully?"

"Cheerful or not, the danger will come. Have you found Tcha?"

"Not yet. I think he may have fled the city for the moment. He'll come back once word spreads that Eater of Souls has been killed."

Meren leaned back in his chair, stretched his legs, and drew a long breath. "Ahhh. No wonder the air smells so fresh. Enjoy the sweet watery breath of the earth, Ky. When Tcha skulks back into Memphis, he'll bring a stench that would knock a vulture from atop a refuse heap."